The Theatricalists

performance works

SERIES EDITORS
Patrick Anderson and
Nicholas Ridout

This series publishes books in theater and performance studies, focused in particular on the material conditions in which performance acts are staged, and to which performance itself might contribute. We define "performance" in the broadest sense, including traditional theatrical productions and performance art, but also cultural ritual, political demonstration, social practice, and other forms of interpersonal, social, and political interaction that may fruitfully be understood in terms of performance.

The Theatricalists

Making Politics Appear

✦

Theron Schmidt

NORTHWESTERN UNIVERSITY PRESS
EVANSTON, ILLINOIS

Northwestern University Press
www.nupress.northwestern.edu

Printed in the United States of America

10   9   8   7   6   5   4   3   2   1

Library of Congress Cataloging-in-Publication Data

Names: Schmidt, Theron U., author.
Title: The theatricalists : making politics appear / Theron Schmidt.
Other titles: Performance works.
Description: Evanston, Illinois : Northwestern University Press, 2024. |
    Series: Performance works | Includes bibliographical references and index.
Identifiers: LCCN 2024013743 | ISBN 9780810147546 (paperback) |
    ISBN 9780810147553 (cloth) | ISBN 9780810147560 (ebook)
Subjects: LCSH: Theater—Political aspects. | Theater—Philosophy.
Classification: LCC PN1643 .S36 2024 | DDC 306.4/848—dc23/eng/20240422
LC record available at https://lccn.loc.gov/2024013743

CONTENTS

INTRODUCING THE LINEUP

It might begin like this:

You might arrive at the theater and take the place assigned to you, along with perhaps a thousand other people who have gathered here in this room. Perhaps the show can be thought to begin before it begins, in the way the architecture directs your gaze, and the way the theater shows you its painted face. The lights might go down and the curtains open, and you may now expect the theater to show you something else—but instead it remains blank, that is, darkened, for the duration of a song about the night; and when the lights do come on, they do so slowly, for the duration of a song about the light; and when the theater finally shows something other than darkness and light, it is when forty or so people assemble on the stage, occupying the space without indicating any purpose other than that of gathering there, and, the director of this particular spectacle might later note, with no instruction other than to stand on stage and be aware that a thousand pairs of eyes are looking at them.

Or it might begin like this:

This time the lights might come up to reveal a group of performers already onstage, distributed in a series of static poses, creating a *tableau vivant*. A couple of the performers might have their hands extended, possibly in greeting or reaching for something; another might have his arms stretched wide. Three of the performers are standing, while the other two are in relaxed poses on the floor. The stage is otherwise empty. There might be several minutes of silence while you look at this image, trying to decipher its meaning, and while the performers are also looking at you, before one of the performers might finally speak. "I imagine we are standing in the middle of a forest," she might say, before she goes on to describe a scene of family reunion. Or another performer might describe a different domestic scene, or a fabulous tale of an animal gathering, or indeed the very activity being played out here: a group of performers gathered on this same stage in this same city. The whole time, of course, they are looking at you, and you are looking at them.

Or it might begin with a pair of deadpan clowns squabbling over the configuration of the performance space, one placing chairs at the front of the stage while the other moves the same chairs to the back, a slapstick contest that might only be resolved when the rest of the ensemble joins the stage so that ten performers take their seats in a row at the front of the stage, looking out at you. One by one they might act out a series of introductions by telling us how they want us to look at them tonight: one of them wants to be seen as manly and virile, maybe, or another performer wants us to be utterly consumed by physical desire for them, or another wants you to wonder if that's the guy you recognize from somewhere else. Or one of the performers might even tell you that she hopes you look at her as a real person, as someone for whom no one has written her lines or told her how to act—in just the same way as she introduces herself every other time this piece is performed.

Or it might begin with first one and then another smartly dressed man bounding onto the stage, their legs shuffling and hands waving, or miming and laughing at each other, or approximating some version of a tap-dance routine but one that keeps threatening to fall out of balance. They might keep looking at you and grinning, and because they are Black, you will probably think that all this shucking-and-jiving and grinning has an uncomfortable resonance with minstrelsy—but it's also infectious. They might be replaced by another performer, who might address you like you're an audience at a stand-up comedy club, "Wassup, [name of your city]?!" he might call out, before he launches gleefully into a series of raunchy stories—about prepubescent sexuality, say, and the differences between White culture and Black culture. If you're White, like me, by now you might be squirming even more uncomfortably, wondering who is the subject of these jokes, and what it might mean to laugh along with them, and the performer might look right at you with a big smile, and say, "I know some of you are thinkin' 'Why do black comedians still do those "White people are like this, and black people are like that" jokes?'" before his smile might drop away: "Well, I'm a tell you why . . . white people be evil."[1]

Indeed, for a period in the first decade of the new millennium, it seemed as if any evening in certain "experimental" versions of US and European theater might be just as likely as not to feature such an encounter: a lineup of performers facing their audience in a configuration that might be teasing, questioning, withholding, or interrogating the nature of the event. An encounter such as this might await you in *The Show Must Go On* (2001) by the French dance-maker Jérôme Bel; or *While We Were Holding It Together* (2006) by the Croatian-Dutch artist Ivana Müller; or *Bloody Mess* (2004) by the British ensemble Forced Entertainment; or *The Shipment* (2009) by the Korean American theater-maker Young Jean Lee, whose openings I have approximated in these previous paragraphs, for "you" is clearly "me," attending theater regularly in London, where I lived between 2002 and 2015, or as a visitor to international festivals in Europe, North America, and so-called Australia.[2] Seated and looking out at the theatrical spectacle, I might be equally likely to have the perform-ers staring right back at me in productions by the British director Katie

Mitchell, whether in her version of Martin Crimp's *Attempts on Her Life* ([1997] 2007) or Euripides's *Women of Troy* (2007); or in the cacophonous dance works of the Flemish company les ballet C de la B under the direction of Alain Platel, in works ranging from *lets op Bach* (1999) to *tauberbach* (2014); or in the nearly static, deliberately wooden acting that characterized Richard Maxwell's New York City Players during this period in theater pieces such as *Drummer Wanted* (2002) and *The End of Reality* (2006).

What should we make of this proliferation of lineups on the stage, repeatedly producing and reinscribing the theatrical situation as a moment of mutual recognition between performers and audience? One of its most frequent practitioners was Forced Entertainment, where such a lineup features prominently in almost all of their works, such as *Showtime* (1996), *Dirty Work* (1998), *First Night* (2001), and the somewhat retrospective *Bloody Mess* (2004) that opens with the squabbling clowns described above. Here is how the company's director, Tim Etchells, described this phenomenon at the time (with notable reference to Jérôme Bel):

> It's not for nothing that a recurring image in much contemporary performance . . . has been the chorus-like line-up of performers at the front of the stage. The line-up is an act of mutual revelation and confirmation for both performers and audience—an initial ocular assertion, testing and probing of the border. We are all here, present and correct—performers arranged at the edge, whilst the audience—you in this case—are all sat in your rows and facing those on stage. It's a blank face-off, a strict orgy of self-presentation and projection, a scene that can be endlessly layered and complex, especially in the hands of an artist like Bel.[3]

The lineup foregrounds the active role of the audience as participants in the theatrical event, whether as co-makers whose imagination activates the signifying functions of the actors' bodies, as in *While We Were Holding It Together*, or as complicit in the questionable politics of spectacle, as in the minstrel-show connotations of the opening of *The Shipment*. More than this, the lineup reminds us that the onlooking of the audience is the occasion for the event, its necessary ontological precondition. In a retrospective interview with Yvane Chapuis, Bel describes how *The Show Must Go On* evolved from his earlier works, such as *Jérôme Bel* (1995), a playful and systematic deconstruction of the signifying elements of the theatrical spectacle: the lights, the music, the body of the actor. Only later did Bel realize that he had left out perhaps the most important element: the audience, or, as Chapuis puts it, "the role given to the person looking at it."[4]

The Theatricalist Turn

In foregrounding the active role of the spectator and the set of relationships between people constructed by the theater-event, the proliferation
of lineups in theater events can be placed in relation to the so-called
social turn of artworks across different media in the late 1990s and early
2000s, as manifested in the use of the art gallery to model interpersonal
encounters in the "relational aesthetics" described by the curator Nicolas
Bourriaud.[5] In his writing, Bourriaud explicitly framed the possibilities
of the art event in relation to Guy Debord's 1967 critique of the society
of the spectacle, in which "all that once was directly lived has become
mere representation,"[6] a diagnosis that Bourriaud implies still holds true
in the 1990s: "This is a society where human relations are no longer
'directly experienced,' but start to become blurred in their 'spectacular'
representation." Bourriaud retains Debord's suspicion of "representation" in favor of the direct or the actual—a recurring tension that will
be explored in this book—as he continues: "Herein lies the most burning
issue to do with art today: is it still possible to generate relationships with
the world, in a practical field art-history traditionally earmarked for their
'representation'"?[7]

We might think of the lineup as one form of this social *turn*: reorienting
the event toward the audience, in a continuation of the disruption of the
European naturalist theater inaugurated by Brecht and Artaud. As Peter
Handke (who will be discussed in more depth in chapter 1) said, "All you
have to do is turn to the spectators and start off; with a perfectly simple
shift of ninety degrees you have a new play, a new dramaturgy."[8] This
"simple" ninety-degree turn makes the relation of these watchers to the
event into the subject of the work's aesthetics. Bourriaud viewed relational
aesthetics as offering an escape from consumer relations, positioning its
relational possibilities in opposition to "the spread of the supplier/client
relations to every level of human life, from work to dwelling-place by way
of all the tacit contracts which define our private life."[9] And yet, in its
theatrical form, this foregrounding of the relationship between artwork
and audience tends to regard these watchers with suspicion—and maybe
even antagonism, to adopt Claire Bishop's skeptical view of the social
turn.[10] For example, the recurring lineups staged by Forced Entertainment mock our desire to get outside these relations, at least so long as
we are configured in this arrangement: "There's a word for people like
you, and that word is audience. An audience likes to sit in the dark and
watch other people do it. Well, if you've paid your money—good luck
to you."[11] The confrontational lineup does not so much break down distinctions between artwork and audience as remind us of them. Nor does
it attempt to undo the laws of spectacle so much as reinforce them, as
in Beth Hoffman's description of *Bloody Mess*: "Their claims tease the

audience, presenting themselves as commodities shaped to satisfy the spectators' desires while simultaneously asserting control over the spectators' experience."[12]

If Bourriaud's writing on relational aesthetics invokes Debord, then these lineups point to other figures from the late 1960s who critiqued the prevalence of "spectacle." With their playful refusals of spectacular displays of skill, their compositions made from everyday movements, and their interest in the distinctiveness and fallibility of the individual performing body, works like *The Show Must Go On* and *While We Were Holding It Together* recall the experimentation of the Judson Dance Theater and others in the New York downtown scene, and reflect the ongoing influence of Yvonne Rainer's groundbreaking *Trio A* (1966–68). And the accusatory lineups that figure so prominently in virtually all of Forced Entertainment's works (including *Bloody Mess* but also *Showtime*, *Dirty Work*, etc.), haranguing their audience and endlessly deferring the promised spectacle, evoke the turn to the spectator in Handke's *Sprechstücke*, or "speech-plays." Haunting all of these lineups, I will argue in the first chapter of this book, is Michael Fried's notorious condemnation of theatricality: "Art degenerates as it approaches the condition of theater," he wrote in the pages of *Artforum* in 1967. And what was it that was so problematic about theater, which he saw as having "corrupted" and "perverted" other forms of art? The problem, for Fried, was that "theater has an audience—it exists for one—in a way that the other arts do not."[13]

Indeed, the lineup is a formal device that engages with the "problem" of audience as a shorthand for the problem of theater and theatricality itself; the problem that Jacques Rancière neatly consolidated as "the paradox of the spectator": "This paradox is easily formulated: there is no theater without spectators."[14] Roughly contemporaneous with the proliferation of lineups on Western stages that I have described is a movement *off* the stage, or perhaps, more accurately, a movement of the stage *out* from the theater, and into other configurations of encounter through an interest in immersive and participatory forms of performance—a tendency that Sophie Nield evocatively described as "the rise of the character named spectator."[15] Like the lineup, these immersive forms also foreground the active and complicit role of the audience in what Adam Alston has described as "productive participation," a tendency that he connects with the increased value placed on individual self-productivity and affective labor within neoliberal economic and political structures.[16] However, there is also a critical difference: whereas immersive and participatory forms offer the promise of emotional and physical "immersion" and "deep" experience—whether or not such a promise is fulfilled[17]—the lineup is a theater of pure frontality, foreclosing any possibility of literal or metaphorical depth in favor of shallowness, surface, and appearance. Pure frontality is another

way of saying pure theatricality, as Bert O. States observed when he identified frontality at the heart of all the problematics of theatrical meaning:
"*presence, representation, repetition, deferral, difference, aporia, supplementation, referentiality, indetermination,*" he wrote, "can be treated as
variations on the principle of frontality."[18]

The face-off between performers and audience is the underscored rein-
scription of the theatrical event itself. Indeed, the lineup is the line that
separates the event *as* theater, its limit-case, the essence of its *theatricality*.
As Josette Féral writes, "theatricality is the result of a series of cleavages
(inscribed by the artist and recognized by the spectator) aimed at making a disjunction in systems of signification, in order to substitute other,
more fluid ones."[19] The lineup is the material manifestation of this cleav-
age, occupying the conceptual and spatial line of demarcation that sets
apart this event as theater. The fascination with the lineup for the artists
mentioned here is one aspect of their more general interest in exploring
the limit-conditions of theater itself. For example, reflecting on *The Show
Must Go On*, Bel observes, "The whole idea of the piece is to re-describe
this process, which I still find mysterious, of theatrical representation."[20]
Writing about the same work, Etchells observes: "[Bel] understands that
theatre is a frame (game) constructed so that people can look at other
people."[21] And in his own polemic about the uses of the lineup, Etchells described his fundamental question as: "How can I break this?" He
writes: "What kind of fun can I have with the rules of this game, this
form? Or how can I modify, expose, weaken or otherwise intervene so
that it can do something that I might really need it to do?"[22] And Patricia
Ybarra describes Young Jean Lee as using theater "to think about racialized and gendered identity, through the index of theatricality," engaging
with the conditions of theatricality as a means to a political theater.[23]
Rather than seeking to *avoid* or *circumvent* the conditions of theatricality, the artists I write about in this book engage with politics *through*
theatricality.

In everyday parlance, machinations in the political realm that are perceived to be only for the sake of appearances and devoid of any substance
or lasting significance are often dismissed as "pure theater" or "only theater." They are only more obfuscation, smoke and mirrors, playing with
appearances, and a distraction from "real" politics. But there's another
way of looking at this, in which the world of politics is not opposed to
the world of appearances, but instead is one in which politics takes place
within and *through* appearance. That is, certain problems of speech and
gesture in the political realm can be engaged as essentially theatrical
problems—problems for theater, but also ideas that theatricality makes
problems *of*—such as problems of representation, presence, and agency. A
theatrical approach to the politics of appearance would consider how to
make these problems appear, and for whom.

The Politics of Appearance

These artists—predominantly European and North American, or else influenced by European theater traditions, and working at the start of the twenty-first century—are often on a self-described search for new forms of political theater. In the European context this search is frequently articulated as "post-Brechtian" (more on this in chapter 1), as exemplified by a provocation from the German curator and dramaturge Florian Malzacher, "No Organum to Follow: Possibilities of Political Theatre Today," whose title references Brecht's influential "Short Organum for the Theatre" (1948).[24] Malzacher's provocation, which introduces a collection of essays from writers and theater-makers who are "looking for the political theatre of today," describes the context in Europe and North America as one in which "society is paralysed by the symptoms of post-political ideologies" such that "the belief in the possibility or even the desirability of political imagination is fading."[25] In contrast to previous periods in which theater's political commitments were overt in their ideological content, Malzacher describes a shift toward an interest in "the medium and the form of theatre itself."[26] For some, this shift toward aesthetic formalism and away from overt political content represents a turn away from politics. For example, the *Village Voice* critic Tom Sellar, in undertaking an overview of New York's theatrical avant-garde in the new millennium, wrote: "Even during a decade of deep social transformation and political upheaval, most American performance groups showed few signs of dissent or engagement. The emphasis remains firmly on cool eclecticism and irony, formalism and fragmentation."[27]

But in this book, I will argue that this apparently "inward turn" toward the mechanisms of the theater is not necessarily an eschewal of politics but instead a practical inquiry into what I call "the politics of appearing." As I discuss in more detail in chapter 3, such an approach to politics can be identified in the mid-twentieth-century writings of Hannah Arendt, which continue to reverberate in more recent Western political theory in the writings of Chantal Mouffe, Judith Butler, Jean-Luc Nancy, and Jacques Rancière. This book follows these thinkers in turning attention away from a politics that is concerned with ideological *content* and instead toward the *conditions* under which political representation and dissent might emerge. Mouffe articulates this in terms of a distinction between politics and what she calls "the political," the relationships of power and the antagonisms that are always present, however much a liberal consensus would seek to transcend them.[28] As Mouffe argues, such consensus is often (if not always) based on an unstated premise of what does and does not constitute "politics" as such, and for Butler, scenes of political dissent—such as the popular uprisings during the so-called movement of the squares—can be understood as contestations over the "prepolitical" or the "extrapolitical."[29] For this reason, Butler emphasizes the sometimes invisible work of care and sustenance upon which these uprisings depend.

Rancière, too, regards these underlying preconditions for the emergence of the political, but is just as interested in the everyday and ongoing "policing" of how we experience the world as he is in overt eruptions of dissensus or conflict: "Policing is not so much the 'disciplining' of bodies as *a rule governing their appearing*, a configuration of occupations and the properties of the spaces where these occupations are distributed."[30] Rancière influentially describes this policing of appearances as "the distribution [or partition] of the sensible,"[31] and as such describes politics as a kind of aesthetic experience: "Politics consist in reconfiguring the partition of the sensible, in bringing on stage new objects and subjects, in making visible that which was not visible, audible as speaking beings they who were merely heard as noisy animals."[32] When Rancière invokes the metaphor of the theater with his reference to "bringing on stage new objects and subjects," we might ask to what extent this is only a metaphor, and to what extent Rancière is suggesting that the *actual* theater could be a useful place for thinking about politics. It is clear from his numerous writings about works of art that he does find useful lessons for politics in artistic works; but he also explicitly rejects the idea that the political value of art might derive from "the messages and feelings that [art] carries on the state of social and political issues" and the "way it represents social structures, conflicts, or identities." Instead, Rancière continues, art "is political as it frames a specific space-time sensorium, as it redefines on this stage the power of speech or the coordinates of perception, shifts the places of the actor and the spectator, etc."[33] That is to say, the relevance of theater to politics derives from its fundamental concern with acts of appearance, with modes of speech and gesture, and with the production of feelings and sensations *as productions*, irrespective of the content of those feelings or sensations. A political theater, in the Rancièrian sense, would be less concerned with making certain claims visible or audible than about reconfiguring the conditions of visibility and audibility—what counts as legitimate speech, and by whom.

The arguments put forward by Mouffe, Butler, and Rancière have been stimulating for art and performance scholars in the way they connect political dissensus and sensory experience. Rancière in particular extends the possibility of "politics" as being something that is potentially available any time that a claim to speech and visibility disrupts the existing distribution of the sensible, and which takes the form of a politics of rupture. It is the very provisionality of this potential that performance scholars often find exciting, because it means that *any* interruption of our processes of experience might be political—and Rancière himself draws examples of these reconfigurations from aesthetic innovations that often have no explicit political intention, such as the exploits of the nineteenth-century acrobatic troupe Hanlon Lees, or Loïe Fuller's swirling choreography of colored textiles and electric lights, to take two examples from Rancière's *Aisthesis*.[34] However, such a Rancièrian celebration of the sensory also locates agency in the role of the spectators, who may have their perception of the world altered when the distribution of the sensible is interrupted—or may not, depending on contingent factors that are out of the control of the artists themselves. But what of those who wish to deliberately interrupt the existing sensibilities? Who cannot afford to wait for history to learn to see differently? Moreover, as in the quotations above, Rancière explicitly rejects any politics based on identity as necessarily rooted in existing distributions of the sensible, and instead favors politics that sit between or outside existing identities (race, gender, dis/ability, etc.). However, as Leah Bassel (following Patricia Hill Collins) asks, what is the place for "claims grounded on experience of multiple forms of oppression, claims *within* matrices of oppression"?[35]

This is the dilemma that this book seeks to unpack—not to resolve, but to follow artists and change-makers as they work their own inventive ways through their situatedness. For we should understand the theater, too, as an intersection of matrices of oppression: of regimes of appearance and invisibility, of power and voicelessness, and of roles distributed into hierarchies of activity and support. "The performance space is never empty," as Ngũgĩ wa Thiong'o observed. "It is always the site of physical, social, and psychic forces in society."[36] How could this apparatus for the production of appearances be used to make the conditions of its own productivity appear? Between a politics of dissensus, seeking to disrupt regimes of visibility in order to make possible different sensibilities and imaginings, and a politics of identity, grounded in experiences of oppression or lack of agency and seeking not only recognition but the power to make positive claims, we find the artists in this book.[37] Theirs is not a political theater that is opposed to some other nonpolitical theater, but an exploration and making-visible of the ways in which theater already is political.

Politics, in this book, is the means by which agency is distributed and exercised, the capacity of individuals and groups to stand from an identity position and at the same time destabilize the constraints on that position—not to dissolve or to transcend those positions, but to allow them to be re-fabricated from within. Theatricality is politicized to the extent that it enables self-awareness about the conditions that allow matrices of power and representation to appear as such, troubling an individualist approach to agency as something held and wielded by discrete selves, and instead figuring agency as eventful, as emergent in relation. Such a relational approach to agency is inspired by so-called new materialist approaches to distributed agency, as in Jane Bennett's analysis of "the agency of assemblages."[38] Viciane Despret calls attention to the etymological connotations of *agencement*, the Deleuzean term often translated as "assemblage," but which also suggests agential emergence: "An *agencement* is a rapport of forces that makes some beings capable of making other beings capable, in a plurivocal manner, in such a way that the *agencement* resists being dismembered, resists clear-cut distribution."[39] In this book I am interested in the political relevance of artistic practices that invest in and explore theater as assemblages of appearance. Such practices amplify artifice and fabrication rather than producing authenticity, disjoin spectatorial feelings from sympathetic identification, and proliferate sensations that may not necessarily coincide with individualized selfhood. As I will describe in the first chapter, formal experiments that explore the spectatorial situation of the theater-event itself are valuable for the cultivation and development of these practices. But I depart from a strictly Rancièrian emphasis on the aesthetic experience of the spectator to consider the ways in which artists who wish to intervene within matrices of violence, oppression, and devaluation have made use of the theatrical apparatus as one that is not isolated but produced within overlapping *dispositifs* of appearance. That is, through the engagement of the theater-event with its own conditions of sensibility, these theatricalists practice a political engagement within wider mechanisms of appearance, which the theater is employed to make visible.

The Lineup of the Book

The lineup is paradigmatic of the theatricality I am interested in: it is a moment when something seems to appear, in its most literal presentation: "Here I am," or "This is me," or even "This is this." This book proceeds through a series of such opening propositions, when someone or something seems to appear as itself, not dressed in artifice or standing in for something hidden from view—*and at the same time* this appearance takes place within an explicitly invoked theatrical frame, a space of representation where an image is made available for viewing by spectators. So the lineup is also an acknowledgment of the spectatorial relation, a self-awareness about *making* an appearance, the act of showing, of making a show of oneself. "This is this," but such an avowal of the circumstances of presentation and reception also reminds us that "this is only theater." But rather than a form of dismissal, as when the phrase is used in relation to politics, the examples discussed in this book offer a more curious exploration and affirmation of such gestures. Forgoing the pretense to be "more than" theater, the artists discussed here might be seen to address the question: What is it that is happening when what is happening is, indeed, *only* theater?

One of the things that is happening is that someone is watching, and indeed, for many Western thinkers and makers, this presence of the audience is the zero-condition for theater, its most minimal requirement. It is worth emphasizing that this is a particularly Western concern; the distinction between a seated audience and staged players, and the designation of separate spaces (such as theaters and their attendant architectures) for aesthetic activity, are not universal practices. But we find a persistent fascination with this zero-condition in the practice of the British theater-maker Tim Crouch and his collaborators, which is the primary focus of chapter 1. His is a "minimal theater," not only because it is often interested in exposing various core operations of the theater apparatus, but also because Crouch explicitly references minimalist art of the 1960s and 1970s. So this chapter also considers a lineage of work from that earlier period which engages with the audience as subject and the peculiar form of passive activity (or active passivity) that is involved in being a spectator. As discussed already in this introduction, some of the key works in this lineage come somewhat paradoxically from practitioners who at first glance might seem to position themselves as *anti*-theatrical, as articulated in Yvonne Rainer's pursuit of a dance without spectacle, typified in her "No Manifesto" and *Trio A*, and Peter Handke's post-dramatic exploration of a "theatre without drama," to borrow Hans-Thies Lehmann's term, in the form of his *Sprechstücke* mentioned earlier. And yet, even as they subtract many of the conventions and expectations of the theatrical event, what is left behind is not the absence of theater, but a theater that takes as its subject its own internal conditions and relationships: the "minimal theater" to which the chapter's title refers. Crouch's plays deploy a self-reflective theatricality to foreground the necessary and active role of the audience, even when that activity consists of nothing more (or less) than being a spectator, but his plays also turn their attention wider, conjoining these activities to other forms of spectating such as viewing atrocities or child pornography, or the consumption of images in the art world.

The minimal theater of chapter 1 necessarily has an inward focus, directing its attention to the specific distributions of roles and agency within the theater-event itself. Chapter 2 continues the exploration of theater that is about "the theater"—that is, theater that is about the *idea* of theater, its spectatorial relations and representational operations. But the theater is not only a place of ideation and abstraction, of representation and spectatorship; it is also a specific place of work, a place where people make their living. In chapter 2, I consider works that make visible this work of theater, its labor—for example, by showing us its stagehands and managers, in productions by the British theater company Quarantine and the behind-the-scenes team of the Manchester International Festival. Rather than the backstage world *behind* appearances, I argue, works like these show us the apparatus that produces appearance; and in numerous projects of the German ensemble Rimini Protokoll, the theater becomes a place where diverse machinations of appearance from outside the theater can be brought into view. I describe this coming-together of different apparatuses of appearance as an *engaged theater*, in the sense that the gearing systems of two different machines might engage or couple with each other. Such engagement is possible because they are already, in some ways, part of the same larger machine. The insight is not so much that "we are acting all the time," but that placing these actions of making-appearance in the theater can engage two different connected systems of representation in order to generate affective and agential possibilities. Finally, in the epic work of the US-based Nature Theater of Oklahoma, we get a vision of a theater that is not separated from everyday life, but which voraciously swallows up all of life—not the theater becoming "real," but the task of making and sustaining a life becoming a matter of theatrical production.

If chapter 2 begins to suggest ways in which the making of theatrical appearances is interconnected with broader social structures, these questions take on an additional urgency in chapter 3, which considers works where the subjects who appear on stage are those who are normally denied visibility and full participation in the wider world—in the case I discuss, because they are perceived to have learning or intellectual disabilities. Indeed, such performers are also denied visibility *on* stage, as well, and so this chapter opens by thinking about who is and isn't perceived as capable of "acting," and considers a number of recent works involving children and young performers in collaborations initiated by the Flemish companies Ontroerend Goed and CAMPO, before moving on to discuss the long-running artistic output of the Australian company Back to Back Theatre. At the core of this chapter is an interrogation into representation and agency, drawing on Hanna Pitkin's distinction between "acting for" and "standing for" in legal and political contexts, and the lineage of political thought from Hannah Arendt through to Judith Butler and Jacques Rancière that focuses on the right to appear. In Back to Back's work, made collaboratively over several decades by a semi-permanent ensemble of performers perceived to have intellectual disability, the ensemble uses theater to illuminate and interrogate cultural presumptions about who has the right to be heard and seen, as well as who has the agency to fabricate and to invent, rather than being trapped in a role they have had no part in writing.

One of the recurring tensions regarding the ways to which theatricality is put to use in the case studies in this book is that between the "real" or authentic and the representation or fabrication. Chapter 4 foregrounds this tension in relation to the deployment of theatricality in contexts outside the theater: it compares the carefully orchestrated state apology performed by the former Australian prime minister Kevin Rudd with more playful versions by the British artist Carey Young and the Lebanese-born theater-maker Rabih Mroué. In Mroué's work in particular, along with that of Walid Raad/The Atlas Group, also originally from Lebanon, the work of fabrication is not opposed to "real" politics, but instead exposes the way in which the ground of politics—"the stage of the 'we,' " to borrow Jean-Luc Nancy's term[40]—is itself fabricated from a mix of performative self-authorizing and collective fictionalization, thus challenging the authenticity of what does and does not "count" as politics. This blurring of boundaries between "mere" theatrical gesture and "sincere" or "authentic" politics is exemplified by the book's final case study, a revisiting of the German multidisciplinary artist Christoph Schlingensief's public provocation *Please Love Austria* (also known as *Ausländer Raus!*), in which theatricality is used as a means to intervene in politically charged debates around national identity. As with the engaged theater discussed in chapter 2, Schlingensief's work is notable for the way in which it turns the apparatus of theatricality outward from self-reflection to incorporate and ingest cultural and mediatized structures of representation, making them all part of his theatrical "game."

A wide range of "theatricality" is on display in this book, from the meta-theatrical "inward turn" of Rainer, Handke, and Crouch—theater *about* theater, dance *about* dance, spectacle *about* spectatorship—to a more explicit engagement with external contexts "in the real world" in Mroué and Schlingensief's works that explore the theatricality of political gestures in the so-called public sphere—as well as various permutations in between, in which the operations of representation that are internal and external to the theater are folded into each other or placed in conflict with each other. But there are a few recurring characteristics, which are the key observations of this book.

First, theatricality can be characterized by self-awareness of the constructedness of the situation; its dependence on being-seen (and being-seen *as* theater) produces a removal of the theater-event from everyday life. In this way it can be contrasted with the (apparently) self-actualizing or self-realizing potential of performativity. More detailed definitions and debates around theatricality and performativity are discussed in chapters 1 and 4, but a concise way of articulating the difference that I'm interested in is that between "something being done" in the case of performativity and "something being seen to be done" in the case of theatricality—a phrase that neatly suggests not only the dependence of theatricality on "being seen," but also the pejorative connotation of something being only *seen* to be done as opposed to *actually* being done.[41] This is not a novel distinction—indeed, the Western lineage of theater analysis more or less begins with Aristotle's definition of drama as an action that is also "an imitation of an action,"[42] introducing the problem of *mimesis*—but the works I discuss here pay particularly careful attention to this condition of *being seen.* That is, something *is* being done in the seeing, which is the activity of seeing itself, and this seeing *does* something. It is generative.

Secondly, this self-absorption into the theater-event might suggest a kind of autonomy—a suggestion that is inherent in the description I just gave of the removal of the theater-event from everyday life. However, this apparent autonomy is dependent on an apparatus that frames what is and is not seen—an apparatus for the production of appearances, which is not an abstraction but a real collection of different kinds of labor and relationships that make this possible. The different forms of theatricality deployed by the works under consideration here are marked in the way they use that very apparatus in order to make the apparatus itself visible. That is, "theater about theater" can also mean theater about the conditions that make it possible for the theater to appear. Or to put it another way, one of the things theater is capable of is to make visible its own conditions of appearance, of framing that within which it itself is framed.

The lineup on the stage is exemplary of such an act, in that it simultaneously presents the appearance of some persons, apparently fully available for view, and at the same time indicates (and even produces) the conditions that enable this appearance: the edge of the stage (especially where the stage is not physically distinct) and an orientation toward frontality, not to mention foregrounding economic and cultural expectations around what it is to be "available" for view. It is for this reason that this book is preoccupied with such lineups and openings, and most of the chapters begin with descriptions of these moments in which a theater-act begins in a way that calls attention to or acknowledges its conditions of production and reception.

In this way, the case studies in this book present ways in which theater can be political, not by suspending or overcoming its theatricality, but through an interrogation of its own conditions of action, speech, and representation. Rather than representations being deceptive or distractions from "real" politics and social relations, these theater-makers explore what is at stake in *making an appearance*. Referring directly to what Rancière has called "the disappearance of politics,"[43] Nicholas Ridout argues that the challenge for political theater is "how to make politics appear."[44] If we are to share a common stage, then these frameworks of appearance must themselves be made to appear.

The works discussed in this book present various responses to this challenge. What these works share is an exploration of a politics of theatricality that consists of the elements I have described here: an exploration of the situation of "being seen" determined by the distinctive mode of being *with* but not *of* that is spectatorship; an engagement of the event with its own conditions of sensibility, interlocking within wider mechanisms of appearance which the theater makes visible; and a politics that is concerned with acts of appearing, with who has the right to be seen and heard and what actions are designated as political in the first place. Crucially, my contention is not that these works serve as mere illustrations of these ideas, or that this book will present a theory or viewpoint that explains or decodes problems that these works unwittingly expose. Rather, these are problems that these theatricalists themselves are thinking through, even as they come at these questions from diverse contexts and areas of work—and the form that their thinking takes is the theater they make. The method, then, is this: begin where they begin, and see where it leads.

Chapter 1

Minimal Theater: Making the Audience Appear

And so we might begin with something as simple as this:

Where ordinarily there might be a division between the playing space and the viewing space, instead there are just two banks of seats facing each other, separated by a few meters, so that if you are sitting in one of them, your view is of another group of audience members symmetrically facing you, like a mirror made of other bodies. The house lights are on, and maybe there is some gentle music playing, so this face-off between audiences is presented as an amusing situation, not a confrontational one. More than likely, there is some general chatter among those members of the audience who arrived together, so it's not clear who is the first person to speak who isn't really one of us; and therefore, the first thing said by the person we will eventually come to know as "Adrian" is more than likely to be lost in the hum of the room, as a kindly spoken "hello" or "good evening," perhaps with a just detectable exaggerated display of kindness, to someone sitting next to him. Eventually, however, Adrian will say something a bit louder, so that the whole room can hear, and even though he claims to speak on behalf of us, this act of speaking-up marks him out as different from us: "I love this!" he might say. "This is great. Isn't this great?"

This is the opening configuration in Tim Crouch's *The Author* (2009), co-directed by Crouch, Karl James, and Andy Smith. As the work unfolds, other performers speak from positions distributed among the audience, and through their disclosures they are all eventually identifiable as having been in some way bound up within a supposed previous piece of theater through various degrees of involvement in it: as the writer/director (Tim), two actors (Esther and Vic), and an audience member (Adrian). This prior play is described as having happened in London's Royal Court Theatre, where *The Author* was also first staged (and is set),[1] and it apparently depicted graphic violence, much like the "in-yer-face" theater of the 1990s that the Royal Court was influential in popularizing.[2] Esther and Vic both recall an experience as actors that exposed them to brutal images of violence in the name of the creative process, including watching online videos of beheadings and the killings of civilians, and interviewing asylum-seekers fleeing violence. Vic recalls playing an abusive soldier and being so affected by the role that he was unable to distinguish between fiction and reality, so that when Adrian (the audience member) excitedly rushed up to him at the stage door after the show, Vic reacted with unthinking violence, assaulting and hospitalizing Adrian. The character of Tim wrestles with a guilty conscience about the emotional cost of the work to which he subjected his actors, and wonders whether it made any difference. In the play's chilling final movement, Tim gives a hazy, blurred account of having watched online child pornography in which an infant is sexually abused, which may or may not have been accompanied by Tim abusing Esther's baby who was in the room with him; and his recollection ends with him recounting his own suicide.

My synopsis of the work's content suggests an emotionally charged encounter with confrontational subject matter, and this is certainly a significant aspect of the experience. However, this charged *content* is complemented by a number of *formal* strategies that generate a sense of lightness and care. This is suggested in the prefatory staging descriptions in the printed version of the play, which emphasize that "there should be plenty of warm, open space"; that "the audience should be beautifully lit and cared for"; as well as instructions for the use of incidental music "as a release valve" that "brings us into the here and now and helps the audience to feel good about being together."[3] Other notes refer to "an easy, playful presence"; and in performance, the actors' speech is characterized by a bright, matter-of-fact delivery, delivered with a careful clarity of enunciation and intention, and frequently punctuated by variations on questions such as "Can you see all right?" or "Is everyone okay?" These aspects of the work's formal presentation, as with the physical arrangement of the space, emphasize that as much as the work seems to be "about" acts of violence, it is the act of watching that is the focus of the work's attention— that is, watching understood as a kind of action, which in this chapter I will describe as "the situation of the spectator."

The fictional play within the play is concerned with the representation of violence: the character of Tim describes his intention to create "an amateur war zone on the stage," "to represent what was happening in the real world";[4] and Adrian recalls how "I've seen everything imaginable here. I've seen bum sex and rimmings and cock sucking and wankings and rapings and stabbings and shootings and bombings."[5] But the larger play of *The Author* is also about the violence of representation. Describing the theater as a "safe space," the character of Adrian reassures himself that "nothing really happens in here, does it? Not really. Nothing real."[6] In contrast, the structure of *The Author* seems designed to refute this claim, and to invite us to consider watching as a form of participation, as a thing that is "really happening." It asks us to consider the consumption of representations of violence in the theater in relation to other images that some of us might encounter, and all of us know about, disseminated in documentaries, YouTube videos, and pornography. The performers' frequent pauses, uses of "Can you see all right?" and invitations (or instructions?) to "look" set up a continuity between the consumption of spectacle in the theater and other kinds of image consumption. As Crouch puts it when describing the play, "a representation of an act of violence is, on some level, still an act of violence."[7]

For commentators such as James Frieze, *The Author* can be read as a critique of the passivity of spectatorship, which relies upon what he describes as "a scripted failure to intervene."[8] Indeed, *The Author* includes an instruction for an audience "plant" who walks out of the theater very early in the play, which can be interpreted as an act that signals permission for others to walk out (which is how Crouch himself describes his intentions),[9] but also as a scripted foreclosure on audience agency, a rhetorical gesture that pointedly reminds the rest of us that we are choosing to remain passive. Cristina Delgado-García suggests that this spectatorial powerlessness can be understood in relation to a larger "crisis of democratic legitimacy," as suggested by references in the play to the historically unprecedented, but ultimately ineffectual, mass demonstrations in 2002 against the UK's participation in the military intervention in Iraq. Delgado-García characterizes this crisis as the juxtaposition of "the *appearance* of political participation and consent" with the absence of meaningful democratic accountability, which *The Author* echoes at a smaller scale.[10]

These kinds of interpretations suggest that while *The Author* may appear to be a play about theater, it is also about spectacle and spectatorship more broadly: it is a play about looking—or better, about "just" looking, and about how just looking is not *just* looking, or without consequences. *The Author* can be seen as a cautionary tale, in which what we do in the theater is a reminder of the dangerous theatricality of our behavior outside the theater. The following lines from Tim gesture to these multiple modes, in which looking functions as both a figurative speculation—a passive taking-stock of the world outside—as well as an active choice being undertaken here, now, in this place:

> Look around you and tell me that this world is not full of horrors. Look around you.
> Look.
> Look.
> Can you see all right?[11]

More than this, these lines also signal the theater as a special kind of "place for looking"—a connection that has often been pointed out in relation to its ancient Greek etymology: the *theatron*, the seeing-place, the place for spectators to gather. But in *The Author*, when we look around us to try to see the "horrors" of the world, what we see is our own looking. That is, the seeing-place of the theater is a place where we might see our own looking. In this way, I will argue that *The Author* can be placed in a lineage of works that appear anti-theatrical, in that they are opposed to the theatricalization of everyday life, but at the same time they emphasize the peculiar particularity of the theater itself as a place where this violence of watching can be interrogated, challenged, and redirected so that it itself becomes visible. Paradoxically, it is because of the prescribed passivity of the spectator that a kind of agency emerges. And so, while *The Author* has convincingly been discussed in relation to a twenty-first-century interest in theatrical participation and "the social turn," I want to locate the issues that it is working-through in relation to a bifurcating moment in the late 1960s when, in the name of a theater without drama, and a dance without spectacle, what came into focus was the figure of the spectator.

Yvonne Rainer's "No to Spectacle"

From this moment when Tim Crouch asks us to consider the horrors of a world in which beheadings and sexual violence are circulated through online videos, let us return to an earlier scene, sometime around 1965, in which the dance-maker Yvonne Rainer, living in New York, buys a television.[12] It is around this time that US troops are being increasingly deployed in Vietnam, following the Gulf of Tonkin incident, and this is the first time that images of war are televised on a daily basis for an audience in the United States: the "living-room war," as Michael Arlen would call it, and which Martha Rosler would so strikingly thematize in her photo-montages.[13] We can try to imagine what it would be like for Rainer to be working with others in the downtown dance scene, coalescing around the Judson Dance Theater, as they experimented with what kinds of move-ment could be counted as dance and how the "everyday body" could be expressed through performance—and then she would return home to these images of atrocity, shown at dinnertime on the nightly news. We can imagine this daily pattern as we read her words, which she included as a program note to *The Mind Is a Muscle*, the 1968 performance evening that included the first performance of what subsequently has been described as her "signature work," *Trio A*. In this program note, she describes her "horror and disbelief" at seeing these images from Vietnam—emotions experienced not, she writes, "at the sight of death," but rather "at the fact that the TV can be shut off afterwards as after a bad Western."[14] Here Rainer is describing a feeling of simultaneous estrangement and complic-ity with the mediated image, an experience that would be given a pithy name a few years later by Guy Debord: "the society of the spectacle," which "unites what is separate, but it unites it only *in its separateness*."[15]

How might performance say "no" to spectacle? This is the famous challenge Rainer put forth in her writing about her work in this period, encapsulated in the influential text that has come to be known as her "No Manifesto":

> NO to spectacle no to virtuosity no to transformations and magic and make-believe no to the glamour and transcendence of the star image no to the heroic no to the anti-heroic no to trash imagery no to involvement of performer or spectator no to style no to camp no to seduction of spectator by the wiles of the performer no to eccentricity no to moving or being moved.[16]

Rainer's provocation is a minimalist, subtractionist one. It seeks to remove everything extraneous about the theatrical encounter, leaving only the "fact" of the performer's body. In the face of mediated atrocity, "my body remains the enduring reality," Rainer concludes her 1968 program notes. What is the relationship between the unfolding brutality of the exterior world and the experimental dance that Rainer and her compatriots were making? Between war as spectacle and spectacle as theatrical event? Rainer's program note explicitly refuses a direct thematic connection: "Just as ideological issues have no bearing on the nature of the work, neither does the tenor of current political and social conditions have any bearing on its execution," she writes. Such a hard-and-fast distinction is less tenable in future iterations of her work, such as the 1970 version of *Trio A* in which Rainer and her dancers performed naked, draped in US American flags, as part of a group show organized as a protest against the arrest of activists for allegedly desecrating the flag.[17] But in 1968, in its first iteration, Rainer suggests that whatever relationship this performance work might have to wider political conditions is not a matter of content, but derives instead from the formal qualities of the work itself. In her notebooks, she summarized these formal qualities:

> Task- or work-like movement with a "factual" quality, in part presented with a smooth, apparently even, energy continuum. Eyes averted from engagement with the audience to create the effect of a blank gaze into the mid-ground.[18]

Two possibilities emerge here. One way of reading this distinction between the formal exploration of "task-like" performance and the broader political context might be to imagine the theater as a quasi-utopian space of presence and community, a common space that is opposed to the alienating spectacle of a mediatized culture. We can imagine the theater being transformed into such a place of co-presence through the introduction of the "enduring reality" of the body and the "factual" quality of action—achieved, for example, in the way that the task of manipulating the bulky weight of mattresses in Rainer's *Parts of Some Sextets* (1965) precludes the possibility of pretense or simulation in the performance. One cannot *pretend* to heave these mattresses about, Rainer wrote: "You just *do* it, with the coordination of a pro and the non-definition of an amateur."[19] Or, as Chantal Pontbriand would later claim about this emerging genre of "performance" more generally,

> performance presents; it does not re-present. This distinction throws some light on the distance which can exist between classical presence, which is dependent on the problem of representation, and this new form of the presence/situation.[20]

This "new form of the presence/situation" that Pontbriand has in mind recalls the earlier efforts of those self-named situation-ists, whom Debord inaugurated with his 1957 "Report on the Construction of Situations/ Towards a Situationist International." The kind of events that Debord called for, he wrote, would begin "au-delà de l'écroulement moderne de la notion de spectacle," that is, "on the other side of the modern collapse of the idea of theater," where the French word for theater, *spectacle*, anticipates Debord's later manifesto.[21] Indeed, Debord's critique of "la société du spectacle" is in many ways a critique of a society of theatricality where, as Debord writes in the book's opening provocation, "all that once was directly lived has become mere representation,"[22] or as Sadie Plant glosses it, "people are spectators of their own lives, and even the most personal gestures are experienced at one remove."[23] The role of situations, according to the Situationist International, was to disrupt both the specific genre of theater and theatricality more broadly. Here is Debord in 1957:

> It is easy to see to what extent the very principle of the theater [*spectacle*]—non-intervention—is attached to the alienation of the old world. Inversely, we see how the most valid of revolutionary cultural explorations have sought to break the spectator's psychological identification with the hero, so as to incite this spectator into activity by provoking his capacities to revolutionize his own life. The situation is thus made to be lived by its constructors. The role of the "public," if not passive at least a walk-on, must ever diminish, while the share of those who cannot be called actors but, in a new meaning of the term, "livers," will increase.[24]

In this way, the constructed frame of the new situation, once its rules of spectacle are collapsed or expunged, might become an oppositional space—a smaller scale model of the utopian possibilities realized, at least briefly, in those other influential "performances" of 1968, the occupation of Paris streets in May '68. Here, for many, was the manifestation of a revolutionary utopia, in which the alienation of everyday life was replaced by a return to the "directly lived" experience of a unified community: "Revolutionary moments are carnivals in which the individual life celebrates its unification with a regenerated society," as the situationist Raoul Vaneigem wrote in *The Revolution of Everyday Life* (1967).[25]

Following this one train of possibility, one could imagine theater aspiring to play a role in such reunification and regeneration—and for examples one might look to other performance works of the period, such as the blurring of art and life in the Happenings of the 1950s and 1960s, made famous by Allan Kaprow, and upon which the situationists looked favorably;[26] or the Living Theatre's *Paradise Now* (1968), with its exhortations to its audience to join in acts of revolutionary expression. As Herbert Blau puts it, such works hoped to create "a communitarian state of ecstasy that would break down the hierarchy of established power."[27] In relation to the more general condition of life becoming "mere representation," these new forms of performance explored ways to circumvent or dismantle their own representational distance from the thing being represented. In place of the representational role of the actor, subsuming their identity to that of a character, new modes of performing were explored. This was exemplified by Michael Kirby's influential spectrum from not-acting to acting, which elucidates the approach of "non-matrixed performance," in which actions do not have their meaning determined by being located within a fictional or representational "matrix," but instead exist in the "here and now" of the performance space. Kirby presents these impulses in contradistinction to the "fakeness" of acting:

> Acting means to feign, to simulate, to represent, to impersonate. As Happenings demonstrated, not all performing is acting. Although acting was sometimes used, the performers in Happenings generally tended to "be" nobody or nothing other than themselves; nor did they represent, or pretend to be in, a time or place different than that of the spectator. They walked, ran, said words, sang, washed dishes, swept, operated machines and stage devices, and so forth, but they did not feign or impersonate.[28]

Yvonne Rainer was taught by Kaprow and Anna Halprin, and some of her initial choreographic works, such as *Parts of Some Sextets* described earlier, can be included within this artistic impulse in which task-like activity is used to avoid acting, feigning, and representation.[29] And to be sure, something of this exploration continues in *Trio A*, a work motivated, as Rainer described, by her "love" for the body, "its actual weight, mass, and unenhanced physicality."[30] Pat Catterson, who would later dance *Trio A* herself, described her first response to seeing Rainer's dance by comparing it to the everyday, non-representational uses of the body:

> It was like watching the ease, calm attention to detail, elegance, efficiency, and flow of someone doing anything in life that is practiced and familiar. It was like seeing my mother make a bed, or a cobbler fix a pair of shoes, or a store clerk ring up and bag your groceries, or someone fold her laundry and noting the beauty of that doing, that performing.[31]

Indeed, Catterson's analogies find a surprising resonance with Rainer's own description; she is reported as saying, "In the studio, I work with aesthetics like a shoemaker works with leather."[32]

However, rather than seeking a theater that establishes itself *outside* of the (tainted) sphere of representation, there is another possibility, which I want to pursue here. Notably, Rainer differed from some of her contemporaries in that she remained fascinated with the elements and mechanics of theatrical representation, including classical music and acknowledgment of an audience, for example. Rainer would later reflect: "I was still wedded to or interested in undermining or making reference to certain kinds of theatricality that I was then becoming more and more in opposition to. I had to incorporate both strands into my work, the theatrical one and the oppositional, polemic, pedestrian one."[33] In incorporating these contradictions of "pedestrian" performance and theatricality, *Trio A* is a crucial work—a crux, a crossroads, a pivot—because something else begins to emerge as an area of interest in this work: the role of the spectator. In particular, in Rainer's work that role is conceived not as an "active" participant, or "liver" (in Debord's term), but *as* a spectator. The spectator may not do anything other than be present as an observer—"Stay in your seats," writes Rainer in a 2008 revision of the "No Manifesto," reproduced later in this chapter—but Rainer understands this presence of the spectator as necessary to the performative act.

Looking back at *Trio A*—which we can do through the cinematic lens of Sally Banes and Robert Alexander, who filmed Rainer performing the work in 1978[34]—we may more or less agree that Rainer has succeeded in her goal of avoiding spectacular images, or heroic virtuosity, or seductive emotion, as promised in her manifesto. But alongside this absence, there's something else present, a quality of performance that feels cool and distant, as if we are watching a body that is operating under compulsion. Unlike, say, the Living Theatre's *Paradise Now*, Rainer proclaims "no to involvement of spectator and performer"—and the unmarked energetic continuity of *Trio A*, the withholding of the performer's gaze, and the task-like behavior of the performing body all work to create an experience of spectatorship that is distanced from the action, rather than unified with it. Flattened of emotion, with Rainer completely absorbed in her task, this dance is, as Ramsay Burt puts it, "choreographed so as to be difficult to watch."[35] This difficulty is deliberate. We are watching a body "at work," and while comparable to the kinds of work to which Catterson refers (fixing shoes or folding laundry), the work that *this* body is doing is a very particular kind of work—that is, the work of theater, the work of being watched.

"Being watched" is the titular phrase of Carrie Lambert-Beatty's provocative rereading of Rainer's work of this period: in puzzling over the irritation Rainer's work caused her contemporaries, and in particular the specific gesture of the "averted gaze" (discussed further below), Lambert-Beatty writes, "I realized that even *Trio A* . . . was an attempt not to escape performance's spectatorial condition, but rather to distill it" to what Lambert-Beatty describes as "the fact of display."[36] Whereas Kaprow proclaimed that "there should not be (and usually cannot be) an audience or audiences to watch a Happening,"[37] Lambert-Beatty argues that, for Rainer, "there was something about the conventional spectatorial situation—one group of people, largely passive, watching another, largely active—that needed to be worked through," in an exploration (rather than a negation) of "*spectatorship as such*."[38] That is to say, *Trio A* is interested not only in the "enduring reality" of the performing body, but also in the role given over to those other bodies in the room, the spectators.

How did Rainer get to this particular juxtaposition? In order to achieve the effects that she wanted, Rainer took explicit inspiration from minimalist sculpture, and she explored parallels between the way physical materials were used in these art forms and the way that she wanted the performing body to appear in her own work. She sets out these parallels in her 1968 essay "A Quasi Survey of Some 'Minimalist' Tendencies in the Quantitatively Minimal Dance Activity midst the Plethora, or An Analysis of *Trio A*," in which the overall conceit is an extended analogy between her dance work and some tendencies in minimalist sculpture—such as those described in "Notes On Sculpture" by the artist Robert Morris, Rainer's romantic partner at the time.[39] Rainer's essay opens with a table depicting the correlation between trends in minimalist sculpture and her own practice. For example, if minimalist sculpture seeks to eliminate or minimize "texture," "figure reference," and "illusionism," then in her dance Rainer sought to eliminate, respectively, "variation and dynamics," "character," and "performance." Where minimal sculpture emphasizes "nonreferential forms" and "literalness," Rainer would foreground "neutral performance" and "task or task-like activity."[40] In the remainder of her essay, she explains her interest in "task" as oriented toward the achievement of "movement-as-object," and her use of repetition is intended to "objectify" movement, to "make it more objectlike."[41]

But Rainer's turn toward minimalist ideas of "objecthood" does more than open possibilities for how the body and movement might be deployed in non-representational ways; it is also this turn that orients the work *toward* spectatorship—an insight best articulated, ironically, by minimalist sculpture's most vehement critic, Michael Fried. In his 1967 *Artforum* essay "Art and Objecthood"—which reached a wider audience through its republication in Gregory Battcock's 1968 *Minimal Art: A Critical Anthology*, coincidentally the same anthology in which Rainer's own "Quasi Survey of Some Minimalist Tendencies" was published—Fried described the confrontation with which minimalist work presents its viewers as "basically a theatrical effect or quality—a kind of *stage* presence." Also drawing on Robert Morris, Fried notes how the effect Morris wants to achieve requires control over "the entire situation"—and this situation is understood, in Fried's words, as "including, it seems, the beholder's *body*."[42] To illustrate this, Fried appropriates a description by the sculptor Tony Smith in which Smith recounts a car ride on the then-unfinished New Jersey Turnpike. For Fried, this story is a paradigmatic scene of the ambitions of the minimalist art that he opposes. Smith is quoted as remarking: "Most painting looks pretty pictorial after that. There is no way you can frame it, you just have to experience it."[43] In Fried's retelling, this experience aims for a re-conceptualization of art that is not just a change in degree, but in kind: "Smith seems to have understood [his revelation] not as laying bare the essence of art, but as announcing its end."[44] Fried continues, "And what was Smith's experience if not the experience of what I have been calling *theater*?"[45]

After recounting Smith's post-industrial experience, Fried's rhetoric becomes increasingly apocalyptic:

> Smith's account of his experience on the turnpike bears witness to theater's profound hostility to the arts and discloses, precisely in the absence of the object and in what takes its place, what might be called the theatricality of objecthood. By the same token, however, the imperative that modernist painting defeat or suspend its objecthood is at bottom the imperative that it *defeat or suspend theater*.[46]

In surprising ways, Fried's rhetoric recalls the urgency of Debord's manifesto of the same year: for example, compare Debord's proclamation that "all that once was directly lived has become mere representation" with Fried's declaration that theatricality has "corrupted or perverted" our modern sensibility, keeping us alienated from an experience of "presentness" that, in his final line, Fried identifies with "grace": "We are all literalists most or all of our lives. Presentness is grace."[47] Some years later, Stephen Melville would characterize "Fried's dream" in terms that resonate with Debord's longing for the "directly lived": "a world to which we can be simply present and in which we can be simply present to one another, undivided and unposed, graceful."[48] To realize this dream, one must transcend one's spectatorial distance, one's situatedness in relation to the work, and instead become "absorbed" in the work, as Fried describes elsewhere in his writings on eighteenth-century painting.[49] (To be sure, as Maaike Bleeker argues, the state of absorption is no less "relational" than that of theatricality; it is just that the relations are disavowed.)[50] But it is this absorption of the spectator that *Trio A* makes impossible, instead insisting that the spectator be aware of their own situation, precisely by foregrounding the performer's own absorption in the work at hand.

By self-reflexively transposing ideas from minimalist art to the idea of the performance-event, Rainer's work reveals that the "theatricality of objecthood" (as Fried puts it) necessarily includes the condition of being watched. Her approach to making, which I have described here as "sub-tractionist," removes all that is nonessential from the action; and what remains is theater's existence for, with, and because of a spectator; "theater has an audience—it exists for one—in a way that the other arts do not," Fried wrote, and Rainer's own startled realization is similar: "My God! Can theater finally come down to the irreducible fact that one group of people is looking at another group?!"[51] For this reason, whether or not one agrees with Fried's disdain, his label of "theatricality" can be applied just as appropriately to Rainer as it is to the sculptures of Judd or Morris: as Bleeker writes, Rainer and the minimalists reflect "a shared engage-ment with spectatorship, rather than a material object, as that which is sculpted."[52] But whereas Fried's use of the term "theatricality" sits in that long line of anti-theatrical prejudice that implies a condition of exhaus-tion, depletion, and cheapness, Rainer's work begins to probe different strategies for political engagement: it neither represents politics through the production of referential images—*Trio A* is not a dance "about" Vietnam—nor does it try to create a situation that is "on the other side of spectacle," in the manner of the situationists. Instead, as Lambert-Beatty and others have argued, Rainer uses spectacle to *work through* spectacle.[53]

It is worth highlighting the role of *work* in this *working through* of spectacle. Whereas previous dance styles might attempt to hide the effort being deployed in the production of the aesthetic image, in *Trio A* the image itself is that of continuous effort, that "worklike" quality in which the body is engaged—not necessarily the display of excessive exertion, but rather a continuous, unrelenting effort. But even this "worklike" image requires hidden labor to produce, as Rainer acknowledged: "I have exposed a type of effort where it has been traditionally concealed and have concealed phrasing where it has been traditionally displayed."[54] Perhaps it is because of the distinctive challenges it poses for the performer that *Trio A* has become its own self-repeating "task" for other dancers to perform, identifiable as Rainer's "most reproduced and reproducible dance"[55]—a "canonical" and "signature work"[56]—thanks in part to a legacy of official "transmitters," who act as custodians of the dance and are "allowed" to re-perform it and teach others to do so.[57] The self-conscious effort of re-performance amplifies this performance of dance-as-effort, or dance-of-effort, calling to mind the observations that Bojana Kunst makes about the politics of effort in contemporary dance: "Dance is not close to work issues because it can function as a representation of work or an image of the working process, but because it *is* work in terms of its material rhythms, efforts and the ways in which it inhabits space and time." It is for this reason, Kunst continues, that "the political potentiality of dance should not be searched for in the abstract or democratic idea of freedom and infinite potentiality of movement, but in the ways in which dance is deeply intertwined with the power and exhaustion of work, with its virtuosity and failure, dependence and autonomy."[58]

These questions of effort and exhaustion, virtuosity and autonomy are ones that *Trio A* inaugurates, and takes as its subject, through its task-like performance. Paradoxically, the introduction of task-like activity does not make the actions more real, nor does it allow us to forget that we are in the theater, but it instead reminds us even more that this *is* theater, and that theater is the place where we watch people work to make images of themselves. I'll return in the next chapter to some of these questions around the particularly paradoxical quality of theatrical labor. At this point, I simply want to mark *Trio A* as a turning point, in which Rainer's inward turn—the averted gaze, the continuous image-making of the body—directs our attention to the situation of the theater itself and to the conditions under which this body moves—conditions that include its being watched. Rather than reading her "no to spectacle" as an anti-theatrical gesture, or as a paradigmatic gesture of 1960s anti-representationalism, we might reinterpret it as a key moment in a subsequent "theatricalist turn" in which the ambiguities and complexities of the theatrical situation itself are increasingly taken as the subject of the work. Indeed, Rainer herself has long disavowed the severity with which her "No Manifesto" has been interpreted: "It was never meant to be a prescription for all time for all choreographers," she writes, but rather "to clear the air at a particular cultural and historical moment."[59] And when she revisits this declaration as part of Hans Ulrich Obrist's 2008 *Manifesto Marathon*, she does so in just such a revisionist spirit:

1965	2008
No to spectacle.	Avoid if at all possible.
No to virtuosity.	Acceptable in limited quantity.

No to transformations and magic and make-believe.	Magic is out; the other two are sometimes tolerable.
No to the glamour and transcendency of the star image.	Acceptable only as quotation.
No to the heroic.	Dancers are ipso facto heroic.
No to the anti-heroic.	Don't agree with that one.
No to trash imagery.	Don't understand that one.
No to involvement of performer or spectator.	Stay in your seats.
No to style.	Style is unavoidable.
No to camp.	A little goes a long way.
No to seduction of spectator by the wiles of the performer.	Unavoidable.
No to eccentricity.	If you mean "unpredictable," that's the name of the game.
No to moving or being moved.	Unavoidable.[60]

Peter Handke's "Unmediated Theatre"

For Rainer, "performance" is linked with "illusionism" as one of the components of art that should be "eliminated or minimized" in the opening schema of her essay, and her solution for what she called "the 'problem' of performance" was "never permitting the performers to confront the audience. Either the gaze was averted or the head was engaged in movement."[61] It was this "inward turn" that creates her desired effect of a "worklike or exhibitionlike presentation." By contrast, at nearly the same time, the Austrian writer Peter Handke was experimenting with a turn in the opposite direction. First performed in Frankfurt in 1966, and then in London in 1970, Handke's *Offending the Audience* (*Publikumsbeschimpfung*) famously presents a face-on confrontation with its spectators in an explicit commentary on its status as spectacle: to return to Handke's declaration quoted in this book's introduction, "All you have to do is turn to the spectators and start off; with a perfectly simple shift of ninety degrees you have a new play, a new dramaturgy."[62] As the first and most sparse of his *Sprechstücke*, or "speak-ins," *Offending the Audience* consists of nothing but the actors speaking directly to the audience about the situation called "theater" in which they are gathered. His later experiments with this form would introduce elements of character, minimal furniture and staging, and some narration—as in *Self-Accusation* (1966) or *Kaspar* (1967) in which the speaker creates himself in language—but all of them seek to minimize or eliminate any fictional pretense. The performances are set not in some other time or place but in the unfolding temporality of the theater-event as it is happening, seeming to take place in real time, and the words the actors speak are not an attempt at verisimilitude of speech "in the real world" but rather a theatrical recitation, a performative "speech-act."[63]

As with Rainer's "No to spectacle," Handke's 90-degree turn can, at first glance, be aligned with the anti-representational shifts of its time, and the rejection of fictional pretense in his works marks them as "non-matrixed" performances (to recall Michael Kirby's terminology cited earlier). Indeed, at a 1966 gathering of postwar German-language writers at Princeton, the younger Handke provocatively attacked the older generation of writers for what he described as an "impotent descriptivism" (*Beschreibungsimpotenz*) underlying realist attempts to represent social and political conditions: "That is the cheapest thing literature can be made of," he said, and instead he called for "new forms of language."[64] At the same time, Handke was equally critical of claims that events within the theater could affect social and political circumstances outside the theater. It was for this reason that he distanced himself from Brechtian theater (at least as it was being practiced at that time—more on this below). Handke acknowledged Brecht's contribution in showing that the state of the world is not "natural" but manufactured, "and [is] precisely therefore manufacturable and alterable";[65] but he argued that practitioners of Brechtian theater were mistaken if they thought that anything "real" could happen in the theater. In his view, the kinds of political gestures that he saw deployed in contemporary productions, such as chanting antiwar slogans, bringing real coal miners onto stage, and espousing Marxism, are all neutralized if they happen in the theater:

> What upsets me is not that it is a Marxist solution which is specified, but that it is specified as a solution in a *play*. I myself would support Marxism every time as the only possible solution to our governing problems . . . but not its proclamation in a play, in the theatre. That is just as false and untrue as chanting slogans for the freedom of Vietnam when this chanting takes place in the *theatre*: or when, as in the Oberhausen recently, "genuine" coal-miners appeared in the *theatre* and struck up a protest song. The theatre's [limited] sphere of relevance is determined by the extent to which everything that is serious, important, unequivocal, conclusive outside the theatre becomes *play*.[66]

In place of the Berliner Ensemble with their Brechtian productions, Handke takes inspiration from the Berliner Kommune and other forms of direct action that intervene in public spaces: "There is now Street Theatre, Lecture-hall Theatre, Church Theatre (more effective than 1,000 Masses), Department Store Theatre, etc.: the only one that doesn't exist anymore is Theatre Theatre."[67]

And yet, despite these protestations, Handke does not commit himself to orchestrating actions in public spaces (as, say, in the work of Christoph Schlingensief some decades later, which I will discuss in a later chapter). Instead, Handke makes works for theater spaces, predominantly taking the form of the *Sprechstück*. Following the logic of his manifesto-like declaration, perhaps these could be considered attempts at making a "Theatre Theatre"—that is, attempts to use the theatrical apparatus to theatricalize theater. This redoubled theatricality is evident from the stage directions to *Offending the Audience*: "The usual theatre atmosphere should prevail," and indeed should be even more emphatically theatrical: "The ushers should be more assiduous than usual, even more formal and ceremonious, should subdue their usual whispering with even more style, so that their behaviour becomes infectious." Handke's directions go on to script the role of the audience—in which their job is precisely to behave as if they were a theater audience: "None of the spectators should call attention to [themselves] or offend the eye by [their] attire. The men should be dressed in dark jackets, with white shirts and inconspicuous ties. The women should shun bright colours."[68]

There are similarities with Rainer here, in that Handke is interested in avoiding representation, and does so through a subtractionist, minimizing method: "*Sprechstucke* lack setting, plot, dialogue, and character—all the elements of traditional drama," notes Bonnie Marranca.[69] This structure of negation—like an extended version of Rainer's "No Manifesto"—shapes *Offending the Audience* from the first words the speakers address to their audience after bidding them welcome:

> You will hear nothing you have not heard here before.
> You will see nothing you have not seen here before.
> You will see nothing of what you have always seen here.
> You will hear nothing of what you have always heard here.
> You will hear what you usually see.
> You will hear what you usually don't see.
> You will see no spectacle.
> Your curiosity will not be satisfied.
> You will see no play.
> There will be no playing here tonight.
> You will see a spectacle without pictures.[70]

The remainder of the play consists of statements about the situation of the theater, statements that insist upon the extent to which no fiction or illusion is being portrayed here.

> We don't represent except what we are. We don't represent ourselves in a state other than the one we are in now and here. This is no manoeuvre. We are not playing ourselves in different situations. . . . We are not acting as if. We are not acting as if we could repeat time or as if we could anticipate time. This is neither make-believe nor a manoeuvre.

At the same time, Handke's text emphasizes contradiction and oscillation, parsing the nuances of what it means to speak *on stage*, even if one is not speaking *in a fiction*:

> On the other hand we do act as if. We act as if we could repeat words. We appear to repeat ourselves. Here is the world of appearances. Here appearance is appearance. Appearance is here appearance.[71]

This awareness of contradiction is similar to Rainer's acknowledgment that her work is not without artifice: it is just that the effort that is usually hidden is shown, and other effort is hidden. Perhaps because he orients himself in relation to theater rather than dance or sculpture, Handke is more explicit about this artificiality, as he emphasizes in his commentary on the work:

> The stage is an artifact; I wanted this play to point out that every word, every utterance onstage is dramaturgy. Every human utterance the theatre presents as natural is not evolved, but produced. I wanted to show the "producedness" of theatre.[72]

This artificiality is the reason he rejects certain kinds of political possibilities from the theater: because theater is a space of "play," any gesture will always be a theatrical gesture; and any reality will always be no more (and no less) than a signifier of itself—"a *theatrical* reality," to use the phrase Handke deploys when asked by an interviewer to describe the basic intention of his plays:

> Making people aware of the world of the theatre—not of the outside world. There is a theatrical reality going on at each moment. A chair on the stage is a theatre chair. A broom on the stage may even carry the name of the theatre in which the play is shown. . . . Onstage, a table has its own theatrical function: it is not a table

to eat at, to show how a hungry person eats—it is to demonstrate what a table onstage can be good for.[73]

Offending the Audience systematically works through this theatrical existence of not only material objects, like the bodies and objects on stage, but also the immaterial aspects of the event, including the speakers' own words: "We express ourselves by speaking. Our speaking is our acting. By speaking, we become theatrical. We are theatrical because we are speaking in a theatre."[74] This self-referential tautology of Handke's *Sprechstück* shares with Rainer's movement-pieces the qualities of literalness, facticity, frontality—precisely those aspects of theatricality that Fried condemned. Whereas Rainer's version of anti-illusionism emerges in relation to minimalist sculpture and task-based performance art, Handke's version sits in a direct lineage with Brechtian theater. However, as I will argue, Handke's literal self-referentiality represents a narrowing of the political ambitions of theater's field of focus from that of Brecht.

The influence of Brecht's politics on his theater practice was twofold: his Marxist affiliations motivated him to develop not just new kinds of stories and theatrical *content* (e.g., the plight of those whose options are delimited by economic class), but also innovations in theatrical *form*. For Brecht, the two were linked: "Simply to comprehend the new areas of subject-matter imposes a new dramatic and theatrical form," he wrote.[75] Or as David Barnett succinctly puts it, Brecht was "not making political theatre but *making theatre politically*."[76] Brecht's numerous innovations were all intended to disrupt the illusory quality of dramatic theater, distinguishing an "epic theater" in which "the spectator was no longer in any way allowed to submit to an experience uncritically . . . by means of simple empathy with the characters in a play."[77] Brecht's theater developed an influential collection of techniques and principles for disrupting empathetic identification: the deep structure of the *Fabel* (fable) that foregrounds contradiction as an organizing principle; the use of a paradigmatic repertoire of gesture or *Gestus* to connect character to social structures rather than to interior psychology; and *Verfremdungseffekt* (an estrangement or distancing effect), which is achieved through particular approaches to acting (as quotation rather than inhabitation), staging (use of banners, titles, etc.), and audience relationship (such as narration) that serve to "make the familiar strange." These various strategies can be summarized by Brecht's famous injunction, "Show that you are showing!"[78]

In these formal innovations, the task of the actors and director is to find ways to explicitly acknowledge this double-showing—and in turn this necessarily shifts attention to the experience of the spectators, who are similarly asked to be continuously aware of their own spectating. Brecht calls this a *Zuschaukunst*, an "art of spectating,"[79] for which the parallel dictum might be "See that you are seeing!" In this regard, Handke's *Sprechstücke* owe an obvious debt to this Brechtian shift; and yet, as in his manifesto quoted earlier, Handke explicitly distanced himself from the Brechtian theater. As Christine Kiebuzinska puts it, Handke was part of a post-Brechtian generation of playwrights who suffered from "Brecht allergy, Brecht antipathy, Brecht *Müdigkeit*, or Brecht fatigue."[80] Partly this had to do with a certain codification of Brechtian techniques into a recognizable style which Handke found wearisome and predictable, as in his criticism of the Berliner Ensemble quoted earlier. Heiner Müller would later make a similar criticism, noting that Brecht had become "a classic in gilt wrapping": "The audience accepts a closed form as a package, commodity, and they can't get between its parts anymore."[81] So this rejection was partly opposed to the familiarity and predictability of Brechtian techniques, which were no longer capable of provoking the kind of self-awareness that even Brecht wanted to produce; instead, new techniques were needed. It's for this reason that Marranca describes Handke's *Sprechstücke* as a "step forward" from Brecht's *Lehrstücke*, "further radicalizing the theatre event and consciously activating moment-to-moment audience response."[82]

But the shift from Brechtian theater to Handke's is more significant than the evolution of theatrical forms; it also marks a deliberate reorienting of the political aspirations of theater from those of Brecht. For, as David Barnett argues, to reduce Brechtian theater to a set of techniques is to miss the point—"Brechtian theatre is a method and not an aggregation of devices"—and what makes a work Brechtian is its commitment to a dialectical view of society and a belief that the revelation of social contradictions can bring about social change.[83] Barnett differentiates here between a Brechtian theater and the idea of "postdramatic theatre" articulated by Hans-Thies Lehmann, because a Brechtian theater is still "dramatic," not only because it tends to work through "characters" and "story"—formal devices that, as Barnett demonstrates, a post-Brechtian theater may approach differently while remaining true to Brechtian beliefs—but more fundamentally because a Brechtian theater retains a belief in a correlation between the theater and a representation of the world. It is just that a Brechtian theater offers a non-illusory, non-naturalistic representation intended to challenge the illusion of the apparently "natural" order of things in the world.[84]

However, Handke is not interested in changing people's perceptions of the order of things beyond the theater. His goal, quoted above, is "making people aware of the world of the theatre—not of the outside world." In his dismissal of the capacity of the theater to be efficacious in circumstances outside its own confines, Handke focuses instead on its own mechanisms of appearance and representation:

> *Offending the Audience* is not a play against theatre. It's a play against the theatre as it is. It's not even a play against the theatre as it is, it's just a play. . . . It's a play against the theatre as it is, only insofar

as it requires no story as an excuse for making theatre. It doesn't make use of the mediation of a story in order to create theatre, it is unmediated theatre. The spectator doesn't need to get into a story first, he doesn't need to have pre-histories or post-histories related to him: on stage there is *only now*, and this is the spectator's now too.[85]

I've emphasized Handke's focus on "only now" to highlight the way he shares with Rainer the goal of creating an experience of an unfolding present. This is accentuated by the undifferentiated perpetual motion of Rainer's body in *Trio A*, or the monologic flow of language in *Offending the Audience*: "Our time up here is your time down there. It expires from one word to the next."[86]

This sensation of immediacy is one characteristic that Lehmann ascribes to "postdramatic theatre," which "offers not a representation but an intentionally unmediated experience of the real (time, space, body)."[87] This focus on a theater that abandons its referentiality beyond the theater walls and generates instead a shared temporality, unfolding in the here and now, is celebrated by Lehmann in a short article on the political potential of post-dramatic theater: "The task of theatre," he writes, "must be to create *situations* rather than spectacles, experience of real time process, instead of merely representing time."[88] In Lehmann's opposition of the situation and the spectacle, we can hear yet another echo of Debord, a distinction that also resonates in this more recent formulation, from Forced Entertainment's director Tim Etchells:

> In the complicity of the performers with their task lies our own complicity—we are watching the people before us, not representing something but going through something. They lay their bodies on the line . . . and we are transformed—*not audience to a spectacle but witnesses to an event.*[89]

This talk of witnesses might evoke Brecht's famous model of the "street scene," in which the ways in which different bystanders might retell a street accident from their respective positions serves as a model for the approach to performance of the Brechtian actor.[90] But the person who plays the role of witness in Brecht's model is the *actor*, holding up facts and interpretations as a way of viewing events in the world. Whereas in the post-dramatic paradigm it is the *spectator* who is the witness; and what is being witnessed is both more immediately apprehensible to the spectator, with the performers' actions no longer symbolic or allegorical, and at the same time more abstracted as a consequence of that separation, making no claim to relevance outside the theater-event itself.[91] In Lehmann's terms, this inward shift in the politics of theater is a shift to a "politics of perception": "Instead of the deceptively comforting duality of here and there, inside and outside, [theater] can move the *mutual implication of actors and spectators in the theatrical production of images* into the centre."[92]

And yet, for all Lehmann's talk of "real-time processes," and elsewhere, "the irruption of the real" and the "event" or "situation,"[93] I would argue that this centering of spectatorship complicates any simple distinction between situation and spectacle posed by this rhetoric. For example, Etchells illustrates his opposition between audience and witness with Chris Burden's 1971 performance *Shoot*, where the small crowd in attendance would have seen Burden shot through the arm with a real bullet fired from a real gun. But in Etchells's own work with Forced Entertainment, thankfully no real firearms are brought onto the stage, and instead such encounters with violence are mediated through an explicitly theatrical artifice. Their 1996 *Showtime*, for example, begins with performer Richard Lowdon entering the stage wearing an exaggerated caricature of a dynamite suicide vest, explaining that the first thirty seconds of a performance are important in order to establish a rapport with the audience and that every performer needs a trademark or "a physical gimmick" to stand out from other performers. Later in his opening speech he offers the often-quoted line: "There's a word for people like you, and that word is audience. . . . An audience likes to sit in the dark and watch other people do it. Well, if you've paid your money—good luck to you."[94] As with *Offending the Audience*, which this play clearly echoes, the only thing one is being asked to witness is the activity of theater being made. The spectator is necessary in order to activate this event, but that role is consistently marked as passive: "We have no wish to enter into a dialogue with you. You are not in collusion with us. You are not eyewitnesses to an event."[95] Or as Rainer puts it: "Stay in your seats." This is not the Debordian situation, in which spectacle is defeated and the audience members become "livers," but instead what I will call "the situation of the spectacle," concerned only with its own conditions of representation.

This is a more limited claim for a political theater than Brecht's, one that disavows its ability to intervene in anything other than its own apparatus of production. For some, this self-absorption within the manufactured event of the theater is questionable, a retreat from the world of "real" politics. Janelle Reinelt, for example, airs this disquiet in her review of the 2013 collection *Postdramatic Theatre in the Political*, referring to a quote from Lehmann cited in the collection's introduction:

> It is, however, still quite difficult, at least for me, to understand how Lehmann's insistence that "the political has an effect in the theatre if and only if it is in no way translatable or re-translatable into the logic, syntax, and terminology of the political discourse of social reality" leaves any room for actual engagement with concrete political struggles.[96]

Indeed, one might well ask whether *Trio A* or *Offending the Audience* are anything more than so much dallying with artistic forms while urgent political issues take place outside the theater; and indeed, Rainer herself seems to acknowledge this through the reference in her program notes to the televised images coming from Vietnam. We could imagine that Handke's reply would be more provocative: if we imagine that we are doing anything about political issues by watching them being represented on stage, he might say, then we are only kidding ourselves. "The theatre, as a social institution, seems to me useless as a way of changing social institutions," he writes.[97] But then again, our sense of Handke as a reliable guide to political commitments is seriously undermined by his own affiliations later in his life when he repeatedly expressed sympathy for Slobodan Milošević, the Serbian leader accused of war crimes for his role in ethnic cleansing committed by Bosnian Serb forces in the Bosnian War.[98]

Nevertheless, at the same time as they deliberately close off some aspects of theater's political ramifications, the reductionist experiments of Rainer and Handke also open new dimensions: theater that explores the dynamics of the theater-event itself, a dance that turns inward to regard its own making, and the foregrounding of spectatorship as the necessary condition for the situation of theater. But, to dwell on Lehmann's phrase, what is it that is so political about perception? We may "see ourselves seeing," but what is enabled by this awareness of the world of appearances and representation? This is not immediately obvious in works like *Trio A* and *Offending the Audience*, but we will see these political dimensions of self-reflective theatricality explored and expanded throughout this book through techniques of task-like performance executed without affectation, or the lineup as acknowledgment of the theatrical event, or the *Sprechstück* as self-description. As I will argue when returning to Tim Crouch's work at the end of this chapter, and in further examples in the chapters to come, subsequent theater-makers have navigated this relationship between theatrical representation and the "concrete political struggles" that Reinelt describes, precisely through this core theatricalist strategy of centering the activities of showing, watching, and being-watched.

"Good" Performance and "Bad" Theatricality

The lasting influence of *Trio A* and *Offending the Audience* can be seen throughout successive works that seek to engage with the "event-ness" of theater, and with the role of the spectator. I wonder how many explorations may have begun with a group of young theater-makers gathered excitedly around Rainer's "No Manifesto," as Matthew Goulish recounts the early days of the theater company Goat Island, for example: "We admired these words. They encouraged us to avoid almost everything," he writes.[99] And across the range of twentieth and twenty-first-century performance, there have perhaps been countless variations on Rainer's insight, "My God! Can theater finally come down to the irreducible fact that one group of people is looking at another group?!"[100] Here's one: reflecting on the process of making *Speak Bitterness* (1995), Forced Entertainment's Tim Etchells remarks: "We've finally come down to some awful irreducible fact of theatre—actors and an audience to whom they must speak, and in this case, confess."[101] Or here's another: an interviewer asks Jérôme Bel, "Pour vous, un spectacle, c'est quoi?" (For you, a show, what is it?), and he replies: "C'est des gens vivants dans l'obscurité qui en regardent d'autres vivants dans la lumière" (It is people living in the dark who watch others living in the light).[102]

Both Forced Entertainment and Bel featured prominently in this book's introduction because they are notable for their use of the onstage lineup as a theatrical form. While Forced Entertainment draws upon (and subverts) a long history of conventions from popular entertainment (including vaudeville, double-acts, and TV variety shows), *Offending the Audience* is certainly a key inspiration for the company.[103] And in her review of the New York premiere of Bel's *The Show Must Go On* (singled out by Etchells for its particularly accomplished use of the lineup), the performance scholar RoseLee Goldberg makes an explicit link to Rainer: "'No to spectacle no to virtuosity . . . no to seduction of spectator'—Jerome Bel takes as a given the commandments of radical dance laid down by Yvonne Rainer in her notes for the 1965 *Parts of Some Sextets*."[104]

For all the supposed anti-theatricality of the 1960s, then, I have argued here that these two key works exemplify a theatricalist turn, an inward turn, in which the event of the theater, and specifically the crucial role of the spectator, become the subject of the work. *Trio A* and *Offending the Audience* remain reference points for works all along the spectrum between theater and performance, particularly for works that seem preoccupied with the role of the audience, and especially where that preoccupation is ambiguous or troubled, as in the work of Bel, Forced Entertainment, Ontroerend Goed, the Sydney Front, and many others. Florian Malzacher describes the roles to which audiences have become accustomed, "at least since Handke," as he puts it:

> Bad witnesses (because we are taxed beyond our abilities), bad voyeurs (because we are not enjoying it) and bad players (because we resist it from inside)—roles constructed through the various strategies that make us aware of the theatre situation.[105]

These works invite us to look again at spectacle, not to call for its collapse but to engage in a generative exploration and inhabitation of what Fried (citing Robert Morris) called "the entire situation," and what I am calling "the situation of the spectacle."

The influence of Fried's "Art and Objecthood" essay itself is more complex. Most commentators in an art historical context describe the effect of his essay as exactly the opposite of what it intended to be: that in setting out to catalog the flaws of minimalist art, Fried inadvertently delineated the territory which subsequent artists found most interesting, as exemplified by *Trio A* and *Offending the Audience*: the incorporation of the viewer's situational perspective, the literal (rather than representational) treatment of bodies and objects, and attention to the temporality of the moment of encounter with the artwork. But at the same time, "theatricality" has remained a term that is regarded with ambivalence and even hostility, particularly when juxtaposed to the idea of "performance," with which it is frequently paired—and indeed, many of the advocates of performance might not much disagree with Fried's notorious accusation that "art degenerates as it approaches the condition of theater."[106]

For Hal Foster, minimalist art introduced a rupture in art history—Foster calls it "the crux of minimalism"—not because of any supposed reductivism in its use of materials, but because of its more fundamental reorientation around "the perceptual conditions and conditional limits of art"—which is exactly what Fried condemned as theater.[107] Looking back twenty years later, Rosalind Krauss remarks that Fried's essay is perceived to have "driven a theoretical wedge into the '60s discourse on art, somehow dividing that period into a *before* and *after*."[108] As discussion of Fried's essay moved out of the pages of *Artforum* and into broader discussion, the consensus around Fried's unintentional diagnosis solidified; for example, in a 1979 issue of *October*, Douglas Crimp declared that "over the past decade we have witnessed a radical break with that modernist tradition, effected precisely by a preoccupation with the 'theatrical.'"[109] And in a 1982 issue of *Modern Drama* that surveyed recent experimental performances by the likes of Richard Foreman, Chantal Pontbriand begins by quoting Fried's essay, if only to point out how wrong he got it:

> Despite what Fried thinks, what has given impetus to—what has even shaken—the arts scene during the sixties and seventies is indeed *a kind of theatricality*, brought about by a re-examination of the codes categorizing the arts: painting, sculpture, architecture, poetry, music, dance, etc.; by a shifting of fields between these codes; and also by emphasis given to a device which is akin to the theatre, that of spectator/stage/spectacle, seen as process. This whole phenomenon is called performance.[110]

As the declaration at the end of this passage indicates, Pontbriand is setting out to differentiate this very special "kind of theatricality" that goes under the name of "performance," and she asserts that "Greenbergian critics like Fried" are missing a "distinction between theatre and performance."[111] In her pithy summary I quoted earlier in my discussion of *Trio A*, Pontbriand locates this distinction in performance's ability to transcend represent-ation: "Performance presents; it does not re-present."[112]

And so, despite her opposition to Fried, Pontbriand ends up giving the same name—"theatricality"—to the thing she wants to avoid: hence, per-formance's possibility of "being removed from the theatre or theatricality" grows larger to the extent that "it withdraws from representation into sim-ple presentation." This withdrawal can produce what Pontbriand labels "a 'good' performance, a performance in which presence differs from what it is in the theatre."[113] This "good" performance is characterized by a desire to discover "not a presence sought after or represented," but instead "a here/now which has no other referent except itself."[114] Elsewhere in the same journal issue, Josette Féral more emphatically lays out an opposi-tion between "performance" and "theatricality," contrasting these two terms in her title. For Féral, "performance explores the under-side of . . . theatre, giving the audience a glimpse of its inside, its reverse side, its hid-den face."[115] Like Pontbriand, Féral argues that by referring to nothing other than its own staged existence, performance "escapes all illusion and representation" and "exposes the conditions of theatricality as they are."[116]

These gestures are typical of a persistent binary in which "perfor-mance" and "performativity" are positioned in opposition to "theater" and "theatricality." In her 1996 introduction to a volume on *Performance and Cultural Politics*, Elin Diamond begins by describing such an opposi-tion (although she is careful to identify it as a distinction made by others, rather than one that is self-evident): where theater has been identified with the modes of production of twentieth-century drama—playwrights, directors, and make-believe—performance "has been honored with dis-mantling textual authority, illusionism, and the canonical actor in favor of the polymorphous body of the performer."[117] That same year, and antici-pating Lehmann's "postdramatic theatre" by a few years, Elinor Fuchs in *The Death of Character* describes "performance theater" that moves away from these conventions, distinguished by "its continuous awareness of itself as performance, and in its unavailability for re-presentation."[118] Taking a more dogmatic position, Richard Schechner argues for (and successfully institutionalizes) the "broad spectrum" approach to performance studies, specifically opposing it to what he considers an outdated and increasingly irrelevant model of theater. His address to the 1992 Association for Theatre in Higher Education conference included this oft-cited provocation: "The fact is that theatre as we have known and practiced it—the staging of written dramas—will be the string quartet of the twenty-first century: a beloved but extremely limited genre, a subdivision of performance."[119]

Some artists have been even more blunt in making a demarcation between theater and performance, no doubt with an intentionally exag-gerated polemical flair. Interviewed at the time of *The Artist Is Present*, her

2010 retrospective at MoMA New York, the performance artist Marina Abramović famously declared that "to be a performance artist, you have to hate theatre." As she went on to explain,

> theatre is fake: there is a black box, you pay for a ticket, and you sit in the dark and see somebody playing somebody else's life. The knife is not real, the blood is not real, and the emotions are not real. Performance is just the opposite: the knife is real, the blood is real, and the emotions are real. It's a very different concept. It's about true reality.[120]

It's not just classical dramatic theater that she rejects, but even its contemporary innovations; Abramović identifies directors such as Jan Fabre and Pina Bausch, typically identified with "postdramatic theatre," as examples of how "theatre has appropriated performance's attitudes . . . without giving any credit to performance." And in his survey of contemporary forms of anti-theatricality, Glen McGillivray quotes a similar sentiment from the Australian performance artist Mike Parr in a 2006 interview:

> Performance in the theatre, that is simulation; performance art, that is performing a task to the end of one's endurance, both mine and the audience's. . . . Theatre is always simulation; performance art is always a drastic version of the real.[121]

In their Manichean outlook, it is not much of a stretch to imagine Fried's words coming from Abramović or Parr's mouths: the imperative of performance art, they might happily say, is to "defeat or suspend theater." And yet, as McGillivray points out, theater remains a "cipher" in this opposition, an "empty term" that is not defined in its own right but only as the negative view of what must be avoided, such as seduction of the spectator, simulation, fakery, and so on.[122] As Shannon Jackson has observed, "critics of relational art ranging from Nicolas Bourriaud to Claire Bishop" are only the latest in a long line of art theorists "who place the theatrical on the opposite side of whatever lines in the sand they are drawing."[123]

And so, despite this recurring intensity of rhetoric around theatricality, these lines between the theatrical and everything else are often blurred ones. Jackson describes elsewhere the "flexible essentialism" of the concept of theatricality,[124] and McGillivray cautions that the opposition between performance and theatricality risks essentializing them to the point of uselessness. He suggests that "rather than enter into debates concerning art versus theatre, theatricality versus performativity, or reality versus (theatrical) simulation," it is better to "critically appraise just how metaphors of theatre and theatricality are used in a particular argument and for what ends."[125] Hence we might attend to what is excluded in this drawing of lines: which are the kinds of practices that are labeled "bad" theater as opposed to "good" performance? Stephen Bottoms performs one of the most excoriating analyses of the biases that might underline such distinctions, arguing that the line drawn by Schechner and others between theater and performance is based on a hetero-masculinist anxiety, if not an explicitly homophobic prejudice, in relation to the supposed effeminacy and queerness of "theatre."[126] In her commentary on Fried's essay, Amelia Jones similarly critiques what she calls a "masculinist determination of theatricality," in which the supposed "virility of 'pure' modernism" has allegedly been degraded by theatricality's "feminine mode of presentation."[127] And Fred Moten has also returned to "Art and Objecthood," noting how Fried's rejection of what is "between the arts" excludes the sonic and phonic dimensions of encounter, instead privileging a disembodied "viewer from nowhere."[128] Moten rereads the work of Adrian Piper—pointedly disappeared, at least at the time he was writing, within modernist/avant-garde histories—in order to describe Piper as working through "the exploration of that specifically black objecthood" and what he calls the "essential theatricality of blackness."[129]

In these debates, then, "theatricality" returns, not merely as the foil for performance, but as a positive term in its own right, in need of rescue from its degraded status—a reversal that Diamond had also anticipated in her earlier introduction: "We might observe that if contemporary versions of performance make it the repressed of conventional theater, theater is also the repressed of performance."[130] Significant milestones in this recuperation of theatricality are a 2002 special issue of *SubStance*—in which Féral, for example, reconsiders her earlier antipathy to theatricality[131]—and the 2003 collection *Theatricality*, edited by Thomas Postlewait and Tracy Davis. In the latter volume, the editors begin their introduction by summarizing what Jonas Barish has influentially catalogued as "the antitheatrical prejudice," the recurring critique of theater as both excessive and deficient: "Theatre reveals an excessive quality that is showy, deceptive, exaggerated, artificial, or affected, [and] it simultaneously conceals or masks an inner emptiness, a deficiency or absence of that to which it refers."[132] However, they note that analyses of anti-theatricality inevitably focus on the motivations and contradictions of theater's detractors, from Plato onward, rather than expanding on a positive definition of what might be meant by theatricality itself.[133] Indeed, it is precisely the broad range of possible meanings, and the looseness with which the term "theatricality" is used, that Davis and Postlewait cite as the impetus for their collection: "The idea of theatricality has achieved an extraordinary range of meanings, making it everything from an act to an attitude, a style to a semiotic system, a medium to a message. . . . Apparently the concept is comprehensive of all meanings yet empty of any specific sense."[134]

Davis's own contribution to the collection, "Theatricality and Civil Society," goes back to first principles, at least etymologically, in order to frame a specific and positively defined concept of theatricality. She differentiates between the long etymology of the word "theatrical" and the relatively short one of "theatricality." The latter etymology, she finds, begins with Carlyle's 1837 descriptions of French Revolutionary pageantry, and it's significant for Davis that this term begins to emerge in a context in which democracy itself is being debated, evaluated, and corrected; it is a time when "how we see ourselves—protean and in flux—is related to how we make the culture in which we express ourselves."[135] Following David Marshall, she works backward from Carlyle to Adam Smith's *Theory of Moral Sentiments* (1759), which for Davis describes the "theatricalization of the self relative to others and in self-conscious *reflection* to the self."[136] And, turning to Jay Fliegelman's analysis of theatricality in American republicanism, Davis concludes: "Theatricality was the right condition for a responsible self-governing people to engage in the acts of democracy as well as the condition of consciousness." In contrast to the anti-theatrical critique of inauthenticity, she continues, "theatricality's 'inauthenticity' was its virtue, recognizing the gap between signifier and signified, truth and effect."[137]

Through this etymological history of ideas, Davis identifies theatricality as fundamental to certain ideas of democracy, sympathy, and self-knowledge. In chapter 3, I will expand on these associations through a discussion of the idea of theater in relation to the appearance of the social, and the micro-politics of appearance itself—particularly in relation to Hannah Arendt's writings on "spaces of appearance" and Jean-Luc Nancy's idea of "compearance" or "co-appearance." For now, the key aspect I want to highlight in Davis's reappraisal of theatricality is the way she identifies a common dynamic throughout the various contexts that she considers, which she describes as *dédoublement*: an experience of *uncoupling* from experience leading to self-awareness—or more, perhaps, the experience of a self constituted by and in (rather than prior to) this awareness. That is to say, theatricality is characterized by an ontological dependence on spectatorship, as is made explicit in Davis's proposed update to the *Oxford English Dictionary* entry for "theatricality":

> A spectator's *dédoublement* resulting from a sympathetic breach (active dissociation, alienation, self-reflexivity) effecting a critical stance toward an episode in the public sphere, including but not limited to the theatre.[138]

Although Davis does not refer here to Brecht, her definition recalls Brecht's opposition to sympathy in favor of critical distance. But Davis's definition locates the essence of theatricality in the spectatorial experience of being divided into two: the spectator is both part of an encounter and removed from that situation, both an actor and audience to oneself. This view also recalls Elizabeth Burns's much earlier and more broadly socio-logical account of theatricality, in which she wrote that "theatricality itself is determined by a particular viewpoint, *a mode of perception.*"[139] It was exactly this perceptual mode, the self-awareness of spectatorship, that Fried rejected in Robert Morris's description of the condition of art: "Art is primarily a situation in which one assumes an attitude of reacting to some of one's awareness as art."[140] Davis's version, however, foregrounds the political and agential possibilities of this "mode of perception." For me, this identification of the dynamic of spectatorial *dédoublement* gets to the heart of the "problem" of theatricality: to its detractors, theatrical-ity describes the failure of the representational to be "real," to be fully present, or to be wholly identical with itself, but it is precisely these sup-posed "failures" that Davis reappraises as a possible source of agency and efficacy.

As I have described here, the project of positively reevaluating theatri-cality had already been undertaken for some time by the likes of Burns, Diamond, Féral, Jackson, and Davis by the time such an argument was given an elevated profile in the form of Jacques Rancière's now widely cited provocation, "The Emancipated Spectator"—first delivered as a keynote address at the 2004 International Summer Academy of Arts in Frankfurt, after which it was widely circulated on the internet and reprinted in *Artforum* in 2007, and finally published in an eponymous collection of Rancière's essays in 2009.[141] As his (frequently misinterpreted) title sug-gests, Rancière is concerned with the role of the spectator in performance, and he begins with another variation on the ontological necessity of the spectator, which he describes as "the paradox of the spectator": "There is no theater without spectators."[142] The reason that Rancière describes this as a paradox is that, in his view, those who would defend the value of theater at the same time tend to position spectatorship as a bad thing, yet spectatorship is that which defines theater. Debord's critique of spectacle returns in Rancière's summary of this position: to be a spectator is to be in passive thrall to spectacle, a dupe to simulacrum, and implies the loss of a sense of unalienated community. According to this argument (of which I gave a version earlier in relation to the artistic movements of the 1960s), the alternative is a "good" theater that is opposed to representation and that restores an experience of immediacy, co-presence, and unalienated togetherness—a view that is encapsulated in the theme of the Frankfurt gathering to which Rancière was invited to respond: "Theatre remains the only place of direct confrontation of the audience with itself as a collective."

However, Rancière's paradox of the spectator is intended to reveal the self-defeating nature of such an ambition:

"Good" theater is posited as a theater that deploys its separate
reality only in order to suppress it, to turn the theatrical form into
a form of life of the community. The paradox of the spectator is
part of this intellectual disposition that is, even in the name of the
theater, in keeping with the Platonic dismissal of the theater.[143]

Rancière goes on to argue that both Brecht and Artaud, while usually
positioned in contrast to each other, exemplify two different approaches
to achieving the same end: to disrupt the passivity of the spectator. For
Brecht, spectators must become more distant from the drama in order
to become aware of their own situation, whereas for Artaud the distance
must be overcome so that spectators are totally immersed in the latent
energy of their communal life. In both positions, Rancière argues, "theater
is held to be an equivalent of the true community, the living body of the
community" as opposed to "the illusion of the mimesis."[144]

Moreover, Rancière's argument is not only against the futility of this
exercise in self-suppression, but also about the hierarchy of power that
it reinstates—even as it intends to redistribute agency. For Rancière, at
the heart of this self-suppressing desire for collective activity is a presupposition of binary oppositions: between "looking" and "knowing" or
"acting," between "appearance" and "reality," and between "activity" and
"passivity." Drawing on the concept that he has developed throughout his
political philosophy, Rancière describes these oppositions as a "partition
of the sensible": "a distribution of places and of the capacities or inca-
pacities attached to those places. Put in other terms, they are allegories
of inequality."[145] Far from modeling equality, the ideal of a lost "communal" life perpetuates a set of normative values that are entrenchments
of power differentials, between dupes and those who know better. Rather
than overcoming the distance between us (which, for Rancière, will always
be achieved through suppression)—that is, rather than fetishizing the (im)
possibility of immediacy—Rancière would have us accept that distance
and mediated coexistence as the necessary starting place for any communication among equals. "Distance is not an evil that should be abolished,"
he writes, nor is it "a gap that calls for an expert in the art of suppressing
it"; instead, it is "the normal condition of communication."[146] What if the
condition of spectatorship is not some degraded position to be overcome,
but instead a place of discovery? What if we are already equal?

Tim Crouch and the Situated Spectator

Or to put it another way, "If it weren't for you, I wouldn't be here," in yet
one more observation of theater's ontological dependence on the spectator. This time it is uttered by two actors who are playing guides to a visual

art exhibition, which is being visited by a group of attendees who have booked in for a theater show. This is the situation at the beginning of Tim Crouch's *ENGLAND: A Play for Galleries* (2007).[147] In the first half of this piece, the two actors function as ersatz gallery guides, leading their audience through whatever exhibition is on display in the (actual) art gallery where the piece is being performed. As with *Offending the Audience*, their lines are not designated to particular characters but are instead a shared text between the actors, written in the second person, and they address themselves to the persons gathered in this specific space and this specific time. Sometimes the actors describe the works on the gallery's walls; sometimes they describe the view from some other place, including fictional places (a church and a hospital) from which they are speaking at the same time. "Look," they keep saying. "Look!" The audience is exhorted to see what is there in front of them, and also to see with their imagination into a conjured space—and, as with Crouch's next play, *The Author*, with which this chapter began, to see themselves seeing.

Crouch is the author and co-director of several plays which address the nature of the theater-event both in their theme and in their experimentation with forms: *My Arm* (2003) is a monologue whose seemingly autobiographical basis is gradually revealed to be illusory; *An Oak Tree* (2005) features hypnotism as its central theme and uses a different and completely unrehearsed second performer in every performance; *ENGLAND* (2007), as I have just described, is a two-person piece always performed in art galleries; in *The Author* (2009), the performers speak from their positions in two audience seating banks that are immediately facing each other (as described at the opening of this chapter); and *Adler & Gibb* (2014) is a play for a conventionally seated audience that centers around a fictitious pair of conceptual artists, told through a performance style that gradually shifts from abstract anti-realism to realism. Across these works, Crouch uses a self-reflexive theatricality in order to use the apparatus of theater to think through its own conditions of production and reception, and to foreground the active role of the spectator, in ways that extend and deepen the questions emerging out of the debates of the 1960s that I have discussed here. Moreover, Crouch refers to these debates as explicit touchstones.

Perhaps because he is often a performer in his own plays, Crouch has built a collaborative relationship with Andy Smith (who also goes by "a smith") and Karl James as co-directors of his plays. Describing the beginning of this relationship, it is notable that Smith recalls the influence of Handke's *Offending the Audience*:

> It was this play that Tim was reading when he and I first worked together, a play I knew well and that we ended up discussing at length, so in some senses it was over this play that we met, and

though it was a number of years before we collaborated on anything, it was perhaps somewhere in that play that something of
our work together began.[148]

If Smith fancifully imagines that his collaboration with Crouch began
before the two of them ever met, with the play that Handke's performers themselves announce as "the prologue to all your future visits to the
theatre,"[149] it is because Smith agrees with the way *Offending the Audience*
announces the centrality of the spectator as an active agent in the work.
As Smith makes clear, he is not interested in making the kind of work that
wants the audience to stop being an audience, that seeks to "emancipate"
them from being duped; instead, Smith writes, "We want to let the audience in; *let them be an audience*; be with them."[150] The skills that the three
co-directors bring to this practice could even be described as exactly the
skills involved in being an audience; for example, as Smith puts it, "We
look and re-look, we listen and re-listen; search and re-search."[151] Elsewhere, Crouch makes a similar statement that affirms this equity between
makers and watchers:

> I have always said that theater practice is just an extension of
> audience practice; that we actors are nothing special; it's just the
> contract that we've agreed on for this show, that I'll be here this
> time and you'll be there. Next time, maybe, it will be the other
> way round.[152]

And in *The Author*, the character Adrian articulates this idea that the
audience is authored by the writer—often badly:

> But I often think—I think—I think that sometimes the most
> fantastical—the most made up thing in the theatre is us! Don't you
> [*addresses audience member*]? I saw a play last year. And I remem-
> ber thinking, "that writer has imagined me." I've been imagined!
> Poorly imagined! The audience has been badly written.[153]

Indeed, one way of thinking about Crouch's body of work with his collaborators is as a series of ways of writing the audience differently, testing
various configurations and distributions of roles between actors and audience. To extend the idea of the "situation of the spectacle," in which the
event of theater is acknowledged and foregrounded as what is really happening, then Crouch's plays all demonstrate different ways of "situating"
the spectator. In *My Arm*, characters and significant objects in the story
are represented by miscellaneous objects collected from audience members
at the beginning of the show. In addition to the use of an unrehearsed
second performer, *An Oak Tree* begins by signaling to the audience that

they are also playing a *different* audience who are attending a hypnotist's show at a pub-theater a year from now. As described above, the first half of *ENGLAND* takes its audience through a gallery exhibition, and in its second half, the now-seated audience members, unbeknownst to them, are collectively assigned one of the roles in the drama. And *The Author* is conjured from among the audience to evoke a different (imagined) audience's experience of a piece that never happened. Even in a more conventionally framed work like *Adler & Gibb*, performed on a traditional stage at the Royal Court in London, Crouch has continually emphasized the active role of the audience:

> As with most of my work, the audience can expect a piece that invites, to some extent, their role as co-authors. Space is left for the audience's input—contradictions that require an audience to resolve. The play is complete but remains as open as I can make it. This openness is there to allow the audience entry.[154]

Notably, both Crouch and Smith recall reading Rancière's *The Emancipated Spectator* at some point in their process.[155] However, if their work exemplifies the kind of equity between audiences and makers that Rancière calls for, it is clear that they have been thinking through these questions for some time, and so it would be more accurate to describe Rancière as exemplifying their thinking rather than the other way around.

Crouch and his collaborators' preoccupation with the role of the audience as the necessary condition of theater, and the politics of spectatorship that might be explored through the theater-event itself, is one line of continuity with the kinds of evaluations of theatricality that I have discussed so far. What's more, Crouch's thinking about (and through) theater is explicitly informed by the questions and approaches of gallery-based art from the 1960s and '70s, and specifically works associated with conceptualism and minimalism—exactly the works that Fried hated. Indeed, in his survey of Crouch's work, Stephen Bottoms describes it as "conceptual drama," noting similarities between Crouch's descriptions of his work and those of Robert Morris's minimalist sculptures, and he also compares the techniques Crouch uses in *My Arm* with the works of conceptual artists like John Baldessari and Marcel Duchamp.[156] Crouch and Smith also draw on this legacy in their own descriptions, characterizing their work as "dematerialized" theater—a reference to Lucy R. Lippard and John Chandler's influential 1968 essay on conceptual art, "The Dematerialization of Art," which documented the shift toward ephemeral and experiential forms of encounter with reference to artists like Judd, Rainer, and Kaprow.[157] In his description of "dematerialized" theater, Smith emphasizes its minimalist ethos: "It is a method of making theatre that at its foundation employs only what we might call the essential elements. It is a theatre that—influenced by the terms of conceptual, information, or idea art . . .—attempts operations using the principle that more might be able to be achieved with less."[158] And Crouch also uses the term "dematerialized" to describe the closeness of what he is doing to the art movements of that earlier period, observing that it is "a loose and imperfect term but, for me, it suggests a theatre that is closer to being a conceptual artwork than a figurative or representational form." Crouch continues: "I have taken great inspiration from visual art (without destabilizing my belief in the potential of theatre)."[159]

This inspiration is perhaps most evident in Crouch's play *An Oak Tree*, which adopts its title from the 1973 installation of the same name by Michael Craig-Martin. Craig-Martin's piece, which Crouch describes in the quotation below, is both conceptualist and minimalist; and for Crouch, it embodies his own ambitions of what theater should do:

> I loved the Craig-Martin piece, and I knew that it spoke directly to my approach to theater and to theater in general. Here were, in essence, the devices of *My Arm*, the devices of all good theater. Craig-Martin displays a glass of water and, in a text next to it, he tells us that he's "transformed the properties of the glass of water into those of a fully grown oak tree." This (playful) transubstantiation is achieved through an act of intention—simple as that. He says it, and it is so. In this respect, theater is the ultimate conceptual art form.[160]

This correspondence between Craig-Martin's conceptual proposition and the operations of theater is illustrated in a clever demonstration by Smith, which begins with reading the text that appears next to the glass of water in Craig-Martin's original installation:

> Q. To begin with, could you describe this work?
> A. Yes, of course. What I've done is change a glass of water into a full-grown oak tree without altering the accidents of the glass of water.
> Q. The accidents?
> A. Yes. The colour, feel, weight, size . . .
> Q. Do you mean that the glass of water is a symbol of an oak tree?
> A. No. It's not a symbol. I've changed the physical substance of the glass of water into that of an oak tree.
> Q. It looks like a glass of water.
> A. Of course it does. I didn't change its appearance. But it's not a glass of water, it's an oak tree.
> . . .
> Q. Isn't this just a case of the emperor's new clothes?

A. No. With the emperor's new clothes people claimed to see some-
    thing that wasn't there because they felt they should. I would be
    very surprised if anyone told me they saw an oak tree.

In the demonstration, Smith then asks for a volunteer to stand next to
him—in this account, the volunteer is named "Kelly"—and announces
that Kelly is now the character Miss Julie from Strindberg's famous play.
Craig-Martin's text is repeated with these substitutions:

Q. To begin with, could you describe this work?
A. Yes, of course. What I've done is change Kelly into a full-grown
    Miss Julie without altering the accidents of Kelly.
Q. The accidents?
A. Yes. The colour, feel, weight, size . . .
Q. Do you mean that Kelly is a symbol of Miss Julie?
A. No. It's not a symbol. I've changed the physical substance of
    Kelly into that of Miss Julie.
Q. It looks like Kelly.
A. Of course it does. I didn't change its appearance. But it's not
    Kelly, it's Miss Julie.
    . . .
Q. Isn't this just a case of the emperor's new clothes?
A. No. With the emperor's new clothes people claimed to see some-
    thing that wasn't there because they felt they should. I would be
    very surprised if anyone told me they saw Miss Julie.[161]

This clever bit of theatrical *legerdemain* underscores a key aspect of
theatricality that Crouch explores: the arbitrary representational functions of objects and people, which arises not from any intention or artistry
of the performer, but purely from the situation of theater—"the entire
situation," to recall Robert Morris's description, quoted by Fried. This
situation equally includes the circumstances of the gallery (signaled in
ENGLAND) or the conventional theater space (in the case of *The Author*
or *Adler & Gibb*). For Crouch, these two situations are intimately linked,
as he indicates in a revealing anecdote in which he recounts a conversation
over dinner with the curator of a gallery in which *ENGLAND* was being
performed:

I said that I was doing a play in her gallery, which she didn't even
seem to know about. She almost visibly sniffed and said "Ah yes,
theatre. All that suspension of disbelief stuff." She said she didn't
go to the theatre, because she felt above "pretending." I told her
that all art requires a buying in, a suspension of disbelief—to see
beyond oil on a canvas, or to see form in a block of stone.[162]

The curator's "almost visible sniff" sounds like a mild case of anti-theatricality, once more signaling an aversion to fakery and pretending, and once more locating the problem not only in the performer's artifice, but also in the spectator's willingness to be duped: "All that suspension of disbelief stuff." But Crouch's "conceptual theatre" sets out to explore the proximity between these acts of looking, to "place the dynamics of visual art and theatre up against each other," as he writes in the program notes for *ENGLAND* (which also extensively quotes from Brian O'Doherty's influential critique of the supposed neutrality of the gallery, *Inside the White Cube*, 1976).[163] Crouch explains that *ENGLAND* is not a hybrid work, an encounter across forms, but rather a version of Craig-Martin's transubstantiation: "I have simply taken what I consider to be the mortal essence of theatre and transplanted it to the gallery." What is this mortal essence? It is the game of looking, and being available to be looked at, to exist within the realm of representation. "Look," the two gallery guides say, over and over again, calling attention to the artwork, to the space, to the activity of performing and the activity of spectating. "All this is art," they say. "All this is art. This is how we look. Look."[164]

If *ENGLAND* transposes the theater into the gallery, then *Adler & Gibb* makes the inverse move. This play was a commission for the main stage of London's Royal Court Theatre, a significant marker in the career of any British playwright, and so it's a bold move to open with a lecture on art history—which is how it begins, with the character of "STUDENT" introducing the fictitious subjects of the play, the two conceptual artists named in the play's title. The character of the student continues to add commentary throughout the play, which follows two contemporary figures, a filmmaker and an actor, who intend to create a biopic of the deceased Adler and over the course of the play break into the couple's house and encounter Gibb, who is still alive. In this way, the play specifically addresses the history of conceptual art: the student tells us that "influenced by the Fluxus movement, [Adler and Gibb] became united in their desire to integrate art and everyday life," and one of the historical actions Crouch invents for them involves the two artists literally consuming a portrait of Fried's critical mentor, Clement Greenberg.[165] The student retells the art historical narrative of conceptual art: the way it marked a shift against commodification and toward dematerialization (including an imagined nod to Lippard herself):

> The work of Janet Adler calls into question the, um, conventional strategies by which society preserves, cares for, and re-presents its culture. Her work was remarkable in its power of resistance to the trend towards a cultural commodification. Um. As described by Lucy Lippard, it was a de-emphasis on material aspects, um, uniqueness, permanence, decorative attractiveness, um, it lies in

the non-material realm of experience and interaction—existing
only for the moment of transmission and prolonged within the
memories of those individuals who experienced it. A shift from
the perceptual to the conceptual, from the physical to the mental, um.[166]

But "the non-material realm of experience and interaction" is also
the realm of the theatrical, even if contemporary art-makers distance the
works they make from such a label.[167] In Crouch's work, that theatricality
is not avoided but amplified, consistently foregrounding the operations of
representation that are at work. Many of his plays incorporate a meta-
theatrical narrative: in *Adler & Gibb*, for example, within the fiction of
the play we have the character of a director who is coaching the character
of an actor (Louise) to play the role of one of the other characters (Adler).
But equally prevalent are formal aspects of the production that highlight
the mechanics of representation: in this play, the performers on stage are
accompanied by two children who assist the actors in preparing for their
scenes by undertaking tasks such as bringing scenery onto the stage while
the actors are performing, applying fake blood or handing a tube of fake
vomit for the actor to use, turning on a smoke machine, or in an extended
sequence, swapping out the props that the actors are using with substi-
tutes that the stage directions indicate should be "more outlandish and
more theatrical" (a plastic fish for a sledgehammer, a plastic gun with an
inflatable toy).[168] And across the overall trajectory of the play, Crouch's
direction asks that the adult actors' performances shift from a stylized,
anti-realist style of presentation to a form of acting that is more "dimensional," perhaps literally enacting Kirby's spectrum from not-acting to
acting. For example, by act 2 of the play, the directions specify that the
performances should be "three dimensional but not quite 'naturalized,'"[169]
and the production ends by leaving the realm of theatrical representation
entirely, as a projected film shows "real" environments (the interior of
buildings, the grass outside) in closely captured detail.

In this way, alongside the emphasis on the active role of the spectator—
and indeed emerging as a necessary corollary to this active role, as I will
discuss below—a recurring formal property of Crouch's work is the foregrounding of an arbitrary relationship of representation. Importantly, he
distinguishes his theatrical representations from a fictional or narrowly
mimetic relationship in which an audience takes the representative object
as being *the same as* the represented thing—that "suspension of disbelief"
that prompted the curator's sniff.[170] Throughout his plays, it's clear that
no relationship of similarity is necessary in order for representation to
take place: from the sundry physical objects standing in for the narrator's
mother and father in *My Arm*, to the unrehearsed second actor in *An Oak
Tree*, to the use of child performers in *Adler & Gibb* to portray various

nonhuman figures—a deer, a dog—which the children do by simply standing on stage, and in no way mimicking animals.

Significantly, for Crouch, this shift away from mimetic representation is coupled with the foregrounding of the active role of the audience.
He actively removes any need for the actors to feel or believe what they
are doing in order to create the conditions "whereby thought and feeling is engendered predominantly in the audience rather than on stage."[171]
Crouch's strategies recall a Brechtian approach, in that they separate the
act of representation from the structures of empathy and identification,
but (as with the distinctions I made in relation to Handke) his choices are
not primarily aimed at fostering an awareness and disidentification with
historical narratives, but instead generate awareness of the theater-event
itself—the "inward turn" of Rainer and Handke. In particular, Crouch
seems interested in that particular state of *dédoublement* described by
Davis in which, paradoxically, an audience is aware of the artifice of representation *and at the same time* continues to enjoy the event—and indeed,
may even have a heightened enjoyment.

For Crouch, this was an important aspect of *My Arm*. At one point in
the story of having decided to keep his arm raised for the rest of his life,
the narrator explains that in order to avoid being "sectioned" (losing his
right to self-determination under mental health legislation), he agrees to
have his now lifeless finger amputated—and to illustrate the point, Crouch
the actor shows the audience his finger, which is still attached to his hand.
As Crouch emphasizes in an interview, "this is a quintessential moment of
theatre for me. This is the moment of theatre which is a transformation
that has a physical container that looks nothing like the thing it says it
represents." He continues:

> In this playful nature it's actually a finger representing a non-finger,
> which is as pure as you can come, almost, in that relationship.
> There's also a moment where I show my back and I talk about try-
> ing to kill myself and failing, but rupturing my spleen and having
> an operation. And I say to the audience, "but you can still see the
> scar," and I stand up and lift my shirt and show them the scar on
> my back, but there isn't a scar on my back. But the rubric of course
> is that the audience all lean forward to see the scar, even though
> that bottle is my dad and this pastry is my mum, and I haven't got
> my arm above my head.[172]

This "quintessential moment" is characteristic of a recurring feature
of Crouch's work, in which claims to reality and claims to the fictional
are staged simultaneously, presented in such a way that neither claim is
privileged over the other, and instead both seem to coexist in a mutually
supportive relationship.

In *An Oak Tree*, Crouch begins by introducing a second performer—and introducing to the audience the idea that the second performer will only ever be speaking as he or she has been instructed to do—either by reading from a script, repeating what he or she hears in an earpiece, or with Crouch giving instructions in plain view, as in: "Ask me what I'm being, say: 'What are you being?' "[173] This dynamic both represents a hypnotist's act and is itself a kind of hypnotism, already acknowledging its staged-ness. This condition is further complicated by incorporating the "real" audience within its structure:

> HYPNOTIST [Crouch]: Let's face out front. Ask who they are, say: "And them?"
> FATHER [played by the second performer]: And them?
> HYPNOTIST: They're upstairs in a pub near the Oxford Road. It's this time next year, say. . . . (*To the audience.*) In a short time I'll ask for volunteers but I'm not asking you. I'm asking some people in a pub a year from now. So don't get up.[174]

The stage act we are seeing is placed in a kind of suspended reality; it is both happening in front of us now, and is a representation of something that is claimed will take place in the future. We get similar spatiotemporal doublings in Crouch's other plays: the gallery guides in *England* describe not only the artworks currently in the gallery but also the quality of light of some fictional spaces (a church and a hospital) from which they seem to be speaking at the same time; and from within the audience, *The Author* conjures the experience of a piece that never happened.

The figure of the Hypnotist in *An Oak Tree*, in particular, seems to be a metonym for the theater as a whole and is a succinct encapsulation of this duality of representation and the real. His routine evokes all that is cheap and tawdry about the theater: the idea of the actor as a mere entertainer, at best, and a charlatan, at worst, which are connections that Crouch has discussed.[175] But at the same time, the power of suggestion that the Hypnotist wields is clearly associated with the power of the performative: its ability to overwrite and overwhelm the real, and to fabricate new realities, and while these can be used for cheap effects (Crouch's hypnotist recalls having convinced audience members that they have defecated on themselves), it can also create layers of complex lyricism:

> HYPNOTIST: When I say so, you're driving.
> It's dusk. The sky is purple, blue, orange, yellow, grey.
> To your right, the rim of the world is blackening. . . .
> FATHER: When I say so, you're walking.
> It's dusk. You're on your way to somewhere.[176]

Like Handke's *Sprechstücke*, the world of Crouch's theater is a world made out of language, and nothing in it happens without the performer suggesting it and without the spectators acceding to that suggestion. We are always invited to follow that suggestion, to imagine ourselves in the drama, and at the same time we're reminded that it is only a suggestion and that it is our choice to participate. Bottoms offers a succinct catalogue of the aspects of Crouch's theatricality:

> The non-coincidence of actor and character, the overt fictional-
> ization of both performance space and audience, the provocative
> juxtaposition of real-world materials with language that facilitates
> alternative perceptions in spectators' minds, and the exploration
> of complex ethical questions surrounding both authorial influence
> and spectatorial engagement.[177]

To Bottoms's list, I would add the particular quality with which spoken text is used in Crouch's plays, which announces itself as theatrical descrip-tion even as it enacts the description by way of a quality of lightness, matter-of-factness, and clarity of enunciation and intention that character-izes the way the texts are performed.

Crouch himself exemplifies this approach, but it is shared by his fellow performers in *ENGLAND* and *The Author*—and it even has a similarity to the unprepared second performer in *An Oak Tree*, who may add some particular inflection but has been relieved, by the performance's setup, of any expectation of emotional investment. Crouch and his performers tend to wear a cheerful expression on their faces, and this expression is matched by a brightness and openness in the way they say their words. Exclamation marks appear frequently in the printed text, and it often feels as if these are audible in performance—but not as if they are carriers of any particular sense of surprise or discovery. Instead they seem to exclaim something like: there is nothing here but this sentence! "Look! My skin is damp with sweat. / Look!" says one of the performers in *ENGLAND*. "I love this! This! All this!" declares Adrian in *The Author*. "I'm an actor! / I didn't tell them that I hadn't worked for a year!" confesses Vic in *The Author*.[178] It is not that the words are meaningless, but that no additional meaning will arise from any particular emotional or stylistic exertion by the performer. What seems important is that the audience hears and understands that their access to the language is equal to that of the performers. Perhaps this speaking style derives from Crouch's parallel experience as a maker and performer in an ongoing series of performances for young audiences—but this is not to say that he talks as if condescendingly addressing a child.[179] Instead, his style of speaking serves to acknowledge the scripted nature of the words: this is prepared speech, it announces, delivered by practiced public speakers, and even when the words describe the here and now, they are not *completely* here: "Here and now needs to be transformed into somewhere else and 'somewhen' else, and that happens in *The Author*," says Crouch.[180] In this way, even the way the performers speak serves to highlight the doubleness and interconnectedness of the representational meaning of the words and their real sound and resonance in the room.

There seems to be something of a contemporary interest in denaturalized speech to which Crouch's theater bears an interesting relationship. We might think here of the curiously flattened yet emphatic speech of the performers in Richard Maxwell's New York City Players, frequently glossed as "deadpan" (much to the frustration of Maxwell himself, who prefers Sophie Nield's negative characterization of it as "not traditionally intoned").[181] Or the bizarre, whimsical speech of the Nature Theater of Oklahoma, discussed in the next chapter, in which initially comical accents and over-exaggerations are sustained over several hours, long past the point of being funny. Or the cheerful singsong of Lone Twin Theatre, which the company's directors described as intended to achieve the effect of the words floating in the air, like a comic-book speech bubble, or as if they had quotation marks around them.[182] Denaturalized speech is certainly nothing new in contemporary theater, or indeed in theater of earlier periods. But what might be new in the cluster of performance styles is that the artistic intention seems not to be about alienation or distance, but instead about proximity and a certain *kind* of reality—that is, the reality of being representational. Maxwell, for example, describes his technique as a reaction against the obvious artificiality of so-called naturalistic drama, an artificiality that (for Maxwell) seems to alienate rather than persuade.[183] By contrast, instead of investing in the reality of the fictional characters, Maxwell draws attention to the reality of the theater-event. In an interview he says: "The reality of it is we are acknowledging the artificiality, and that's what makes it real. The highest reality is that there is a play happening."[184] Crouch similarly insists that "there is only one 'site' in theatre, and that is the audience. *That's* where the play takes place."[185]

Much like Yvonne Rainer before them, Crouch and his collaborators explicitly look to the operations of minimalist and conceptual art for theatrical analogues, and so perhaps this style of speaking can be compared with Rainer's so-called pedestrian dance: it has a kind of presentness, avoiding spectacular demonstrations of technical skill, and simply announcing itself as a variety of human action. But also like Rainer, these are actions oriented toward and in relation to another activity, that of spectating. Rather than a means to an end—an interruption or intervention into theater, a transformation of spectatorship into some other form of involvement—Crouch is interested in the ethical and political complexity of this particular form of action. In one interview, Crouch makes a comparison with Forum Theater, the participatory format created by Augusto

Boal and adapted by many other artists working in a range of contexts. Crouch affirms that these kinds of participatory events are valuable in many circumstances, but this is not what he is setting out to achieve. The structure of the theater-event is what is fascinating for him, not its capacity to become something else. He continues:

> That's a kind of danger for me. If we do see theatre as a debating tool, then there's something else happening, on a much deeper internal level, in *The Author* than just provoking some questions around responsibilities of watching. Do you know what I mean? Which is about how you are, how we are, how we are together, what we see in each other. [It's about] the form of the structure of the piece, [which] can be read on a surface level but on another level I hope is working quite deeply in how uncomfortable we're feeling, or how released and warm we're feeling. And those for me are, in a way, the . . . the prods that are most exciting for me. I'm not trying to shake the audience to suddenly have a revelation around child pornography. I'm not trying to prod them to have a revelation about how the theatre is made. I hope I'm having a little prod to go, You know you're in this really deep now. We are in this really deep now.[186]

I've reproduced Crouch's comments at such length because of the many ways in which this passage is relevant to the argument at hand. At its core are two negations: for Crouch, the ethical urgency of *The Author* is not about its dramatic content: it is not *about* child pornography. However, Crouch continues, neither is the work about using the example of child pornography to produce an ethical realization about the nature of the theater. Indeed, what is most clear is that there is no realization being pushed onto the audience; whatever there is to be realized has already been realized (in the double sense of *making real*) through the act of coming together as an audience. And it is the act of coming together as an audience that makes this event, which exists for an audience, come into existence. Rather than the representation of politics outside the theater, the ethical challenges and precarious power dynamics that Crouch stages are already problems of representation, and of representationality itself; and so to represent them in the theater is not to transform them, but simply to continue to practice them within the situation of the spectacle.

Chapter 2

✦

Engaged Theater: Making the Work Appear

If the last chapter opened with no stage at all, just an audience facing itself, then this one begins with a scene that shows us everything else: an open playing space, with all the machinery of the theater exposed; the back wall and emergency exits; the fluorescent worker lights as well as the theatrical lighting rig; the sound systems and safety barriers. A man walks across the stage. He walks with a particular quality of awareness: seemingly without any special consideration of how he walks, his is a functional walk that does little more than take him from one side of the space to the other. His loose gaze takes in the room—not the audience, or any particular detail of the staging apparatus, but instead a practiced alertness for anything that might be amiss. A few moments later, tracing a different trajectory, another man walks across the space (and they are mostly men in this production). And after him, a couple more, and then finally a congregation gathers in the middle of the space. Their conversation is too quiet to hear from the audience, and so projected surtitles represent their words. "Is everyone here?" one asks, and upon agreeing that they are, they proceed to plan the evening's event. "Let's make it comfortable," says the captioned text. "We can use the things we have here. Props, sound, lighting." Someone asks about dressing up. "Not necessarily," is the reply. "Then let's stay here. We could even use the machinery."

This scene I am describing is not Peter Brook's famously romanticized vision of "the empty space," stripped of all but the essential act of theater (another version of the ontological necessity of the spectator, described in the previous chapter): "A man walks across this empty space whilst someone else is watching him, and this is all that is needed for an act of theatre to be engaged."[1] Instead, this space is a workplace, filled with machinery of all kinds used for the manufacture of appearances; and the (mostly) men who walk across the stage are the people who make their living by working here: not the performing companies, who come and go, but its permanent technical workers, or *technique* in French, and this piece, Philippe Quesne's *Pièce pour la technique du Schauspiel de Hanovre* (2011), is made for them.[2] The show's conceit is that these workers are setting up for their Christmas party, and so, while we watch, they try out the theater's various functions, not for the purpose of creating an illusion or spectacle, but as something to play with, experimenting with its different capabilities: the way that the curtains and stage mechanisms perform, for example, by obstructing and revealing, by framing and directing the gaze. In the middle of the piece, these theatrical elements are combined to create a cozy shed, with a warm light coming from inside as it is surrounded by the fog and gentle snow of a winter storm. However, this setting is not used to play out any fictional scene, but is merely an act of composition for its own sake, as the workers move trees and other elements around and comment on the arrangement, beginning to disassemble the image even as other parts are being added. Nor are these *actors* pretending to be stagehands, as in Pirandello's *Six Characters in Search of an Author*; sometimes, it is true, they are stagehands pretending to be stagehands, as in occasional elements of fictive drama: a section where the workers act as if the stage lift has broken down, for example, complete with illusionistic sparks and sound effects. And we also know that they are not *really* planning their Christmas party to happen here, even as they end by creating a careful onstage reproduction of a backstage canteen area. Nevertheless, we know that they really are the technical workers employed by the theater, as the work's title promises, and this correlation is crucial to the pleasure of watching them at work.

This piece stages the convergence of two different kinds of work that, after Marx, we might think we understand with regard to the production of value. The first kind is the work that a laborer is doing when no one is watching apart from other workers; for example, when being paid an hourly wage to build a stage set, or all the other kinds of work involved in running a theater: project management, delivering outcomes, producing marketing materials, meeting deadlines. This is *just* work: labor power, a variable and anonymous form of capital—and, Marx tells us, because the activity itself is objectified by being sold, it is also the site of the worker's estrangement from his or her own activity: "The worker is related to the *product of labour* as to an *alien* object," Marx writes, and this alienation from one's labor results in "*alienated man*, estranged labour, estranged life, *estranged man*."[3] The second type of work is that which the finished art object is doing when it is available for display, and is part of an exchange of capital: it might be up for sale, or honoring a commission, or viewable for the price of a ticket. This is no longer "work" but "*a* work": the commodity form, circulating independently and defined precisely by its abstraction from the labor that went into it, and hence alienated by a second degree. This chapter asks: what might be made possible by collapsing these two categories, when labor is incorporated into art such that "work" becomes "a work," or when "a work" consists of "the work" that makes it? When the workers working *is* the artwork?

There are two primary ways in which the interrelation between theater/ performance and labor has been conceived, and which are playing themselves out in various configurations in contemporary art and theater works. The first of these, based in 1960s art practices, draws upon the blunt materiality of "task-based" activity in order to resist the artifice of theater, mimesis, or acting. In this model, the impurity of representation is allegedly displaced by performativity, the presence of the action itself; such an approach was discussed in the previous chapter in relation to works such as Yvonne Rainer's *Parts of Some Sextets* (1965), or the Happenings by Allan Kaprow and others. The second and more recent model draws parallels with ideas of immaterial or affective labor, exploring the ways in which the performance-event is symptomatic of wider changes in economic production. Some of the initial proponents of "relational aesthetics" excitedly predicted that the artistic sphere might hold open the possibility of an alternative space uncorrupted by commodification. As Nicolas Bourriaud wrote in inaugurating relational aesthetics in the 1990s: "The enemy we have to fight first and foremost is embodied in a social form: it is the spread of the supplier/client relations to every level of human life, from work to dwelling-place by way of all the tacit contracts which define our private life."[4] For Bourriaud and others, the claimed autonomy of artistic spaces offered the potential for escape from these relations, if only temporarily—and, somewhat paradoxically, this escape might be achieved not by doing away with labor altogether, but instead by making a shift toward labor that was relational, interactive, and immaterial. Chantal Pontbriand's introduction to a 2006 issue of the contemporary art journal *Parachute* captures this enthusiasm, as she celebrates a post-industrial society which "has almost entirely emancipated humans from the production of objects and from an economy based on the circulation of objects and commodities, and has given rise to an economy that is ever more immaterial."[5]

Almost immediately, however, this optimism was attacked both on the basis of its overstated claim to art's autonomy from social conditions, as in Stewart Martin's Adorno-inspired critique of relational aesthetics;[6] and on the basis that this "immaterial" labor was not in fact an alternative to dominant market forces, but simply symptomatic of that modern form, characterized by Maurizio Lazzarato and subsequently popularized by Antonio Negri and Michael Hardt as post-Fordist or "immaterial labor."[7] Subsequent critics would argue that artists, performance-based or otherwise, cannot claim some vantage point outside of advanced capitalism, but are its most exemplary laborers; Claire Bishop, for example, concludes that "the virtuosic contemporary artist has become the role model for the flexible, mobile, non-specialised labourer who can creatively adapt to multiple situations, and become his/her own brand."[8] And Bojana Kunst has identified artistic processes as paradigmatic of neoliberal emphases on self-improvement and continual reinvention, as well as contemporary capitalism's shift toward the production of sociality itself:

> What Bourriaud fails to stress is the question of exploitation: the social effort invested to create the audience of the museum, to create the new dispersed and autonomous public for the contemporary institution. This social is therefore not *a priori* emancipatory (or political in Bourriaud's sense), but part of the exploitation, going hand in hand with other processes of human exploitation in this post-Fordist mode of working.[9]

This chapter draws on both of these ways of thinking about staged labor: as task-based activity, apparently manifesting itself as "real" work, and as affective labor, in which private endeavor is no longer dissociable from investment in social and material economies. I will explore these aspects across three different modes of theatricalized labor: the transposition of work from outside the theater into the theatrical frame; the making visible of the support structures that make possible the artistic work; and, finally, the expansion of theatricality to a scale that it might occupy an entire life. If a Marxist critique of productive labor is that it is abstracted and alienated, experienced as "estranged labor" rather than "life activity" or "productive life itself,"[10] then the theater would appear to be the last place where such alienation might be resisted, given its long association with dynamics of abstraction, representation, and reproduction. However, as I will argue, the representational function of theater—the way it decouples action from its function and transforms it into the *appearance* of action—can render inoperative the typical productive function of labor. This is not to argue for the autonomy of the theater from its conditions of production; quite the opposite, I want to suggest that one of the things theater is capable of is making visible its own conditions of appearance—that is, of engaging with the material conditions within which it itself is held.

The "Reality Theatre" of Rimini Protokoll

From out of the darkness, the sound of a man's voice. Though it rises and falls like song, the tones are unfamiliar, and since I don't know Arabic, the meanings of the Quranic verses are a mystery to me. The voice is joined by others throughout the auditorium, with semitonal differences emerging between them. The lights come slowly up, and the chanters move onto the carpeted stage. They are all men: one of them is apparently blind; another has a beard and a permanent bruise on his forehead from touching the ground during prayer; another is dressed in carefully presented brown and white robes, with a white cap. They line up and face us.

In relation to the larger questions of this book about the political potential of theater, these opening moments of Rimini Protokoll's *Radio Muezzin* at the 2009 Dublin Theatre Festival set up an encounter in which the politics of the theatrical event are entangled with the politics of the world outside the theater. The production toured throughout Europe at a time when the status of Muslim populations in European cultures was a prominent subject of debate by non-Muslims; and that same year (during which the production played in Zurich, among many other cities) a popular referendum was passed in Switzerland banning the construction of minarets—the same towers from which the muezzin to which the show's title refers would call the faithful to prayer.[11] In this way, Rimini Protokoll's productions can be seen to participate in a politics of representation by the way in which they bring into visibility groups that might otherwise be hidden from the dominant gaze (an idea discussed more fully in the next chapter). Other examples from their works presented to English-speaking audiences include *Cargo Sofia* (Dublin Theatre Festival, 2007), which features Bulgarian truck drivers telling their stories, and *Call Cutta in a Box* (Dublin, 2008; New York, 2009; Minneapolis, 2010), in which, as I will describe in more detail below, audience members have one-to-one phone conversations with Indian call-center operators. Still other projects offer a "behind the scenes" perspective on the processes of representation: *Breaking News* (Brighton Festival, 2009) directly stages reporting on world events, its onstage cast of news workers giving live commentary on the stories of the day; and in *Best Before* (Brighton Festival, 2010), each audience member controls an individual avatar in a collective video game, participating in a series of collective decisions within the micro-society modeled by the game. As Christiane Kühl points out, Rimini Protokoll's interest in representation is typically based on group identity: "The world is always presented by Rimini Protokoll in groups: occupational groups, age groups, nationalities, etc."[12] This is exemplified by their most widely toured work, the *100%* series, which has taken place in more than thirty-five cities: *100% Berlin* (2008), *100% London* (2012), *100% Gwangju* (2014), *100% São Paulo* (2016), and so on. Performers are selected for this series through an exhaustive pre-production process, unique for each city where it is staged, in order to represent different demographic aspects of the city's population; in the final staged event, the performers on stage manifest different spatial, statistical, and discursive ways of representing the city's demographic diversity.

What's more, the encounter offered by Rimini Protokoll's works does not seem to be with a second-degree representation of these issues, at least at first glance, but rather with the real circumstances of the lived experiences of those who appear on stage. As Jens Roselt observes, "They were real people" is likely to be the way anyone who has seen a Rimini Protokoll piece for the first time describes their experience.[13] The performers in

Rimini Protokoll shows are not actors, trained in the art of standing in for others; nor are the effects of policies and politics on their lives illustrated by stories written by outside observers. The truck drivers really are truck drivers, telling their stories while they drive their audience around in the back of a truck; the news workers really do have careers in the television news industry; the Indian call center employees really are working in an Indian call center when they speak over the phone to their audiences of one at a time; the performers leading the audience through the video game are people who work in or near the video game industry; and the Muslim declaimers really are the ones who call the faithful to prayer from the minarets of Cairo's mosques.

All of these factors seem to point to a theater that seeks to transcend itself, that is more than theater: not a representation or simulation of politics, but the staging of politics itself. However, my interest in the work of Rimini Protokoll is in the way the social issues and political problems that are staged in their works turn out to be interrelated with theatrical dynamics of presentation and representation, the production of authenticity, and affective labor and its consumption. The work that this theater does, then, is to make visible the continuity between the apparatuses of appearance within which these performers labor *outside* the theater and the related dynamics *inside* the theater. That is to say, these performers' respective professions are *already* defined by the need to negotiate their own representations and the production of a "reality" effect, such that the theater becomes not so much a contrast with their "real lives," but instead a folding of different systems of representation into and onto themselves, in a process that I will describe as "engagement."

Rimini Protokoll is a collaboration between Helgard Haug, Stefan Kaegi, and Daniel Wetzel (as well as their early collaborator Bernd Ernst, who left the company in 2002).[14] As has been frequently commented upon, their distinctive style is based on the use of nonprofessional actors, who are referred to by Rimini Protokoll as "experts." In a typical production process, the company will decide upon a particular theme, recruit experts who have some relation to that theme, work with the experts to construct narrative and theatrical elements out of their own life experiences, and combine these in a theatrical composition in which the experts themselves perform. In *Breaking News*, for example, the experts were selected based on their experience in television reporting, editing, producing, interpreting, and so on. The theater production introduced the experts as allegedly all living in the same apartment complex in Berlin, and the stage design somewhat mirrored this arrangement. During the performance, the experts presented their own stories, and they also collaborated in real time to produce a live news program about the stories of the day using footage from various networks around the world.[15] Or in *Best Before*, the audience is led through their interactive video game experience by four experts: a video game programmer, a games tester, a lobbyist for the games industry, and a flagperson employed as part of construction work that took place outside the offices of the video game production company.[16]

A recurring thematic element of Rimini Protokoll's work is their interest in experimenting with, modeling, or restaging processes of democracy and representation (as with the collective decision-making facilitated by *Best Before*). In the *100%* series, one hundred inhabitants of the city are chosen by a kind of chain-selection process, with the constraint that the final group has to proportionally represent the city's demographics with regard to age, sex, nationality, place of abode, and civil status. The production itself emphasized that its participants are "not just numbers," but "people with the power to make [their] own decisions."[17] In discussing *100% London* (2012), Marissia Fragkou and Philip Hager compare its mode of representative assembly with its contemporary backdrops of the 2012 London Olympic Games and the 2011 Occupy London Stock Exchange, describing all of these as various forms of staging citizenship.[18] In another work, *Annual Shareholders' Meeting* (2009), Rimini Protokoll bought shares in the Daimler corporation and sought out shareholders willing to donate their right to attend the annual meeting; the rights to attend the meeting were transferred to "audience" members, who then attended the meeting "as" theater, complete with theater programs provided by Rimini Protokoll.[19] This exploration of multiple meanings of representation began with one of the company's first works, *Deutschland 2* (2002), which proposed to have over 200 volunteers performing a simultaneous reenactment of a debate in the newly relocated German Bundestag; whatever was said in the Bundestag was to be transmitted to the earphone of the respective volunteer, so the volunteer (in Bonn) would speak exactly the words being spoken by his or her representative (in Berlin). However, the performance never happened, as the Bundestag president, Wolfgang Thierse, personally intervened on the grounds that the performance would "impair the dignity and prestige of the German Bundestag."[20]

This approach seems to be stretching the limits of the theatrical, turning it into something else, something more "real" than ordinary theater. Histories of Rimini Protokoll tend to place the company within a specific German tradition that turns against representation and artifice, emphasizing, for example, the fact that all of its members attended the Giessen Institute for Applied Theatre Studies. As Florian Malzacher describes it, "the trap of representation (and that was essentially the whole of the German theatre landscape) was to be avoided at any price, and was considered at Giessen, more than anywhere else, the primary cause of all theatrical ills."[21] For Thomas Irmer, Rimini Protokoll exemplifies a third phase of German "documentary theatre." In the first period, dominated by Erwin Piscator in the 1920s, images from public political life were transplanted into the theater, as in the technique referred to as "living newspapers."

During the 1960s, documentary plays such as those by Peter Weiss (who staged the Auschwitz trial in *Die Ermittlung*, 1965) used historical documents as the source texts for staged performances (a format that continues in Anglophone theater, such as the "tribunal theatre" that London's Tricycle Theatre has been developing since the 1990s). In Irmer's third period, beginning in the late 1990s, history and politics are viewed less monolithically and more critically, and the works often addressed "smaller subjects with complex social contexts that demonstrated the heterogeneity of contemporary events."[22] Rimini Protokoll's work is thus often located in an overall category that is characterized by its proximity to "reality": Irmer's history is titled "a search for new realities," and many mainstream reviews invoke the idea of "reality theatre."[23] This emphasis on the real is frequently underscored in quotations used in the company's publicity material, such as "Rimini Protokoll brings real life to the stage in a way that no other theatre form has been able to."[24]

However, the experience of their work is much more complex than simply the transplantation of "reality" onto the stage, as most in-depth accounts testify. In the examples I described above, common themes emerge that have less to do with reality and more to do with the forms of media and representation by which reality is made to appear: television news, interactive video games, demographic proportionality. Malzacher's history of the company, while emphasizing their reaction against "the trap of representation," nonetheless depicts an early interest in the inner workings of that trap's machinery: the company's Giessen experiments included various ways of making theatrical mechanisms that were themselves the object of the performance, within which humans functioned as operators rather than subjects or characters. This interest in the apparatus of the theater, the machine for manifesting appearance, has persisted throughout their work: for example, obvious uses of lighting and sound are deployed to signal dramatic frames in *Breaking News* and *Best Before*, and *100%* translates the sociographic choreography that precedes the event into an actual choreography through the configuration of bodies on the main stage of the theater as civic space. Malzacher calls attention to one particular repeated "quotation" in their work, that of the red theater curtain, which frequently draws apart or closes before us.[25] This is but one recurring invocation of the theatrical: again and again, in sometimes whimsical ways, such as highly artificial lighting, or in subtle ways, such as the use of subtitles and reenactments, we are reminded that this is all taking place within a particular apparatus: the theater.

Rather than departing from theater, then, this work turns out to have been about theater all along. Jens Roselt points out some of these paradoxes, which quickly reveal themselves following the initial observation (quoted above) that "They were real people." "Don't you always see real people in the theatre?" Roselt asks. "Is a repertory actor somehow a fake person? Is not the performer's identity and physicality inextricably linked to their performance?"[26] Roselt goes on to catalogue the similarities, rather than differences, between Rimini Protokoll's experts and professional actors, writing that "'real' life is not making a breakthrough onto the stage with Rimini Protokoll's 'real' people, rather every type of staging is being explored, which presents 'real' daily life."[27] Other commentators likewise note the extent to which these productions are the result of layers of theatrical craft: researching a theme, adapting text into script, constructing a drama, choreographing an event. Malzacher writes:

> Even though viewing Rimini Protokoll's work is in the first instance through viewing the experts, the perceived authenticity of these characters—and they are characters—is not only the physical creation of the performers themselves. It is also the result of a dramaturgy, the result of a production and the result of a text that does not arise spontaneously and does not simply flow from people's mouths. . . . It is, rather, the specific theatrical work of Haug/Kaegi/Wetzel that has led to a specific type of text. *Reality has to be scripted.*[28]

For this reason, a recurring theme in critical commentary on Rimini Protokoll is the extent to which the opposition between fiction and reality is destabilized. Writing about *Breaking News*, Katia Arfara describes the way that fictional constructs (such as the claim that the characters all live in the same apartment complex) help to desaturate any aura of authenticity: "The Rimini experts do not attempt to reinvest the stage with an *auratic* quality but rather call into question the very nature of their *aura* tied up with the dimension of their physical, unmediated presence."[29] For Matt Cornish, *Call Cutta in a Box* reveals the paradoxical extent to which careful artifice is required to produce the "feeling" of reality: "Only virtuosically sculptured artifice feels authentic; everything else is as boring, unmemorable, and fake as a typical blind date."[30] For Lyn Gardner, "one of the interesting things about *Radio Muezzin* is its recognition that the truth is a fabric that's full of holes."[31] And writing about a collaboration between Kaegi and Lola Arias called *Chambermaids*, Ulrike Garde and Meg Mumford describe a rupture in the distinction between real and fictional that "is achieved because they create ontologically unstable phenomena that appear to oscillate between or simultaneously inhabit the authentic . . . and the patently staged or manufactured."[32]

But in relation to the politics of appearance that I am pursuing in this book, my interest in Rimini Protokoll's work has less to do with resolving the opposition between artifice and reality, and more to do with the way that they explore theater as a mechanism of appearance. Specifically, I find that "theater" has two related functions in their work: first, it is one among many machines for producing appearances, and is continuous with (rather than distinct from) other apparatuses that frame reality for us in all aspects of our lives. We might think here of Giorgio Agamben's general description of the Foucauldian understanding of apparatus as "literally anything that has in some way the capacity to capture, orient, determine, intercept, model, control, or secure the gestures, behaviors, opinions, or discourses of living beings."[33] So the theater sits alongside, and is interconnected with, other representational apparatuses such as video games, TV broadcasts, voting and shareholding, and so on. And second, theater is at the same time a quite specific kind of machine, one that is invoked (with both positive and negative connotations) whenever there is the production of appearances; and it is distinct in its self-awareness (the *dédoublement* discussed in the previous chapter) by which the production of appearance can itself be made to appear. Thus, "theatricality" is not limited to those instances of actual theater. Bringing problems of representation, appearance, and co-relatedness from "the real world" into the theater, I argue, engages these problems as *theatrical* problems; the theater, therefore, is an appropriate place to regard the social and political issues that Rimini Protokoll confronts because these issues are, in this sense, already theatrical ones.

These overlapping forms of apparatus are at work in the Rimini Protokoll work *Call Cutta in a Box*, which I experienced at the 2009 Kunstenfestivaldesarts in Brussels. I will argue that what takes place in this work is less a transplantation of reality into theater, or a transfiguration of reality as it becomes framed by theater, than it is an extended interlinking of the processes of the theater and the already theatrical processes of the "real" world. My experience of *Call Cutta in a Box* is one that is customized just for me—in exactly the same way as it is for every other visitor. Having booked an appointment, I show up at a nondescript office block, and, at my appointed time, I enter a room. The room is configured like a corporate office: a desk, filing cabinets, a sofa, and photos and logos on the wall. I am alone, and then the phone rings. For most of the hour that I have purchased, I will be on the phone, speaking with an operator in Kolkata, and the conversation is directed along lines that evoke both the telemarketing profession's appropriation of personal contact and the broader global economic factors of which outsourced Indian call centers are symptomatic. "What is the weather like where you are?" she asks. "I hope you are healthy. Are you healthy?" And later, "Do you believe in reincarnation?" I am wary of answering these questions, knowing that in doing so I might accede to a proposition which is not yet fully known to me. As anyone who has participated in service economies knows, I am aware that the friendliness with which the questions are asked is not genuine, but is designed to set up a situation in which I may find myself doing something I do not want to do.

As usual with the company's work, this experience is clearly framed as an overtly theatrical experience. In this case, there is pleasure to be had in entering into the conceit of a make-believe office environment, as if one is entering a theatrical set, and, as with the subjunctive mood of so much theater, I am invited to take a seat in the office chair "as if" this were my office, my desk, my corporation. The greater the degree of verisimilitude with a real office, the more I am aware of (and enjoy) the painstaking fabrication of this environment. Throughout the experience, there are minor acts of theatrical magic, such as when my interlocutor from across the globe offers me a cup of tea, and at the same time an electric kettle switches on in the room I am in, as if remotely activated by her. The recurrent motif in Rimini Protokoll's work of the theatrical curtain is manifested here when she asks me to lift up a desk plant; doing so, I find beneath the plant a tiny box adorned with miniature red curtains. Pulling them apart exposes the lens of a web camera, by means of which my companion becomes able to see me, just as I am, by this point in the experience, looking at a live image of her on the computer screen in the room I am in. She reveals things about her life—where she lives, what her workplace is like, what projects are happening in Kolkata—and sends photos representing these aspects to the printer on the desk. As the mediated encounter edges toward its conclusion, it becomes clear that she wants to solicit some kind of exposure from me, something that she alluded to at the beginning of the conversation; it's the equivalent of the "sale" in this telemarketing exchange. Finally, I agree to her request that I sing something to her. When I finish, she asks me, "Do you hear that?" holding the phone above her cubicle. "That is what we do when one of us makes a sale." The sound I hear, piped over the internet from several continents away, is applause.

There are multiple overlapping frames that produce who we are, and who we are to each other, in this brief relationship. This might be a version of "relational aesthetics," in that what is produced is an immaterial relationship between us; however, it is pointedly not the escape from "supplier/client relations" for which Bourriaud hoped. Instead, it is a relationship mediated by consumer-product expectations, and by inequalities of power on both local and general scales: my wish not to be embarrassed puts me at a disadvantage in this encounter, but on the other hand, this is only leisurely entertainment for me, while she is doing this for a living. As in most Rimini Protokoll productions, she is both herself and playing herself; however, because of her job as a call-center employee, the requirement that she enact a performance of self is also part of her daily life. Throughout the experience, I catch myself feeling uneasy about my complicity in an arrangement in which, I presume, differences in currency and labor-value mean that she is being paid comparably low wages for my entertainment. But would I feel uneasy if her profession were that of an actor, and if not, why not? I feel voyeuristic when she sends photographs of herself in social situations because it reminds me that she has a life outside of this job. But when an actor is working, why do I need to assume that this is what they most want to be doing? Isn't the fantasy that acting is its own reward, or even that the actor is taking pleasure in revealing their true self, simply part of the "sale" that the actor is trying to make me—and which also gets rewarded with applause?

It is this doubling of affective labor that distinguishes the work being done here. Exemplary of the service economy in general, the call center industry understands that we need to feel like we're talking to a real person, that authenticity is an effect, and so it manufactures a kind of commodified form of "reality." But the theater, too, is a site of affective labor, the production of feelings and emotional connections: "Long before we began to speak of globalization, the laborers of the theatre could be found engaging in all kinds of material production to create an immaterial product," writes Shannon Jackson.[34] And Erin Hurley describes the "feeling-labour" of theater, "the work theatre does in making, managing, and moving feeling in all its types (affect, emotions, moods, sensations) in a publicly observable display that is sold to an audience for a wage."[35] Indeed, the kind of "reality theatre" with which Rimini Protokoll is associated is charged even more than other types of theater with producing a "feeling" of authenticity, even if that authenticity is understood as only a production—but this is no different from the understanding I have in its other service economy contexts, in which I know very well that the employee's seeming interest in meeting my needs or resolving my problems is something for which I have paid, but I am nonetheless grateful when it feels "authentic," not least because it helps ease my embarrassment about the situation.[36] Writing about reality theater in general, Ulrike Garde and Meg Mumford observe that it produces "authenticity-effects," which they contrast with Brechtian *Verfremdungseffekte*. The description they give of this kind of theater, I would argue, could be applied to all forms of affective labor that generate similar effects: "The 'authentic' is not a given and fixed entity, but rather the product of a contract between performers and spectators which has to be renewed for each 'authenticating act.' "[37]

In this way, what is striking about the experience constructed by *Call Cutta in a Box* is that while it is framed as a theatrical experience, the extent to which it is a comment on theater is also the extent to which it is a comment on economics and geopolitics, and vice versa. In this chapter, I want to explore this interconnection between the apparatus of the theater and other apparatuses of visibility and relationality as a distinct type of *engagement*. I want to distinguish this form of engagement from its more common meanings in the context of "socially engaged art," where it might refer to an intention of the work to include or activate its spectators. Instead, I am interested in experiences in which the spectators might also experience their literal or relational distance from the event, as in the experience of using a call center service. This idea of engagement can also be distinguished from a desire to use the aesthetic experience in order to empower or emancipate the community within which it is located; instead, as *Call Cutta in a Box* demonstrates, the work might make visible the structures of disempowerment and unequal distribution of wealth and power of which it is a part. This kind of engagement involves the self-reflexive demonstration of the event's own conditions of visibility: the structures of representation within which it is itself already (and irretrievably) implicated, and yet within which it manages to introduce a momentary gap—even if that gap only allows a brief glimpse of how irretrievably it is entangled with context.

The idea of engagement that I am proposing here takes inspiration from the evocative choice of a word at the center of Tracy Davis's definition of theatricality, discussed in the previous chapter:

> A spectator's *dédoublement* resulting from a sympathetic breach (active dissociation, alienation, self-reflexivity) effecting a critical stance toward an episode in the public sphere, including but not limited to the theatre.[38]

The meanings of *dédoublement* include splitting or dividing into two, and indeed there are various "doublings" that signal theatricality is at work. One of the term's common usages in French is in the phrase *dédoublement de la personnalité*, or dual or split personality, and I have discussed in chapter 1 this kind of splitting in relation to the spectatorial experience of co-distance. It can also be a way of thinking about the phenomenon of actors who play themselves, which is a characteristic of the works discussed in this and the next chapter. However, *dédoublement* is also a word with mechanical resonances, used, for example, to describe the uncoupling of train carriages, and so it suggests the capacity for parts of an apparatus to be removed, reconfigured, and reconnected in a different way. The word "engagement," too, has these mechanistic connotations, as a description of the interface of two different parts of a system—the way two or more gear systems might *engage* in order to transfer power from one assembly to another—and I want to extend this image to think about the engagement of the theatrical apparatus with other machinery of appearances at play. In developing this idea of engagement, I hope to follow Shannon Jackson's model in sidestepping questions about the autonomy and heteronomy of the work of art in relation to its cultural and economic conditions—distinctions that, as Jackson notes, are often the basis for a pejorative value judgment about "applied" or community practice.[39] Arguing against a "disavowal of support" in favor of works that participate in an "infrastructural aesthetic," Jackson calls attention to the "support structures" within which art finds itself and the ways in which some works might contribute to the "unsettling of inside/outside divisions."[40] In this way, the relationship between the politics *within* the theatrical event and those *outside* the event is not one of a separation that must be reconciled, nor an irruption into the theater of the real from outside, but is instead a continuity of structures of looking and being-seen, and the attendant distributions (and potential redistribution) of power relations associated with those ways of seeing.

What kind of apparatus is the theater? Drawing on the work of Barbara Freedman, Maaike Bleeker has described the theater as a kind of "vision machine" that "stages ways of looking that respond to a particular culturally and historically specific spectator consciousness." In this analogy, she continues, the relation between the theatrical and "reality" is one of continuity and complementarity rather than separation: "Theatre and reality appear as parallel constructions appealing to similar ways of looking. Theatre presents a *staging* of the construction that is also constitutive of the real."[41] To return to the overlapping types of "customer experience" offered by *Call Cutta in a Box*, it can be seen to deploy two systems of affect that are interconnected, and to an extent irretrievable from each other: the theater and the call center, working in consort as part of the minutiae of everyday operations with which many of us participate. However, in the event's overt theatricality, the two systems are discernible: rather than disappearing behind the normalizing function of their "authenticity-effects," they are made to appear. I want to emphasize that I am not arguing that this instance of the form of encounter somehow replaces the mediated (false) relationship with an unmediated (real) one (as in the promise of relational aesthetics); rather, it adds another, overlapping mediation. Neither the theatrical frame nor the call center frame is erased or eclipsed by the juxtaposition, but the effect of the double framing is that both the artifice of the encounter, and its inseparable "real world" double, are made visible. As I described earlier, the work of Rimini Protokoll is sometimes described as staging a friction between fabrication and reality, but in my reading, the two are not opposed but contiguous with each other. That is, it is not the case that the commodified relationship is exposed as "fictional" or "artificial," in the sense of being different from some "real" relationship that might potentially be possible, and which theater might be able to deliver through its claimed autonomy from the distributions of global capitalism and service economies. Instead, what this work's theatricality exposes are the mechanisms of appearance and representation that constitute our relatedness—mechanisms that are, we might say, *really theatrical*.

11 Rooms: Precarious Labor and the "Work" of Art

For Shannon Jackson, affective labor is a notable element of Rimini Protokoll's work, not only for the way in which it is theatricalized within their specific productions, but also for the way in which it is part of the relation-ships of production that support the company's works: in other words, "the way its production process actually interacts with—and sometimes mimics—the processes, delivery systems, and affects of a global service economy."[42] *Call Cutta in a Box*, and more indicatively the way the *100%* concept has been restaged in more than thirty-five cities around the world, demonstrate the company's distinctively twenty-first-century capacity for global distribution, in which the "concept" or "brand" can travel globally, supported by local "casting." As Jackson points out, then, the company's use of "experts" and "real people" does not stop at the level of visible performers, but also includes flexible and interchangeable support teams that enable this "simultaneous circulation": "At any point on the calendar, one can find six to ten productions 'touring'; that is, their propositions circulate thanks to helpful technical directors who transport expert actors or find new experts in each site."[43]

In this section, I will consider two examples in which these support structures are themselves foregrounded as the subject of the work of art, as with this chapter's opening example, *Pièce pour la technique du Schau-spiel de Hanovre*. In these examples, even more than in Quesne's work, the "work" of art consists of the ordinarily hidden labor that goes into producing it. The first of these is taken from a gallery-based context, the *11 Rooms* exhibition curated by Klaus Biesenbach and Hans Ulrich Obrist and shown as part of the 2011 Manchester International Festival. The particular room I will focus on was empty of objects or performers, and instead used its walls to display printouts of the email correspondences from project managers and technical workers who had been attempting to make possible an ultimately unrealized work of art. My second example will be the performance *Entitled* by the theater company Quarantine, also first presented in 2011. *Entitled* reconfigures itself somewhat in each site where it happens, but it always involves an opening monologue from the production manager, who narrates the process of setting up the various pieces of technology as if in anticipation of a performance that, in *Entitled*, never arrives.

In each case, I will argue that one potential reading would be to under-stand the visibility of the paid labor as puncturing the mimetic artifice of the art event and calling attention to the "real" social and economic relations that surround it. Such an interruption is at least implied, if not explicitly promised, by the curatorial statements around each event. For example, in *11 Rooms* the foregrounding of supporting labor might be seen as interrupting and grounding the ostensibly dematerialized value structures of the gallery—although I will argue that this intervention is nevertheless a limited one. Moreover, such an interruption of artifice is complicated, if not entirely foreclosed, by the explicit theatrical frame of the second example, *Entitled*. I want to describe the activities of this show's production manager, because they take place on a stage, as constituting *acting*, even though they are ontologically indistinguishable from the same set of actions he and his colleagues might perform in the same space were an audience not present and were he not narrating. Because of the explicit theatrical frame, I will argue that the "real" labor fails to appear. However, this failure of the real has generative possibility, where the theater might be a place where we can give up our consumptive desire for the real because it is a place that can never deliver it. What remains in its stead is pure speculation, emptied of the promise of a return, and instead present in its collective act of self-representation.

The first example, *11 Rooms*, was the third of a series of commissions from the biennial Manchester International Festival (MIF) that staged some form of encounter between the world of high-profile visual arts and the activity of theater. In 2007 this was *Il Tempo del Postino*, co-curated by Hans Ulrich Obrist and Philippe Parreno, in which contemporary gallery-based artists were asked to create works for the proscenium stage of the Manchester Opera House. And in 2009, Marina Abramović placed durational and performance-based practices on permanent display (during opening hours) in the otherwise empty Whitworth Art Gallery under the banner *Marina Abramović Presents*. In 2011, *11 Rooms* combined these approaches, as co-curators Klaus Biesenbach and Hans Ulrich Obrist commissioned eleven highly regarded artists, whose practice is primarily based in galleries, to make installations involving human bodies on display in eleven rooms of the Manchester Art Gallery. Some of these included re-performances of previous works, such as Joan Jonas's *Mirror Check* (1970) and Marina Abramović's *Luminosity* (1997); some involved quite straightforward displays of realistic acting in a set, as in the bed-bound actor who recited monologues in Simon Fujiwara's *Playing the Martyr* (2011); some involved choreographed, anonymous bodies as in Allora & Calzadilla's *Revolving Door* (2011); and some involved performers whose specific identity in "real" life was crucial, as in Santiago Sierra's use of professional soldiers in *Veterans of the Wars of Northern Ireland, Afghanistan and Iraq Facing the Corner* (2011) or Tino Sehgal's use of school-age children for *Ann Lee* (2011).

When gallery practices incorporate performance, it is notable that they tend to distance themselves from theatrical practices (and above all from acting), much like the performance artists discussed in chapter 1. For example, *11 Rooms* is introduced by the curators in this way:

> From morning to afternoon, these rooms will house "sculptures" like any other sculpture gallery, but this is a sculptural display with a difference. For when the last visitors leave and the gallery closes its doors for the evening, the sculptures will all walk out as well, because they too are alive.[44]

No doubt this is intended as a playful analogy, but there is nevertheless something revealing about this encouragement to imagine these human performers, exhibiting behavior in front of an audience, as sculptures—rather than, for example, actors.

Indeed, the piece in the exhibition on which I want to focus attention is one that proposed to do away altogether with the possibility of acting, and the taint of fakery that comes with it. This was an installation nominally "by" John Baldessari, in which the organizers attempted to stage a previously unrealized concept by Baldessari, dating from 1970, that proposed the display of a real human corpse. Baldessari's original proposal began by describing it as "possibly an impossible project," and indeed, for various reasons, the MIF was ultimately unable to do so, although not for want of trying. Instead, the walls of the gallery in which this installation was meant to take place were covered with printouts selected from a year of correspondence, in which the bulk of the activity was undertaken by relatively anonymous members of the curatorial and technical staff attempting to negotiate the legal restrictions on sourcing and displaying a cadaver for the purposes of art instead of science. The display begins with a list of the involved parties—something like a cast list, which includes gallery directors, a mortuary manager, professors of law and bioethics, and other assorted players, such as the president of something called the "Biological Resource Center of Illinois LLC." The correspondence tracks a dramatic journey through optimism and desperation, as new potential sources for the cadaver are discovered only to lead to further complications. A typical reply reads:

> This exhibit sounds fantastic. Unfortunately, for our institution to support the cadaveric needs, we require *demonstration of patient benefit*. For an art exhibition there isn't a direct tie to patient benefit. We will not be able to assist you with this endeavor.[45]

Right to the very end, the central figure in this drama is Polyanna Clayton-Stamm, hired temporarily as a "consultant producer" for the MIF. As the number of options diminish, she remains hopeful:

> I am working on the assumption that Wednesday 29th of June will be our cut off point. . . . We both feel confident that constructing the room, with all its details, along with installing the necessary refrigeration unit/extractor fan, can be achieved within seven days. Allowing the eighth, and final day, to take receipt and prepare (makeup artist) the full cadaver.[46]

The project manager—flexible, task-based, always working—exemplifies the post-Fordist or neoliberal worker, and the world of contemporary art production simultaneously critiques and parallels the rise of what Negri and Hardt have characterized as immaterial labor: "The production of services result[ing] in no material and durable good."[47] This repurposing of the Baldessari piece makes this dynamic very clear, in the way it shows that what the "work" of art normally looks like is not primarily undertaken by the artist—Baldessari's rough sketch takes up only a couple of pages in the display—but by a frenzy of hidden activity of communication, negotiation, and professional virtuosity.

In this way, one way of reading this presentation is as a critique of the way in which celebrated artists and curators derive surplus value from the (waged) labor of those working for them. Clayton-Stamm, as project manager for the Baldessari installation, is typical of the kind of invisible (and temporary) work that supports the art world. One of the functions of this public display of previously private correspondence is to make her function visible—perhaps analogous to those modes of institutional critique deployed by an artist like Mierle Laderman Ukeles in her "maintenance art," in which the artist took on exaggerated, manual versions of the kinds of maintenance tasks normally hidden from view in the art gallery, such as scrubbing the gallery steps and floor by hand.[48] I think there is value in the way in which this dynamic is exposed; and yet, I would also note that this exposure of the support apparatus is immediately reappropriated by the valuing systems of the exhibition, precisely through its exposure being presented *as art*. In terms of the distinction laid out at the beginning of this chapter, when the work becomes *a* work, its challenge to hierarchies of productivity and value becomes subsumed within the encompassing authority of what Jacques Rancière has called "the aesthetic regime of art": the autonomous separation of a distinctively aesthetic *sensibility*, no longer dependent on criteria based on skill or representational verisimilitude.[49] Ukeles benefited from this additional valuing system, gaining financial and reputational recognition as an artist to supplement the undervalued work of maintenance: "Maintenance jobs = minimal wages, housewives = no pay," she wrote; then, an epiphany: "I have the freedom to name maintenance as art."[50] Unpaid work might become paid (or at least valued) when reframed as art. However, the presentation of the correspondence in *11 Rooms* serves to extract surplus value from that same labor all over again, being put to work twice, but paid only once.

Of course, artists and curators are very much aware that contemporary art is closely mirroring the development of advanced capitalism, and, for some, such a parallel allows an opportunity for critique. For example, Nicolas Bourriaud followed his declaration of the domain of "relational aesthetics" with an interest in what he calls "precarious art," celebrating rather than resisting precarity as a positive value. "Today," he writes, "we need to reconsider culture (and ethics) on the basis of a positive idea of the transitory, instead of holding on to the opposition between the ephemeral and the durable."[51] More cautiously, the artist Liam Gillick—a central figure in the debate around relational aesthetics—acknowledges the potential problem of "a series of practices that coincide quite neatly with the requirements of the neoliberal, predatory, continually mutating capitalism of the every moment."[52] Nevertheless, for Gillick, artistic practices continue to hold the potential to take a critical position toward the forms they adopt, primarily when artists identify themselves on the side of the observers of social relations rather than claiming some privileged viewpoint outside the system. Although we can't get outside the system, Gillick wants art to say, let's find a way together to look at the system from within:

> Art is not a zone of autonomy. It does not create structures that are exceptional or perceivable outside their own context. . . . For example, with regard to the undifferentiated flexible knowledge-worker who operates in permanent anxiety in the midst of a muddling of work and leisure, art both points at this figure and operates alongside him or her as an experiential phantom.[53]

In relation to the Baldessari emails, one could argue for a reading that the display offers the kind of critique that Gillick suggests: in this reading, the work of art creates a parallel entity to those structures of exploitation and value-extraction, as a ghost or a "phantom" rather than the real thing. Such a critique asks art to wrestle with the idea of "work" itself, with how labor is valued and the function it serves within the work.

However, even though labor is made visible in the example from *11 Rooms*, in my view this labor is not actually a critical subject of inquiry, but is instead deployed as a signifier of the real—that is, as a signifier of "real" human activity and industry that stands in for, and trades upon, the unavailability of the absent corpse that was unable to be procured. Notably, the allure of the idea of a corpse is itself its supposed "realness," even if Baldessari himself was ambivalent about this realness: "What is intended is a double play of sorts," he wrote in his original proposal, suggesting that the corpse's representational status is as much a factor as its material reality. Baldessari's notes and sketches show an engagement with rules of perspective, placing the body firmly within histories of the representation of Christ, and his suggested use of a peephole might recall Duchamp's *Étant donnés* (1946–66) with its self-conscious reflection on voyeuristic spectatorship. Baldessari wrote: "The subject is not the cadaver. The subject is rather the issue of breaking and mending aesthetic distance."[54] Nevertheless, in this revisitation of Baldessari's idea, the emails necessarily focus on the central question of the cadaver, and in its very absence, what is evoked is a possibility of the limit of representation that the corpse represents, the ultimate in real performance—as in "you can't get more

real than this," or "there's no denying the reality of it," or "we're not deal-
ing with artistic representation anymore." Curator Biesenbach writes in
one of the emails:

> I am seriously worried that the point of john baldessari's piece is
> the courageous displacement of something that has no other place
> in society, neither profane nor art spheres anymore. If there is any
> way we could still achieve this, that would make the exhibition
> truly unique and groundbreaking.[55]

In this way, I would argue that the emails function to invoke the mundane reality of organizational work, its supposed facticity, circulating
around the apparently impossible hope of realizing the cadaver display.
Rather than a critical reflection on labor conditions, the work seems more
aligned with the idea that the function of art is to overcome its artificiality and deliver us into encounters with the real—and if the real corpse is
not available, in its stead the work offers the (supposedly) real labor of
the project manager, in its material traces. Indeed, something curious has
happened to the status of the "material" of that labor. As I began research
on this work, I (rather naively) asked a contact at the MIF if I might have
a copy of the project manager's emails for reference. I was told, regretfully,
no, that these emails, which presumably still exist in multiple digital copies on the computers of multiple recipients, now constitute the artwork!
Although I was generously invited to review the physical copies of the
emails, they obviously remain valuable to the work's owners as intellectual
property, and 11 Rooms has continued to circulate as an expanding exhibition: as 12 Rooms (2012) for the Ruhr Trienalle, as 13 Rooms (2013)
for the Kaldor Public Art Projects in Sydney (where the Baldessari contribution was replaced with a different piece of his), and as 14 Rooms (2014)
at Art Basel. Where the corpse itself has not materialized, the emails must
undergo a transubstantiation from ephemeral, immaterial labor into a
material art object.

Quarantine's *Entitled*: Stagehands and the
Non-Productivity of Theatrical Labor

In what follows, I want to continue to unpack this association between
labor and "the real" to suggest that this desire to overcome representation—
which might also be described as performance's desire to overcome
theatricality—can be seen to parallel Marx's own dream of unalienated
labor. "Let us finally imagine, for a change," Marx writes, in a reverie
inspired by *Robinson Crusoe*, "an association of free men, working with
the means of production held in common, and expending their many

different forms of labour-power in full self-awareness as one single social labour force."[56] Indeed, theater itself seems to be tainted by being exemplary of the commodity form, even in the way Marx borrows language from the theater in order to describe the transformations and abstractions that characterize the fetishization of the commodity: "The complete metamorphosis of a commodity, in its simplest form, implies four *dénouements* and three *dramatis personae*."[57] A more spectacular image is conveyed by his famous description of the dancing table as a metaphor for the twofold nature of the commodity:

> The form of wood, for instance, is altered if a table is made out of it. Nevertheless the table continues to be wood, an ordinary, sensuous thing. But as soon as it emerges as a commodity, it changes into a thing which transcends sensuousness. It not only stands with its feet on the ground, but, in relation to all other commodities, it stands on its head, and evolves out of its wooden brain grotesque ideas, far more wonderful than if it were to begin dancing of its own free will.[58]

Marx describes the commodity as having two lives, one as something useful and one based on what it represents in terms of exchange value, which is not intrinsic to the object. Referring to the commodity's two faces, Nicholas Ridout has remarked, "There is something theatrical about the double life of the commodity."[59] And the anti-theatricality of Marx's theory of commodities is pursued at length across Derrida's *Specters of Marx*,[60] upon which Alice Rayner draws when she describes the "specifically theatrical" image of the commodity-fetish: "The blending of use and exchange values constitutes what it means to be on stage."[61]

If the alienated world of the theater is analogous, or even homologous, to alienated labor lived and sold as a commodity, then a dream that haunts both systems is the idea of a backstage or offstage, where our bodies, and the objects we make, are not representations of themselves or part of a symbolic currency, but are "simply themselves." Rayner addresses exactly this idea, describing the allure of the backstage, and the figure of the stagehand, as holding out the promise of something more real than what is onstage. However—and crucially—Rayner argues that this apparent reality is no more than a stage-effect generated from the division of spaces into the visible and the invisible. Rayner writes:

> Visiting the costume shop where clothes are being made, or seeing the prop storage where objects once seen on stage are in full view, and so obviously made of papier-mâché, holds its own kind of appeal that arises *not because the objects and people backstage are actually more real than the objects and people on stage in*

performance, but because the spatial model of inside and outside creates a geometry of seeming difference. The spatial image not only incites the desire to see more, and to see the truth, but also reinforces the conviction that what is conventionally hidden and then revealed is more true and real than any representation. This sense of the real, which is felt as privilege, thus actually requires a hidden space, an invisible practice, where desire might find its object.[62]

In this way, Rayner writes, the quality of "realness" that adheres to off-stage objects and people is not inherent to them, but is the result of "a differential function."[63] That is, the idea of the offstage, a space and time where labor is itself and not alienated, is an effect of the stage itself. As such, the allure of unalienated labor may be one of capitalism's most dangerous seductions. Rayner's hypothetical figures of the stagehands find material manifestation in shows that make their labor visible, as in Philippe Quesne's work for the professional team at the Hanover Schauspiel, described in the introduction. But whereas Quesne's work relies on the conceit of the workers' holiday party, which gives license to the production of fantastical images (a characteristic of Quesne's work), a more austere self-reflective logic governs Quarantine's *Entitled* (2011), which I will discuss now.

Entitled consists of the "get-in" for its own production: the placement of the various pieces of equipment and scenery, the testing of sound levels, and the warming-up and walking of the space undertaken by performers before the show, usually done in the absence of an audience. As the audience enters, members of the production team are already engaged in these kinds of activities, such as sweeping the floor. This experience of entering while activity is in progress is not an unfamiliar one in contemporary theater, and, with the house lights on, members of the audience, at least the one of which I was a part, continue talking among themselves; the technicians, in plain view, are invisible—or, better, visibly not-there. As Rayner writes, "an audience, largely for its own benefit, agrees to ignore the presence of the technicians and to accept instead that only the visible or auditory results of their work will be counted as performance."[64] But then the production manager, Greg Akehurst, introduces himself and his role and addresses the audience:

> Before we start does anyone have any questions?
> I'm Greg Akehurst, the production manager. Before we start there's a few things that I need to go through with you.
> At the moment the space is like this because that's how we begin.
> Soon we'll bring in some lighting and sound equipment and assemble large bits of scenery.

> [*Akehurst indicates the distance from the front row of seats with a measuring tape.*] We'll never put anything closer to you than this. That's the legal distance.
>
> This means you'll always have a clear route to the emergency exit.
>
> The entrances here are the performers' entrances and this one leads to the dressing room.
>
> The first thing that Chris and Lisa will do is bring in our sound system. It's a Nexo sound system.
>
> They'll position the sub speaker here and the top speaker here.
>
> During this performance it never has a sustained exposure of more than 100 decibels.
>
> It will be loud but nothing to worry about.[65]

Akehurst, along with the lighting and sound technicians, describe the details of the various pieces of technology—their brand names, what they like about them, why they were chosen. They ask the performers to start checking the mic levels, and this allows the performers to start speaking associatively, eventually building into more structured pieces of narration, while still ostensibly remaining within the conceit of the get-in.

One association that this performance might have is with the kinds of task-based performances developed in the 1960s and '70s which made a virtue of non-virtuosic action and, as discussed in the previous chapter, were described by Michael Kirby as "non-matrixed performances."[66] Rather than acting, one might be tempted to say, the performers in *Entitled* are simply exhibiting behavior. Indeed, whereas the convention of an audience entering while behavior is already in process may be characteristic of much non-illusionist theater, *Entitled* takes this one step further, in that the behavior being staged when we enter is the one kind of behavior that can be proper to this place, that does not stand out as "restored" or "matrixed" behavior; it's usual to walk into a theater and find people dressed in black T-shirts configuring the space. (In fact, the other kind of behavior that seems so natural as not to be worthy of attention is our own behavior: to enter as a group, to sit, and to watch what is happening with disinterested interest.) So one way of reading this piece is as an attempt to minimize theater's artifice and maximize its reality, as Kirby emphasized with his opposition between performing and acting (with the latter described as "to feign, to simulate, to represent, to impersonate").[67] The theater-makers have themselves recognized the alignment of their work with this genre of the "theatre of the real"; in *Entitled*'s program notes, for example, director Richard Gregory writes:

> Over the past 13 years, Quarantine has worked with all kinds of people, some of whom are rarely seen in theatres. . . . We've perhaps developed a reputation for working with "real people"

> as opposed to actors on stage, portraying fictional characters. . . .
> For this piece, I wanted to explore some of the real stories of its
> performers—somehow turning theatre inside out.[68]

Indeed, one of the things that the piece might be seen to insist upon, particularly in its second half, is the reality of what is happening and the
authenticity of what is being shared, as the performers share personal
details apparently from their own life experiences, contributing to an
atmosphere of confessional intimacy.

And yet, as invested as the company is in the use of "real" performers
and their stories, a consistent thread across Quarantine's projects is an
interest in challenging distinctions between different kinds of work and
their relative value. For example, in *Susan and Darren* (2008), the two
title figures are Darren, who has trained extensively as a performer, and his
mother, Susan, who has not. In her analysis of this work, Geraldine Harris argues that the appearance of authenticity that seems to characterize
the work might be understood as exactly that, as *appearance*: "Paradoxically, it is the focus on surface, 'show,' or appearances rather than what is
'behind' them and indeed 'behind' the show as a whole, socially, politically,
personally or emotionally, that gives a sense of an 'authentic' encounter
with Susan and Darren."[69] Her article is accompanied by running commentary in the form of footnotes from Quarantine's artistic directors,
Richard Gregory and Renny O'Shea, and they use these notes to make
a key intervention in the form of a challenge to Harris's use of the term
"non-professional" performers:

> There is a problem of definition. "Non-professional" or even
> "amateur" often imply either unpaid or inept. Susan and Darren
> were neither. We pay all our performers (when we're allowed to:
> with *EatEat*'s performers, this was illegal). "Non-performer" is
> absurd, because they clearly are performers in the context they're
> encountered in (and if the argument is made that this isn't what
> they do most of the time, let me line up some thousands of self-
> defined "actors" who haven't done any work paid or unpaid for
> donkey's years): "untrained" is not specific enough, and what
> kind of training counts . . . ? We prefer Rimini Protokoll's term
> "experts in everyday life." Susan is there because nobody else
> could replace her.[70]

Any claim that there is something more "real" or "authentic" about
"these" kinds of people as opposed to others would have to be based upon
an evaluative distinction between these different skills and experiences,
a distinction between art and non-art—and it is clear that Gregory and
O'Shea pointedly refuse such a distinction.

For this reason, rather than concluding that the labor of the stage technicians lends authenticity to the piece's abstractions through "non-performing," I want to suggest instead that the frame of the theater produces such labor as fabrication, as mimetic, as less "real" or concrete than it may appear. Theatricality has the effect of flattening and equalizing whatever behavior is undertaken within its frame—the dancer dancing, the singer singing, the storyteller telling stories, the production manager managing the production. At the same time as they are what they are, they also appear as representations, or at least as demonstrations: as people not just *being* people but as people *acting* themselves. Inspired by Peter Handke, Bert O. States once declared that a chair on stage is a chair pretending to be a chair.[71] But this is quite different from Marx's dancing table, where it is pretending to be more than a table, to be capable of singing and dancing, and where that pretense reflects the relationships of alienation and abstraction that Marx wishes to puncture. In the overtly theatrical act of self-representation, there is not an illusion that hides the fact that this is only a table made of wood, but the opposite: an awareness that the table has been doubled, its presentational *dédoublement* producing something additional that haunts the onstage body. When something is on stage, "it is present, but also other," says Rayner; "something else is manifestly present but not necessarily identical to what is manifest."[72]

In a retrospective discussion of *Entitled* almost ten years after its first performance, Gregory, the show's director, recalled his fascination with this double life of the action; as he described it, the technicians are really doing their job, and at the same time they aren't really doing their job. They are "both doing it, and standing outside doing it," as he put it. And Akehurst himself was also conscious of this distinction: "I was really clear: I didn't want to turn up and for people to say, 'Oh, here are the performing technicians.' I wanted to be doing my job."[73] But what I am interested in here is the way this *dédoublement* produces a kind of non-productivity: no matter how much the stagehand sweeps the stage, it is not really *this* stage that he is cleaning. Instead, *Entitled* is haunted by the imaginary show for which the technical team is doing the get-in, which is ostensibly *this* show, the one they are doing, but which remains fictional. (This, too, was the subject of much discussion in the company's retrospection: the way their devising process continuously circled around the absent show, and what kinds of lights, sound system, and design it involved in order to necessitate the get-in being performed.) Nicholas Ridout describes this in-built capacity of the theater for failure—the way it never quite shows us the thing it promises to show—as its constitutive feature: "That there is something wrong with theatre is the sign that it is theatre."[74]

I want to propose that one way to think about this failure is not with reference to the logic of task-based performance—a performativity that explicitly opposes itself to theatricality (as discussed in the previous chapter), in the claim that "performance presents; it does not re-present"[75]—but instead with reference to the logic of the readymade, the term designated by Marcel Duchamp for the co-option of already manufactured objects as works of art. John Roberts offers an evocative description of the ready-made as "copying without copying": "The object still retains its material and phenomenological form, but because it is no longer just an object of productive labor, *it exists as other to itself*, and therefore could be said to be a repetition of its original form."[76] Roberts's description of the object that "exists as other to itself" echoes Marx's description of alienation, in which it is an undesirable feature, but it also echoes Rayner's description of that "something else" that is "manifestly present," even while it is not the same as what is manifest. We can see the logic of the readymade at work in Baldessari's proposal, with its appropriation of a corpse as art, as well as in the MIF's strategy of re-presenting the product of curatorial labor as installation. However, there is a distinction between the form of appropriation that takes place with the exhibition of a readymade in a gal-lery and that which takes place with a theater-event (like *Entitled*), which is contingent on the temporal dimensions of the theater-event. That is to say, as I argued in chapter 1, the transformation of the thing into some-thing "other to itself" is achieved through spectatorial self-consciousness, as a result of the fact that we spectators are here watching, rather than the authorial self-nomination of the artist—that is, through a set of affective rather than valuational social relations.

As Michael Shane Boyle has pointed out in response to an earlier ver-sion of the ideas in this chapter, the performers' labor indeed remains productive when viewed in the wider frame of the capitalist systems of investment and profit within which the show *Entitled* is financed (through public and private funding), its workers (of all kinds) recompensed, and its spectators drawn to purchase tickets.[77] Like other forms of production, theater abstracts surplus value from people's actions, such as the way that people sitting around and talking with each other about their fictional lives becomes "a work," and though some forms of theater prefer to dis-avow it, theater is always showing us people at work. It is for this reason that Boyle suggests that theater may be exemplary of capitalist processes of the abstraction and extraction of value; as he puts it, "Theatre can put to work on the stage almost any activity that can be found off of it."[78] I agree; however, what these demonstrations of labor do *not* reveal is the backstage of capitalist exploitation, a scene of unalienated labor, or an act of unmediated expression. The abstraction of capital is doubly abstracted by theater, leaving us not with the real but with a copy of something for which there is no original, a copy made with no effort at all—except for the apparently effortless activity of gathering together, as spectators, to watch, and *so long as we are watching*. This time on stage is unproductive time, and theater is also a set of *temporal* relations—a temporary suspension of "real" work, and the space opened by this suspension, the possibility of a speculative present, permeated with other pasts and futures.

This temporal aspect is foregrounded in the form that *Entitled* takes—the show is all anticipation, preparing for an event that does not arrive—but it is also a recurrent subject of the show's content. In addition to the actions of the technical crew, the show also has various "performers" who speak and move while ostensibly warming up, walking through actions that might be part of the performance, testing out the microphones, or checking that the lighting is illuminating the space as desired. And when using the mics, they often engage in acts of reminiscence about the past. For example, while testing the mic, dancer Joanne Fong shifts from a present-tense narration of her immediate present—"I'm going all the way over to stage left and I'm talking with words, keeping going, speaking," or "My voice is coming out of this speaker here, and my voice is coming out of that speaker there"—to a broader comment on her present circumstances—"I'm growing up again, getting older, got old legs. I'm not quite as pretty as I used to be." While trying out various positions under different lights, Fiona Wright ruminates on the broader set of conditions that enable this activity: "I think about light, the electricity," she muses out loud. "Someone has to make electricity in the power station. There's a woman there, right now, in a room, in front of a screen, watching the national grid flicker." Another performer, Sonia Hughes, has her monologue delivered by a test of the projected surtitles, so that as she looks on, her life story is played out in printed text while other setup activity is being conducted on stage. When it finishes, she adds to what has been written: "Of course that's not all of me, that's just my CV—it doesn't tell you everything." She shares some of the personal details of her life that we wouldn't know, such as her relationship with her siblings, or her son; and she reflects that everyone present in the audience has life circumstances which she will never know.

Continuing her reflection, Sonia recalls a time when she was involved in political activism, participating in marches and demonstrations, and once having the feeling during a face-off with police that if she took a decisive action at that point, she could have started a riot—but she didn't. "We lost and I went to jail," she recalls, "and I thought I'll never do anything heroic." She's been feeling like this again recently, she says, "But what shall I do?" But from this recollection of political action in the "real world," Sonia shifts her attention to the room she is in. "Or what could *we* do? There's about 60 of us in the room?" she guesses, based on wherever the show is being performed. Her hands waft in a delicate waver, like a musical conductor, as she searches for the words. "And we could . . . together . . . make . . . we could create something that lasts beyond the end of this show. Past the drink in the bar, past the sleep tonight, past breakfast and linger even into tomorrow afternoon." She looks out at the audience. "It doesn't have to be monumental. We've only got a certain amount of time." Relaxing her gaze, she suggests, "Perhaps we could just be quiet together." For the next minute, all the preparations stop, as Sonia stands on the stage, at once in the room with us, and at the same time in a room that has been transformed into a representational space through the activity of the production crew: the lights shine on her, she is at the center of attention, and, as her own attention falls on each member of the audience, we too are held in this apparatus. In what sense does this moment of silence last beyond the end of the show? It is not literally the quiet itself, nor even the feeling of collectivity that it produces, as these both will dispel as soon as we leave. But rather the possibility of this distance from our lives, where we become audience to ourselves, and can speculate into other futures . . . this is what remains.

Watching, gathering, being quiet together: these are some of the things we do as an audience, foregrounded in the kinds of situated spectatorship I discussed in the previous chapter. In *Entitled*, the object of that spectatorship has been removed from view: there is no "show" being shown, only the act of assembling the apparatus of showing. Indeed, after the show that never arrives, and following the actors' sound checks and walkthroughs which have drifted off into personal memories and anecdotes, *Entitled* ends with the technicians breaking down the set again. "If you do the chairs and the costumes, Lisa," Akehurst says, "we'll do the floors. Then it's just the star cloth and the PA, and if we all get on the mark-up, then in 35 minutes I will stop." As they finish these tasks, they play a game in which they imagine where they will be a few hours after the show, and then a few days, and onward through months and years until they imagine the time after their lives have finished. In the version I saw and the version recorded in the working script, if not in every performance, this speculation concludes with an image of one of their great-grandchildren clearing out the loft and finding a box of old photos.

> And they'll spend an evening in front of the fire with the curtains shut looking through it
> And they'll see me, stood here, on this stage
> It's hard to think forward from there.
> Is there anything left to do?
> We'll finish it tomorrow.[79]

Entitled was devised in the aftermath of the 2008 global financial crisis. Several commentators have pointed out that one of the consequences of late capitalism has been the dissolution of the future as a source of hope. Instead, most people's lives are bound up in structures of indebtedness, with the present mortgaged to the future, in an existence that is increasingly precarious; as Ridout and Schneider put it, "precarity is life lived in relation to a future that cannot be propped securely upon the past."[80] That is, speculative investment holds the present in thrall to possible futures, and as these imagined futures fluctuate, those in the present prosper or suffer. This is the inequity of speculation: the wagering of lives for profit, and an unequal distribution of risk and reward. But as Franco "Bifo" Berardi has argued, perhaps the idea of a better future is itself an illusion of the organization of life around the accumulation of capital and the pursuit of surplus value: "The idea that the future will be better than the present is not a natural idea, but the imaginary effect of the peculiarity of the bourgeois production model."[81] Here, too, the structure of investment borrows from the theater—even in its very language of *investiture*, the "dressing up" of capital in other garments in the hope that it might return, further bejeweled, from its adventures in faraway markets. As with Rayner's discussion of the structure of the backstage, we might long for an end to this speculation, for an art or politics that would show us our work, maybe even capital itself, stripped bare, divested of its abstracted value.

And yet, the structure of *Entitled* suggests a different kind of temporality, one in which the value of the investment is not in the future, or in the offstage, but in the doubled present, "present, but also other" (Rayner): this temporary stage that is a copy of the "real" one (which never arrives). The possibilities it holds out are not beyond this time and space, as the workers' final lines reinforce through their dramatic return to now, but are instead in the speculative space of the theater-event, where we might dream not a different future but a different present. For its limited duration, we are all speculators—or, to use a more familiar term, spectators. What is important here is not the backstage to which we might long to escape, but the space inside this room, the place where representations appear as themselves. Importantly, this work reminds us that such a space does not arise spontaneously, such that someone like Joanne or Fiona or Sonia is always able to speak and to be heard, but rather that it takes work to hold such a space open. This, then, is the value of the stagehands' labor, and indeed that of the *11 Rooms* project manager: not in its apparent realness, its potential rupture of the artificial space in which it appears, but in the holding open of the space of our own attention.

The "Almost Limitless" Theater of the Nature Theater of Oklahoma

If these carefully constructed situations give an indication of the potential interruption of labor introduced by theatrical *dédoublement*, in which the theatrical frame holds open a space in which labor's productivity fails to appear, then how might it be possible to extend this frame beyond the stage? What would it look like to make all of life a theater, in which one works hard at only gesturing at work, without such work being reabsorbed into the service of the production of surplus? Such an impossible project is given form in the reverie at the end of Franz Kafka's unfinished novel *America*, in which the protagonist, Karl Rossmann, having tried but failed throughout the novel to find meaningful employment, at last stumbles across this enticing advertisement:

> The Oklahoma Theatre will engage members for its company today at Clayton race-course from six o'clock in the morning until midnight. The great Theatre of Oklahoma calls you! Today only and never again! If you miss your chance now you miss it for ever! If you think of your future you are one of us! Everyone is welcome! If you want to be an artist, join our company! Our Theatre can find employment for everyone, a place for everyone![82]

Though other viewers of this advertisement notice that there is no mention of payment—"No one wanted to be an artist, but every man wanted to be paid for his labours"—Karl is drawn in by the promise that "Everyone is welcome" and so takes a calculated risk. Spending most of his remaining money on train fare to the advertised town of Clayton, he arrives early in the morning to find something that vaguely resembles a theatrical spectacle: at the entrance to the racecourse, a platform has been set up "on which hundreds of women dressed as angels in white robes with great wings on their shoulders were blowing on long trumpets that glittered like gold."[83] But, in that dream-logic that is so characteristic of Kafka, this, and a later glimpse Karl gets of a photograph of an ornate box seat "reserved in the Theatre for the President of the United States,"[84] is the closest the adventure gets to anything like theater. Karl proceeds through a series of bureaucratic hurdles and various "recruiting squads," and eventually succeeds in being engaged by the Theatre of Oklahoma as a technical laborer—another of the theater's stagehands. Well-fed at an ornate banquet for new members of the troupe, he boards a train for Oklahoma . . . and there Kafka's narration breaks off, leaving the train to race through vast imagined landscapes.

What is it that makes this "Nature Theatre" a theater? For Walter Benjamin, writing after Kafka's death, it is theater's capacious appetite, its ability to contain gesture *as* gesture, that characterizes it as such. Benjamin clearly sees analogies between Kafka's world and Brecht's "epic theater" which he so much admired. "Epic theater is by definition a gestic theater,"[85] Benjamin wrote about Brecht, and in Kafka's world, "each gesture is an event—one might even say, a drama—in itself."[86] Benjamin suggests that this idea of gestic theater might indeed be a conceptual space that could contain much of Kafka's writing:

One can go even further and say that a good number of Kafka's shorter studies and stories are seen in their full light only when they are, so to speak, put on as acts in the "Nature Theater of Oklahoma." Only then will one recognize with certainty that Kafka's entire work constitutes a code of gestures which surely had no symbolic meaning for the author from the outset; rather, the author tried to derive such a meaning from them in ever-changing contexts and experimental groupings. The theater is the logical place for such groupings.[87]

Such a characterization of theater anticipates a semiological understanding of theatricality, as articulated by Roland Barthes as "theater-minus-text," which is figured as a theater of assembly: "It is a density of signs and sensations built up on stage starting from the written argument; it is that ecumenical perception of sensuous artifice—gesture, tone, distance, substance, light—which submerges the text beneath the profusion of its external language."[88] More: this is theater *as* assembly, or "theatre as organization," as Samuel Weber puts it in his description of Kafka's vision.[89] For Weber, who is seeking to describe the capaciousness of theater as a medium that stubbornly resists being reduced to a form for the expression of narrative,[90] Kafka's image of the Presidential box seat is exemplary:

The "loge" no longer has any contents except itself: its ability to contain. It is pure organization, pure theater, pure place. It is a vessel that contains nothing except itself or, rather, the nothing that *is* itself.[91]

Theater is thus a name for containment and separation from "life," for mediation itself, distinct from any idea or content to be mediated. This theater is not dependent on the actions of its participants, and no demonstration of skill or dramatic talent is required; instead it is the conceptual frame of the "organizing theater" that does the work. So when, in the recruitment process, Karl confesses that he has no wish to be an actor, this doesn't seem to be a problem for the company. Instead, what characterizes the Nature Theatre of Oklahoma is that "everyone is welcome"; it seems that whatever one wants to do anyway can become "employment" by being framed within this "theater"—or, as recorded by the Nature Theatre's clerk when Rossman's application is accepted, anyone can be *Aufgenommen*—"included," "recorded," "taken in," or, as Edwin Muir translates it, "engaged."[92] Benjamin notes that "all that is expected of the applicants is the ability to play themselves."[93] But what is it to *play* oneself? In that familiar theatrical operation of *dédoublement*, discussed earlier, it is not the same as *being* oneself. As Alan Read observes, "to be present to the Theatre of Oklahoma is at once to recognize the gestic quality of life and yet to continue living that life."[94] The challenge thrown down by Kafka in the early twentieth century is not to find a living truthfulness that interrupts theater's artifice to give it some meaning. It is instead to live a life as theater. It is into that unfinished horizon that Kafka's happiest protagonist disappears (Kafka's working title for the novel was *Der Verschollene*, "The Missing Person," sometimes rendered as "The Man Who Disappeared"). As to what might have become of Karl, Max Brod recalls in his postscript: "In enigmatic language, Kafka used to hint smilingly that within this 'almost limitless' theater his young hero was going to find again a profession, a stand-by, his freedom, even his old home and his parents, as if by some celestial witchery."[95]

Jump ahead one hundred years, to a scene that confronts us with what might be a version of this "almost limitless" theater, a theater into which a life has disappeared, and a theater which is now animated by that single life:

> Um . . . So . . .
> Shall I start?
> Okay. Um . . .
> So . . . let's see.
> Okay. Well—[96]

So begins *Life and Times*, a multi-episode theater project by the contemporary company Nature Theater of Oklahoma, which has co-opted not only the name of Kafka's imagined troupe but also its clarion call advertisement reproduced above ("The Great Nature Theater of Oklahoma is calling you!" etc.), at times emblazoned on the company's website and reprinted in its playscripts. Though this inspired appropriation of the catchy name and clarion call need not mandate that the company continue the project imagined in Kafka's pages, I will suggest that the company's works, and *Life and Times* in particular, nevertheless give a glimpse into what such an "almost limitless" theater might look like. Whereas other theatrical projects have attempted to push beyond the boundaries of theater—to surpass its limits, to get outside it—what I argue is going on in this work is the amplification of theatricality itself, expanding the capacity of theater as container, so that it even includes the labor of the workers, and the shared labor of the audience, in holding itself open.

Indeed, the ambitious project of *Life and Times* is to contain an entire life, based on recordings from a series of extended conversations (totaling 16 hours) in which one of the company's associated artists attempts to recall her life story, and to translate the text of these recollections into what was ambitiously planned to be a 24-hour, ten-episode performance event. Each episode retains the recorded text verbatim, with all its hesitancies, false starts, and chronological leaps, and takes a radically different genre: *Episode 1* (2009) is presented as low-fi, jaunty musical theater, with live accompaniment on mostly acoustic instruments, bringing in elements of eastern European synchronized choreography. *Episode 2* (2010) retains song as its format but adds a dance-floor pop aesthetic, with chorus lines, handclaps, and electronic beats. *Episodes 3 & 4* (2012) take place in a cheaply rendered set of *The Mousetrap*, with the actors as stock characters moving through static tableaus. The next episodes feature no actors: *Episode 4.5* (2013) is a hand-drawn animated film of scenes from everyday life; and *Episode 5* (2013) is, surprisingly, a book, a mashup of a medieval illuminated manuscript and a guide to sexual positions, copies of which are distributed to the audience to read while seated in the theater for a delimited period of time, illuminated by individual clip-lights and accompanied by live organ music. As the company began work on *Episode 6*, they discovered that the source recording was completely blank. From there, the company moved more into film, with *Episode 7* (2015, 132 min.) adopting the conventions of classic Hollywood black-and-white cinema, *Episode 8* (2015, 118 min.) filmed outdoors and referencing early color Cinemascope, and *Episode 9* (2015, 19 min.) mimicking the form of a rap video.

The project seems to have concluded after nine episodes rather than ten, and the final three exist as collaboratively created films. My focus here is on the first five and a half episodes, those that rely on the live presence of the performers. These episodes can be broken up into discrete units for stand-alone performances over sequential evenings, but the company has also presented the work back to back as a continuous performance, typically described as a "marathon showing" by venues that offered this option. A viewing of the marathon production takes twelve hours, including meals and snack breaks served by the company. For example, in Norwich (UK) where I saw the continuous production, *Episode 1* began at 1:30 p.m. and lasted three and a half hours with an intermission, after which the cast cooked and served a barbecued meal; *Episode 2* lasted two hours, followed by brownies and ice cream; *Episodes 3 & 4* ran together for two and a half hours without interval, followed by a break for hot chocolate; and the individualized reading experience of *Episode 5* finished in the early hours of the morning, with the company's cast and co-directors, Pavol Liska and Kelly Copper, exhausted but cheerfully bidding us goodnight.

There are three different levels at which this theater might be said to contain life. The first of these is that of the everydayness of "real" life—most obviously, that of Kristin Worrall, the subject interviewed in the source recordings. Each episode covers a discrete period of Worrall's life—birth to age 8, ages 8 to 14, ages 14 to 18, and so on—and is as thorough a record as possible of all that Worrall remembers, while also an invitation to associate one's own memories of that age with the specifics of Worrall's circumstances. "Since her life is quite normal and unexceptional, her story contains many bits of your own," the publicity material reads.[97] And it's true: Worrall's effort to recall the names of long-forgotten friends—Taxon Haligan, best friend Johnna Mollicone, Mrs. Broderick (illustrated with jazz hands), grade-school beauty Tanja Zorbeedian ("I wish I could be Tanya Zor— / [All (in a choral fanfare)]: Zorbeedian!"),[98] Pete Jackson, with whom she had her first kiss—triggers for me a similar list of people I haven't thought about for a long time, who were once so important to me but whom I don't think I would recognize if I were to see them now. The life she recalls is one made of tiny moments of delight or delirium, fragments of which are recalled and held up in the buoyant singing of the company. An early reverie of discovering insects under a rock: "Like oh my god! It's sooo beautiful! / And I never found them again."[99] The child's fixation with her father: "What—does he like—think? When he sits there silently?";[100] and an everyday moment of looking at her mother preparing dinner, memorable exactly for its banality: "And I remember, one time, thinking— / Like I was staring at her, while I was holding on to the beams, / And I was like— / 'I have to remember this moment for the rest of my life!' "[101] The feeling of elation coming home from one's first formal dance: "I saw something new, and I felt— / Like all these like emotions / That I had only dreamed about, you know. / But I had FELT them! / For the first time, so. / It was very exciting."[102] These are exemplary experiences, whose value is in their very banality, their mundanity, their individuality; precisely because they are so particular to Worrall, they create a fabric of memory in which my own memories can be held. It is the dormant memories of my own past life, which are all of it that lives on, that this theater contains, too.

The everyday sense of "real life" is evoked not only by Worrall's recollections but also by the mundane quality of the verbatim text as it is re-performed. The everyday lives not just in the content of the recollections but in their form of expression: its hesitancy, the gaps and jumps, and the signifiers that reveal Worrall's own self-consciousness in remembering. These all contribute to those "authenticity-effects" described by Garde and Mumford (cited earlier), and perhaps most so when the "contract" is renewed through revelations of the circumstances of the recording. *Episode 1* ends with the inclusion of text in which Worrall is speaking to others who are in the room with her while she is on the phone with our interlocutor: "Hold on one second . . . / Are you guys ready to go? / Okay. / I'm—I'll go with you guys. / Okay. / Um. I have to go pretty soon. / But—uhhh."[103] And *Episode 3*, after an interval, opens with a renewal of that context, both between the interviewer and her subject, and between performers and the audience, playfully evoking our own renewed acquaintance and shared fatigue:

ALISON: Hey!
ANNE: Hello.
ALISON: Hel-LO. How are you?
ANNE: Good!
ALISON: Good.
(breath)
ANNE: Good!
ALISON: I hope you're not too tired—
ANNE: No! / Are you?
ALISON: No! Never for you!
ANNE: OK.
ALISON: Yeah.
ANNE: Yeah, um.
ALISON: I just don't want you to have— / To rush!
ANNE: No! / No—
ALISON: —'Cause the longer it is, the better! / You know?
ANNE: Yeah, I mean— / Sounds good.
(pause)
   Um . . .
ALISON: So don't—don't—don't leave out any— / Don't— / Don't
   feel like you have to abridge it for me, or anything.[104]

It is this textual quality of verisimilitude that draws the attention of many commentators. In a blog for the *New Yorker*, Hilton Als describes the play as allowing its audiences to hear everyday speech "in all its terrible richness and peculiarity and flatness as it struggles to express itself, or hide from its own emotional life and specious truths."[105] Charles Isherwood of the *New York Times* makes a similar observation: "Language unshaped by an aesthetic formula is shown to have its own funky fascination by being presented in a context in which we expect to encounter an aesthetic experience."[106] To some extent, this texture of everyday speech is one of the interests of the theater-makers; in an interview, Liska reflects:

> I wanted the breakdown of language, I wanted her to have trouble, I was really listening for the times when she couldn't remember, not the sections that she remembered fluently and fluidly. I wanted to find out how she generates language and how language is going to come out of the brain when it's in a crisis, when it's uncomfortable, when it doesn't know what to say.[107]

Together, the ordinary quality of Worrall's own experiences (and those that are stimulated in our own memories) and the banal texture of everyday speech constitute what I would characterize as the first way in which "real life" is contained within this theater.

And yet, superimposed on top of this "life" of the everyday is another, diametrically opposed layer: that of theatricality. For, as the theater company's co-directors make clear, the thing they are interested in is not the content of Worrall's text and its claims to authenticity, but instead the text as theater, and specifically as a challenge for the apparatus of theater to absorb:

> [COPPER:] I'm aware of this *[interest in verbatim theater]*, here sometimes it's called documentary theatre: I think where we differ from at least some of the companies that do that kind of work in the US is that it's not for us a journalistic project. It's more that the material exists as a kind of restriction and it offers us a resistance: I can't rewrite this. We're not out to tell the story of Kristin, down to even not representing her on stage. It's something else.
>
> [LISKA:] Also we're not interested in the "poetry of the everyday." People do take that away, that's fine, but there's no romanticism in [it]. It's very easy to do, it's easy to record. It's not that it's better than anything else.[108]

In this way, what drew them to this text was a continuation of the company's practice of using constraint and restriction as generative elements in making theater. Several of these techniques are documented in Rachel Anderson-Rabern's 2010 survey of the company's work, which predates the *Life and Times* project but includes their earlier works *Poetics: A Ballet Brût* (2005), *No Dice* (2007), *Chorègraphie* (2008), *Rambo Solo* (2008), and *Romeo and Juliet* (2008). Some of these restrictions are determined by the company's material circumstances, and Anderson-Rabern notes that the company often chooses to embrace and foreground its "shoestring" budget, for example. But she notes that the company also "purposefully *generates* obstacles to enhance their creative material,"[109] through practices such as deliberately restricting the movement vocabulary available to performers, imposing accents that are the most difficult ones for the performers to execute, and overloading the performers with multiple simultaneous tasks. In this context, we can understand the use of verbatim text as another of these generative constraints. The company began to explore this with *No Dice*, in which the performance text was edited from hundreds of hours of phone calls, and the actors performed with in-ear headphones dictating the pace and rhythm of delivery, over which they performed in ridiculously exaggerated accents.

In *Life and Times*, further ways in which the company sets obstacles for themselves include directing the movement sequences live during *Episode 1* by holding up prompts drawn at random; rehearsing *Episodes 3 & 4* without Worrall's text, and instead using the text of Agatha Christie's famously long-running play *The Mousetrap*, so that the actors are not familiar with the text and only see it on cue cards during performance; and, most prominently, the decision to foreground the use of live music, which was a challenge given that most of the company had no experience with singing before undertaking the project. (Even the composer, although he did have musical experience, decided to compose the work on the ukulele, an instrument that he was learning to play at the same time as undertaking the composition.) The animation and manuscript techniques for *Episodes 4.5* and *5* were also completely new to Copper and Liska, who learned by doing them, and the labor took its toll: Copper developed ganglion cysts on the tendons of her hand from the relentless challenge of drawing day after day.

For Florian Malzacher, this insistence on difficulty is not only part of an aesthetic of work, but also an ethical proposition:

> They do not believe that something that is too easy can truly have value—in life as well as in theater. They want to see actors work, especially if the point is to be entertaining. They are not interested in apparently effortless virtuosity. This would be a sign for them that one obviously is not challenging oneself enough and has not yet reached one's limits.[110]

Malzacher situates the kinds of practices they pursue in relation to historical antecedents of the avant-garde and neo-avant-garde that include the readymade and the appropriation of "found" objects, chance-based operations, and an interest in the materiality of both text and objects. Indeed, their aesthetic could be placed in relation to the kind of "task or task-like activity" advocated by Yvonne Rainer, which I discussed at greater length in chapter 1.[111] But whereas Rainer's approach might be characterized as subtractionist—how can the unwanted "spectacle" be removed from performance?—the approach in Nature Theater of Oklahoma might better be described as "additionalist"—what is the threshold at which speech or gesture transforms into theater? In a 2009 interview with Young Jean Lee, Copper describes their approach this way:

> We start out with some extremely basic question, like: What's the least thing we can do and have it be a show? Will it be a show if there is no script? If we just stand there in front of a curtain? If we open the curtain, is it then a show? If we use only our phone conversations for dialogue but we're wearing costumes, does that make them into a play? At the heart of our investigation is this wondering about the tipping point—when does it turn into theater?[112]

By the time it comes to *Life and Times*, these minimal operations have accumulated into the excesses of musical theater, stylized costume drama, and film. The aim here is not the removal of the inauthentic from theater through the introduction of everyday life, but instead an exploration of the theatricality of the everyday.

The choice of hyper-stylized genre, coupled with the extravagant investment in duration—three and half hours of singing, two hours of static tableaus and fixed grimaces—function as a Brechtian defamiliarization technique, creating a distance between the actor and the character, between the life of the performance and the life being performed. For example, the repeated instances of "um," "like," and "blah blah blah" accumulate the potency of a Brechtian *gestus*—not a signifier of authenticity but instead, through repetition, finally becoming visible and audible as the gap between language and experience, not their proximity. If there is a paradigmatic moment of this, it is the conclusion of *Episode 2* when a chorus of all eighteen performers join together for a glorious final "Um," their voices rising together in a resonant articulation of this empty signifier—a container of nothing, of nothing itself, and as such "pure theatre," as Weber described it. But more than this, the hyper-theatricality of the company's performance also amplifies a tendency toward genrefication already latent in Worrall's story: the way her own life is already experienced through mediated forms, and her recognition of repeated acts of self-dramatization. Worrall's enchantment with soap operas recurs a few times throughout her story, and their episodic logic clearly informs *Life and Times*: an early infatuation with reading Agatha Christie prefigures the *Mousetrap*-inspired *staging* of *Episodes 3 & 4*;[113] and her own experience of being a young teen is mediated through a desire to realize the fantasies of popular culture, such as her memory of her first dance standing out for her because it featured the soundtrack from *16 Candles*, with Worrall longing to be the teen actor Molly Ringwald.[114] Her experience of her first menstrual period—the event that is the heart of the "mystery" in *Episode 3*'s appropriation of mystery theater—is also experienced almost as if seeing herself from above, as in a movie: "I was like lying and sunning myself on the— / Front of the boat. / And then um. / I looked down. / And there's like a STREAM of blood!"[115] Not only are her experiences understood and incorporated via popular genres, but she also reflects on her acts of composing her life at the same time as she is living it. For example, she recalls giving names to episodes of her life: "And I would always call it like / 'The Feeling That Something's Missing' / And, um. / So, anyway. / Um. That was third grade"; "In sixth grade . . . was like— / Yeah, just like— / The Beginning of the Dark Period."[116] She also remembers calculatedly constructing events, such as trying to arrange situations where her best friend's cute cousin will oversee her changing out of her bathing suit.[117] And in an interesting precursor to this future project, she remembers being "absolutely enamored" with a tape recorder into which she would talk endlessly, fictionalizing her life.[118]

In this way, one effect of the hyper-theatricality of the company's staging is to underscore the theatricality already at work in Worrall's remembered life. Indeed, one implication might be that "real life" actually has more affinities with a non-narrative, "post-dramatic" aesthetic than with realist theater, something that Worrall hints at when, in a somewhat frustrated moment, she says:

> I feel like I TOOOtally babble to you, like . . .
> That was like a—
> Just a MESS of nothing I just told you.
> Like it's NOT my life story!
> Just these weird . . .
> These weird like FLASHES of
> Experience I guess.[119]

Having this sentiment conveyed through a static actor, dressed in a garish costume inside a drawing room with furniture painted on the walls, reinforces the idea that what we think of as "story" is only "flashes of experience," loosely held together through a retrospective artifice. As opposed to the first layer of "real life" described above, this second layer is wholly concerned with theater and theatricality.

And yet, there is a third layer of the interrelation between "life" and "theater" at work in this event—one which has to do with the other half of the project's title, its "Times." For it is not only the enclosing of verbatim verisimilitude within exaggerated theatricality that distinguishes this project, but also its ambitious duration and episodic rhythm. There is something deliberately relentless about the effect this experience has on its audience: "We are so arduously entertaining that it becomes painful," as Malzacher characterizes it.[120] The overwhelming accumulation of mundane details within each episode, and the cumulative effect of episode after episode, makes it impossible to maintain a full state of attentiveness, and this must be considered one of its intended effects. The company makes deliberate choices about the organization of dynamics within the episodes, introducing variety-within-sameness by changing the number of performers on stage, or introducing unexpected interventions (*Episode 4* finishes with figures in rubber alien masks speaking in booming voices from outside the *Mousetrap* set). But at the same time, inhabiting the duration of the event is a responsibility that is placed onto the audience:

> [LISKA:] Exactly: you put the responsibility on them as well. It's like telling people how long the show is: if you say it's 10 and a half hours, there's no way I can feel responsible for entertaining you for 10 and a half hours. I hope you understand—you, the audience member—there is just no way that I am going to be

> able to keep it up. At some point you will have to jump in and
> supply your own excitement—unless you have absolutely no
> excitement whatever within you: then we can't work together.
> [COPPER:] We always assume that within that 10 and a half hours
> there's some room for you and you're going to take it upon
> yourself to claim that space. It's not all the time the actor giv-
> ing you something, at a certain point you'll give back, even to
> yourself.[121]

The regulation of time extends to the intervals between episodes, as well:
held within the episodic structure, they also become episodes of their own
within this theatrical life. And so a sense of inexhaustible theatricality—the
show keeps going and going, long after it feels as if it should have come to
an end—spills over into everything. I feel this theatricality in the exchanges
I have with the performers who are serving me the barbecue dinner, whom
I have just seen onstage in costume and covered in sweat, and who are now
here in a different kind of costume (aprons and cooking paraphernalia)
and covered in sweat. They bicker with each other and with the customers (because we are placing orders, we are customers now, aren't we?),
and I can no longer tell if this is the playfulness that arises "naturally" in
everyday life or if we are still "playing" a role. It spills over into the conversations I have with my companions at the theater, too, as we mimic the *um*s
and *like*s of the verbatim text—but of course we are enacting our own ver-
bal tics, our own voices sounding estranged from us. It spills over into the
encounters with Liska and Copper, who seem somehow to be everywhere
in their matching tracksuits, flamboyantly colored, and different between
each episode. "The performance really shifts, for us, from the stage, to the
screen, and finally out into the house," Copper says.[122] And it spills over
into my return to the auditorium, to my role—my job—as spectator. Less is
asked of me than of the performers on stage, of course, but as we all enter
exhaustion together, our states feel like they grow nearer to each other.
This is hard work, for all of us, to live together like this.

> [LISKA:] But theatre's weird, it's like the least natural form of
> behaviour that we humans engage in. That's why I'm curious
> about it: everything else is kind of easy to understand and it's
> nice but theatre is awkward, it's weird, it's dirty, it's grounded—
> [COPPER:] —you're sitting next to other people who smell funny—
> [LISKA:] —it's the opposite of heaven, it's like theatre is hell and is
> a very interesting place to be.
> [COPPER:] Or at least purgatory or limbo. It's a liminal state.
> [LISKA:] It's hell. Theatre is heavy, it's material, it's all materialistic—
> [COPPER:] —it takes money to make it, it takes money to bring it
> anywhere—

[LISKA:] —it takes space, it's heavy—

[COPPER:] —people can only experience it for a brief moment, a window in time, and if they're in the same city. . . . I think we're constantly trying to discover why [we do it]: some days I do it because it feels good to me and it amuses me; equally there's some days when it does not make any sense to me at all why somebody would be bringing 15 doofuses around the world to put up a little fake thing and do it for you. There are days when I'm embarrassed that somebody pays as much money as they do.[123]

Crucially, duration functions differently in *Life and Times* than in other forms of durational work that set out to promote a sense of focus, mindfulness, and presence in the moment. For example, Marina Abramović has developed a training "drill" of exercises in slowness; participating in this drill was a requirement for entry to *Marina Abramović Presents*, her takeover of the Wentworth Gallery for the 2009 Manchester International Festival, which, like *11 Rooms* in the 2011 festival, was preoccupied with staging performance as installation.[124] Something similar was promoted via the carefully regulated tempo of Robert Wilson's *Walking* for the 2012 Norfolk & Norwich Festival, where *Life and Times* would play in 2013, and which Louise Owen describes as being framed as a retreat from everyday life.[125] But this is not the intention behind *Life and Times*, which takes place not in "real time" but in *constructed* time; such is the effect of its epic form. Our job is not, *cannot* be, to be present; this work's scale makes that an impossible task, and the defamiliarization of the idea of "life story" makes the very idea of such a thing seem ever more impossible the more it is pursued. But this doubled, deferred time becomes the experience of not only Worrall's life as it is played out before us, but also our own lives that have become part of this "nature theater" in which we are all living for a time. As the hours accumulate, I find that ideas about being the author of one's life, a player in the life of another, and a spectator to life passing by begin to detach from each other and commingle. The present always fails to coincide with itself, such that we catch it some time later, or find ourselves unable to think back to it. *Are the words they are saying now the same or different from what they just said?* I find myself thinking. *Am I thinking about my own memory or was it something that Worrall remembered? Who are these people really?*

The foregrounded artifice of the event, and the visibility of the work that it takes to maintain it, ensure that we never forget that this is theater; it is not some condition to be transcended. And yet within this theater we begin to *live* together—to eat, to talk, sometimes to sleep as the show carries on into the night. This attention to the conditions of theater can be seen as a continuation of the project of *No Dice*, in which the verbatim text was taken from multiple phone conversations in which the actors and their friends discussed all the things they were doing (usually for money) instead of making theater. As Nicholas Ridout comments, the trick of *No Dice* was to make that "wasted time" into theater, such that "the subject matter of this performance is the conditions in which it was made."[126] But in folding those conditions into the theater itself, Ridout suggests this offers a vision of theater that becomes itself a site of political action, rather than "seeking to extend itself into any part of the so-called real world." Instead, it is *already* real: "Theatre does not stand to one side of the 'real' world or offer an alternative to it: the theatre is a real place, where real people go to work, and where their work takes the form of 'conversation.'"[127] The challenge is how to open up that logic of the theater into a domain that others can co-occupy, into a shared workspace.

Entitled offers a glimpse of this shared time and space: "We've only got a certain amount of time," Sonia reminds us, but still we could make something together, opening, as I have argued, a speculative window into the present. The multiyear project of *Life and Times*, and its extended playing durations in the marathon performances, open different possibilities. Regarding the reasons for undertaking a long-term project like *Life and Times*, Copper comments on this possibility of opening the theatrical apparatus to others:

> And actually, one of the reasons that we did it initially is because we both felt like theatre can be an incredibly hermetic experience: you're writing these plays and you're doing your little private work and then at a certain point you open it up to the world. We were interested in how we [could] stay attached to the world; I mean, it was a way of making our work more permeable to and inviting the world into the work. You just grow tired of this art as self-expression all the time: theatre is a social event and it's a social art form and it's an oral art form, so can we stay entirely in this social and oral if that's what it does and that's its essence?[128]

What is the "work" which Copper wants to make "permeable" and into which she wants to "invite the world"? We are returned here to the dual meaning with which this chapter began: between work as surplus object produced by labor, and work as the labor itself. I have suggested that the labor in the theater, emptied of the promise of return, interrupts the logic of productive labor; this exploration of ways in which that labor might be shared between performer and spectator is an extension of that interruption of the everyday that is enabled by the theater as pure container (as Weber puts it). But what is the nature of this work, to which, as Kafka's advertisement declares, "everyone is welcome"? It is no more and no less than the work of maintaining life—represented figuratively through the support structure that contains *a* life via Worrall's "life story," but also the work that we are all doing by living together, co-distant in this theatrical space.

Like the labor of the stagehand, this is the work of caretaking, of maintaining life. Indeed, recent critiques of labor have looked to "care" as a model for subverting the logic of productive labor under capitalism, such as Bruni Gullì's argument that creative labor is a special case of a "general economy of care," and that a caring mode of production might offer a way of thinking beyond the dichotomy of productive/nonproductive labor.[129] Or Bojana Kunst differentiates between the temporal logic of the "project," oriented toward a future gain, and the work of maintaining life:

> No matter how much they may experiment with the present, all projects are projections and steps into the future, entailing a promise of the future and the possibility of what is still to come. In contrast, we can understand work primarily as the preservation and maintenance of the present or a life balance that is preserved through a continuous consumption of human powers. Such understanding closely connects work with the practice of life and its consumption. It contains no other promise but that of having to maintain and preserve life.[130]

Or as Liska puts it: "I think all the work—the shows, the animations, all this—the one thing they have in common is that *we take care of every single moment.*"[131] The invitation opened to us is, like the artists, to take care, to play a part in this life—our own lives—as if we were its stagehands.

Chapter 3

✦

Real Theater: Making the Actor Appear

And then, sometimes it can seem as if the stage is being invaded by a forceful interruption from outside. Swaggering, playful, ebullient, the performers burst onto the playing space individually or in small groups and take their places in a lineup of empty chairs facing the audience; to a pounding rock soundtrack, they fight, make out with each other, shout to the audience, and generally act like restless, reckless, and spontaneous teenagers. This is the explosion of wildly rambunctious adolescent energy that happens at the opening of the provocatively titled *Once and for All We're Gonna Tell You Who We Are So Shut Up and Listen* (2008) by the Flemish theater company Ontroerend Goed. For Bert O. States, children belong to a category of persons or objects that resist being fully incorporated into the representational apparatus; along with clocks, running water, animals, and so on, they have an "abnormal durability," so that they "do not always or entirely surrender their objective nature to the sign/image function."[1] Similarly, in the context of child actors on film, Karen Lury describes the way they possess an "abnormally interesting" quality, where this quality is dependent upon the extent to which they appear not to be acting.[2] As Lury writes, child actors "confuse or threaten the understanding of what acting or performing is, and how it can be distinguished from not-acting or from 'being.'"[3] There is something that appears nontheatrical, or even anti-theatrical, about the appearance of children and teenagers on stage or in works of art, as if an apparent absence of guile or fakery threatens to unsettle the theatrical event, to exceed the constraints of the event, to spill out into the auditorium.

In this chapter, I am concerned with theater that pushes at the limits of representation, and that thinks through the nature of representation itself, through the appearance in the theater of certain kinds of bodies which for one reason or another are not "supposed" to appear—because they are not yet adults, as discussed in the first part of the chapter, or because they are perceived to have disabilities that prompt ableist assumptions about the performers' capacities to represent themselves, addressed in the second half of the chapter. As I will discuss, some interpretations

of these appearances on stage emphasize the "realness" of such performers as a challenge to theatricality as artifice. This is similar to the way in
which the real (not fake) suffering of the performer is a strategy of some
artists to separate "performance" from "theater," described in chapter
1—as emphasized in Mike Parr's dismissal of theater as "simulation," or
in Marina Abramović's insistence that a performance artist must "hate"
theater because "the knife is not real, the blood is not real, and the emotions are not real," or the image of Chris Burden having himself shot in
the arm that inspired Tim Etchells's distinction between spectators and
witnesses.[4] But the works I discuss in this chapter are not intended to
deceive, to pass off fake blood as real, but instead attempt something more
complicated: to reverse or subvert socially imagined characteristics, and in
that sense to pass off real people as imagined ones. Like the work of the
stagehands or Rimini Protokoll's "experts" discussed in the previous chapter, these examples foreground the machinery of representation, making its
workings visible. But if the previous chapter focused on the ways that artists have explored the inner workings of the theatrical apparatus in order
to engage with wider structures of representation, then the artists in this
chapter demonstrate ways of leveraging this machinery of representation
to escape—or at least make visible—the "trap" of representation.

The appearance of children or disabled performers on stage produces
a tension between "the real" and the representational, because these performers appear to retain their extra-theatrical "realness" and are perhaps
perceived not even to be "performing," or at least performing themselves.
This tendency to incorporate elements of reality from outside the theater,
references to factual events via documents and media, or staged versions
of non-theatrical situations is a recurring feature of contemporary performance. Hans-Thies Lehmann has described this as the "irruption of the
real," in which "the level of the real" is intentionally cast as a "co-player."[5]
Carol Martin refers to it as "the theatre of the real," cataloging works
that "recycle reality" through techniques such as "theatre created from the
verbatim use of transcripts, facts, trials, autobiography, and interviews;
theatre created from reenacting the experiences of witnesses, portraying historic events, and reconstructing real places; theatre created from
the Internet including YouTube and Facebook; and any combination of
these."[6] And Ulrike Garde and Meg Mumford have described the phenomenon of a "theatre of real people," which foregrounds "contemporary
people who have a verifiable physical existence, and who usually have
not received institutional theatre training and have little or no prior stage
experience," and which is characterized by "the self-representational and
either fully or partially self-devised nature of their presentations."[7]

These various terms emphasize the significance of the *real*—which, as
Paul Rae notes, presupposes an oppositional relation between the theatrical and the real, resting on the general assumption that "one of theatre's

defining characteristics, relative to other social phenomena in the social world, is that it is 'not real.' "[8] In this chapter, I am interested in the mode of "self-representational" performance described by Garde and Mumford, and particularly those performances that call attention to their own theatricality by foregrounding the process of constructing their own representation. Rather than presuming a distinction between the theatrical and the real, in this chapter I continue to explore the connections begun in the previous chapter between problems of representation raised by theatrical appearances and problems of representation more broadly as they affect people's lived experiences. In this way, my interest here is less in the way in which the real might interrupt the theatrical (ostensibly to rehabilitate, rescue, or transform it) than in the performance of agency—that is, the agency that arises *through* performance—that is realized through the act of "making an appearance" of oneself.

Children Playing Children:
Ontroerend Goed, Tim Etchells, and Milo Rau

Bert O. States's description of theatrical signs that display "abnormal durability" is framed within a discussion of theater as an apparatus that swallows up the real, "a matter of gestation" by which things are turned into signs: "Theater ingests the world of objects and signs only to bring images to life."[9] As a somewhat problematic illustration, States uses the image of nonhuman animals on display in a zoo: "Do we not," he asks, "in some such way, see animals in the intentional space of a zoo as vaguely oscillating between animals and images or signs of animals?"[10] For example, he writes, a dingo, when contained in a cage with a sign next to it that reads "DINGO: Wild Dog of Australia," appears both as the "actual" animal and as a sign of itself, a representation of the sort of creature one might encounter in Australia. While States insists that this is not a matter of "the animal losing its actuality," but "a perceptual change," he describes the presence of a dog within a theatrical space as having a more depreciative effect: "The act of theatricalizing it—putting it into an intentional space—neutralizes its objectivity and claims it as a *likeness* of a dog."[11] States goes on to describe the history of the theater as a continual search for new elements of the actual to "colonize," such that previously shocking or energizing images become worn down with familiarity over time, and the theater must seek out new ones:

> The dog on the stage is a nearly perfect symptom of the cutting edge of theater, the bite that it takes into actuality in order to sustain itself in the dynamic order of its own ever-dying signs and images. One could define the history of theater—especially where

we find it overthrowing its own traditions—as a progressive colonization of the real world.[12]

States's image of colonization is a problematic one, for even if he is deploying this metaphor critically, he does not explicitly name the histories of
European appropriation of non-European theatrical and cultural practices
in order to revitalize itself.[13] Furthermore, his language of "colonization"
sits uneasily with the choice of an example from Australia, a land brutally
colonized in the absence of any treaty with its Indigenous peoples, and
with ongoing destructive effects on its natural environment.

But despite the problematic metaphor, we can see something of the
dynamic he describes in the periodic "waves" by which trends sweep
through Western theater. For example, Ontroerend Goed's *Once and for
All . . .* was just one of numerous instances of the appearance of children
on European stages in the 2000s, in works by Romeo Castellucci/Sòcietas
Raffaello Sanzio, Boris Charmatz, and Fevered Sleep, for example, as
well as numerous collaborations with contemporary theater-makers initiated by the Flemish company CAMPO (formerly called Victoria). Among
these CAMPO collaborations have been Josse De Pauw's *üBUNG* (2002),
Gob Squad's *Before Your Very Eyes* (2011), Philippe Quesne's *Next Day*
(2014), and two that I will discuss in more detail below, Tim Etchells's
That Night Follows Day (2007) and Milo Rau's *Five Easy Pieces* (2016).
Following States, perhaps we can read this phenomenon as just such a
moment in the history of theater when it takes a "bite" in order to sustain
itself. In bringing child actors on stage, contemporary theater practices
also echo, whether self-consciously or not, other historical traditions of
exhibition and spectacle, a point that Nicholas Ridout underscores in his
interest in the way that both animals and children seem to reappear on
European stages at around the same period.[14]

Interestingly, in reviewing the Edinburgh premiere of *Once and for
All . . .*, Brian Logan also deploys the metaphor of the zoo:

> The achievement of this remarkable event from Belgium is to put
> teenage [*sic*] on the stage. It's not a play about adolescence, it is
> adolescence itself: making out, fighting, getting high, dancing, and
> defying its adult audience not to be utterly absorbed. Watching
> the show is like visiting the zoo—teens can seem like a different
> species—or perhaps the circus, as these 13 performers walk the
> tightrope between innocence and experience.[15]

Logan continues to use anti-theatrical terms to describe the performance,
highlighting the resistance of the young people to being absorbed within
the representational apparatus of the theater: "These kids aren't performing, they're just *being*," he writes. In my view, however, the dramaturgy

of *Once and for All* . . . is more ambiguous with regard to the relationship between "performing" and "being," so that they are not necessarily oppositional. For example, after the seemingly uncontained outburst of energy onto the stage with which the show begins, a loud klaxon calls the performers offstage—only for them to re-perform the sequence of actions in exactly the same way, perfectly replicated in every detail. Again and again this motif is repeated, as the basic structure of the opening sequence is reproduced through a series of variations in style and execution: in slow motion, as overacted theater, as hyper-sexualized exhibition, or with every gesture or prop exaggerated and amplified. What was perhaps once a spontaneous improvisation (though more likely a composite of directed and improvised actions developed in rehearsal) is revealed as carefully crafted and repeatable, both in subsequent variations in a single performance and in numerous performances throughout Europe, the United States, Australia, and New Zealand over the production's three years of touring.[16]

To continue States's metaphor, we might think of the repetition of the initial sequence as a staging of the process of ingestion, as the mechanism of the theater grinds against the apparent spontaneity of the teenagers—but even as it does so, I would call attention to the way that this theatricalized repetition also offers an opportunity for the teenagers to play out their resistance, their "abnormal durability"—not by rejecting the conditions of theater but by embracing them. In a direct address to the audience early in the performance, nearly drowned out by the music, one performer lists the conventions and stereotypes at play: you look at us, she says, and see that "we are 'free as birds,'" that "we have 'nothing to lose,'" that "we make you feel old." There is an echo of *Offending the Audience* here; rather than reproducing a glamorized version of adolescent rebellion, the production turns its gaze on the apparatus of representation itself and the desire of spectators to romanticize what they're seeing. In this self-critical gaze, some space is held open for the teenagers to exist not in spite of being performers on stage, but precisely *through* the act of performing. For unlike the dog in States's example, these performers are aware of the act of symbolization within which they are participating, and the theater becomes a place where they can self-reflexively critique this process. In this way, John Bailey rejects the idea that the work is comparable to visiting a zoo or museum:

> This work could easily have been a condescending glance backward, either treating teenagers as exotic specimens from another world or using them to remind us of a nostalgic youth we all apparently shared. Instead, it allows its performers to exist on their own terms, as individuals, as a group, as able performers and as fallible humans. They do not become signs of a generation, nor of an abstract principle.[17]

Engaging with the apparatus within which they appear, the teenagers in *Once and for All* . . . find a kind of agency through the act of self-representation, not necessarily by resisting the apparatus but instead by showing it to us—and showing us our own complicity, in which, as the title suggests, our role is "to shut up and listen."

The complicity of the audience is amplified through the use of sustained direct address in *That Night Follows Day* (2007), written and directed by Tim Etchells in collaboration with the Flemish company Victoria (later renamed CAMPO). This work has some initial similarities to *Once and for All* . . . , but whereas the latter used teenage performers, the children in *That Night Follows Day* are all aged between 8 and 14, and thus appear less rebellious and seductive, and more innocent and vulnerable. If the broad theme of *Once and for All* . . . is the energy of youthfulness, with the relation between the performers and their adult audience framed as circulating around nostalgia and envy (as in the performer's opening lines quoted above), then the obvious theme of *That Night Follows Day* is the responsibility that adults have toward children—both in the sense of individual duties of care, and also in the more general sense of taking responsibility for the state of the world that new generations must inhabit.

This theme is made obvious from the play's opening lines, which are spoken in a uniform chant. When I saw it in London, the children spoke Flemish while the English translation was projected onto a school chalkboard above their heads:

> You feed us.
> You dress us.
> You choose clothes for us.
> You wash us.
> You bathe us.
> You clean our teeth.
> You sing to us.
> You watch us when we are sleeping.
> You tell us that once the world was full of dinosaurs.
> That whales may soon be extinct.
> That some snakes are poisonous.
> That water and electricity are not good together.[18]

This is the format for the remainder of the show: in unison or in alternating individual voices, the children speak in sentences that are almost always in the second person; and though they are speaking *to* me, they also seem to be speaking *about* me, about my power as an adult. They are speaking about the world they have been born into: a world that they did not make, a world they must be told about. Within this structural constraint, both the words spoken by the performers and the way they speak them range from the playful to the tragic, from the accusatory to the melancholic, from the vulgar to the virtuosic. Some of the statements are drawn from the banal, such as the children reciting their multiplication tables ("You teach us that 6 × 3 is 18. You teach us that 7 × 3 is 21," etc.), but these are juxtaposed with more complex ideas that require an adult understanding:

> You teach us that certain words must not be said at all.
> That certain words can be said at home, in private but not in front of other people, and certainly not in front of the teacher.
> That certain words can mean something different than what they seem to mean.
> Or that certain words can mean different things in different contexts.
> Or that certain words might not mean anything much at all anymore,
> but that sometimes they still need to be said.[19]

If the onstage lineup is one trope of contemporary performance, as Etchells himself has identified (discussed in this book's introduction), then *That Night Follows Day* exemplifies another recurring format, that of text organized in the form of a list. As the children's encyclopedic listing of information that is required of them goes on, it becomes absurdly impossible, seeming to include the knowledge of right and wrong, of the delicacies of every social situation, of the history of the world and all of scientific discovery. It's a totality that threatens to overreach itself. How do they ever learn all this? How do any of us ever learn all this?

But just when I think that this is a particularly adult thing to be aware of, the text adopts this adult perspective, with the speakers describing the things that "we" think about "them," our backwards-looking thoughts that have nothing to do with the lived experience of childhood. And so the text keeps shifting, one step ahead of me. Each time I start to think of a question about what I'm watching, the text anticipates this question: I start to think about the challenge of the performance task, the memorization effort required of the children—and then the text becomes exaggeratedly virtuosic, spilling off into elaborately long constructions and displays of wordplay. I think about the taboos about what children should and shouldn't think—and the text becomes peppered with obscenities, with bigotries, with the petty prejudices and hypocritical judgments of the "adult" world. I think about the theatricality of the situation—and the performers say, "You give us words to memorise. You arrange us. You make us stand in lines. You tell us that an actor is only a parrot speaking words he cannot understand."[20]

In this way, the formal rigor of the piece and its message or content might be understood to be working toward contrasting purposes, producing a complex juxtaposition. At the level of content, the piece proposes an encounter with childhood and a comment on the multiplicity of relationships that adults and children have with each other. In relation to this wider spectrum of relationships, theater functions as a kind of metaphor for power relations in general—but the theatrical event is also a specific instance of such an encounter in a concentrated form. For example, the lines

> You trick us.
> You trap us.
> You take advantage of our trust.

are immediately followed by

> You teach us that a theatre is a place where all the things that happen are just part of a story and where all the people are not real and all the emotions are pretended.[21]

There are obvious echoes here of Handke's *Sprechstücke* (discussed in chapter 1), not only in the mode of second-person address, but also thematically in the self-reflexive turn to regard the theater's own formal properties. The artifice of the theater and the apparent realness of the children are in tension with each other. One way of resolving this would be to conclude that even though the children's authenticity is always bracketed by the contrivance of the situation, their authenticity lends it enough truth-value that the artifice is sufficiently disrupted: in *other* theater, the people are not real but just pretending, such an argument would suggest, but how could we doubt the reality of what is happening here in this theater? After all, these *really* are children, and look: this is what children are *really* like. This would be similar to the view espoused in Logan's review of *Once and for All . . .* , quoted earlier: "It is not a play about adolescence, it is adolescence itself." Such an interpretation would adhere to the possibility of looking *through* the theatrical encounter and getting a glimpse of some essential truths—as exemplified by a quotation, reproduced in the production's publicity material, which enthuses that this is "perhaps the finest show about parenthood and childhood ever produced in Europe."[22]

However, the cumulative effect of the work's structural rigor overwhelms and incapacitates, rather than activates or elucidates, any idea that childhood is an obvious and coherent category. The longer these performers speak, and the more they inhabit their function of representing childhood, the less they seem to actually *be* children. Instead, I have the eerie feeling that the children whose bodies walked onto the stage are not really *here*. Instead, what persists and accumulates is the idea of a child speaking—as an apparition, the image of a child speaking. This image may be achieved through the presence of a speaking child, but it is not the same thing as a child speaking. Paradoxically, the longer the children are here with me, the more they generate about them a kind of not-here-ness. Partly this has to do with the peculiar doubling inherent in the mechanics of acting: these words are not *their* words, and any of the performers could just as easily be a different child, from a different school, even speaking a different language. Indeed, they were partially a different group when the work was premiered two years before I saw it, with cast members who were consequently too old to perform with those whom I saw on stage in London. Where were they when the piece was performed? Still in Belgium, running and playing with their friends? And what spectral trace of the original cast haunted its subsequent performances by different groups of children in Abu Dhabi (2014), Gwangju (2015), and its restaging in London (2018) ten years later with a cast of British children?[23]

Furthermore, these distinctions and disparities are amplified by the piece's formalism: the choreographed lineup, punctuated by equally choreographed eruptions into apparently spontaneous behavior (running, climbing, playing), reinforces the nature of this event as spectacle, as image; and the anaphoric repetition of the text always reminds us that this text has been crafted, that its affective efficacy has been deliberately orchestrated, and that it is all, after all, built from quotation. By describing these children as "not really here," I do not mean to imply that something is missing from this particular situation. On the contrary, their not-here-ness is something additional, something layered over their here-ness—"present, but also other," as in the description from Alice Rayner quoted in the previous chapter.[24] This self-representation makes the distinction between *here* and *not-here* difficult to sustain in a version of that "peculiar but necessary double negativity that characterizes symbolic actions," as Richard Schechner puts it.[25]

What becomes possible in this theatrical event—and, I want to insist, possible *because* it is theater—is not so much a question of whether or not these particular children are performing, pretending, and so on, but instead the performative quality of the category "childhood" itself. That is, childhood as a social category is a matter of appearance, and there is always a context in which it is made to appear, in which the idea of childhood is deployed, in the service of some message, or some corrective, or some comment. From this perspective, to explore "childhood" is not to explore some essential state of innocence, but instead to catalogue the instances in which the idea of childhood makes an appearance, and the uses to which these manifestations are put. One way of reading the exhaustive list that makes up the text of *That Night Follows Day* is as just such a catalogue (as well as itself adding one more entry to that catalogue).

Indeed, one theater critic makes just such a comment about the appro-
priateness of this particular use of childhood. Writing in the *Observer*,
Clare Brennan concludes:

> The effect is like watching newsreels of communism's Young Pio-
> neers. It impressed on me how precious and fragile the openness
> and trustfulness of childhood is, and how important it is not to
> impose on that trust by using children to promote our own aims
> however worthy they may be.[26]

Brennan suggests that this performance might be ethically suspect because
it imposes its own project over whatever desires its actors might have. But
in raising this critique, Brennan necessarily makes her own political claim.
Her argument rests on the assumption that there exists some essential
state of childhood, characterized by "openness and trustfulness"—but she
also immediately couples the existence of such a state with the idea that
it requires protection, as well as an implicit self-nomination to the role of
protector. Whether or not this is her intention, her definition of childhood
is one that mandates an authority to monitor and defend it, and to delimit
what is an appropriate use of childhood. In this way, the apparently obvious idea of childhood turns out to be bound up with a set of authoritative
claims—including what is and isn't a worthy theater project.

These anxieties about the protection of children, and the necessity of
authority over the kinds of experiences they can have, are widespread.
Writing about a preponderance of British plays that address childhood
(although not exclusively focused on the use of child performers), Helen
Freshwater writes: "Anxieties about children and childhood have been
central to some of the boldest experiments in dramatic form on the British
stage during the last 15 years."[27] For Freshwater, such anxieties are intertwined with what Lee Edelman and Robin Bernstein have described as
the "secular theology" of the innocent child, a "framework of belief [that]
can be deployed to support a wide range of political positions."[28] Theatrical experiments benefit from "the extraordinary affective weight currently
carried by the figure of the child and idealized fantasies of childhood";
and at the same time, Freshwater proposes that "theatrical representation of the child can trouble and resist these forces of abstraction and
idealization."[29] Following Freshwater, I am interested here in exploring
the interruptive power of the image of the child, not in relation to its
supposed realness puncturing the representational frame of the theater,
but as an intervention within the larger cultural politics of representation:
its relation to potent ideas of futurity and nostalgia, to innocence and
vulnerability—and indeed to the very idea of "the real," as something that
children supposedly have special access to, but which I would argue should
also be understood as an "abstraction and idealization." In emphasizing

the ways in which theater is continuous with broader politics of representation, one of the implications is that the theater does not stand outside of these politics, and must itself be understood as a place where these power relations are exercised and reproduced.

In Etchells's *Sprechstück*, these politics of care and responsibility are primarily something that is engaged discursively—it is a play about speaking, about what "you tell us"—but they take a more embodied and enacted form in *Five Easy Pieces* (2016) by Milo Rau, another in the series of collaborations that CAMPO initiated with experimental directors. Rau, trained as a sociologist, has gained a reputation for controversy: a *New York Times* profile leads with the clickbait headline, "Is Milo Rau Really the Most Controversial Director in Theater?" citing some of Rau's provocative aesthetic choices such as advertising for returned ISIS fighters to appear in his first production for NTGent.[30] Rau's tenure at NTGent was announced by the publication of the "Ghent Manifesto," whose opening declaration articulates the tension between the representational and the real: "It's not just about portraying the world anymore. It's about changing it. The aim is not to depict the real, but to make the representation itself real."[31] The manifesto goes on to place an emphasis on the process of theater-making itself, rather than thematic content: it makes commitments to publicly accessible rehearsals (including a requirement that some rehearsals take place outside the theater space, and that at least one production be rehearsed or performed in a conflict zone); no adaptations of "classics"; at least two different languages being spoken in every production; and at least two of the performers in every production being nonprofessional actors (and adding, "animals don't count, though they are welcome").[32]

Five Easy Pieces exemplifies the last of these requirements. Its cast of seven children, ranging in age between 8 and 17, appears on stage alongside one adult performer, Peter Seynaeve, who was Rau's assistant director on the project. The young performers auditioned for the project—dramatically reenacted in the piece's opening sequence—but did not have prior performing experience. Through a series of five scenes, the piece calls on them to tell the story of the kidnapping, torture, and rape of six young girls, four of whom died, by Marc Dutroux in Belgium in 1995 and 1996. The Belgian public was horrified by these events, and they blamed the police for mishandling the investigations of the abductions and failing to protect their children, leading to the so-called White March, in which 275,000 people demonstrated in Brussels. The issue of adult responsibility for children, as described in an everyday sense by Etchells in the above quotation, is regarded here in its most malevolent extreme; but, like Etchells, Rau makes an overt connection between the dynamics of power, care, and control in adult-child relationships in the world at large and those being played out within the theatrical setting.

This power dynamic is most explicitly enacted in one of the *Five Easy Pieces* which is most frequently commented upon: the third scene, right in the middle of the overall work, in which the youngest performer, eight-year-old Rachel Dedain, recites some of the letters written by one of the kidnapped girls, twelve-year-old Sabine Dardenne, who was rescued after having been kept chained in a makeshift dungeon for seventy-nine days. As Rachel/Sabine recounts, the letters were written in response to the promise by Dutroux that in exchange for sexual favors from Sabine he would send the letters to her parents. Like all five scenes, the staging uses the conceit of a film shoot, with various pieces of furniture and props used to compose a scene, and the adult actor Seynaeve operating an onstage camera that is the source for a live video image projected above the stage. As this scene begins, Dedain is sitting on a mattress surrounded by various detritus. Seynaeve prompts the young actor: "Rachel, this is your scene." He repeats the reminder, as if she has forgotten something. "Stop," he says. "Take off your clothes. Do it like in rehearsals."[33] She says nothing, but lies back and pulls off her leggings, with Seynaeve helping to remove them. He indicates for her to move so she is again in the center of the camera frame, and then asks her questions to set the scene: " 'Who are you?' / 'I'm Sabine.' / 'Where are you?' / 'In Marc Dutroux's cellar.' " The director calls for sound, camera, and the scene clapper. "Take your T-shirt off after all," Seynaeve instructs. Dedain/Rachel pulls off her vest. "Action," Seynaeve calls. Wearing only her underpants, pulling her knees to her chest and wrapping her arms around them, Dedain begins to speak Rachel's letters.

If the power relations staged in *That Night Follows Day* are under-scored through the repetitive structure of "You tell us . . . ," then they find their most sinister form in these letters written from captivity: "He told me you have accepted that I've gone," Dedain/Sabine says. "And I shouldn't look at the clock too much. But what else do I have to do? [*Pause.*] And I should 'find the sex fun.' " There is no question that this is a different order of domination than that of the theater director, one that has become predatory violence; however, Rau's production intentionally invites a com-parison between the two activities in which the child is made to "perform." For example, from which domain does the instruction for Dedain/Sabine to remove her shirt come? It is issued after she has announced that we are now in the cellar and the director has called to start the camera, plac-ing Seynaeve (and the instruction) ambiguously both outside and inside the represented scene: does the instruction come from Seynaeve (outside the scene), or from Dutroux (inside it)? And the large projected image above the stage, which has had the effect of amplifying the theatrical setup throughout the scenes so far, serves here to amplify our own spectato-rial position, as Dedain looks straight at us, and we look directly at her nearly naked and apparently vulnerable face and body. We are confronted with a representation of a scene of suffering, in which the apparatus of representation is always visible, reminding us that this is (only) a representation; but the representational apparatus is also marked as an apparatus of power, a fact revealed by the presence of the child within it.

As mentioned earlier, *Five Easy Pieces* is one of many European works that feature children as performers, and many of these foreground the vulnerability of children: Romeo Castellucci's predominantly hyper-realist *Purgatorio* (2008) has an extended sequence at its center in which child sexual abuse is evoked by offstage audio.[34] Boris Charmatz's dance work *enfant* (2011) begins with adult dancers and mechanical hoists manipulating the inert bodies of children, with the dynamics reversed in the second half.[35] Fevered Sleep's *Men & Girls Dance* (2013) explicitly sought to counter the cultural discomfort provoked by physical contact between adult men and young girls and instead explore whether it is possible to give "permission for play, tenderness, trust, empathy and love."[36] And as noted before, both *That Night Follows Day* and *Five Easy Pieces* are just two of a number of collaborative works produced by CAMPO that bring together experimental performance-makers with casts of young people.[37] But what is distinctive about *Five Easy Pieces* is that it positions this relationship of vulnerability in an exploration of how theatrical appearances are constructed, in which the young performers demonstrate the ways in which they are learning *how to act*, in the theatrical sense of the phrase, as well as its wider implications.

This emphasis begins with the prelude to the piece, as each young performer takes turns coming to the center of the stage, while Seynaeve asks them questions from behind a desk at the perimeter of the playing area. Consulting papers as he asks them questions, and taking notes of their responses, this approximates the form of an interrogation; the questions solicit biographical details from each performer, which eventually turn into questions about things they would like to do in performance, or what they think acting is. "What does theatre mean to you?" Seynaeve asks Winne Vanacker. "That's simple," he replies. "Theatre is like puppetry, but with real people instead of puppets." For Polly Persyn, acting is "mainly a question of keeping calm and concentrating." And for others, acting is the chance to dance, to dress up as a king, to play a policeman. Rachel Dedain—who plays Sabine in the scene above—describes theater as a democratic space: "Everyone deserves their place on the stage," she says.

As the production unfolds, the responses given by the young performers in the opening sequence are revealed to have informed the staging decisions. For example, Maurice Leerman describes having had a prenatal lung condition from which he nearly died, and Seynaeve asks him to demonstrate how he might have coughed in the womb; disregarding the fact that we don't breathe or cough until after being born, Leerman coughs in a very realistic way, to the point that we might have concern for his well-being if he continued. Seyaneve asks him, "What do you think is the hardest thing for an actor to play?" Leerman replies, "Something that is unlike yourself. . . . Playing someone old when you're young. Or acting that you're ill when you're healthy." This comment reminds us that he has just played at being ill, and throughout the opening sequence he applies facial makeup to make himself look like an elderly man. All of this discussion with Leerman is revealed to be a setup for the first scene, in which Leerman portrays Marc Dutroux's elderly and infirm father, whom the company had interviewed as part of the development of the work.

Each of the five scenes begins with a projected title: "Father & Son," "What Is Acting?" "Essay on Submission," "Alone in the Night," and "What Are Clouds?" As Rau describes in interviews, each of these pieces is organized around a lesson:

> The first lesson is mimicry, how to play old and sick. The second is about biographical design: you are playing a policeman who is finding the murdered children, how do you construct his character on stage? The third is called "essay on submission," and is about the relationship between actor and director. The fourth is about emotion: the children have to play parents who have lost their children, they have to cry on stage. Then comes the last lesson, rebellion: how to revolt against everything they have just been asked to do.[38]

In this way, the staging and dramaturgy of *Five Easy Pieces* share with other post-dramatic work an emphasis on the theatrical apparatus itself, rather than representing a fictive world, or creating a "model of the real."[39] But what is interesting here is the way in which the piece superimposes the lessons in being an actor upon the experience of childhood; indeed, this superposition is literally manifested in several scenes in which prerecorded adult actors are shown on the projection screen carrying out the same actions as the child performers who are live on stage. So while this piece is partly a self-referential work about the construction of representations, it invites us not to reflect on representation as something detached from the real world outside the theater, but instead to think about the reality of representation— "to make the representation itself real," as the "Ghent Manifesto" puts it. Evaluating *Five Easy Pieces* in relation to Carol Martin's "theatre of the real," Debra Levine describes it as "theatre of the even realer" because of the way the child performers are acting out their own agency:

> Rau banks on the fear he knows we as adults bring to the theatre: that the children might become "broken," in some manner traumatized, by the show's content. Instead however, we see that participation appears to build resilience and teaches how cultural mechanisms and narrative frameworks are constructed for specific political effects.[40]

In other words, this is not a work that *simulates* the agency or vulnerability of children, but rather one where that agency and vulnerability are literalized through the *actual* process that the actors are going through. And at the same time, that agency is achieved *through* the act of simulation, through the fabrication of a self-representation.

If, as quoted earlier, States used the metaphor of colonization to describe the process by which theater "ingests" the real world,[41] then *Five Easy Pieces* presents a resistance to that colonization by means of a reverse occupation. Indeed, the politics of colonization is an explicit reference in much of Rau's work, including *Five Easy Pieces*, which is framed in its opening sequence in relation to Belgium's colonization of the Congo and its likely role in the assassination of the independence leader Patrice Lumumba. This framing of the work is based on a historical connection, in that the kidnapper Dutroux was born in the Congo, but there is also a thematic connection, as Andrew Haydon observes:

> Of course, the piece isn't suggesting anything as crass as "Belgian colonialism made a child-murderer of Marc Dutroux" (although it doesn't deny it, but logically it's no kind of point to make); it does, however, cause you to realise the level of similarity between the narcissistic desires of a child-murderer and paedophile, and those of an imperialist power; the arrested-development of a mind, or a culture, that allows it just to say "I want" and to take that thing and keep it in captivity.[42]

As the scene with Sabine in front of the camera evokes so powerfully, the theater can be a place of captivity, where we hold others within the representational functions to which they are being put. But as I will discuss in the next section, the self-doubling dynamics of theatrical representation can also be a means to self-determination.

Standing for Oneself: Representation and the Arendtian Turn

Works such as these involving young performers are often cited in relation to the incorporation of the "real," sometimes in opposition to that which is "merely" representation. Logan's statement "These kids aren't performing, they're just *being*," for example, echoes Chantal Pontbriand's declaration that "performance presents; it does not re-present," discussed in chapter 1.[43] But Rau's version brings these terms into a slightly different relation: "to make the representation itself real." Examples such as *Five Easy Pieces* mix together (at least) two different meanings of representation: *theatrical* (or mimetic) representation, by which a simulated action stands in for another real event or person, and *political* representation, in which a person or group appears in some way within a political domain, so that their views, lived experiences, or desires are counted within a social process. In this section, I want to explore the ways in which these two meanings of representation have been intermingled in political theory, drawing substantially on Hanna Pitkin and Hannah Arendt, as well as what I describe as an "Arendtian turn" in the recent political thinking of Jean-Luc Nancy, Judith Butler, Chantal Mouffe, and Jacques Rancière.

In the lineage of ordinary language philosophy that includes J. L. Austin, John Searle, and Stanley Cavell, Hanna Pitkin's *The Concept of Representation* (1967) seeks to correct some of the misunderstandings and inconsistencies in the use of the term "representation" in political philosophy by drawing on the ways in which we use that word in everyday speech. She begins, for example, by laying out what she calls "the authorization view" of representation, in which a set of preceding formal agreements means that a person or persons are authorized to act on behalf of another. One difficulty with such a formalistic view, she points out, is that—provided that the necessary arrangements and agreements have been made—it does not allow for the possibility of *misrepresentation*; this concept simply does not make sense under the authorization view, and yet it is clearly part of our understanding of the concept of representation, and indeed is one of the most frequent complaints we make of both aesthetic and political processes of representation. Moreover, she points out, there are wildly diverse meanings of representation that are ignored by this view, but which must be considered in relation to each other:

> We also speak of a representative case, a representative sample, representational art, a work "representing someone's best efforts," a painter "representing his subject" in a certain way, a flag representing the nation, symbols on a map representing iron-ore deposits. No definition formulated in terms of agreements, rights, obligations, authority, and actions can explain why the word "represent" should have anything to do with such things—why these, too, should be instances of representation.[44]

In contrast to the authorization view, which Pitkin glosses as "acting for," she considers modes of representation that take the form of "standing for," where the representative person or object is related to that which is represented through resemblance or a more symbolic association. In these cases, representing is not "acting with authority, or acting before being held to account, or any kind of acting at all." Instead, "it depends on the representative's characteristics, on what he *is* or is *like*"—as played out in arguments for proportional representation in democratic legislatures, as well as arguments about representational diversity in art and popular culture.[45]

Emerging from this view of representation is the idea that there can be "degrees of representationality," so that one can ask "how *well* does something represent something else?" which is not a question that is relevant in the authorization view. Interestingly, Pitkin develops this view by considering aesthetic representation, noting that verisimilitude is not the most important standard by which art is judged.[46] However, the "standing for" view also presents shortcomings in capturing the range of meanings of political representation, in that it only pertains to the qualities of the representative, not to the actual *activity* of representation: "It has no room for any kind of representing as acting for, or on behalf of, others; which means that in the political realm it has no room for the creative activities of a representative legislature, the forging of consensus, the formulating of policy, the activity we roughly designate by 'governing.' "[47]

With her dichotomy of "acting for" and "standing for," Pitkin argues that any definition of representation that focuses exclusively on only one of these will be incomplete, but that it is also difficult to reconcile the two in the same concept. This is due to a fundamental paradox in the idea of representation:

> Representation, taken generally, means the making present *in some sense* of something which is nevertheless *not* present literally or in fact. Now, to say that something is simultaneously both present and not present is to utter a paradox, and thus a fundamental dualism is built into the meaning of representation.[48]

This "fundamental dualism" of representation is shared across its various manifestations, whether in the political sense of representative democracy, in legal or economic senses in which someone performs as an agent on behalf of another, or in artistic and theatrical senses in which the work of art evokes a person or situation that is not co-present (as in *Five Easy Pieces*, for example). Pitkin does not resolve this paradox in any universal way, but instead looks at how specific cases might demonstrate what she calls "substantive representation" or "substantive acting for others," in which "the represented thing or person is present in the *action* rather than in the characteristics of the actor, or how [the actor] is regarded, or the formal arrangements which precede or follow the action."[49]

Pitkin also emphasizes the "re-" in representation in order to argue for the necessary preexistence of the thing which is being represented, and therefore an obligation of fidelity of some kind on the part of the representation. For this reason, although she finds theatrical examples to be useful in identifying some aspects of representation, she generally discounts ideas of representation as being generative or performative. For example, she devotes just a brief discussion to the idea that representation might be said to occur *only* if there is a third party to witness and be convinced by it;

that is, an audience, the ontological requisite of theater that was discussed in chapter 1.[50] And she explicitly condemns the idea that representation might be a form of "symbol-making" in which the thing being represented does not precede the representation but is conjured through belief in the representation, because for Pitkin this reification of belief leads potentially to fascism.[51]

In this way, Pitkin herself is not that interested in theatrical representation, even as she addresses questions of "acting for" and "standing for" others—ideas to which I will return, particularly in the case of self-representational performances in which one is "standing for" oneself. However, a more performative, even theatrical, understanding of political representation can be found in the work of one of Pitkin's main influences, Hannah Arendt.[52] As I will now discuss, the impact of Arendt's thinking can be felt in contemporary political philosophy that emphasizes just such a performative understanding of political action. One of the legacies of Arendt's work as a political philosopher is to shift the idea of the political itself away from specific structures of governance and representation and toward a more general category of "action." In *The Human Condition* (1958), this shift is expressed through her influential idea of "spaces of appearance," which "come into being whenever [persons] are together in the manner of speech and action, and therefore predates and precedes all formal constitution of the public realm and the various forms of government." Rather than a preexisting "public realm," into which people might move and from which they might remove themselves, Arendt is interested in the way that ephemeral moments of gathering and expression create the very possibility of politics: "Wherever people gather together it is potentially there, but only potentially, not necessarily and not forever."[53]

In contrast to Pitkin, Arendt's formulation points toward a politics that is fundamentally performative: that is, the appearance of "action" through public speech and gesture is not political because it expresses or articulates some underlying politics or represents politics that is at stake elsewhere, but instead it is such action that is constitutive of the political as such. In these moments, politics makes an appearance—or better, politics is *made of* appearances. Because of her interest in speech and action undertaken in public, Arendt points to the dynamics of the theater as exemplifying the political: "Theatre is the political art par excellence; only there is the political sphere of human life transposed into art."[54] In her final work, *The Life of the Mind* (published posthumously in 1978), Arendt expands on these themes of appearance and theatricality. She begins with an ontology that cannot imagine "being" without "appearing":

> In this world which we enter, appearing from a nowhere, and from which we disappear into a nowhere, *Being and Appearing coincide*. Dead matter, natural and artificial, changing and unchanging,

depends in its being, that is, in its appearingness, on the presence
of living creatures. Nothing and nobody exists in this world whose
very being does not presuppose a *spectator*.[55]

The metaphor of the theater is continued throughout her analysis: "To
be alive," she writes, "means to be possessed by an urge toward self-
display which answers the fact of one's own appearingness. Living things
make their appearance like actors on a stage set for them."[56] Anticipating
subsequent post-structuralist theories, such as Karen Barad's critique of
"representationalism," Arendt draws on accounts of scientific experimentation to reject the dichotomy between Being and Appearing—the idea
that there is some truth beyond "mere appearance"—as advocated by
Plato, Kant, Marx, and so on.[57] Instead, Arendt reverses the metaphysical
hierarchy between surface and depth, arguing that the world of surfaces
is the one we live in.

I would argue that recent political theory has taken an "Arendtian turn,"
whether or not there is an explicit acknowledgment of her work, that is
marked by the search for politics in the conditions that enable action to
be possible (rather than the actions per se) and by the idea that politics
is the *appearance* of the political as such.[58] Moreover, this "urge toward
self-display" marks our dependence upon others, the condition of plurality that is the defining condition of human existence according to Arendt.
The influence of Arendt's insistence on plurality, which she expresses so
emphatically in all her works, can be widely felt within twentieth and
twenty-first-century political philosophy.

Take the work of Jean-Luc Nancy, for example, who argues for an idea
of political community that is not based on "immanentism," a coherent
identity that imbues all members of a community with their individuality,
but instead is built from the ground up on the basis of selves (or "singu-
larities") that are defined by their finitude rather than their autonomy; this
finitude "always presents itself as being-in-common," Nancy writes.[59] The
fundamental experience of being, as Nancy describes it, is of exposure to
other beings, which he terms *com-parution*, variously translated into English as "compearance" or "co-appearance." "Compearance . . . consists in
the appearance of the *between* as such: you *and* I (between us)—a formula
in which the *and* does not imply juxtaposition, but exposition."[60] In place
of ideas of wholeness, completion, or communion, Nancy proposes an
idea of Being whose very being-ness exists through its exposure to others: "Finitude compears, that is to say it is exposed: that is the essence of
community."[61]

Elsewhere in his writing, Nancy connects this metaphysical rethinking of
being with the experience of the theater, and describes this co-appearing as
taking place upon "the stage of the 'we.' "[62] In the central essay of *Being Singular Plural* (1996), Nancy pursues an explicit parallel with the theater by

way of a reinterpretation of the lesson of classical Athenian theater. He re-
iterates that compearance is not some form of revelation or manifestation,
the "becoming-visible" of something that has an ongoing, invisible existence
separate from its appearance. Instead, it is only through co-appearance that
our being-together, our experience of sociality, has any meaning:

> In this sense, there is no society without spectacle; or more pre-
> cisely, there is no society without the spectacle of society. Although
> already a popular ethnological claim or, in the Western tradition,
> a claim about the theater, this proposition must be understood
> as ontologically radical. There is no society without the spectacle
> because society is the spectacle of itself.[63]

Nancy goes on to write that "the various critiques of 'spectacular' alienation are, in the end, grounded on the distinction between a good spectacle
and a bad spectacle."[64] In the passage above, he clearly has Guy Debord's
The Society of the Spectacle in mind as a paradigmatic articulation of the
"bad" spectacle, but such a distinction has a long lineage. For example,
Jean-Jacques Rousseau's Lettre à M. d'Alembert sur les spectacles (1758)
famously condemned the idea of introducing theaters to Geneva, identifying the theater as a source of corruption and dilution of human virtues and
relationships. David Marshall comments that it is not the "literal instance
of theater" which is problematic for Rousseau, but "the exchange of
regards, the awareness of others as beholders, that creates a theatrical consciousness."[65] As an alternative to the theater, Rousseau proposes another
kind of spectacle: village fêtes, outdoor festivals, displays of gymnastics,
"balls for young marriageable persons," and the like.[66] About Rousseau's
vision, Jonas Barish writes:

> The key to this newer, and at the same time older, form of spectacle
> is total participation, the breaking down of the arbitrary barrier
> between stage and audience. All the actors now become specta-
> tors, and all the spectators actors. No one any longer represents
> anyone other than himself.[67]

In Nancy's analysis of the typical distinction between the "good" spectacle and the "bad" spectacle, Rousseau might typify the position that
the "good" spectacle (as exemplified by the republican festivals prescribed in the Lettre à M. d'Alembert) is a faithful representation of "the
people itself," a community that exists independently of its spectacular-
ization; while Debord stands for the position that the "bad" spectacle
(i.e., commoditized media culture) is an unfaithful representation of our
true potential. However, Nancy argues that the distinction between spectacle and community that underpins ideas of both a "good" and "bad"

spectacle is erroneous. Instead, the spectacle of community is all there is: for Nancy, this is the only basis for an idea of community that is not derived from immanentism, and that does not therefore prepare the ground for totalitarianism.

In support of his argument, Nancy revisits the paradigmatic origin of politics, the one place (so the Western mythos claims) in which the representation of community and the presence of community are aligned: the Athenian theater. He writes: "There is certainly nothing accidental in the fact that our modern way of grounding the so-called Western tradition involves a triple reference: to philosophy as the shared exercise of *logos*, to politics as the opening of the city, and to the theater as the place of the symbolic-imaginary appropriation of collective existence."[68] The significance of the Athenian theater, Nancy writes, is its apparent conjunction of *logos* and *mimesis*; however, he argues, "when we see it in this way, we systematically efface the moment of *mimesis* in favor of the moment of *logos*."[69] Nancy argues that this is another example of the way in which we perpetuate a distinction between "good" spectacle and "bad" spectacle: we hypothesize a "good" mimesis that the Athenians somehow had access to, but which is now lost to us, and a "bad" mimesis, which is pervasive and must be overcome in the name of true politics. In contrast to this false opposition, Nancy proposes an understanding of community that is fundamentally mimetic, and fundamentally spectacular. Nancy's political community, like Arendt's, is constituted through and in the act of co-appearance.

However, there is a shared problem for the philosophies of both Arendt and Nancy, which is the presumption of equality of access to these ontological acts of appearance: "The stage is common to all who are alive," writes Arendt, and Nancy's ontology is similarly universalist.[70] The question of who has access to the domain of the political has been taken up by Judith Butler, Chantal Mouffe, and Jacques Rancière, whose arguments I will summarize here. With the most direct reference to Arendt, Butler elucidates this problem in their rereading of "spaces of appearance" in relation to the "movements of the squares," the phenomena of popular uprisings such as those that took place in Tahrir Square in Egypt, Zuccotti Park in the United States, Syntagma Square in Athens, Porta del Sol in Madrid, and Gezi Park in Istanbul. Butler points out that certain actors and actions are deemed "prepolitical" or "extrapolitical" because "they break into the sphere of appearance as from the outside."[71] Butler argues that "any conception of the political has to take into account what operation of power demarcates the political from the prepolitical."[72] For Butler, politics erupts when those who are invisible, whose claims are not seen as legitimate, nevertheless come together in assembly and insist on their right to appear—or what Arendt elsewhere, writing about the plight of stateless refugees (of which she herself was one), calls "the right to have rights."[73]

Similar distinctions are made by Chantal Mouffe, who argues that "the political" is premised on a consensus about what does and does not constitute politics: "Instead of trying to erase the traces of power and exclusion," Mouffe argues, "democratic politics requires us to bring them to the fore, to *make them visible* so that they can enter the terrain of contestation."[74] And Jacques Rancière echoes Arendt in describing "the part of those who have no part": those to whom no political valence has been assigned by a particular order of representation.[75] Again deploying the metaphor of the theatrical stage, Rancière argues that politics consists in reconfiguring what he calls "the partition of the sensible" by "bringing on stage new objects and subjects, in making visible that which was not visible, audible as speaking beings they who were merely heard as noisy animals."[76] Rancière's work is often cited in relation to artistic practice because he explicitly connects the kinds of transformations in perception that are made possible in artistic experience with wider political realities:

> Political statements and literary locutions produce effects in reality. They define models of speech or action but also regimes of sensible intensity. They draft maps of the visible, trajectories between the visible and the sayable, relationships between modes of being, modes of saying, and modes of doing and making. They define variations of sensible intensities, perceptions, and the abilities of bodies.[77]

Perhaps Rancière's provocations have excited performance scholars because there is a limitless speculative quality to his description of political action: potentially *anything* that disrupts our customary ways of seeing, hearing, and otherwise experiencing the world *could* be political, but the effect will only be known once it is affirmed by those who are standing-on, who see for themselves a new configuration of experience. In his own lived experience, Rancière has put his own body in alliance with those at the front line of protest, but his writing is more concerned with tracing the agency of spectators (as in his widely cited *The Emancipated Spectator* [2009], discussed in chapter 1). Peter Hallward has described this view of politics as a "theatrocracy": "Before it is a matter of representative institutions, legal procedures or militant organizations, politics [for Rancière] is a matter of building a stage and sustaining a spectacle or 'show.'"[78] Many have emphasized Rancière's focus on spectatorship, which is where dissensus is registered; but Hallward's criticism calls attention to the work required in "building" and "sustaining" the disruptive spectacle, which is the activity that I want to attend to in this chapter.

In tracing the interrelation between these performative locutions and the material conditions of everyday experience of those whose lives are shaped by them, perhaps the strongest articulation comes from Butler's earlier work on the effects of hate speech. Responding to a context in the United States in which conservative politicians and judiciaries defended racialized actions (notably, cross-burning) as "free speech," at the same time as they restricted sexualized speech (including the act of military personnel naming themselves as gay, which was classified as itself a "homosexual act"), Butler inquires more deeply into the capacity of words to wound. "Could language injure us if we were not, in some sense, linguistic beings, beings who require language in order to be?" Butler begins by asking. "Is our vulnerability to language a consequence of our being constituted within its terms?"[79] But while Butler's point of departure is speech and language, and how these constitute the conditions for "the social existence of the body," the larger question is the Arendtian one of appearance within the social: "One 'exists,'" Butler continues, "not only by virtue of being recognized, but, in a prior sense, *by being recognizable.*"[80] Thus for both Butler and Rancière, politics rests on the prior question of inclusion or exclusion from recognizability: "Politics exists when the natural order of domination is interrupted by the institution of a part of those who have no part," writes Rancière;[81] while Butler more cautiously describes the potential for "resignification": "Opening new contexts, speaking in ways that have never yet been legitimated, and hence producing legitimation in new and future forms."[82]

The previous chapter described artistic strategies for engaging with the mechanisms of representation, connecting the apparatus of the theater with broader systems and economies of narrative and self-presentation. As Florian Malzacher put it, describing the ethos of the Giessen Institute from which Rimini Protokoll's work emerged, "the trap of representation . . . was to be avoided at any price."[83] For others, such as the Nature Theater of Oklahoma, the process of making theater becomes intertwined with the process of making a life—not to mention literally making a living, for those technical workers for whom the theater is a workplace. There remains something theoretical about the "trap of representation" to which Malzacher refers, primarily thinking about the conceptual domain of the theater; and in the case of Rimini Protokoll, it is a concern brought by the theater-makers to their subject matter, rather than necessarily a concern held by the participating "experts." However, as I will discuss now, this trap is more than an abstract concern for those who have no part, who are excluded from both aesthetic and political representation, and for whom the act of appearing on stage, let alone making a living through creating theater, is itself a hard-won legitimation.

Acting, Disabled: Back to Back Theatre

At the top of this show, the stage is empty. As the house lights dim and the audience grows quiet, there is the sound of a few simple sequences of

piano notes and percussive rumblings, gradually building into a minimalist but pervasive sound score being performed live by the improvisational
trio The Necks. Mark Deans walks onto the stage, which is a wide, shallow playing space with only a few meters between the curtains and the
front of the stage. Squirming, and making a few funny faces at the audience, he squints into the lights. Space. Nothing happens. He looks down,
picks up something from the floor that is too small for me to see, and
moves it to stage right. He stands there, looking pleased with himself, still
illuminated but no longer blinded by the lights. He looks down again in
order to position himself precisely, and I smile with the realization that the
thing he moved was the "spike," the small pieces of electrical tape used to
mark where a performer should stand or a prop should be placed.[84]

Among the things I notice is that Mark has the recognizable facial characteristics of Down syndrome.[85] He is joined on the stage by Scott Price,
who enters from behind a curtain, stands, and faces the audience for several moments. He walks over to a microphone on the ground and picks it
up. "Yes, yes, yes," he says. "Oh, come on. Yeah, that's good." Scott and
Mark sit at opposite edges of the playing space. Entering from between the
curtains, Nicki Holland stands stage center for a long time. Staring deadpan at the audience, she is dressed in tight black sweatpants and a golden,
glittering leotard, her body made somewhat lumpy by the tightness of the
fabric around her hips, waist, and breasts. She turns to profile, her stat-
ure slightly hunched, her expression matter-of-fact. She stands there for
a few beats: this is her body. This is who she is. She turns to the back. A
few more beats, and then she moves stage right and sits in a chair. A few
moments later, performer Sonia Teuben enters through the curtain, dressed
in a matching stretchy leotard within which all the distinctiveness of her
body, too, is obvious.[86] She repeats the sequence of poses, then joins Nicki
to begin the scene.

This is the opening of *Food Court* (2010) by Back to Back Theatre, an
ensemble based on actors who identify as having intellectual disability,
and located in Geelong in Victoria, Australia.[87] Back to Back was founded
in the 1980s in the context of a policy emphasis in disability outreach
services on "normalization" and "deinstitutionalizing."[88] But its original
artistic collaborators made a deliberate choice to distance themselves
somewhat from these support structures: "We insisted that it wasn't some
sort of disability support organization—that it was a professional theatre
company," recalls Ian Pidd, one of its early artistic directors.[89] Since 1999,
Back to Back has worked with Bruce Gladwin as its artistic director, and
they have increasingly presented their work in the European and North
American performance festival context, particularly following their breakout work *small metal objects* (2007), which I will describe further below.
As Tony McCaffrey notes in a recent survey, "it would appear that theatre
involving people with intellectual disabilities is a theatre whose time has

come." To illustrate the surge in interest in disabled-led theater on the European stage, he cites the following examples, all from the same year: in 2017, Back to Back performed at Theater der Welt in Hamburg, the Wiener Festwochen in Vienna, and the Holland Festival in Amsterdam, and also released their first feature film; Theatre HORA's collaboration with Jérôme Bel, *Disabled Theatre*, played the Festival d'Automne in Paris, having previously toured widely since 2012; and the European Union-funded Crossing the Line showcase festival took place in northern France.[90] In this context, Back to Back's recent work has been intentionally oriented toward a nondisabled audience, and over time their public descriptions of their work have shifted the focus from "disability" to the distinct perspective they might offer on nondisabled culture. The word "disabled" has gradually been removed from their self-descriptions, and even where it was present in a previous version of their public "Artistic Rationale," this shift in emphasis is clearly articulated:

> Driven by a core ensemble of people with disabilities, Back to Back is uniquely placed to comment on the social, cultural, ethical and value-based structures that define the institution known as "the majority." Family, career, sex, politics, religion, education, academia and culture are all subject to a lateral analysis from an artistic team whose defining characteristic is separation from the spectacle of their subject matter.[91]

In writing about their work, I am aware that I write from the perspective of a nondisabled spectator, and that these particular works, devised for an international audience, address me as such.[92]

The opening actions of *Food Court*, like the "90-degree turn" described by Peter Handke in chapter 1, embody this orientation, emphasizing the encounter between performer and audience. The "reality" of who they are is apparently on display: their body shapes which appear unusual to my nondisabled perception, their facial expressions, and above all, their prolonged stares extend the duration of this moment of looking and being-looked-at. "Staring," writes Rosemarie Garland-Thomson in her book-length study of how people with disabilities are regarded, is "an intense visual exchange that makes meaning." That is, this visual exchange is not simply the reading or taking in of the meanings of appearances, but the place where that meaning is made: "At the heart of this anatomy is the *matter of appearance*, of the ways we see each other and the ways we are seen."[93] *These people are really disabled. This is what disabled people really look like*, I might think as I stare, and am stared at, in the beginning of *Food Court*. And yet, these stage entrances emphasize that disability is a "matter of appearance": it matters how I have come to see these people, in both the figurative and literal senses of this process. Here, they are revealed, and also masked, by their sparkling golden tops, by their illumination in the stage lights, and by their intentional activity of representing themselves.

Garland-Thomson's anatomy of staring repeatedly draws insight from the dynamics of the apprehension of disability. Often, she writes, starers will experience discomfort in their encounters with bodies they perceive as disabled:

> Discomfort comes in part from the social illegibility of the disabled body. The social rituals in which we accord one another recognition depend on an accurate reading of bodily and gestural cues. Unpredictable or indecipherable cues create anxiety. It is not that disability itself creates unease, but rather people's inability to read such cues disrupts the expected, routine nature of social relations.[94]

Garland-Thomson describes the ways in which some people have become expert "starees," proficient at the art of being stared at, deploying a range of techniques to interrupt the social organization of bodies around the logic of what she elsewhere calls the "normate": a presumed subject position constructed in opposition to "deviant others," but which is actually "a very narrowly defined profile that describes only a minority of actual people."[95] Such starees are frequently compelled to practice the endurance, interruption, or redirecting of the gaze throughout everyday life, but the arts provide a particular platform for "visual activism"; they "rework the way we usually stare," keeping us "looking rather than looking away."[96]

Prior to *Food Court*, Back to Back's *small metal objects* foregrounded these questions of visibility. Rather than taking place in a theater, the piece uses a raised bank of audience seating in a busy public place, with the audience members listening through headphones to performers outfitted with wireless microphones as they intermingle with the everyday crowds that might be found in such a place. In East London where I saw it, the site was Stratford Train Station, busy with commuters rushing between trains or queuing at the exit gates. Seated with my headphones on, I could hear the voices of the actors before I could distinguish them in the crowds of commuters, so the countless non-performers are transformed into performers as I look from person to person, wondering who is "in" on the piece. Bree Hadley emphasizes:

> The difficulty of seeing the actors is central to the performance. It is, Tim Milful says, "the point [of the performance]. The actors are invisible, just as intellectual disability is often not visible in our everyday world"—physically, discursively or economically—as long as it is attached to the pervasive stereotype of a sweet, simple but socially unuseful set of people.[97]

Indeed, it soon becomes clear that it is we audience members who are the spectacle, more so than those we are looking at, as passersby stop and stare at this strange assembly of passive theatergoers, prominently displayed and available to be pointed out, photographed, called out to. As Jen Harvie writes, one of the significant effects of the piece is to expose the disparities in cultural capital in Greater London: an elite, arts-consuming public who buy their tickets from the metropolitan Barbican Centre is transplanted to the marginal, lower-income, and more ethnically mixed East End area of Stratford.[98] Such a contrast between different worlds is also pursued in the narrative content of the work, which depicts a friendship between two characters, Gary and Steve. Their dialogue, which we overhear through the headphones, is intimate and everyday, ranging from recollecting what they did the night before, to expressing more deeply felt desires and anxieties:

> STEVE: I'm missing something, a feeling.
> GARY: A good feeling?
> STEVE: A feeling that I've felt, sensed and known that I've always had.
> GARY: Hmm.
> STEVE: It's my task to be a total man.
> GARY: OK.
> STEVE: I want people to see me. I want to be a full human being.[99]

As the play continues, Gary is solicited for illegal drugs by an arrogant city worker, a businessman of some sort, who is later joined by a female colleague, both of whom are played by nondisabled actors. For reasons that he does not explain, Steve decides midway through the negotiation that he is unwilling to move from the spot where he is standing, and Gary refuses to leave him on his own. And so, despite the increasingly desperate and crude persuasions of the man and woman ("Come to the locker and I'll suck your fucking dick," the woman offers),[100] the exchange doesn't take place. The apparent irrationality of Steve's decision serves as a theatrical foil against which is reflected the objectifying and petty-minded attitudes of consumer culture, in which, as Gary and Steve repeat to each other at one point, "Everything has a fucking value."[101]

Steve's decision not to move, his standing still, is also a zero-degree point for "acting" in the theatrical sense. In an interview, Gladwin, the company's director, describes this (non-)action as the starting place for the play:

> There was something so amazing about watching Simon [Laherty, the actor playing Steve] standing. No matter what else was going on in the rehearsal I would be drawn back to Simon. When he did stuff, I'd say, no, just stand. Don't move. That's how it started. Watching Simon standing . . .[102]

Surveying contemporary theater made by and with actors with intellectual disabilities, Matt Hargrave observes that the static performer is a recurring motif in these works. Hargrave draws upon Michael Kirby's continuum between "acting" and "not-acting" (discussed in chapter 1), and in particular the distinction between "complex acting" involving multiple tasks and registers, and "simple acting" involving a single dimension of performance.[103] Careful to point out that Kirby does not intend "simple" as an evaluative term, Hargrave notes that "most performers in these shows are engaged in acting that Kirby would define as simple."[104] Writing about Laherty's performance in *small metal objects*, Hargrave observes:

> Laherty, the most minimal performer, hardly "does" anything. He is still for such a large percentage of the play that he comes close to an even more pared down point on [Kirby's] continuum: that of "received acting." This is where the performer, an extra, for example, might walk on and stand in costume. They appear to be acting because their image is aesthetically framed, but they are not *actively* feigning or representing something.[105]

In *small metal objects*, what is at stake in Steve/Laherty's standing still is an insistence on one's right to appear in public—not to represent the right to visibility, but actually *to be visible*. It is an instance of what Garland-Thomson terms "visual activism": activism that not only takes visual form, but where the intervention also seeks to reorder the realm of the visual itself, interrupting what Rancière describes as "the partition of the sensible" that determines who and what experiences can be seen.[106] Writing about another context, but with similar concerns, Eve Kosofsky Sedgwick articulates the urgency of queer activists staging their own visibility on public access television: "With the force of our bodies, . . . and in that sense performatively, our object was not merely to demand representation, representation elsewhere, but ourselves to give, to *be* representation."[107] This representation is achieved through being seen: as Steve says in the line quoted above, "I want people to see me. I want to be a full human being."

The opening sequence of *Food Court* is a series of these standings-still, as the appearance of each actor is marked by a moment of directed gaze toward and from the audience—a "lineup" unfolding in serial form. But rather than insisting on their right to appear and to be seen in a public space, making that space into a stage (as in the metaphorical descriptions offered by Arendt, Nancy, and Rancière), here these actions are taking place on a literal stage, that of the proscenium theater. This is an intentional choice. *Food Court* followed a number of experiments by the company with less traditional forms of staging, like the public space work of *small metal objects* and the use of large inflatable sculptures to create an immersive environment in *soft* (2002). In a post-show discussion after the production of *Food Court* that I saw, director Bruce Gladwin described this return to a traditional proscenium theater as an intentional choice, as "the most challenging and thrilling thing we could do."[108] I will argue that the *dédoublement* of the theatrical situation, described in previous chapters, is used by Back to Back as a generative tension to intervene in the politics of representation.

In that same post-show discussion, Gladwin described the way that the company intentionally produces audience uncertainty about whether we are watching an actor with a disability portray a character with a disability, or whether disability is incidental to the action being portrayed.

> I think there's a tension that sits in the piece. When the actors first come through the split in the curtain, I anticipate there's a kind of reading in the audience where the audience is going, "There's a guy with Down syndrome. I wonder if he's playing a person with Down syndrome?" I think that's a tension that the audience is never released from. Who are these characters? What is this world that they're in? And is the intention that they are people with disabilities or that they're not? And that's something that we're interested in playing with in our work.[109]

In *Food Court*, the actors' opening actions underscore this instability by accentuating the mechanisms of theatrical representation—spikes, props, microphones, costumes—and throughout the piece, the theatricality of the event is always similarly highlighted, so that whenever something is shown or said, we are always aware that it is being shown or said *on a stage*. For example, as Nicki and Sonia talk, Mark and Scott hold a boom microphone over their heads, moving the mic from actor to actor—even though they are quite visibly equipped with individual wireless mics. And throughout the play, all the dialogue is projected as surtitles. It is a representational world within which these individual bodies appear, and their bodies, too, are part of this apparatus.

From a semiotic perspective (similar to States's arguments earlier), Hargrave argues that "the appearance of a learning-disabled actor destabilises our categorisations of signs." Noting that the common definition of "disabled" is "incapable of performing or functioning," he asks, "What might it mean then for a disabled person to stand in front of an audience and begin to speak?" It is worth quoting at length his discussion of the semiotics of disability:

> The fact that he is on stage speaking directly to us denotes iconically that he is disabled: he is a disabled man because he *looks like* one. But does his obvious impairment mean that he must *remain* iconic, unable to break out of the label, "disabled man"?

His disability also indexes or *points* to itself. And his appearance
is symbolically loaded: disability carries connotations of "dependency," "affliction," or premature death. Because disability is
used as a metaphor in so many stories and cultural references,
the disabled actor is literally trapped in a prison house of signs.
Semiotically encumbered from the start, any "characterisation" is
smothered by the "fact" of his disability. He may perform but will
he always perform one thing: as in the phrase [which Hargrave
reports was told to one director before she began working with
disabled performers], "these actors will only play themselves."[110]

When a disabled person appears on stage and begins to speak, then, it is not
only the material reality of his or her disability that appears, but also the
way that disability is already bound up within representational structures.
For nondisabled performers appearing as themselves in other instances of
the "theatre of the real," where their ability to represent themselves is not
questioned, Pitkin's dichotomy of "acting for" and "standing for" seem to
be collapsed into the same thing; as in Barish's gloss on Rousseau quoted
earlier, "No one any longer *represents* anyone other than himself."[111] But
as Hargrave argues, the situation is more complex in relation to actors
perceived to have disabilities; here the actor is "semiotically encumbered"
so that they are always "standing for" a culturally defined and perpetu-
ated idea of disability, what it looks like and what it is capable of; and
furthermore, in the case of intellectual disability, a prejudicial question
hangs over whether these actors are even able to "act for" themselves.
As with the child performers discussed earlier, lurking behind any anti-
theatrical "realness" attributed to these performances are presumptions
about naivete and innocence, taking the form of a presumed inability to
dissemble.

However, even as the theater is part of a "prison house of signs," as in
Hargrave's description, its theatricality and artifice might also be deployed
as interruptions within this representation structure through a deliberate acknowledgment of that artifice—as exemplified in these opening
moments of *Food Court*. At stake here is not just appearance within the
realm of visibility, but the active *making* of appearance, the "urge toward
self-display" that Arendt describes. As Elin Diamond argues in her discussion of feminist mimesis, the constructivist processes of the theater can
destabilize essentialist ideas of identity, or at least stage the convergence of
different ways of seeing on the body of the actor:

The body, particularly the female body, by virtue of entering
the stage space, enters representation—it is not just "there," a
live, unmediated presence, but rather (1) a signifying element in
a dramatic fiction; (2) a part of a theatrical sign system whose

conventions of gesturing, voicing, and impersonating are referents for both performer and audience; and (3) a sign in the system governed by a particular apparatus, usually owned and operated by men.[112]

Despite the restrictions of these normal conventions, the theater holds potential as a place where representations are made and remade, where they are malleable, particularly when the theatrical apparatus itself is foregrounded. As Diamond puts it, "When gender is 'alienated' or fore-grounded, the spectator is able to see what s/he can't see: a sign system *as* a sign system."[113] Rather than the appearance of the real, then, what I would like to emphasize in Back to Back's work is their use of representation as a type of *fabrication*. With regard to disability, what becomes possible within the theatrical frame is the capacity to deploy it, to make it stand for something else, to falsify it, to stand to one side of it, to wear it as a costume, to use it as a dance.

Let's continue with the action. After the actors' series of entrances, the first dialogue in *Food Court* is a conversation between Nicki and Sonia in which they are talking about food. It feels like verbatim text, with Mark moving between them with the boom mic, and the words appearing over their heads as they speak. "Have you ever had a hamburger? / No. / Have you ever had hot chips? / No."[114] As they speak, the accompanying music performed live by The Necks accumulates slowly from sparse notes and simple rhythms into more complex sequences. Nicki and Sonia's attention is drawn to Sarah Mainwearing, who takes a seat stage left, the opposite side of the stage from them. She is not wearing distinctive clothing; she is of a slim build; and her hands and head are constantly moving and rotating in tiny circles.[115] "She's fat," says Sonia. The two other women tease her, gradually building into bullying; Sarah never says anything (or appears to respond in any way), and the two other women comment that she "doesn't speak." The scene climaxes with the following tirade, noted in the script as partly improvised, with, as always, surtitles and microphones:

Fat person	Fat guts
Fat head	Fat arms
Fat face	Fat knee
Fat ears	Fat feet
Fat nose	Fat kidney
Fat brain	Fat liver
Fat daughter	Fat you

Fat skeleton   Fat diarrhoea

Fat Muslim   Fat tumor

Fat Christian   Fat shit

Fat European   Fat smell

Fat history   Fat priest

Fat maggot   Fat evil

Fat beast   Fat world

Fat cancer   Fat nation

Fat monster   Fat boring

Fat freak   Fat breast

Fat witch   Fat bone

That's for you.

Look at them looking at you.[116]

After this tirade, the piece makes a transition to its second half, mediated by Mark, who speaks for the first and only time, reading lines from the surtitles as each word bounces as if it were on a karaoke machine. Mark's words indicate a shift away from the current scene: "Past the juice bar, past the Asian Hut, past the car park, past the last house, past the factories, over the creek and down the dirt road to the forest . . ." The curtains part to reveal the full height and depth of the theatrical playing space. A translucent screen covers the proscenium opening, and the remainder of the action takes place behind this gauzy covering: the figures are shadowy, dimly lit, casting shadows against the back of the theater. Surtitles of the actors' words are visible at the front of the stage, but also pass through the screen so they are visible on the back wall, along with large video projections of shifting, indistinct branches.

In this murky world, the two women accuse Sarah of having soiled herself and force her to take off her clothes. They then order her to dance; in a dim spotlight, but obscured by the screen, we see her slowly shifting her weight from side to side, her arms moving in erratic spirals through the air. To the side of the stage, an audience of shadows slowly assembles. The music builds, and after some time, they stop Sarah dancing. They appear to beat her. Mark and Scott, standing some distance away, provide the sound effects using boxing gloves and the microphone. They leave her for dead: "Wild animals will kill you. / You'll get burned. / You're evil. /

We can't rescue you. / I'm not your mother, your sister or your friend. / We're not your carers. / Guilty! / As ever!"[117] They leave the stage, and Price comes over to her prone body, describing his sexual inexperience and his desire to learn more. "I need some encouragement. I'm confused of what is appropriate sexually. I'm pretty immature."[118] He leaves. Sarah rises, walks toward the screen separating her from the audience, and, while walking, for the first time, speaks. Her words, the last words in the show, are taken from Caliban, the speech that begins: "Be not afeard; the isle is full of noises . . ." She speaks slowly, putting each word together sound by sound, and the letters of the surtitles swarm and swim across the screen until they form each word. The screen falls away, and the piece ends with Sarah alone on stage, looking out at us.

These representations of abuse and victimization are hard to watch, and they're meant to be. As Elaine Scarry observes in *The Body In Pain*, the unknowability of another's suffering evades representation, and evades language in particular.[119] However, asks Judith Butler, "how do we account for the specific kind of injury that language itself performs?"[120] Butler draws upon Toni Morrison's observations in her 1993 Nobel Lecture on Literature: "Oppressive language does more than represent violence; it is violence; does more than represent the limits of knowledge; it limits knowledge."[121] As Butler elaborates, the power of words to do harm does not reside in their individual usage, or even the intention of the speaker, but from their citationality—which, Butler insists, is not to absolve the speaker of responsibility because the harm did not originate with them, but instead to shift attention to the way in which one participates within the circulation of citations.[122] And while they are always careful to separate ideas of agency from individual sovereignty, Butler's thoughts on re-signification suggest that the power of words might be redirected: "If the text acts once, it can act again, and possibly against its prior act."[123] The challenge Butler poses, then, is how to create contexts for re-signification. Revisiting Morrison's formulation, is it possible to turn the violence of language back into the representation of violence, without eliding the interchangeability of the two? Without, that is, making it *only* representation, and thereby forgetting the harm that these speech-acts do?

This re-signifying of speech and action is the realm that is explored by post-dramatic theater, in Lehmann's formulation, with its strategies of parataxis, non-hierarchization, and "play with the density of signs" that serve to separate language from dramatic fictions.[124] In understanding *"speech acts as actions,"* Lehmann writes, "a split emerges that is important for postdramatic theatre: it provokes by bringing to light that the word does not belong to the speaker. It does not organically reside in his/her body but remains a *foreign body*."[125] In deploying post-dramatic techniques, the play of textuality in *Food Court* creates an environment of unstable signification. As the list of "fat" insults accumulates, the words slide around the theater, slipping in and out of their horrific affect. We see the words as text to be read. We hear them as amplified sounds (aided by the microphones held by Price and Deans). We do not know if the speaker is talking to the other woman, or to a character who is represented by the woman, or is repeating the things that she has been called; nor can we tell to whom Price's sexual address is directed; and the effort it takes Sarah to sound out Shakespeare's words, carefully forming each one in her mouth, stages this action as the reclaiming of poetry, recalling the lines Shakespeare gives Caliban earlier in *The Tempest*: "You taught me language; and my profit on't / Is, I know how to curse."

Moreover, there are reversals and reconfigurations of hierarchical subject-positions here: as a nondisabled spectator, my experience includes confronting my own expectations about the actors I am watching, such as my assumption that people like them are more likely to be the recipients of violent words rather than the speakers of them. This is intentional, Gladwin reveals in the post-show discussion, explaining that one of the driving interests behind *Food Court* was to push at assumed boundaries of characterization with regard to disabled actors and/or characters by presenting disabled actors/characters who are perpetrators as well as victims of abuse. He explains, "If you can't act evil, then you're sub-human, in a way, because we're all capable of being evil." Such an intention emerged directly out of *small metal objects*, which Gladwin refers to as a "feel-good piece." Gladwin feels that audiences enjoy it because of the voyeuristic pleasures of its site-specificity, as well as the way in which it presents characters played by disabled actors as the "good guys" in contrast to the selfish and reprehensible characters that are played by the nondisabled actors.

One of the questions this work raises, then, is who is assumed to suffer, and who is capable of wounding? As Licia Carlson argues, a persistent prejudice surrounding disability is the presumption that the lives of those with disabilities *inevitably* involve suffering, and this assumption is particularly pronounced with regard to intellectual disability. Carlson steadfastly rejects this prejudice: "The claim 'all intellectually disabled persons will inevitably suffer' is simply untenable, unless it is intended only insofar as all human beings suffer."[126] She argues that such a view tends to be reinforced by what she calls "prototype effects," in which some of the extreme possibilities doctors predict based on prenatal genetic testing, for example, are taken not as hypotheticals but as predictions of lived experience. More perniciously, the presumption of suffering in biomedical ethics discourse tends to ignore the fact that, historically, the cause of much of the suffering of disabled persons has been the actions of medical practitioners *themselves* through systemic practices of physical isolation, removal from human connection, and other acts of inhumane treatment. Indeed, the association of disability with suffering is itself used to justify further discrimination against people with disabilities, and for this reason, as Carlson writes, "a primary objective of many disability rights activists and theorists has been to challenge the conflation made by the non-disabled world between having a disability and suffering."[127]

Part of the reason why the presumption of suffering is pervasive with regard to intellectual disabilities is that challenges around communication make it hard for nondisabled persons to imagine the lived experience of those living with disability, a situation compounded by the fact that the lives of most nondisabled people do not overlap with the lives of those with intellectual disabilities. "By discussing only the severe cases, generalizing about their condition (to the point that they are stripped of all actual and potential human capacities), and choosing examples that do not reflect their actual historical treatment . . . , it is easy to divorce persons labeled intellectually disabled from our concrete human world," Carlson writes.[128] Instead, when we nondisabled people try to imagine (rather than actually listen to) the lived experience of people with disabilities, we tend to focus on the things that we imagine we would no longer be able to do or to enjoy, and we therefore figure disability as deprivation (while simultaneously reifying our current capacities as "normal"). But to imagine the suffering of others, even when undertaken in the name of sympathy, also displaces the experience of others, turning them into supporting characters in our own ableist narratives about what matters.

With regard to the complicity of the nondisabled, the most significant shift in reframing disability over the past few decades has been the so-called social model, which locates the causes of suffering not in individual instances of impairment, as "personal tragedy," but instead in exclusionary social structures. For example, Michael Oliver's influential book *The Politics of Disablement* (1990) presents disability as an artifact not of individual impairment but of capitalist modes of production, within which disability is constituted as a result of a system that is not capable of finding productive uses for some people. In a different system, Oliver argued, individuals would still have impairments, but disability would be constituted differently or would not be constituted at all—that is to say, disability is a function of social apparatuses rather than of individual conditions.[129] As Carlson puts it, "the distinction is made between an impairment (any biological, physiological, or psychological pathology) and a disability, which is the result of having such an impairment." By locating the causes of suffering in cultural configurations, she continues, the social model "calls into question the assumption so often made by non-disabled persons that people with disabilities, by virtue of their impairments, *necessarily* suffer."[130]

The social model has driven radical change in disability rights by emphasizing the extent to which disability is socially constructed, as in this articulation from a report commissioned by UNESCO for the 1995 World Summit on Social Development:

> The term disability is now used by many disabled people to rep-
> resent a complex system of social restrictions imposed on people
> with impairments by a highly discriminatory society. Disability,
> therefore, is a concept distinct from any particular medical condi-
> tion. It is a social construct that varies across cultures and through
> time, in the same way, for example, as gender, class or caste.[131]

In this way, the social model has parallels with the kinds of arguments
about the social construction of identity found in Butler and elsewhere:
on an individual level, disability (and intellectual disability in particular)
might name a set of material conditions manifest in the body, but it is also
a cultural concept with associated values and hierarchies. The concept of
disability is constructed and maintained through linguistic and semiotic
practices—how we talk about it, how it is represented—and according
to the social model, these cultural practices are equally consequential for
shaping what the lived experience of disability is like. Carlson asks, "Must
one choose between pure constructs and real entities?" and goes on to
describe the ways in which the impact of representations is *real*:

> There are real people who have been labeled as "mentally
> retarded" and have been directly affected by that label. There
> are individuals who have various intellectual limitations, some a
> result of endogenous biological or genetic causes, others caused by
> external factors (e.g., poverty, deprivation, prenatal or postnatal
> trauma), and some for which there is no identifiable cause. There
> are persons who face social barriers, institutionalization, and vio-
> lence because of their limitations, and/or because they are labeled
> "mentally retarded."[132]

Such an entanglement complicates the dichotomy of "real" and "representation," like that which would underlie a question such as "Is there *really*
such a thing as intellectual disability, or is it *only* a representation"? In the
social model of disability, such a dualism cannot be sustained.

"We're People Who Do Shows": The Work of Representation

Despite opening up these possibilities for agency by recognizing and changing the discourse around disability, the social model has also been criticized
from within disability rights movements, most notably for the way it figures disability as primarily (if not exclusively) a form of oppression, so
that even reparative attention paid to impairment itself can be seen as a
distraction from, or even a perpetuation of, these forms of oppression.[133]
Matt Hargrave illustrates this critique in relation to a hypothetical person

"X" who has the diagnosis of autism: "If the predicament of 'X' is reduced to one of attitudinal barriers, then autism too is reduced: effectively, once the barriers (curriculum, class size, and so on) have been removed, it *disappears*."[134] In contrast, Hargrave cites what John Swain and Sally French call the "affirmation model," which "focuses on the need for a disabled person to feel a sense of pride; to reclaim identity as something validating, not stigmatising."[135] As Swain and French write, such an affirmation "is necessarily collective as well as individual."[136] It is within the context of just such a collective effort that the work of a theater company might be located, not only in the creation of new representations on stage, but also in the ongoing work of making a living as theater-makers: people who show up to work together, support each other, and reclaim and validate each other's identities as artists.

What is the place of a theater practice like that of Back to Back in relation to these interconnected issues of representation and collective agency? We can think of a work such as *Food Court* operating within the politics of representation at three different levels. First, it puts different kinds of images on stage, not only expanding *who* is represented by "standing for" (in Pitkin's language) the kinds of people and experiences that have typically been obscured from view, but also using techniques of post-dramatic theater to disrupt and reconfigure the conventions of signification attached to disabled bodies. Secondly, as with the techniques discussed in chapter 1, it calls attention to the spectator's role in creating an instance of co-appearance; that is, it is our spectatorial identification of this activity as an instance of theater that creates the conditions for the acts of self-fabrication that the actors undertake, and the meta-theatrical acknowledgments of the theatrical frame serve to remind us of the part we are to play. And third, in addition to the instance of theater as an aesthetic and semiotic process, it is also a material one, as discussed in chapter 2. Theater is not just an instance of an artwork that can be considered autonomously, but is bound up in ongoing social conditions, such as the lives of the performers and the conditions that make it possible for them to be onstage in any one performance—and that constitute, as Butler emphasizes, the networks and processes of support that are necessary to enable the conditions for an Arendtian "space of appearance" to be sustained.

Furthermore, the paradox of (non)productivity discussed in the previous chapter returns in a more charged way here, so that the peculiar kind of labor involved in the theater might serve to reflect, and even reverse, some of the ways that disability is socially produced. In the iconic representation described by Hargrave above, the actor is put to work to stand in for disability *in general*, such that some kind of surplus value is extracted at the cost of the actor's individuality; that is, the actor could be anyone with a disability, interchangeably representing the idea of disability. One way to resist this reductive signification would be to foreground the individuality of the actor. The actor would then be obstinately nonproductive within the economy of the theater: they are not "really" acting, and therefore not doing the work they should be doing in the theater, and might instead be described as doing a kind of performativity (a position discussed in the previous chapter). But this resistance is also a position of resignation: as in Hargrave's quote from the director who was told "these actors will only be themselves," the options for agency are limited. A third possibility, one that sits between these two positions and destabilizes them, is to produce the performers precisely *as* actors, neither identifiable as themselves nor as an abstraction, but occupying a specific and contingent representational function within a framework of appearance. In this way, what is apparent in the work is not the actor's productivity or stubborn non-productivity, but the economy of production itself.

This dynamic is similar to the production of meaning around childhood discussed earlier in the chapter; but these economies of production are particularly interesting in the case of a company like Back to Back because of the longevity of its existence as a company. This means that, unlike the child performers who appear in one or more productions and then inevitably age and are no longer children, the ongoing work of Back to Back becomes a place for the ensemble members to reflect and process not only their own lived experiences outside of the theater, but also their existence within the theater. Moreover, the two become intertwined, as the task of self-presentation within the theatrical context is, as I have argued in this chapter, not a representation of a political act of self-definition, but an instance of it. These blurrings of the theatrical and the everyday are apparent in collaborative statements issued by the company:

> We're people who do shows.
> We're all quite short, but each one is
> a little bit taller than the one before.
> We're agile and we work
> professionally as a theatre company.
> There are other things we do as well . . . warm-ups, research,
> trips to Melbourne, lots of meetings and time off when we need it.
> Sometimes we have noodles for lunch.[137]

This declaration, "We're people who do shows," was selected as the title of the volume on the company's work, and in its simplicity it is also powerfully suggestive: they are people who happen to do shows, but also, perhaps, they are people who define themselves through the doing of shows. "We go deep into the work," they say in another statement. "We go to places you can't go in real life."[138] And reflecting on his role as artistic director, Gladwin describes each process as a task of continuous reinvention: "The actors and I are a group of people who have to find a way of working together," he writes. "Each time we start a new work, we begin again."[139]

What is striking about Back to Back's work is the way it is a longitudinal process, one that is cyclical and iterative. In the post-show discussion I attended after *Food Court*, this aspect of their work was apparent in the way they discussed how much of the content of the work was informed by interests and challenges that were specific to the actors' own development as actors, and Gladwin described his job as director as being "to put forward challenges for the actors that will help them grow and develop as performers."[140] For example, the character ultimately played by Sarah Mainwearing was initially developed by Sonia Teuben, whom Gladwin describes as highly regarded among the company for her oratory skills; however, the character she developed is mute (until the end) as a result of the decision to have Teuben work with the productive constraint of not speaking during the improvisations that made up the devising process. Similarly, the opening exchange around food arose out of a desire to work with dialogue, particularly because one of the actors who originally played the scene (Rita Halabarec) tended to work primarily with monologue rather than dialogue. Gladwin describes Mark Deans's strength as being with physical performance and creating strong relationships with audiences, and his text—the karaoke-like moment that marks the transition between scenes—arose because Deans had never spoken in previous performances. The use of surtitles and text-captioning was a way to support him in speaking on stage. And the agonizing scene in which the two women force Mainwearing to strip and dance is revealed to have come almost directly out of a company improvisation. Mainwearing has a background in experimental performance that includes, for example, using her naked body as a tool for painting; when the actors in the improvisation ordered her to take her clothes off, they were surprised to find that she nonchalantly complied.

These glimpses of the devising process, which took place over three years, reveal the extent to which the performance is the direct result of the actors engaging with challenges of theatrical appearance and representation. In addition to staging disability, the performance stages the complexity and challenges of staging itself. Instead of directly approaching broader issues of disability in culture, this piece can be understood as an account of the ways in which the actors negotiated their own experience of speaking on stage, of acting on stage, of "being oneself" on stage. Furthermore, the ways in which these challenges of representing oneself on stage are interconnected with a broader politics of representation—who gets to appear, who gets to speak—were made painfully clear by some audience responses to *Food Court*. In the post-show discussion for the performance I attended, one audience member identified himself as an actor and then asked the performers how they remembered their lines.

His question rests on a presupposition about what the actors are capable of—and also misses the support structures that were visibly present to enable the delivery of this text. More revealing was a comment during a post-show discussion in Brussels: "I don't believe these people made this work," the audience member is reported to have said. "I have worked with people like this and I don't think they are capable of it." Gladwin also describes a comment from a festival director, which is less blunt but similar in sentiment: "I really like it," the director reportedly said, "but I do have concerns about whether the actors know and understand what they're saying and doing."[141]

The company has written, "as an ongoing dialogue with our audience, each new project is an investigation seeking answers to questions raised in previous works,"[142] and this audience response to *Food Court*—which understandably infuriated the company members—was cited as an impetus for the company's next works. Both *Ganesh Versus the Third Reich* (2011) and *Super Discount* (2013) made use of the meta-theatrical conceit of representing the process of making a play, with the nondisabled actor David Woods joining company members for these two productions in order to play the director of the two different fictional productions. In *Ganesh*, scenes set in a rehearsal room are interspersed with scenes from the play within the play, which tells the story of the eponymous elephant-headed deity traveling to Nazi Germany to reclaim the Hindu symbol of the swastika. Along the way, Ganesh meets the Jewish prisoner Levi and Josef Mengele, the notorious SS physician who conducted horrific medical experiments on his prisoners, including disabled people. *Super Discount* is set entirely within a rehearsal room, where the company members (as well as the director) debate and workshop ideas for a piece that would represent a disabled superhero based on company member Mark Deans.

The depiction of a fictionalized rehearsal room allows both pieces to stage different ideas around theatrical representation, what is involved in acting, and who has the right to represent what—with the wider sense of cultural representation being addressed in *Ganesh*'s exploration of Hindu and Nazi symbols and stories. Both plays also stage questions about the actors' abilities, and those of Deans in particular, as in a scene in *Ganesh* in which Scott Price performs an echo of the condescending remark from the Brussels audience member. Following a previous scene in which Deans was asked to play Hitler, Scott (the character) says, "Mark should be removed. Like, he doesn't understand what is fiction and what is not." (I must emphasize that this dismissal comes from the dramatic persona of Scott, since the actual person Scott was in anything but agreement with the Brussels audience member. A reviewer reports, "One of the actors, Scott Price, livid at the presumption, stood up, grabbed the microphone and said: 'Well mate, you can just get out of here because what you just said is so wrong and so offensive.' ")[143] The conversation carries on between Brian (playing another member of the ensemble) and David (playing the nondisabled director).

> SCOTT: You look at it. Mark's mind is probably, OK like, working like a goldfish.
> BRIAN: A goldfish? Does anyone ever call you a dumb arse?
> SCOTT: I didn't say it literally.
> BRIAN: What if someone said you had the mind of an earthworm?
> SCOTT: I'm walking away. Just ignore him. Just ignore him. I'm just going to ignore him.
> DAVID: I want to. I think I can answer your quibbles with the help of Mark. Mark, do you think of yourself as having the mind of a goldfish?
> MARK: Goldfish, whale, penguin . . .
> SCOTT: See, what did I tell you . . .
> BRIAN/SIMON: Hang on . . .
> DAVID: Let him answer. Let him answer. Yeah, go on, Mark.
> MARK: Octopus, seal, whale, shark, Sea World.
> DAVID: And sometimes when we are working, what's real and what's not gets confusing?
> MARK: Sea World.
> DAVID: But afterwards, you are clear what was real and what wasn't—afterwards?
> MARK: Yeah.[144]

Putting the words of the Brussels audience member into Scott's mouth, and creating a semi-fictionalized version of their own ensemble, is one way in which the company quite literally theatricalizes the politics of representation.

What's more, the difficulty with deciding "what was real and what wasn't," as David queries Mark, is inherent to the theatrical form, and the scene goes on to redirect this difficulty with distinguishing, shifting it from the actors to the audience. David asks the other company members to imagine that there is an audience watching them, and turns to the seats in which we are presently sitting in order to illustrate his point.

> DAVID: I was imagining that there were people in these empty seats, right.
> SIMON: They're not empty seats.
> DAVID: No, they are empty seats.
> SCOTT: Simon, please!
> DAVID: There's nobody in these seats.
> SIMON: Right.[145]

David continues by saying that when the show is on, each of the seats will have a person in them, pointing to a series of actual audience members in turn: "You know there will be somebody sitting there, and somebody sitting there, and somebody sitting there and there and there and there." David uses this projection of a hypothetical audience onto the real one to accuse us of being "perverts," having come to see a "freak show." "Like this person sitting here, this person sitting here," David says, pointing to an audience member: "You are a pervert. You have come here to see a bit of freak porn."[146] With the lines delivered swiftly and the conversation moving across four different participants, this is a scene that is funny because of its rapid-fire pace and rapid shifts in topic and focus; it is dizzying to follow—disorienting, even—as we try to keep track of who is standing in for what, who is in on the joke, and whom the joke is on. The effect of this disorientation is to make it evident that it is not the *performers* who are at risk of being unclear about what is and isn't real, but rather us, the *audience*. In making the conditions of acting, appearing, and watching the subject of the work, the self-reflexive meta-theatricality of these works shares with Rainer and Handke that "inward turn" that I described in chapter 1, as well as the infrastructural aesthetics of Rimini Protokoll and Quarantine described in chapter 2, in which it is the political distinctions and distributions of the theatrical event that are scrutinized. But Back to Back's theatrical world is a leaky one, and these deliberate confusions create lines of continuity between the fictional appearances of the theatrical stage and the political appearances (and disappearances) of the world outside.

This connection between issues of representation in the theater and the spectrum of meanings of representation outside the theater is perhaps most vividly demonstrated in *The Shadow Whose Prey the Hunter Becomes* (2019). Here, the company members appear to be setting up for a public meeting in their hometown of Geelong, beginning (as with *Food Court*) with the actors bringing chairs onto the stage, making their entrance one by one, and including a long pause while one of the performers works with electrical tape—this time, using a single line of tape to create the flimsiest possible manifestation of the line of demarcation between performers and audience. In this theatrical representation of another place of assembly, which is hardly distinct from this one, they rehearse their act of self-presentation. Their conversation with each other is by turns supportive, interrogative, speculative, and sometimes bickering and cruel. They remind each other of the proprieties of public behavior: "You can't touch people in the crotch area. It's a very sensitive place. It's also inappropriate to touch your own crotch in a public space."[147] They stumble through meeting protocols: housekeeping and Acknowledgement of Country, a practice adopted in public forums in Australia to acknowledge Traditional and First Nations custodianship, even when it can appear as only a ceremonial gesture (as it is played by the company here; I discuss

Acknowledgement of Country and tokenism in more depth in the conclusion to this book). As with previous shows, there is a debate about
whether Mark understands what is going on. "Who thinks it's important
we empower Mark in the meeting?" Scott asks. They all vote yes, except
for new company member Michael, who first wants to be sure that Mark
is interested in having a voice and that it is not something forced upon
him. There is a conversation about how they should describe themselves,
which is worth reproducing at length for the way in which they explore
how the performative consequences of terminology create the conditions
for "the social existence of the body" (as Butler puts it):

> MICHAEL: We are a group of people with intellectual disabilities. Is
> everyone OK for me to say that?
> SCOTT: I don't mind sharing my diagnosis.
> SARAH: I have a head injury.
> MICHAEL: Are you okay with the word disability?
> SIMON: I don't think it describes me.
> MICHAEL: Right.
> SIMON: I don't want to use the word.
> SCOTT: Why?
> SIMON: I just don't like it.
> SCOTT: I'm comfortable.
> MICHAEL: I am talking to anyone who is not comfortable.
> SARAH: What about "Neuro-diverse"?
> SCOTT: I need to think about it.
> SARAH: Neuro-diverse describes everyone.
> SCOTT: Look, I am a "disabled person," I am proud and I don't
> want to have to weave my way around language.
> SIMON: Shall we just say some of us here have a disability and
> some are without?
> SCOTT: Well that's not true.
> SIMON: Some who are and some who are not?
> SCOTT: It's just not accurate. We are all disabled even if we don't
> want to use the term.
> MICHAEL: I agree. My brain doesn't work like other people's and
> if you don't mind me saying, Sarah and Scott, you're the same,
> and Simon, we all have an intellectual disability.
> SIMON: I'm okay with saying that I have a disability as long as I
> don't have to talk about it.
> SCOTT: Are you okay with other people talking about it?
> SIMON: I am coming to terms with it.[148]

Terms such as "disabled" can be a source of pride for Scott, demonstrating
the power of the "affirmative model" of group identification as a source of

agency; but even as the company members find solidarity in their shared practice, it is important for them to insist on variation and difference, and resist the kinds of aggregate imaginings of the prototypical "intellectually disabled person" that Licia Carlson critiques in the argument summarized earlier. In that argument, Carlson also points out the danger of separating any of these discursive categories from their histories of discriminatory and abusive treatment. When we do so, Carlson writes in the passage, it becomes dangerously easy to separate such persons from "our concrete human world."[149]

Such a separation is addressed in the middle of *The Shadow Whose Prey the Hunter Becomes*, in which Scott delivers perhaps one of the most politically explicit commentaries in Back to Back's oeuvre on the politics of disablement. From a precarious position atop a kind of towering lectern that the company has been steadily assembling during the first part of the piece, Scott recounts this history of abusive treatment: "For thousands of years," he says, "people with disabilities have been abandoned in woods, kept in cellars, tied to beds, experimented on, isolated, gassed, drugged, devalued, victimised, dehumanised, stigmatized, sterilized and euthanised."[150] And these are not incidents from distant history, he continues. Scott's speech cites one recent example of the Magdalene laundries in Ireland, where women (including many with intellectual and other disabilities) were forced to work in brutal conditions; even after the laundries were disbanded, one of them was converted into a manufacturing plant for the Hasbro games corporation where workers were paid a pittance as recently as 2012.[151] In another example that Scott describes, 32 people with intellectual disabilities worked in a meatpacking plant in Iowa for just $65 per month for more than 30 years until it was shut down in 2009.[152]

As Tony McCaffrey documents, the theater is itself imbricated in this history of institutionalization. McCaffrey describes the role of theaters within mental asylums, such as the 300-seat theater built at Normansfield Hospital by John Haydon Langdon Down, the physician who classified the genetic condition now named after him, and this is one instance of the broader way in which the cultural definition of "what disability looks like" is intertwined with conventions of medical display. As McCaffrey writes, contemporary forms of theater that involve performers with intellectual disabilities must contend with this history of institutionalization, and indeed, "theatre itself is an institution: of representation, expression, and communication, often in the service of normalisation or celebration of what is held in common."[153] As described above, in its founding, Back to Back made a deliberate choice to distance itself from institutions of care. But the company retains an interest in the institution of theater as an apparatus of display and self-representation. For me, the relevance of their performances to issues of disability is not in the way that they might

bring "reality" onto stage, puncturing the theater's representational operations, but in the way in which they reveal that sense of reality to always
be an apprehension, a matter of perspective, a matter of "the way we see"
disability.

As discussed in the previous chapter, theater is both a place in which
we see these appearances and a place that allows us to see the mechanisms
of appearance. Back to Back's work is designed to increase access to the
mechanisms of appearance, to use existing theatrical structures, and to
invent new ones that generate agency with regard to appearance: not as
representative of some other agency that might be achieved elsewhere,
but to utilize representation as an agential act in itself. Furthermore, as
a work like *The Shadow Whose Prey the Hunter Becomes* demonstrates,
this theatricalist politics, while it can be subject to particular examination
and reconfiguration within the institution called "the theater," is continuous with other spaces of appearance: the workplace, the public forum, the
town hall. In the next chapter, I look at examples where theatricality is at
play in relation to the politics of the public sphere, and indeed the nation-
state itself.

Chapter 4

✦

Political Theater: Making the Public Appear

Sometimes words are not just words; for example, when they are spoken not on a theatrical stage, but at the center of political power, where the leader of a newly elected government convenes a special meeting of the nation's parliament and delivers on a promise made during the preceding election campaign. That promise was to utter some words that the political party previously in power had consistently refused to speak. Now, as a representative of the state, and with the full force of the democratic assembly, the leader says these words live in Parliament and to millions watching via televised address: "We say sorry." This public apology on behalf of the Australian government for its history of neglect and abuse of Indigenous people was offered by Prime Minister Kevin Rudd in 2008, along with testimony from victims of the "Stolen Generations," Aboriginal and Torres Strait Islander peoples who as children were removed from their families and their cultures and forcibly assimilated into settler-colonial institutions. As a public acknowledgment by a government of its accountability for its past actions, where too often there has been only silence, Rudd's apology was a significant milestone.

It would also appear to be an exemplary instance of those uses of language famously described by J. L. Austin as "performative," where the act of uttering certain words by an appropriately empowered speaker functions not merely to represent or to communicate *about* something, but to actually *do* something. Austin's analysis excluded from consideration any deliberately ambiguous, fictional, or theatricalized speech-acts, such as speaking on stage or in works of literature, calling these "parasitic uses of language" and therefore "not serious."[1] In such a view, the theatrical might make references to structures of power, but it does not participate in them, while the performative is not at a second-order remove, but offers the promise of immediate and self-contained autonomy, an action that is complete in itself. And yet, as I will discuss here, Rudd's apology is in fact dependent on theatrical supplementation, and the self-authorizing force with which it speaks can itself be considered a stage effect. I will move from this "official" example to interventions and performances that are deliberately "not serious," in Austin's sense, including artworks by Carey Young, Rabih Mroué, Walid Raad, and Christoph Schlingensief, and I will consider the relationship between authority and authenticity that is exposed and undermined in these works. I return here to some of the questions of the "Arendtian turn" discussed in the previous chapter, arguing that the distinction between the "serious" performative and the "not serious" theatrical is not one between the political and the nonpolitical; instead, it is the determination of this distinction in the first place—that is, what counts as serious and what counts as legitimate—which is *itself* the domain of politics. As opposed to the customary dismissive meaning of theater when it is applied to "real" politics, here I will argue that the dynamics of theatricality that I have been exploring in this book are generative in that they enable new readings of political events and new approaches to politics itself.

"We Say Sorry": Kevin Rudd, Carey Young, and Rabih Mroué

I begin by exploring the theatricality at work in three examples of publicly performed discourse: Kevin Rudd's parliamentary apology to the Indigenous peoples of Australia; a gallery-based artwork by Carey Young which consists in its entirety of a legal disclaimer of its status as art; and a text and video work by the Lebanese-born artist Rabih Mroué in which the artist offers an apology for the Lebanese Civil War in the absence of any official version. Each of these examples is a variation on apology: Rudd's is an official gesture of the state in relation to past wrongs; Young's is a preemptive disavowal of any potential misunderstanding; and Mroué's is an apparently personal confession, but one that complicates its authenticity through its presentation as a work of art. All three examples consist entirely of spoken or printed text, and all three invoke a legal framework that appears to elevate the potency of the words from that of everyday speech and, as such, to be instances of Austinian performativity in their almost tautological self-actualization: an apology is apologized, a legal agreement is legally agreed, a confession is confessed.

In contrast to "ordinary" statements, which have the potential to be true or false, Austin argued that the category of performatives is distinguished by their susceptibility to "infelicities," that is, "things that can be and go wrong on the occasion of such utterances,"[2] and an utterance that goes wrong, rather than being *false*, would be *unhappy*. In relation to this infelicity, however, fictional or theatricalized speech acts are neither "happy" nor "unhappy," since they don't even mean to go right, and it is for this reason that Austin dismisses them as "parasitic" and "not serious." Whereas Austin would say that something different is going on in Rudd's apology, compared with the two artistic examples that are "not serious," I will argue that all three share a theatrical quality that complicates the apparently self-fulfilling autonomy of Austin's performative. Underpinning the happy performance of law, I will argue, is a mutually supportive relationship between authority and authenticity, each pointing to the other in a circular loop of legitimation. I will suggest that by taking the same attitude toward Rudd's apology as we do toward these seemingly "not serious" apologies, this relationship is exposed. In this way, what I offer is not so much a critique of whether Rudd's apology is a "good" or "happy" performance, but instead an exploration of the fabrication of nationhood—and the possibility for alternative fabrications that it raises.

As leader of the Australian Labor Party, Kevin Rudd promised to issue an official apology to Australia's Indigenous peoples as part of his campaign during the 2007 federal election. The voting into power of the Labor Party brought an end to eleven years of government under the Liberal Party's John Howard, who had stubbornly resisted growing public pressure to issue such an apology. A year after taking power, Rudd honored his commitment. Issued as an act of Parliament, the prime minister's apology was televised live throughout the country and was a national (and international) event; "parliamentary business became spectacle, spilled into the community to become compelling social performance," wrote the theater scholar Gay McAuley.[3] Here is an excerpt from the official transcript of Rudd's apology:

Apology to Australia's Indigenous Peoples, House of Representatives, Parliament House, Canberra 13 February 2008

—I move:
That today we honour the Indigenous peoples of this land, the oldest continuing cultures in human history.

We reflect on their past mistreatment.

We reflect in particular on the mistreatment of those who were Stolen Generations—this blemished chapter in our nation's history.

The time has now come for the nation to turn a new page in Australia's history by righting the wrongs of the past and so moving forward with confidence to the future.

We apologise for the laws and policies of successive Parliaments and governments that have inflicted profound grief, suffering and loss on these our fellow Australians.

We apologise especially for the removal of Aboriginal and Torres Strait Islander children from their families, their communities and their country.

For the pain, suffering and hurt of these Stolen Generations, their descendants and for their families left behind, we say sorry.

>   To the mothers and the fathers, the brothers and the sisters, for
> the breaking up of families and communities, we say sorry.
>   And for the indignity and degradation thus inflicted on a proud
> people and a proud culture, we say sorry.
>   We the Parliament of Australia respectfully request that this
> apology be received in the spirit in which it is offered as part of
> the healing of the nation.[4]

In purely technical terms, this apology is exemplary. It demonstrates none of the typical pitfalls of public apologies, such as those outlined by philosopher Nick Smith in his wide-ranging treatise on apology, *I Was Wrong: The Meaning of Apologies* (2008). Smith's book catalogues numerous failures to "properly" apologize by political leaders and celebrities, of which the most common type of failure is the conditional apology, as in "I apologize *if* I caused offence," which often seeks to shift responsibility onto the offended—that is, "I apologize if *you* took offence." Smith gives the example of Pope Benedict's disastrous attempts in 2006 to remedy the offense caused by the inclusion in one of his speeches of a passage that criticized the Prophet Muhammad. Subsequent statements by the Vatican and the pope were consistently rejected as being not sincerely apologetic, which is hardly surprising given that these statements included phrases such as: "I am deeply sorry for *the reactions* in some countries to a few passages of my address."[5] Rudd's apology, by contrast, makes no such blunders, and instead seems to satisfy all twelve of the conditions Smith proposes for the "categorical apology," including such dimensions as "acceptance of blame," a "shared commitment to moral principles underlying each harm," "categorical regret," and "an appropriate degree" of "empathy and sympathy for the victim."[6] Rudd's apology is certainly a more satisfying declaration than the Howard government's 1999 "Motion of Reconciliation," which "expresses its deep and sincere regret that indigenous Australians suffered injustices under the practices of past generations," but pointedly refused to include the word "sorry."[7] (In a subsequent TV interview, Mike Munro pushed Howard on exactly this point: "A deep and sincere regret. Is this an apology?" Munro asked. In response, Howard would only say, "Well, it's a deep and sincere regret.")[8]

Despite its technical proficiency, however, the political value of Rudd's apology has been widely criticized. Many reactions to the apology argue that without changes in policy, the apology itself is meaningless; instead, to return to one of the themes this book is addressing, it is "only theater." The political commentator Tara McCormack, for example, noted that the new Rudd government's policies toward Indigenous peoples in the Northern Territory were essentially the same as those of the Howard government, and still maintained a paternalistic, interventionist agenda. McCormack writes: "Rhetoric costs nothing; Rudd's apology can be seen as an attempt to appease people's consciences on the cheap."[9] Writing from a legal theory perspective, Alex Reilly argues that Rudd's apology effectively historicizes any wrongdoing, and so it leaves undisturbed the concept of absolute state sovereignty that led to the wrongdoings in the first place. And Gay McAuley notes that Rudd's actions in Parliament largely ignored the simultaneous convergence of Aboriginal and Islander representatives, who had assembled outside Parliament to protest.[10]

The failure of the Rudd government to substantively change its policies in keeping with the spirit of its apology would, in Austin's terms, render the apology "infelicitous": the speech-act properly considered must include what Austin calls "the total speech situation,"[11] including the context and conventions for the utterance, as well as whether or not the future actions of all parties are consistent with what was said. As someone who lived in so-called Australia for some time, I witnessed firsthand the ongoing failure of its settler-colonialist culture to acknowledge and address its historical and ongoing structures of systemic racism.[12] However, rather than cataloging the failure of action to accompany the apology, I want to look more closely at the performative elements of the apology itself. As I will argue, Rudd's speech seeks to frame itself as an autonomous, self-completing performative, one that exhaustively fulfills the requirement of apology in order to draw a line under the actions of past governments and, in Rudd's words, "resolv[e] that this new page in the history of our great continent can now be written."[13] If this act of apology is "only theater," then what might it reveal about the theatricality involved when the state attempts to perform itself, to assert its legitimacy—and indeed, its very existence? What contradictions might be exposed between the authoritative autonomy of the performative and its more theatrical appeal to emotional sympathy?

Throughout his search to define the performative, Austin gives ontological priority to those forms of utterance that best demonstrate autonomy and self-sufficiency, in which the actual action takes place at precisely the same time as the words are spoken. So, for example, he makes a distinction between the utterance "I apologize," which is a "pure" performative, and "I am sorry," which is "not pure but half descriptive," in that it might more accurately be understood as a descriptive statement about the speaker's state of mind rather than the performance of apologizing.[14] Although Austin gradually abandons his initial distinction between performatives and descriptive statements, he maintains a differentiation between three different kinds of performative forces that may be involved in every utterance: its locutionary dimension, the extent to which it performs an act *of* saying something; its illocutionary dimension, the extent to which it performs an act *in* saying something; and its perlocutionary dimension, the extent to which it performs an act *by* saying something—with this last component including all the intended and unintended consequences, interpretations, and inferences of a speech-act.[15] Even in this expanded consideration of performative discourse, however, the illocutionary retains a special privilege for Austin: all utterances are locutionary, and any utterance may manifest perlocutionary effects, but only certain utterances have an illocutionary dimension. Whereas Austin would demarcate the illocutionary effects of a speech-act from its perlocutionary ones, the example of Rudd's apology reveals how the two are intermingled and mutually dependent; indeed, the way in which it *appears* to be illocutionary—to have "resolved" the act of apology through the saying of the words in the carefully controlled circumstances—can be understood as *itself* a perlocutionary effect.

Looking again at the text of Rudd's speech, we find that it is full of uses of language that Austin would identify as characteristic of performatives, in such expressions as "we honour," "we reflect," "we request" and, of course, the three repetitions of "we say sorry." These can be further categorized according to subcategories proposed by Austin. For example, the repeated central apologetic utterance—"we apologise"—represents instances of what Austin describes as the *behabitive* type, "a kind of performance concerned roughly with reactions to behavior and with behavior towards others and designed to exhibit attitudes and feelings."[16] And these instances are framed within an ever-expanding bracket of other speech-acts: Rudd's speech is suspended within the overarching clause, "I move," which is uttered by him in his role as prime minister and government leader and would be classified by Austin as *exercitive*—"the exercising of powers, rights, or influence."[17] The event also begins with additional procedural performatives that are not recorded in the published text, but which can be seen in the officially archived video: the Speaker of the House "recognizes" the Clerk, who announces the motion, and the Speaker then recognizes the prime minister. These acts of recognition are fundamental to the proceedings: if the words are not spoken and the authorizing people who speak them are not present, then the event does not "count." Expanding the frame further, the execution of the apology is the fulfilment of Rudd's campaign promise, so the whole event is further bracketed within the class of *commissives*, the name Austin gives to promises, contracts, and oaths.[18] And indeed, the fact that it is Rudd rather than the leader of the opposition who is prime minister is the consequence of millions of individual performative actions, each with their own requirements for felicity and authentication, which are equivalent to the utterance "I cast my vote for this candidate."

In Austin's analysis, it turns out that not all of these performative types have the same degree of purity with regard to their performativity, and he proposes an evaluative spectrum along which different kinds of speech-acts would fall. At one end, Austin identifies the verdictive or exercitive types, in which an authority's pronouncement is judged to be felicitous based on (apparently) objective and verifiable criteria, such as whether the person is authorized to make such a judgment or pronouncement. However, the behabitive category, to which apologies belong, falls within the more problematic end of the spectrum, which Austin calls "troublesome" because they have a "special scope for insincerity."[19] The criteria for judging these as successful—again, in Austin's sense of whether one could definitively conclude that the act was "happily" performed—are less obvious and verifiable. The person must mean what they say; but how can we know this? And the listener must believe what they hear; but again, which listener, and how are we to know what they believe?

For Jacques Derrida, Austin's attempt to distinguish between performatives that are more prone to infelicity and those that are less prone (and more autonomous) prevents Austin from recognizing his own most crucial insight. Rather than excluding the risk of infelicity as "accidental" or "exterior," Derrida famously declares such possibility to be the "law" of utterance, the law of communication itself; infelicity "is *always* possible, and is in some sense a necessary possibility."[20] For Derrida, there is no possibility of an Austinian "pure" performative: "A successful performative is necessarily an 'impure' performative."[21] Elsewhere, Derrida considers the illocutionary act that is the US Declaration of Independence—which, like Rudd's apology, is an act of state attempting to articulate itself. Derrida asks, "who signs, and with what so-called proper name, the declarative act that founds an institution?"[22] The signer is authorized to sign, Derrida claims, only by virtue of the signature that he or she has not yet made; Derrida describes this as "a sort of fabulous retroactivity," deliberately suggesting connotations of "fabricated" and "fable-like."[23] For Derrida, such a speech-act functions as *both* a constative and a performative, and the confusion between the two functions is not accidental but necessary: "This obscurity, this undecidability between, let us say, a performative structure and a constative structure, is *required* to produce the sought-after effect."[24]

Stanley Fish expands Derrida's arguments, emphasizing that it is not only Austin's distinction between performative and constative that is unsustainable, but even the distinction between "serious" and "not serious" utterances. Fish revisits Austin's declaration that "not serious" utterances lack the autonomy of true performatives and are somehow "parasitic" upon their capacity. Fish remarks:

> The reasoning behind this declaration is clear enough: a speaker in a poem or an actor on a stage does not produce his utterance with a full and present intention but with the intention of someone behind him, a poet or a playwright; his is a *stage utterance*, and [the argument would be that] in order to get at its true meaning we have to go behind the stage to its originating source in the consciousness of the author.[25]

However, Fish continues, we are always and already at such a remove: "If by 'stage utterances' one understands utterances whose illocutionary force must be inferred or constructed, then all utterances are stage utterances, and one cannot mark them off from utterances that are 'serious.' "[26] It is, of course, vital to the functioning of "serious" discourse that it designate itself as having a special access to the real, but for Fish, these are characteristics of genre rather than ontological distinctions.[27] As with the discussion of the allure of the supposedly "real" backstage in chapter 2, such distinctions emerge *from* the conditions of differentiation, rather than preceding them.

Returning to Austin's normative spectrum of performatives, it seems that the critical attribute at the exercitive end of the spectrum is *authority*: is the person authorized to perform the speech-act? At the other end of the spectrum is *authenticity*: does the person mean what they say, or might they be insincere, "not serious," like an actor on a stage? At first glance, the exercitive type would seem to possess the self-sufficiency that would exemplify the apparent immediacy of the purely illocutionary: it speaks with the force of law. But in Rudd's apology, the two types of performatives are intermingled and mutually dependent upon each other. For the state to apologize, the rules for exercitives would stipulate only that the words "The State apologises" be passed by Parliament and that would be that. But such an apology would clearly be insufficient, and its failure to demonstrate authenticity would undermine the authority of the state; as Alan Read writes, "law has to be *seen* to be done."[28] As Austin acknowledges, an apology cannot be felicitous without knowing whether its sentiment is meant by the speaker; however, the only way to demonstrate conviction is through acts which are more and more prone to infelicity—which are, for example, statements about the speaker. For the illocutionary dimension of Rudd's apology to be felicitous, that success must be based on his perlocutionary proficiency, on his performance of sincerity. In this way the closure of the act never exists; it has a kind of deferral away from itself, a prolongation away from the purely illocutionary "We say sorry."

In fact, the core apology—the motion tabled in Parliament and excerpted above—was presented within the context of a longer event, and Rudd's speech itself went on for another thirty minutes. In the remainder of his speech, Rudd addressed the question of why he felt an apology was necessary, deploying a range of rhetorical techniques to answer this question. These include recounting the story of one woman from the Stolen Generation who was taken from her parents in the 1930s by government agents; quotations from egregiously racist government policies of the past; and finally, an argument about reconciliation, which is articulated in terms of promoting a core Australian value, what Rudd calls "a fair go for all." Rudd makes the following appeal:

I ask those non-Indigenous Australians to imagine for a moment
if this had happened to you. I say to honourable members here
present: imagine if this had happened to us. Imagine the crippling
effect. Imagine how hard it would be to forgive. But my proposal
is this: if the apology we extend today is accepted in the spirit of
reconciliation, in which it is offered, we can today resolve together
that there be a new beginning for Australia. And it is to such a new
beginning that I believe the nation is now calling us.[29]

The purely illocutionary moment of apology is thus supplemented with
rhetorical extension, becoming less a single performed act and more an
extended sequence that might suitably be described as "theatrical." Paradoxically, this perlocutionary supplementation is necessary for the success
of the performative, and at the same time detrimental to the purity of that
illocutionary autonomy. The version of the state that is presented here is
no longer composed of self-contained and self-determining actions, but
instead consists of statements about other people. Rudd's speech becomes
crowded with voices and characters, including the dramatic narrative of a
particular Indigenous woman, the invoked presence of his non-Indigenous
listeners, and claims on behalf of, and appeals for sympathy from, Australia's non-Indigenous citizens.

And so, the intermingling of exercitives and behabitives is not accidental but necessary, with authority and authenticity not at opposing ends of
a spectrum but rather mutually dependent upon each other, each referring to the other. Authenticity presents itself as self-sameness, the quality
of a thing or person or action to be what it purports to be—there is no
backstage illusion, no knife pretending to be a knife or a person pretending to be someone else. And yet, precisely when this self-identity is most
critical, we find that it must be guaranteed by reference to some *external*
authority: an oath on the Bible, the veracity of a signature, the testimony
of an expert. Authority, on the other hand, is presented in Austin's illocutionary examples as something that is objectively known, and the internal
authenticity of a speech-act is irrelevant as long as it can be verified against
the authorizing circumstances: someone may not mean their marriage
vows, but they are still married by speaking them, and a wrongful verdict
issued by a judge in a trial still carries the force of law. But in the case of
Rudd's apology, the fact of having the authority of office is not enough:
a persuasive display of authenticity is required to legitimate the apology,
and Rudd must "play the part" of the remorseful representative of the
state. In this way, authority—"I am really the Prime Minister and not an
actor on stage"—is not the only precondition for what constitutes "serious" action, which is instead dependent upon a successful performance of
authenticity—indeed, very much like being an actor on stage, and behav-
ing the way an authority is expected to behave.

Austin's analysis of performativity has been extended to numerous aspects of culture and identity, including gender, race, and dis/ability, but perhaps nothing is more purely performative than the nation-state, because it has no material existence and is a completely fabricated category, as Derrida suggests. As such, it relies on props and rituals to give it material substance, in the form of flags, anthems, buildings, and ceremonies—such as this parliamentary apology. This codependence is manifested in the way the framework of the democratic process and the rhetorical signifiers of sincerity are mutually supportive, each deriving legitimacy from the other. Looking more broadly, we might see this interdependence between authority and authenticity to be frequently at play, each appearing to be self-constitutive but ultimately depending upon the other. As Judith Butler emphasizes, the "force of law" is not inherent in the words themselves, but is acquired through citation:

> If a performative provisionally succeeds (and I will suggest that "success" is always and only provisional), then it is not because an intention successfully governs the action of speech, but only because that action echoes prior actions, and *accumulates the force of authority through the repetition or citation of a prior and authoritative set of practices.*[30]

In this way, the ritual of the apology is not a decorative supplement to the act itself, but is necessary for the act, as part of what Butler calls "the accumulating and *dissimulating* historicity of force."[31] As I described briefly in the previous chapter, in considering all performatives as (dis)semblances, Butler makes the case for acts of "resignification"—not imagined as "the fantasy of transcending power altogether," but instead a way of "replaying power," of "restaging it again and again in new and productive ways."[32] Butler distinguishes their view from someone like Pierre Bourdieu, who, as with Austin, would differentiate between legitimate and illegitimate speech-acts on the basis of the social power held by the speaker. In contrast, Butler asks:

> But is there a sure way of distinguishing between the imposter and the real authority? And are there moments in which the utterance forces a blurring between the two, where the utterance calls into question the established grounds of legitimacy, where the utterance, in fact, performatively produces a shift in the terms of legitimacy as an *effect* of the utterance itself?[33]

To put it another way, these speech-acts do not so much rely on a *prior* legitimacy, as legitimation is an *effect* created through repetition and citation. In Rudd's apology, these gestures work to cover over and conceal other measures of legitimacy, such as changes in actual policy, or the specific demands of the Aboriginal and Torres Strait Islander representatives gathered outside. But, crucially, the performance of apology has a structural ambiguity that cannot help but be revealed, even as—and perhaps *especially* as—it works to obscure that structural flaw. The structure of repetition opens the possibility of new inflections, including new voices, who claim a right to be heard as political beings, and to participate in the "fabrication" of a different kind of "we."

Fabricated Authority: The Lecture-Performances of Rabih Mroué and Walid Raad

The fabric of authenticity is material that can be woven differently. Artists show us how. Consider Carey Young's *Disclaimer* series (2004), a set of three works of art consisting only of printed text that borrows the discursive authority of legal disclaimers. On the surface, these declarations appear to have all the necessary characteristics of an Austinian performative. For example, one of the works in the series, titled *Ontology*, reads as follows:

> This piece is provided "as is." The artist does not represent this to be a work of art. S/he hereby disclaims any liability for considering this piece as a work of art and excludes any guarantee or warranty, both expressed or implied, as to the fact that this may be exhibited or marketed as a work of art.[34]

Disclaimer is typical of Young's artwork in the way it interrogates the status of the work of art within legal and economic frameworks, and it was created in close consultation with legal experts. In its exploration of context, Young's work recalls the conceptual art of the 1960s that began to treat the encounter with the spectator as part of the domain of the work—and as such, it would be another example of the kind of work that Michael Fried would condemn as theater.

Indeed, Fried explicitly criticizes a lack of "true" seriousness when he defines the "*stage* presence" that he despises in minimalist art. As discussed in chapter 1, Fried describes minimalist art's theatrical effect as a result of "the special complicity that the work extorts from the beholder," which produces a demand for seriousness, but one that Fried dismisses as shallow and insincere:

> Something is said to have presence when it demands that the beholder take it into account, that he take it seriously—and when the fulfilment of that demand consists simply in being aware of the work and, so to speak, in acting accordingly.[35]

This "false" seriousness prevents a deeper appreciation, such as the one that Fried would find in the modernist art that he praises, and he continues: "Certain modes of seriousness are closed to the beholder by the work itself, i.e., those established by the finest painting and sculpture of the recent past."[36] The works in *Disclaimer* could easily be dismissed as "not serious," as a joke, both as a work of art and a legal declaration. They do not offer a complex, autonomous aesthetic experience within which the viewer can be "absorbed," as Fried advocated, and one cannot take them as seriously as Fried would take a sculpture by Anthony Caro, for example. Instead, *Disclaimer*'s seriousness is mock seriousness, pretend seriousness, unfaithful seriousness. In Austin's distinctions, this would be a work that is as "hollow and void" as a stage utterance. It may have appropriated legal discourse, but it is only "parasitic" upon such discourse, falling under the category of stunted "etiolations" of language.[37]

And yet, *Disclaimer*'s parasitism is so precise that it is indistinguishable from its host. Were a court of law to be forced to make a determination about its status as a work of art, how seriously, or not seriously, could this "disclaimer" be taken? Surprisingly, this is not necessarily a hypothetical question, and in fact there have been instances where courts have had to make a determination about whether something constitutes a work of art or not, particularly in situations where the object's status as art is linked to different categories of tax liability—and watching a court use the tools of legal precedent to wrestle with such a complex aesthetic judgment can be bizarre.[38] If such a dispute arose about *Disclaimer*, what would a court decide? Is it, or is it not, a work of art? Young's other works present similar quandaries through other appropriations of legal discourse, such as *Mutual Release*, in which the artist and the gallery both sign "as a deed" an agreement "to each other's complete mutual release."[39] As I described above, the guise of seriousness is typically deployed by politicians and lawmakers in order to obscure the performative speech-act's foundational capacity for infelicity, but in works like *Disclaimer* and *Mutual Release*, that capacity for infelicity is foregrounded, and their theatricality reveals that the "serious" discourse of law and the "not serious" discourse of art are both, in the end, only forms of discourse. The significance of such indeterminacy may not seem consequential compared to the example of a national apology; but Young's work pokes away at the distinction between "serious" and "not serious," between what counts as legitimate legal or political speech or action and what does not. As I argued in the previous chapter, the political is not a category of action, or a certain kind of content, but instead the very distinction that labels some actions as political and some as not.

This play with the politics of legitimation is more overt in Rabih Mroué's *I, the Undersigned*, a performed apology which more closely mirrors Rudd's official act.[40] The work consists of two parts. The first of these is a signed statement, mounted on the gallery wall, in which Mroué declares, "I, the undersigned, Rabih Mroué, present a public and sincere apology to all of you, and to all the Lebanese people." In this statement, he explains that, in the absence of any official apology for the Lebanese Civil War that raged between 1975 and 1990, he has decided to present his own apology. In this half of the work, then, Mroué adopts the guise of seriousness and sincerity. It is notable that the work is titled after the act of signature, and that this signed declaration is always visible alongside the second part of the piece, for the signature is the double carrier of both authenticity and authority. That is, the signature authenticates the work under its own authority—its "fabulous" authority, as Derrida would say.

If the signed statement works through seriousness, then the second part of the piece is quite different. A video monitor next to the signed statement displays Mroué's apology, which consists of a sequence of concise mini-apologies, a *Sprechstück* by prerecorded statement. Some of the elements are as follows:

1. I apologise to all those who were my victims, whether they knew it or not, whether I knew them or not, whether I had hurt them directly or through mediators.
2. I apologise for I what have done during the Lebanese war, whether in the name of Lebanon or Arabness or the Cause, etc.
3. I apologise for my ignorance of the meaning of many words and my total ignorance of concepts I was fighting for.
4. I apologise for not knowing the roots and reasons for the civil war, which I had claimed to understand.

In these first few elements, the apology is marked by its personal scrutiny and by a sense of sincerity and reflection. As the apology continues, these reflections become more personal and specific, as Smith, the author of *I Was Wrong*, might prescribe that an apology "should"; but in this instance, the increasing specificity has the paradoxical effect of making the whole performance more dubious.

6. I apologise for considering that my comrades and I were right and forever in the right.
7. I apologise because I fired bullets towards the sky in glee over Brazil's victory over Germany.
8. I apologise for promoting and chanting in private and public gatherings political and revolutionary songs that excite crowds and push them to continue with the war until victory is won.

Rather than supporting the authentic performance of apology, the increased sincerity and detail of these comments creates fault lines within the performance; these confessions feel plausible, so that we may well believe that he fired a gun after Brazil's World Cup victory, but did he also "go to Cuba for a month to train in guerrilla warfare" as he later confesses?

After he apologizes for not having been injured, kidnapped, or personally threatened during the war, these fissures of doubt and ambiguity are accentuated by Mroué's critical self-reflection about the genre itself:

> 15. I apologise because I sometimes steal other people's writings and pretend they are my own.
> 16. I apologise because I enjoy playing with other people's feelings.
> 17. I apologise for working in a medium that I dislike.
> 18. I apologise for presenting this apology in a medium that I almost ignore.
> 19. I apologise for insisting that this is not a confession, and this is not an apology.
> 20. I apologise because these are only words, words, words . . .

Like Young's disclaimers, the theatricality of this apology is a result of its awareness of its own conditions of production and encounter. But whereas Young's version works through perfect mimesis, adopting the guise of legal discourse so faithfully that it is, in fact, a legal agreement, Mroué's apology is too knowing: it knows itself as representation, is aware of the codes of its genre, and names its own rhetorical gestures. It would fail the tests for felicity specified by Austin because it is a "misfire," that is, because "the particular persons and circumstances in a given case" are not "appropriate for the invocation of the particular procedure invoked"; and additionally it is an "abuse" because it is not clear that the "person participating in and so invoking the procedure" does "in fact have those [designated] thoughts or feelings."[41] Mroué may, he admits, be using someone else's words, recounting someone else's experiences.

And yet, this piece even apologizes for these infidelities. It is not insincere by means of caricatured sincerity or ironic sincerity, but instead produces an insincerity through over-sincerity, through its full commitment to the performance of apology, which necessarily includes apologizing for the inadequacy of apology itself. If *I, the Undersigned* is theatrical—in the sense that I have been using it in this book, to refer to the way it makes visible and thereby critiques its own conditions of appearance—this does not mean that Mroué turns the apology into something else that has *become* theatricalized. Rather, it exposes the theatricality of apology itself. An apology must *perform* remorse, but if it is to be felicitous, it must also *represent* that remorse. For this reason, an apology must always be a double performance of both the apology itself and a representation of what it means to be apologetic; and as discussed in previous chapters, it is this double life of the "real" and "representation" that is the characteristic feature of the theatrical.

Though now established as a successful artist in international visual arts culture, Mroué's background is as a theater-maker, and he retains an interest in the operations of theater, but in an expanded sense that includes the theatricality of discourse itself:

> My theatrical works no longer require an actual theatrical place . . . Not necessarily actors, stage, or big production and so on . . . I do not care where the performance will take place, or how many performances there will be.
>
> What's important is the talk taking place after the work; the talk that describes the art-work to be an accomplished event; the talk that is here and there at once; the talk that will produce ideas; the talk that becomes the performance itself, and without which it's as if the art-work never took place.[42]

Given the emphasis Mroué places on "talk," it is not surprising that one of the forms that he has repeatedly explored is that of the performance-lecture, or as he calls it, the "non-academic lecture." Typically, the subjects of these lectures are acts or processes of representation, focusing on works of art, political posters, or videotaped messages from would-be martyrs, and folding Mroué's own encounters and experiences into the narration. Mroué's preoccupation with representation is evident in the titles of his works: *Who's Afraid of Representation?* (2005), for example, in which he and co-performer Lina Saneh juxtapose first-person narrations of canonical Western performance art with the true story of a Lebanese civil servant who gunned down his coworkers after being fired from his job; and *The Inhabitants of Images* (2009), in which Mroué imagines the afterlife of the occupants of political posters, as if the juxtapositions portrayed by the montages in the posters might be capable of generating other realities. But these lectures are not only *about* acts of representation but are also performances of appearance themselves; like Handke's *Sprechstücke*, they are frequently self-reflective about their own theatricality. A key motif for Mroué is the idea of *fabrication*, as set out in his statement "The Fabrication of Truth" (2002), which revisits a source for an early performance, a 1985 videotape by a combatant for the National Resistance Front of Lebanon, Jamal El Sati. In this video, which El Sati recorded just before he carried out a suicide action against occupying Israeli forces, El Sati repeats his performance for the camera three times before deciding which one to make public. Mroué is fascinated by this element of repetition:

> [El Sati's] repeated attempts question the possibility of construct-ing an artistic work that aims to be critical about the notion of "truth," a work that claims to convey the "truth" without any editing, even while being itself a "fabricated truth."[43]

Concerned with the way in which truth is fabricated, Mroué's own works are explicitly constructed as fabrications themselves. Indeed, a major retrospective exhibition of his work (as well as the accompanying book) is titled *Fabrications*, a word "that for Rabih Mroué contains strength and spell, the straight line and the curse," writes the book's editor.[44] Crucially, *fabricated* is not the same as *false*, and Mroué is not in pursuit of the "real" truth that might lie behind the fabrication, but instead an idea of truth and meaning as *essentially fabricated* in the relationship we have with and through images and representation.

Mroué's work *The Pixelated Revolution* (2011) exemplifies this interest in fabrication and representation. A "non-academic lecture," as Mroué puts it, the work recounts the phenomenon of videos made on camera phones and other widely available media by protesters in the early phases of the uprising against Bashar al-Assad's government in Syria; these were distributed via YouTube and other forms of social media, and sometimes seemed to show the deaths of these protesters and resistance fighters. As Mroué recalls at the opening of the lecture, "It all started with this sentence that I heard by chance: 'The Syrian protesters are recording their own deaths.'"[45] These amateur videos are a form of resistance to dominant distributions of images in a very literal sense, providing an alternative account of events on the ground; but what Mroué is interested in is the way in which they might present not only an alternative set of subjects for images from the government narrative, but also an alternative sense of what an image might *be* and *do*—what its effects are and how shifting ontologies of the image might shape and reshape reality. While these acts of recording one's own death are a form of testimony and witness, Mroué uses his lecture-performance to explore what the effects of this mediation might be on our understanding of the acts of testifying or witnessing.

At the heart of his lecture is an event he calls "Double Shooting," a one-minute 24-second video available on YouTube, in which an unseen cameraman swiftly scans an adjacent building with his phone's camera, trying to find a hidden sniper who has just fired a shot. Eventually finding the sniper in its lens, the camera records the sniper at the same time as the sniper notices the camera; the sniper lifts his gun and fires at the camera, which falls to the ground. Mroué interprets this assault on the image, as well as the image-maker, as symbolic of a wider war of images being pursued by both the Syrian regime and protesters: "It seems that this is a war against the image itself."[46] But he also suggests that the logic of mediation, by which the screen is a proxy for the eye, means that the cameraman is not dead: "Our eyes are an extension of the cameraman's eyes and . . . his eyes are an extension of his mobile phone's lens. . . . As we are not killed after watching the video, I assume that the cameraman is not killed either."[47]

The basis for this claim is clearly fanciful, but it is not fanciful without purpose. As Maaike Bleeker notes, such a fantastic hypothesis serves to bring into focus something quite relevant about the performativity of images, the way they do not merely describe reality but produce it: "Images are places where truths are fabricated, which come into being in and through them."[48] They are part of the fabric of reality, a "*dispositif* of visibility," to quote Rancière. "What is called an image is an element in a system that creates a certain sense of reality, a certain common sense."[49] Mroué's "fabrications," by making their fabricated nature apparent, give a visibility to the role of more authoritative images as intersections of modes of seeing and knowing. By teasing at various threads with his playful propositions, he begins to unravel some of the ways these systems are interwoven. Again, I would argue that this is not a critique such as one that Debord might make with regard to the apparently false illusion of the image, in search of a "truth" before representation, but instead a play with the fabric of "the real" and the possibility of fabrication itself.

Mroué's post-Debordian position is shared—among other striking parallels—with another artist, Walid Raad. Like Mroué, Raad was born in Lebanon in 1967—Mroué was born in Beirut, Raad in nearby Chbaniyeh—and he too has developed a practice of lecture-performances and documentary art that works with fabricated artifacts and inquiries. Is it a coincidence that, in responding to the unresolved legacy of the Lebanese Civil War, both Mroué and Raad are drawn to this form of the unreliable narrator? Perhaps the impulse is not only an individual interest in the form, but also a response to a particular moment in the relation between art and politics in which there is a structural demand in Western art and theater markets for testimony from the global majority—a phenomenon that might also explain the rise of the "reality theatre" of Rimini Protokoll, Back to Back, and others discussed in previous chapters. Raad himself remarks:

> I was surprised when I was invited to present this lecture/presentation in the performance and alternative theater circuit, but my surprise was due to the fact that I knew very little about experimental theater and performance art. I soon found out that others in the performance and theater circuit—in Lebanon, the US, and Europe—are thinking along similar lines.[50]

As André Lepecki has described, Raad's lecture-performances are a "game of mirrors," adopting the pose of a historian sifting through artifacts while hinting at its own fabrications, and even involving audience "plants" who ask prepared questions during the Q&A, often based on questions that Raad had been asked in previous lectures but needed more time to answer.[51] Lepecki calls particular attention to Raad's accent, which he observes becomes slightly more affected during these performances; as

Lepecki notes, "it points at a theatrics of alterity while at the same time it legitimizes his talk as coming from a place of authenticity and therefore of *truth*."[52]

Raad's lectures describe various documents, such as photographs, objects, and audio recordings, that are attributed to "the Atlas Group," and which have been widely displayed as solo exhibitions or elements of group shows. These archives are similarly legitimated by frameworks of authenticity, calling upon a dense organizational system of cataloging, acknowledgment of origin, and presentation of material. Britta Schmitz writes that this system is "far from arbitrary" but "seeks to deconstruct the obligatory forms of the authentic." The result is that "the dividing line between fact and fiction becomes blurred, actuating and sustaining a fluctuating movement."[53] In his lecture-performances, Raad is actually quite explicit about this invented element, but always in carefully attenuated language that many listeners fail to notice. Here I will use italics to draw attention to this ambiguity in one version, for example, in which he introduces the Atlas Group as "a project that today *I present as* having taken place between 1989 and 2004," though "sometimes *I feel I should say*" that it takes place in other time frames. He describes the activity of the group as having "found *and produced* documents that help us think through the limits about the possibilities and limits of writing the history of contemporary Lebanon," focusing on the wars of the past thirty years.[54]

One element of the archive is a file attributed to Dr. Fadl Fakhouri, who supposedly documented the reported practice among Lebanese historians of gambling on the distance between the winning horse and the finish line in newspaper photographs of horse races. This is presented as "Notebook Volume 72, "Missing Lebanese Wars" (1989), under the Atlas Group category A, for works that are attributed to named sources. When Raad introduces the Fakhouri file in his lecture, his language is similarly delicate, making careful use of the passive voice and self-referentiality: he describes the documents as coming "from this particular . . . [pause] . . . *character*, who *is introduced as* one of the most renowned historians of contemporary Lebanon."[55] This deliberate use of the passive tense both foregrounds and conceals that it is Raad himself who authored this introduction, but in his role as the unnamed curator of the Atlas Group archive, so that one invented character is deployed as a source who legitimates another character.

Even when Raad is explicit about the fictional elements of his undertaking, audiences remain confused about what is real and what is invented. In an interview, Raad says:

> I also always mention in exhibitions and lectures that the Atlas Group documents are ones that I produced and that I attribute to various imaginary individuals. But even this direct statement

fails, in many instances, to make evident for readers or an audience the imaginary nature of the Atlas Group and its documents. This confirms to me the weighty associations with authority and authenticity of certain modes of address (the lecture, the conference) and display (the white walls of a museum or gallery, vinyl text, the picture frame), modes that I choose to lean on and play with at the same time.[56]

Writing in *Artforum*, Lee Smith describes two alternative temptations with regard to understanding Raad's work. The first is to see "the forged institution" as a critique of certain "markers" of authority and authenticity. "The other critical temptation," Smith writes, "is to assert that the work, grounded in the realities of violence, the Middle East, and geopolitics, is an emanation of the really real, where authority and authenticity are taken for granted."[57] Yet, as Smith writes, Raad is clear that his primary intention has nothing to do with manipulating gullibility. He is explicit in his declaration that he is *not* setting out to criticize the ways in which authenticity is constructed in order to reveal to us our own susceptibility to authority, to disabuse us of our illusions. But neither does he identify himself with the second interpretation, in which fiction is necessary because it is somehow a more "true" or "authentic" form of documentation of history. What other positions are there?

Writing about the binary opposition between fact and belief, Bruno Latour has argued that we should not align ourselves with one side or the other; for Latour, both the iconoclast who disabuses others of their false fetishes and the social constructivist who argues that all facts are social fictions are not concerned ultimately with truth or authenticity, but instead with authority and mastery over others. Latour argues that "the role of the intellectual is not, then, to grab a hammer and break beliefs with facts, or to grab a sickle and undercut facts with beliefs . . . , but to be *factishes*—and maybe also a bit facetious—*themselves*."[58] Raad's facetious performative presence and the factish-ous archives of the Atlas Group seem to offer a response to this call. He describes himself as producing a mix of "historical facts" and "aesthetic facts,"[59] and the way in which fictions are enveloped within fictions in a cascading sequence of frames further blurs these distinctions. It is not that the authentic is exposed as artificial, nor that the artificial is elevated to the status of the authentic; instead, Raad constructs a fabrication of such intertwined dependency that the two categories are no longer distinguishable, or even relevant. In this way, Raad is engaged in the production of his own representational system, but is also participating within existing representational systems, and it is not clear where one begins and the other ends. As he declares in the voice of the Atlas Group, "We do not consider 'The Lebanese Civil War' to be a settled chronology of events, dates, personalities, massacres, invasions, but rather we also want to consider it as an abstraction constituted by various discourses, and, more importantly, by various modes of assimilating the data of the world."[60]

I want to describe the performance-lectures of Raad and Mroué as *theatrical*, then, not on the basis of whether or not they feature actors and fictional narratives, but because they critically interrogate their own representational status as a way of intervening in a broader system of representations. In a post-show discussion after a performance of *The Pixelated Revolution* that I attended, Mroué emphasized that his intention is not to supplant the official, authoritative story of things with another, more authentic version: "I assure you that we saw nothing of what it is like in Syria," he tells us. "It's really not the real thing."[61] In a personal interview I had with him the next day, he underscored the importance of having these post-show discussions, which are informal and usually not advertised, but for him are crucial to the work. "You don't learn anything about the Syrian situation from *The Pixelated Revolution*," he emphasizes; instead he is interested in the processes of "association" and "sharing" that arise in the discussion afterward. "They take this story and put it inside their mind. . . . This is what makes it live and interesting, and not 'teaching.' "[62] As with Raad's insistence on making public lectures part of the work of the Atlas Group, a critical dimension of the theatricality of this work is the encounter with the viewing (and listening) spectator. Pablo Martínez writes that the spectator "is not a passive figure for Mroué, but someone who, situated in front of him, accompanies him in his *wanting to see* and *wanting to know more*."[63] It is the constitution of that assemblage of spectators that opens a space for reconfiguring the politics of the image.

In our interview, Mroué told me that what is most important is not the intervention in some other system of power, but what is made possible *here*, in the theatrical event itself. The theater may not have any truth to teach us about the conflict, but what is striking is the way in which Mroué identifies the activity of theater—as an act of imagination, of fabrication—as exactly that which is denied by situations of conflict. Mroué cites Rancière's argument that the political begins with a fair distribution of time: "When you have free time, it's your time: to contemplate, to get bored. Here starts the political," Mroué said to me. But the imposition of emergency laws in Syria or Egypt, he says, "mean you are forbidden to think. Under the pretext that we are in a state of war, they suspended the human culture. They stole the time from their people."[64] Mroué is not sentimental in recognizing that his theater performances will be of no help to the people living under oppression and conflict; but this act of coming together, of holding open the space for everyone to imagine together as equals, is for him a way for us to realize and practice the politics that is denied to the besieged. In this way, the "inhabitants of images" referred to by one of Mroué's titles might be thought of as a fantastical community—"the citizenry of photography," as Ariella Azoulay calls it[65]—a fabricated "we" that includes not only the subjects of the photographs and videos that Mroué describes, but also this temporary community of strangers that forms in relationship to the work.

Christoph Schlingensief: "A Machinery to Disrupt Images"

The final case study here brings together many of the theatricalist strategies that have been described both in this chapter and throughout the book, including the deployment of a structural ambiguity with regard to its authenticity, the blurring of lines between the serious and the not-serious in relation to "the political," and the way in which theatricality can productively complicate assumptions about the category of "we." This example is Christoph Schlingensief's week-long participatory installation *Bitte Liebt Österreich* (2000; *Please Love Austria*), in which theatricality is used as a means to intervene in politically charged debates about national identity. This event is also commonly referred to as *Ausländer Raus*, or "Foreigners Out," after the xenophobic slogan that occupied a prominent position in the installation; this phrase was adopted as the title of an influential documentary about the event by the filmmaker Paul Poet, through which the event has become more widely known. Although it is clear that *Bitte Liebt Österreich* stands in relation to a specific context of "serious" politics—xenophobia and the rights of those seeking asylum, nationalism, electoral politics, and so on—the nature of that relationship is less clear, with interpretations ranging from the way in which it might be a model for promoting debate in the public sphere, to the way in which it shirks the assigned role of the artist in relation to politics. I will argue that its theatrical ambiguity—the uncertainty over whether this is an example of real politics or merely "theatrics"—is *itself* its political intervention, in the way that it stages and challenges the ambivalent relationship between authority and authenticity that has been described so far.

The body of Schlingensief's artistic output included a number of films created mostly in the 1980s and 1990s, actions and public provocations such as *Bitte Liebt Österreich* predominantly in the 1990s and 2000s, and ongoing explorations into theater and opera carried out under the shadow of a diagnosis of lung cancer in 2008, of which Schlingensief died in 2010.[66] Throughout these works, Schlingensief blended the serious and the not-serious in such a way that they are no longer distinguishable. He takes on urgent political and social issues, but in a way that appears to be done in bad taste, with the audiences unable to decide whether he is being overly earnest and obvious or if he is employing parody and mockery in relation to his subjects. Across the body of his work, issues of German identity and the legacy of fascism recur as prominent subjects. His early films included the *Deutschlandtrilogie* (1989–92; *German Trilogy*), of which, for example, the second film (*Kühnen 94, Bring Me the Head of Adolf Hitler*) took its name from a notorious neo-Nazi leader, Michael Kühnen. Schlingensief's actions and provocations originate from a preoccupation with media culture, as in *Freakstars 3000* (aired in 2002), a reality television show modeled on mainstream talent-casting shows, but featuring only people with disabilities; and two early variations on the talk-show format, *Talk 2000* (1997) and *U3000* (2000), the latter of which was filmed on a Berlin underground train and aired on MTV Germany. Although several decades old, these works eerily anticipate twenty-first-century politics, which has seen the return of strongman authoritarianism, xenophobic populism, and overtly White supremacist policies and demonstrations.

The best known of Schlingensief's public actions is *Bitte Liebt Österreich*, not least because Paul Poet's documentary film of the event has been distributed internationally (and with translated subtitles), but Schlingensief's notoriety in Germany had already been established by *Chance 2000* (1998). This project, which had the full title of *Chance 2000—Partei der letzten Chance* (*The Party of the Last Chance*), paralleled the 1998 German national elections by founding a political party that encouraged anyone to become electoral candidates, particularly including the disabled, the mentally ill, and the unemployed.[67] The project's action blurred the lines between theater and politics, beginning with Schlingensief entering the election circus by launching the campaign in a literal circus tent in Berlin's Prater Garden, complete with Schlingensief dressed as a ringmaster and riding a pony. During the opening night of the "Election Campaign Circus," Schlingensief is quoted as declaring: "This night is more political than it seems. . . . It contains theatrical parts, and it contains political parts. Now, the question is where the former begins and the latter ends!"[68] Taking his performance on "tour" to regional theater venues doubled as a means of collecting signatures on the party ledger, with the result that his party managed to gather enough signatures to officially be allowed to run in the federal election. Solveig Gade lists the range of elements that formed the overall project, which ranged from "the circus, the theatre, and the freak show, to television, action art, political rally, learning lab, think tank, and revivalist meeting." The events generated confusion wherever they went, to the extent that journalists were uncertain which section of their newspapers and magazines—art, politics, news?—was appropriate for describing them, and it was true of both *Chance 2000* and Schlingensief's work in general that "the public was never offered a clear answer as to whether the project was intended seriously or was just an arty gag."[69] Gade's description is echoed by Thomas Irmer, one of the editors of the Berlin magazine *Theater der Zeit*, writing for a US audience in *Theater*: "Germany is full of earnest attempts to make theater political again. Christoph Schlingensief is the only person, however, who theatricalizes politics."[70]

However, the notoriety of *Chance 2000* came at a cost, according to the introduction to Schlingensief given in Poet's documentary. For two years after *Chance 2000*, Schlingensief was unable to find any partners for his work, and the documentary suggests that this was because he was perceived as only a prankster and provocateur, not a "serious" artist.[71] The opportunity finally came with the 2000 Vienna Arts Festival, and it was for this event that Schlingensief developed *Bitte Liebt Österreich*. This project brought together several elements that had been developed in his earlier works. Like his television programs, *Bitte Liebt Österreich* adopted and exaggerated the format of popular reality television. In this case, the format was taken from *Big Brother*, one of the early breakout successes of reality TV, in which a number of contestants share a living arrangement, are constantly monitored by numerous cameras, and are gradually voted out by the viewing audience to narrow the pool of contestants to a winner. Similarly, the premise of Schlingensief's action was that twelve people seeking political asylum in Austria were to be housed inside a container in a prominent location outside the Vienna Opera House, with constant video surveillance of their activities being broadcast on the project website. As with *Big Brother*, audiences were encouraged to vote each day for their preference of which of the "contestants" should be evicted, but the implications were more dramatically communicated by the fact that the website button was labeled "deport"; the publicity around the project alleged that at the end of each of the six days of the project, two of the hopeful asylum seekers "will be driven directly to the borderline and deported."[72] The contestant remaining at the end of the week, it was claimed, would receive a cash prize and the option to marry an Austrian citizen in order to gain the right to remain in Austria. In addition to the video surveillance and online option, members of the public were marshaled by Schlingensief and his team into the container complex, where they could peer at the contestants through gaps and barred windows. The container installation itself was festooned with right-wing quotations and fascist references, including, most prominently, a huge banner reading "Ausländer Raus."

This banner and the various right-wing slogans were specific references to the political context in Austria at the time, and Poet's documentary stresses the importance of this context. *Bitte Liebt Österreich* took place in June 2000; in February of that year, following a breakdown in negotiations between the conservative Austrian People's Party (ÖVP) and the center-left opposition Social Democrats (SPÖ), the ÖVP formed a government by entering into coalition with the far-right, anti-foreigner Austrian Freedom Party (FPÖ). The FPÖ was led by the controversial figure Jörg Haider, a demagogue and Nazi apologist, and although Haider himself was not part of the new government, the inclusion of a far-right party in a coalition government was cause for international concern and eventually led to sanctions being imposed by the European Union.[73] In addition to the rise of the FPÖ, the other significant contextual background that Poet's documentary focuses on is the popularity of the right-wing tabloid *Die Kronen Zeitung*—a newspaper with which Schlingensief already had an antagonistic relationship as a result of his previous antics. The mise-en-scène of the *Bitte Liebt Österreich* installation in Vienna deliberately referenced all of these elements: logos from both the FPÖ and *Die Kronen Zeitung* were prominently displayed, Haider's image and quotations were reproduced all over the surfaces of the containers, broadcasts of his speeches were played each morning in the Opera House square, and Schlingensief repeatedly announced to the crowd that the entire event was being "brought to you" by "the FPÖ in association with the *Kronen Zeitung*."[74]

Poet's documentary records the range of reactions to the installation in the square, as well as Schlingensief's own reflections and commentary from artists and critics involved in the project. For Matthias Lilienthal, dramatic director for the project, the experience was one of proximity to celebrity in the form of huge crowds and the overwhelming presence of cameras, which he describes as "an experience I had not had before except by watching television." The evocation of celebrity culture was heightened by having the "asylum seekers" obscure their faces with fashion magazines and disguise themselves with outrageous wigs as they ran a gauntlet of photographers and onlookers to enter the container—and to leave it when they were expelled. At a press conference launching the festival, Luc Bondy, the festival director, addressed the political context to which the work responds; he declared that the festival needs to be a political place, for "when such things happen [like the rise of the FPÖ], you need room to openly think about all these procedures." And the director of the Berliner Volksbühne, the theater that had supported Schlingensief since 1997, recalls that he thought the project would fail: "I thought this would be too obvious, too intended. Everybody would feel preached to, because everybody would know what this whole thing is about."[75]

But everyone did not know what it was about. For many spectators, Schlingensief's intervention did not appear to be addressed *to* the FPÖ, but instead was interpreted as an expression of the FPÖ's views, and the documentary shows members of the public consistently reacting to the event as if it were anti-immigration rather than anti-anti-immigration. Schlingensief's constant presence as ringleader and barker, shouting through a megaphone from the top of the container or leaning casually against a blackboard, deliberately amplified this uncertainty: "Step in, ladies and gentlemen! Get inside the peepshow! Pick and watch your own asylum seeker! It's absolutely free!" Tourists were a frequent target, as Schlingensief asked them to take photos and share them with the rest of the world: "Show them what is happening in good old Austria! Land of the Nazis! Land of the fascists! Here is Nazi central! Here refugee camps burn every night! Here blacks, Africans, all kinds of people are murdered with ease." As this particular scene continued, Schlingensief was approached by an elderly man in slipshod military dress, an Austrian flag draped around his shoulders. Schlingensief continues to casually address tourists through his megaphone: "Tourists are ok. They bring the cash. They won't be prey to homosexual, drug-addicted blacks anymore!" And then the old man starts shouting along with Schlingensief: "We got Austria! Foreigners out!" Schlingensief notices him and starts to form a duet with his outcries:

SCHLINGENSIEF: Away with 'em!
MAN IN UNIFORM: With transportation cars—away!
SCHLINGENSIEF: Away with 'em!
MAN IN UNIFORM: We're going to kill 'em all! Heads off!
SCHLINGENSIEF: Official executions in public! This is the place!
    Every day the execution of 20 to 30 foreigners!
MAN IN UNIFORM: Cut the heads off!
SCHLINGENSIEF: The square of heavenly execution!
The old man unfurls his flag and starts waving it.
SCHLINGENSIEF: The square of divine execution!
Schlingensief gives the megaphone to the man and walks off.
MAN IN UNIFORM *(with megaphone)*: We only need Austrians!
    Nothing else! We got Austria!

Again and again, these kinds of exhortations and misreadings are depicted in the documentary, as Schlingensief and his team create an environment of confusion and chaos, a characteristic mode across all of his work that Anna Teresa Scheer calls "theatrical phantasmagoria."[76] One man shouts, "You are an enemy to Austria and you have to be deported!" Someone who hates the xenophobic messages breaks in at night and tries to set the containers alight. Another attacks the structures with acid. A protester is shown being taken away in a police car after defending the rights of foreigners, and wanting to dismantle the site. "Where are the dirty pigs who authorized this?" he shouts as he is dragged away. Filmed after the event, Schlingensief talks about the protest scene and indirectly refers to André Breton's famous declaration:

The only real surrealist deed possible is to randomly shoot into a crowd. If this is a form of radicalism, it has worked here in the end. You could not hear the shot, but an incredible lot of people were stumbling around heavily wounded. Screaming "ouch." Hollering.

One of the "wounded" at the protest scene is a woman who first appears by declaring that she only wants peace, but is shown becoming more and more irate. She begins addressing the crowd: "Those who already stay here shall remain here, and they shall have equal rights to the Austrians," but then, seemingly unaware of the contradiction in her own xenophobic language, she shouts, "Those *Piefkes* [a derogative term for German people, comparable to *Krauts*] always start these things!" She demands that the container be taken down, "otherwise there is going to be a war between us! We want to have our peace," she shrieks, smashing her hand violently against the placards on the fence surrounding the container. Soon she is marching through the crowd, chanting "Kick out the *Piefkes*! Foreigners in!" As she is removed by security staff, she gets in one last jab: "You German swine! You *artist*!"

Schlingensief himself would not disagree with these labels. It is clear that he conceives of this as an artistic project rather than a political project in any traditional sense, and he uses this distinction to justify a certain amount of irresponsibility. In his description, he echoes and accepts his accuser's label of "swine":

> Amnesty International would have done it differently. This was no AI-thing. This was no project of the kind "show me your wounds"! It wasn't that we wanted to get green cards for all twelve of them. In some aspects this venture was swinish to the highest degree.[77]

Throughout the documentary, Schlingensief is depicted interacting with the crowd in ways that emphasize the artificial nature of the project. This is similar to Raad's subtle acknowledgment of the fabrications in his lecture-performances, but Schlingensief does so with an exuberant and paradoxical assertiveness that is his customary mode of operation. In one scene, for example, he enthusiastically combines paradoxical elements: "So now we will initiate an act that is real. I'm saying it again: this is a performance of the Wiener Festwochen [Vienna Festival Week]. This is an actor! This is the absolute truth!" The reaction of Michael Häupl, Vienna's mayor and a member of the center-left SPÖ, is interesting in this regard. Evidently concerned about misinterpretations of the event, the mayor's office hired a car designed to display advertisements and had it parked in the square near the container. The advertisement message on the car read:

> This is not reality.
> This is a game.
> A dangerous game with emotions.
> Austria is different![78]

On the one hand, this message sets out to inform spectators that this is only an art project, and that it is not "for real." But at the same time, both Häupl and Schlingensief acknowledge that it *is* for real, even at the same time as it is artificial; it is "an act that is real," and the "game" is "dangerous" enough that it warrants an official disclaimer. Likewise, the woman who called for the expulsion of the *Piefkes* seems to acknowledge that this is only an image, since her final insult is to call Schlingensief an artist; and yet she is nonetheless determined to tear down the container. Irmer writes: "Nobody really understood to what extent everything was staged, so the boundaries between aesthetics (the container game) and reality (the German and Austrian political situation) could be explored only by destroying the entire project."[79]

Schlingensief's "container game," which was deliberately ambiguous and conscious of itself as theater, poses a particular challenge to describe in terms of its political efficacy. How does one write about its effects without subsuming its representational play and its deliberate ambiguity to criteria that are based on its "actual" consequences? Some critics point to its innovation in activating public debate; citing Janelle Reinelt, for example, Denise Varney argues that the work "would conceivably fulfil the social function of theatre of being 'a place of democratic struggle' in which spectators 'deliberate on matters of state in an aesthetic mode.' "[80] In a similar argument, quoting a contemporary journalist's description of the event as "a total mobilization of the Austrian public sphere," Tara Forrest presents it as an example of "mobilizing the public sphere" as a "catalyst for public debate":[81]

> By staging the performance outside of what he describes as the "künstlerische Sackgasse" (artistic dead-end) of the classical the-atre, Schlingensief was able to extend the reach of political theatre into the public realm (within which political debate is too often stifled by the agendas of politicians and the conservative press).[82]

Varney and Forrest's accounts can be read as defenses of Schlingensief's controversial actions on the basis that his goal was ultimately aligned with a "responsible" political position. However, for the critical collective BAVO, Schlingensief is an example of exactly the opposite approach. BAVO argues that one of the urgent challenges facing artistic practice is how to escape the bind of a "pragmatic post-politics"; as they describe it, this bind restricts the role of artists to helping to find solutions to problems within existing social orders, so long as they don't challenge the underlying conditions of those social orders.[83] They write:

> On the one hand, art is seen as one of democracy's most essential pillars: it is the space *par excellence* for the free expression of ideas, the experimentation with new models of society. However, when an artist takes this role too seriously and becomes too straightforwardly political, s/he is accused of demagogy or simply discarded as bad art.[84]

As they put it, artists are typically restricted to an ameliorative role, providing "direct, concrete, artistic interventions that help disadvantaged populations and communities to deal with the problems they are facing"; they characterize this position as "NGO art" or "Art without Borders."[85] However, BAVO is critical of such practices because they only serve to sustain neoliberal structures of inequality and oppression by making them more tolerable. In contrast to this approach, which they call "making the best of a bad situation," they advocate the opposite approach: "No longer trying to make the best of the current order, but precisely to *make the worst* of it, to turn it into the worst possible version of itself."[86] Borrowing a concept from Slavoj Žižek, they call this approach "over-identification": rather than resisting or disputing the goals and values of capitalism or neoliberalism, this approach involves taking them at face value. BAVO describes Schlingensief's *Bitte Liebt Österreich* as characterized by what they call a "deliberate structural ambiguity": "Schlingensief creates situations that not only are not clear, but also *cannot* be made clear."[87]

In a television debate from 2000, Schlingensief articulated his own tactic of "over-identification" with the racist positions of FPÖ leader Jörg Haider: "We produce images that simply take Haider and his slogans at their word. . . . I take Haider's lines and I simply say: 'I'm playing out Haider.' That was the basic idea of this container."[88] In the lines quoted above—"Amnesty International would have done it differently"— Schlingensief distances himself from the activities of NGOs, and NGO art, and in Poet's documentary, Schlingensief is frequently dismissive of left-wing campaigners. With regard to the relationship between art and politics, one of the most telling moments came on the penultimate day, when a large group of left-wing activists assembled with banners, whistles, and chants, and eventually stormed the installation in an attempt to "free" the "asylum seekers." The documentary depicts this as the moment of greatest actual danger, as the protesters climbed onto a structure that was not designed to support so many people. Matthias Lilienthal recalls the way the situation was defused by selecting a delegation of six protesters to bring their message to the "asylum seekers": "We want to liberate you! We want to bring you freedom! We are from the anti-fascistic front!" they shout. Schlingensief's team appears to assent to the release of the "asylum seekers," and even though this is shown to amount to little more than bundling them into the same black Mercedes as was used to take previous "losers" to be "deported," one of the protesters is shown happy and smiling, declaring that "Now they will all be freed."

Earlier in the documentary, Schlingensief is shown announcing through his megaphone: "This is film! This is film! We produce the images that Austria definitely does not need!" In the contest over images, the protesters' efforts can be seen as an attempt to efface the images they "do not need," and to replace them with an image of liberation—protesters climbing fences, delivering manifestos, meeting with the "authorities" (in this case, Schlingensief's team). However, for Schlingensief, they fail to understand that the whole operation is working under the logic of the image, within which they are themselves inevitably co-participants, and they are only liberating the representations of refugees. Schlingensief comments:

> Sure it's easy to misinterpret the whole thing, but I have not the least [bit] of understanding for the whole bunch of peace activists and those charmingly sweet resistance fighters. I just don't get their way. When I am bugged by something, when something just doesn't seem right, I need to disturb the picture [Bild], presented as the wholesome and right one. The whole container thing was a machinery to disrupt images![89]

From Schlingensief's own comments, it is apparent that the intervention he wants to make is one that is primarily within the domain of representation—as he puts it, to build a machine to "disrupt images"—rather than within the realm of "real" politics—although the two are clearly related, as I have argued throughout this book.

Some of the participants seem to become aware that they are operating within a representational apparatus. Poet's documentary depicts the scene inside the camp offices as the protesters who forced the "release" of the "asylum seekers" try to come to terms with what is actually happening; in the aftermath, one of the participants in the event comments to the others and to the camera, "They have become a part of the play without recognizing it." Another scene in the documentary reproduces a television spot featuring a heated debate between Schlingensief, a representative of the far-right FPÖ, and a representative of the ÖVP (the mainstream conservative party that invited the FPÖ to form a coalition government). As Schlingensief whips the conversation into a frenzy—a conversation that, appropriately enough, is about provocation—Helmut Salcher, the ÖVP representative, says, "You just do your play! I won't step into that trap. I won't be acting in your play."[90] Having this television broadcast reproduced in Poet's documentary makes it obvious that, of course, he is already acting in Schlingensief's play—not just because he is included in the documentary, but because his engagement with the project, as with that of the irate members of the public in the Viennese square, is the project. Furthermore, Schlingensief's methods of appropriation and over-identification mean that it is not a matter of "politicizing theater" but of "theatricalizing politics" (as Irmer puts it in his review, quoted above): the theater of Bitte Liebt Österreich is constituted out of the rhetoric, figures, and positions of the Austrian political and media scene, and its theatricality is the theatricality that is already latent within these positions. Salcher must always appear as the representative of conservative politics, just as the protesters must always appear as the representatives of resistance (*Wider-stand*, or "resistance," is the word they graffiti over the "Ausländer Raus" banner). What appears, what becomes visible, as "political activity" might be understood as the playing out of what is possible within a distribution of representative positions. Schlingensief's work makes that distribution itself visible.

And so there is a politics to this theatricality. In BAVO's argument, one approach to politicized art is to refuse to fit within the assigned role of the artist. Schlingensief's critique offers no solution, and so avoids the ideological trap described by BAVO whereby the existing circumstances are automatically presumed (and therefore reinforced) as the starting place for any improvement. But I would also argue for the politics of the form taken by this work: the way that it both participates in and compli-cates assumptions about public space, that supposedly universal backdrop within which politics takes place. For one week only, and at the hotspot of a pan-European debate about immigration and national identity, *Bitte Liebt Österreich* produced a representation of the public sphere, not with the goal of restoring a lost sense of community, but in order to explore the workings of representationality itself: to build, as Schlingensief put it above, "a machinery to disrupt images." And above all, one might say that the image that Schlingensief most spectacularly disrupts is that of the public sphere itself. I would argue that what *Bitte Liebt Österreich* gener-ates is not a mobilization of the public sphere, or an intervention *in* public space—which would imply that it is circumscribed by that public space—but instead a critical dismantling of the very idea of the public sphere and the contradictions of so-called public space.

In addressing *Bitte Liebt Österreich*, Kirsten Weiss summarizes the particular difficulties German artists confront with regard to contribut-ing to an idea of a "public": "Although the problem of defining the public is not limited to Germany, Germans cannot help but be paranoid about the combined concepts of national identity and public art," she writes.[91] Although there is a strong lineage of German artists who have thematized public involvement (Joseph Beuys, Hans Haacke, etc.), Weiss writes that these explorations are characterized by circumspection around the idea of the public and the processes of representation. For these reasons, Weiss's discussion of Schlingensief's work is very careful in the language it uses to describe these works, always referring to them as images, simulations, or representations. For example, she contextualizes his work in relation to "the possibility of staging *images* of a *representative* public," and she describes what he does as "facilitat[ing] a *reenacting* of a *simulation* of public sphere."[92] I've added emphasis to Weiss's descriptions because I think this language helps get to one of the most interesting—and most theatrical—aspects of Schlingensief's intervention. Rather than emphasiz-ing the way that Schlingensief's work generates a "live moment of public debate" (Varney) or "mobilizes the public sphere" (Forrest), Weiss's language suggests that, at a more basic level, *Bitte Liebt Österreich* can be understood as a skeptical scrutiny of the notion of "public" itself.

Bitte Liebt Österreich does not just produce representations of asylum seekers (in the form of the contestants) and right-wing politics (in the form of the "Ausländer Raus" banner), which are then introduced into the public sphere for consideration. Instead, it invites us to understand the public sphere itself as a representational system, with each element playing its part. Indeed, if we accept BAVO's characterization of Schlingensief's approach as "over-identification," then the implication is that whatever simulative, representational, and theatrical qualities he highlights are *already there* in the culture. In this way, it is not so much that the politicians, protesters, and general public are playing a part in Schlingensief's "container game" (even as they protest that they won't "step into that trap"), but rather that Schlingensief is using the spectacle of the container to play his own part in a larger representational apparatus, amplifying and making tangible the theatrical quality of supposedly "real" politics. If it is a "simulation," as Weiss puts it, then the relationship I am suggesting between the artwork and politics is not one in which the artwork simulates politics—such that the political effects might be located outside the artwork, in the events that it refers to or in public reactions to the simulation—but that in its simulated-ness it is *already* political.

There is a long tradition of Austro-German unease about the deployment of the idea of "community" as an aesthetic object: as Walter Benjamin famously diagnosed in 1935, one of fascism's innovations—indeed, perhaps its defining innovation—was the aestheticization of politics: "The logical result of Fascism is the introduction of aesthetics into political life."[93] Philippe Lacoue-Labarthe has written more specifically about the mythic power of community in the formation of Nazism, which he describes as "national aestheticism."[94] For Lacoue-Labarthe, Nazism was characterized by a mythical belief in the authenticity of a particular race of people, and, as such, was dependent on a mythical belief in authenticity itself:

> The myth (of the race) is the myth of myths, or the myth of the formative power of myths. It is the myth of "mythopoiesis" itself, of which the type, by the very logic of aesthetico-political immanentism, is both productive and produced by fiction.[95]

As with Derrida's reading of the "fabulous" authority of the US Declaration of Independence, here authority and authenticity are bound together: it is the myth of an authentic community that authorizes the Nazi program, and it is the authority of myth itself that underwrites the authenticity of that racially defined community. Drawing on Lacoue-Labarthe's arguments, Michael Hirsch seeks to locate an alternative role for aesthetic activity in relation to this dynamic. If the fascistic aestheticization of politics has as its aim "the fiction of a community, of a common essence or identity of the people," then Hirsch writes that the challenge for politicized art is not to make such a fiction into reality, but instead to affirm a community that is fictional, "neither integrated by natural common identities nor by common beliefs or opinions." Instead, following Jean-Luc Nancy, the "bonds of this community" are "not the representation of a real, but the real of representation."[96]

The idea of theater as a model of a unified community has been rebuffed a few times in this book: in Nancy's critique of "immanentism" in the previous chapter, and in Rancière's rejection of the idea that "theatre remains the only place of direct confrontation of the audience with itself as a collective" (discussed in chapter 1). In this chapter, I have argued that *both* forms of community, the (supposedly) authentic and the representational, are underwritten by fiction. The authentic community has a "fabulous" origin, one that the ongoing force of authority seeks to cover over, but one that continually reveals its dependence on identification. "Imagine if this had happened to you," Kevin Rudd asks, and by acceding to that collective sympathy, the myth of "a new beginning for Australia" is reinforced. Rabih Mroué's apology is not fundamentally different from Rudd's apology, I have argued, any more than Schlingensief's rhetoric is fundamentally different from that of *Big Brother* or Jörg Haider—but these "hyper-authentic" versions invite us to understand what is happening when Rudd or Haider speaks.[97] As in Tracy Davis's prescription for theatricality, these works set up the possibility for a "sympathetic breach," a failure of identification, a persistence of the ambiguous. Once again, the theatrical does not offer a return to the authentic community but instead makes a problem of that community, and interventions such as Schlingensief's operate precisely, as he himself announced, by making it impossible to tell where the political parts end and the theatrical parts begin.

If the works that I have considered reveal ambiguities in the social and political structures to which they refer, I have argued that this is not in the service of an argument that an unambiguous, "real" politics could be located somewhere else. My argument about the "fable" of Australia in Rudd's speech is not a suggestion that this fable is powerless, or that its power derives from our not knowing that it is a fable; it is no less powerful as a fable than as a fact. Likewise, the fabrications of Rabih Mroué and Walid Raad's documents might alert us to the artifice at work in apparently official history, but, as I argued, the point is not that these fabrications are more "real" than other kinds of facts; nor do they intend to discredit other forms of factual documentation by revealing the extent to which they are artificially constructed—that is, to disillusion us of our belief in facts. In their own ways, the artists I have discussed here are interested in the exploration of representationality, and move us away from an unhelpful dichotomy between the real and the representational. Instead, the representational politics in the work of these artists is not standing in the place of a "real" politics taking place outside the theater, or that might be provoked by the works. Representation is a political end in itself.

CODA: ACKNOWLEDGMENT(S)

One more beginning. An actor enters a darkened room, kicks off one shoe, and lies down awkwardly on the floor. She lays out her supplies: dishes of various powders, syringes filled with red and brown creams, an assortment of latex appendages wrapped up in cling-film. Methodically, over the course of an hour, she applies these materials to her supine body to create the semblance of various injuries. A long, ugly gash on her leg. A wound to her stomach, with blood pooling beneath her. Clothes cut with scissors to give the impression of being torn. A bullet wound to the head. And sprinkled over the whole image, a light dusting of ash and soil. The finished image is striking in its verisimilitude, and its painstaking (though painless) attention to detail is complemented by two other elements of the performance: a projected film (by Annik Leroy) in which photographs of war atrocities are casually handled and examined, and a voice-over (by Virginie Thirion) in which the narrator gives an exhaustively detailed and yet dispassionate description of a single snapshot of a scene of violence. The work is *Regarding*, performed by Isabelle Dumont, for which I was a spectator at the 2008 Kunstenfestivaldesarts in Brussels. There are no surprises in this performance, no suggestion that anything more is being done than that an image is being reproduced, and no appeal for the spectator to do anything other than simply regard it, as its title suggests.

And yet, as I have argued in this book, regarding is *not* simple. I am absorbed by the matter-of-fact task of the application of makeup and prosthesis, captivated by the dexterity and ingenuity of the performer as the various elements come together. I never believe that these are real wounds, of course, but *believability* nevertheless arises as an issue: is that too much blood for a wound such as this? What would cause this? What are the mechanics of what happens to a body when it is violated? And in the midst of this critical thought, something else, something corporeal: an unexpected turn in my stomach that suddenly punctuates the steady accumulation of detail. It's hard to pinpoint what causes this reaction: maybe it's the pus oozing from the actor's abdominal wound, even though I just saw it being applied as a fabricated substance taken from a jar, or the efficient cruelty of the bullet to the temple, even though this is only the representation of cruelty.

Regarding takes its title from Susan Sontag's book-length essay, *Regarding the Pain of Others* (2003). In this, the final book she would publish in her lifetime, Sontag's central concern is the ethical or political value, if there is any, that arises from the particularly modern phenomenon of being able to view scenes of violence and suffering that are presently taking place somewhere else in the world. Sontag worries about two alternative responses to this proliferation of images. On the one hand, she is concerned about the extent to which we might become numb to these images, anesthetized against any response. In an implicit critique of Guy Debord, she argues against an aesthetic perspective that cynically accepts the diminishing effectiveness of the image in a society saturated with spectacle. She writes that the effect of this proliferation is not that image has replaced reality, but rather that it is "the sense of reality that is eroded."[1] She rejects the kind of resignation inherent in the idea of a "society of the spectacle" as a position only possible from the perspective of privilege:

> To speak of reality becoming a spectacle is a breath-taking provincialism. It universalizes the viewing habits of a small, educated population living in the rich part of the world, where news has been converted into entertainment. . . . It suggests, perversely, unseriously, that there is no real suffering in the world.[2]

In this way, she argues that criticisms of the alienating effects of spectacle may actually perpetuate that distancing effect, by reinforcing a claim to be outside the effects: "Critics of modernity, consumers of violence as spectacle, adepts of proximity without risk, are schooled to be cynical about the possibility of sincerity. *Some people will do anything to keep themselves from being moved*."[3]

But Sontag is equally concerned about the opposite reaction, in which rather than distancing oneself, the viewer overly identifies with the reality of the suffering being represented. Here the problem is not with those who avoid being moved, but instead the very way in which being moved—and having an emotional or sympathetic reaction—can be yet another way of avoiding the implications of the image. Imagining that our sympathy makes a connection between ourselves and the sufferer is "one more mystification of our real relations to power," she writes. "So far as we feel sympathy, we feel we are not accomplices to what caused the suffering. Our sympathy proclaims our innocence as well as our impotence."[4] This tension runs throughout the book, making it difficult to discern if Sontag believes there could ever be an appropriate response to representations of suffering and violence that is anything other than direct action against the causes of violence. If no other response is adequate, then the question remains: What is the value of perpetuating representations of bodies under duress, and what is the value of looking at such representations?

Sontag argues that part of the difficulty of having an appropriate response to images of suffering is that there is not an appropriate *place* for viewing such images. As possible locations, Sontag dismisses galleries, with their taint of exploitation; magazines, with their awkward juxtaposition with advertisements; and even apparently dignified museums, which are always part of larger economies of leisure: "A social situation, riddled with distractions, in the course of which art is seen and commented on."[5] And yet, if the threat of distraction or lack of appropriate seriousness seems to be the problem, then the example with which she concludes her book, and which she suggests might be a more productive approach to the representation of violence, is somewhat surprising, for it is playful at the same time as it is horrific, acknowledging its own representationality at the same time as it reproduces death in graphic detail. The work Sontag describes is Jeff Wall's *Dead Troops Talk (A Vision after an Ambush of a Red Army Patrol near Moqor, Afghanistan, Winter 1986)* (1992), a large photographic mural that depicts thirteen dead or dying Russian soldiers in a jagged landscape, in which the soldiers appear to be still actively conversing and joking with each other, despite some of them having severed limbs or missing large sections of their skulls. As Sontag notes, the image was entirely staged; Wall never visited Afghanistan, and the image was produced in his studio by the painstaking compositing of carefully produced images. It's an unexpected example with which to conclude, as its staged-ness and aesthetic indulgence might seem to be even further away from the serious response that Sontag is looking for. And yet, it is these artificial—I would say theatrical—elements that might be exactly the most relevant ones. Sontag writes, "These dead are supremely uninterested in the living: in those who took their lives, in witnesses—and in us."[6] Nothing is asked of us by these figures, who, anyway, aren't even real—and perhaps Sontag is suggesting that the image's ethical value arises from this *absence* of an appeal to us. To recall the distinction I discussed in chapter 1, we are spectators, not witnesses, to a representation that evokes the real, while making no claim to be the real—indeed, while making no claim of any kind. If *Regarding the Pain of Others* is about the appropriate response to representations of suffering, then this example suggests that one such response is the one embedded in the double meaning of Sontag's title: to do nothing more than regard, but to understand that *regarding*—in this case, regarding the pain of others—is an ethically implicated action.

The problem with the kinds of situations for encountering representations of suffering that Sontag dismisses—galleries, museums, magazines, books—is that we are distracted by other kinds of activity, including our own feelings. She does not consider the theater as a site, and no doubt the same risks are inherent in being a theatrical audience. Nevertheless, given her remarks about the value of separation from the scene, there is something about the particularly passive role of theater spectatorship that is helpful here. To return to Dumont's carefully fabricated representation of atrocity at the Kunstenfestivaldesarts, it could be understood to function like a version of Jeff Wall's photographic montage enacted in real time. Performed in a theater, before a live audience, it amplifies what I described in chapter 1 as "the situation of the spectacle." My spectatorship is necessary for the action to unfold, since it is a presentation of the image to a collected body of what suffering looks like, rather than an attempt by the artist to feel that suffering; but my role as spectator is defined by my inability to intervene. Critically, I am unable to interrupt the violence being represented, because what is happening here is not real, and to intervene would change nothing of the real suffering that is happening elsewhere. My only possible response to it is to *regard* the act of representation.

In thinking about this particular form of inaction, I am reminded of philosopher Stanley Cavell's writing on the uses of tragedy in "The Avoidance of Love." Cavell's essay is primarily a reading of Shakespeare's *King Lear*—but writing in 1966 and 1967, it is also (like Yvonne Rainer's writings on *Trio A* discussed in chapter 1) an attempt to think through the situation of being a bystander to the war in Vietnam. Cavell identifies issues that are similar to Sontag's: he is concerned with the ways in which we avoid our responsibilities, a theme that he pursues through his reading of the characters' acts of avoidance in *King Lear*; and also the ways in which in our real lives we theatricalize others by turning them into characters in our own narratives (of guilt, shame, our own helplessness to do anything, etc.). But the theater, as paradoxical as it may seem, is where we might be free of this theatricalization of others, because, as an audience, our own inaction is already accounted for. Elsewhere in the essay, he illustrates this with the example of someone unfamiliar with the conventions of the theater who might try to save Desdemona in a production of *Othello*, which is clearly not possible. Cavell is quite careful in how he describes this inaction: "I know the true point of my helplessness only if I have acknowledged totally the fact and the true cause of their suffering. Otherwise I am not emptied of help, but withholding of it."[7] And within the dramatic world of *Lear*, according to Cavell, the "tragedy" stems from a refusal of acknowledgment based on a reluctance of the characters to reveal themselves, to allow themselves to be recognized by others and to acknowledge their relations.

The word "acknowledge" has a special significance for Cavell, which he expands in "Knowing and Acknowledging" (1969). In this essay, he takes issue with the position of those he describes as "skeptics" who contest the grounds on which we might make a claim to "know" the suffering of another. Such a skeptical position is useful, Cavell agrees, in order to force us to question the basis of our claims and the ways in which we use language. But he argues that to say "I know you are in pain," for example, is not (only) an epistemological claim, but also an action, indeed a performative (though Cavell does not use that term). The action it performs is

acknowledgment, and it comes with consequences in a way that an epistemological claim does not:

> One could say: Acknowledgment goes beyond knowledge. (Goes
> beyond not, so to speak, in the order of knowledge, but in its
> requirement that I *do* something or reveal something on the basis
> of that knowledge.)[8]

The many tragedies within the dramatic world of *Lear*, according to Cavell
in his other essay, stem from the refusal of the characters to reveal themselves, to allow themselves to be recognized by others and to acknowledge
their relations. But for we spectators, what action is possible? To echo
Cordelia's famous words, "Nothing." But our nothing is a different
nothing, because it is one predicated upon a prior agreement, namely, that,
as spectators, we have given over the space of action to others:

> If I do nothing because there is nothing to do, where that means
> that I have given over the time and space in which action is mine
> and consequently that I am in awe before the fact that I cannot
> do and suffer what it is another's to do and suffer, then I con-
> firm the final fact of our separateness. And that is the unity of our
> condition.[9]

Spectatorship is not an empty passivity. Our role may be "only watching,"
as in *merely* watching, but it is also *only* watching, as in giving our full
attention—our regard—to what is happening, and in doing so, to give over
time and space to others, and to acknowledge the claim they make on us:
"It is not enough that I *know* (am certain) that you suffer—I must do or
reveal something (whatever can be done). In a word, I must *acknowledge*
it, otherwise I do not know what '(you or his) being in pain' means."[10]
Theater is a strange case: in Dumont's *Regarding*, I know the performer is
not suffering, but this does not prevent the work from making a claim on
me. Perhaps we might say this: theater is a place where we can rehearse
acknowledgment, when all there is to do is to silently acknowledge that
what is happening is happening, to regard the suffering, speaking, acting,
and appearing of others.

　　From these rehearsals of acknowledgment, let us return to the opening
of the Australian Parliament in 2008, discussed in chapter 4, which was
marked not only by the prime minister's meticulously staged apology on
February 13, but also, on the prior day, by the introduction of another
political fabrication. On February 12, the 42nd federal Parliament officially began, for the first time in its history, with a "Welcome to Country"
ceremony, led by the Ngambri-Ngunnawal elder Matilda House-Williams.
The idea of "Country" invoked by the "Welcome to Country" has specific

resonances in the context of Aboriginal and Torres Strait Islander cultures, referring to both the physical landscape as well as a sense of belonging and a way of relating to living creatures, stories, ancestors, and the connections between them. "Country in Aboriginal English is not only a common noun but also a proper noun," observes Deborah Bird Rose.

> People talk about country in the same way that they would talk about a person: they speak to country, sing to country, visit country, worry about country, feel sorry for country, and long for country. People say that country knows, hears, smells, takes notice, takes care, is sorry or happy. Country is not a generalised or undifferentiated type of place, such as one might indicate with terms like "spending a day in the country" or "going up the country." Rather, country is a living entity with a yesterday, today and tomorrow, with a consciousness, and a will toward life.[11]

The Welcome to Country ceremony, as performed at the opening of Parliament, is based on traditional Aboriginal and Torres Strait Islander practices of welcoming visitors from other Aboriginal or Islander nations, and has a few one-off antecedents in the late twentieth century, but is primarily a twenty-first-century invention in the form of a standardized protocol in which an Aboriginal or Torres Strait Islander elder of the land on which a gathering is taking place performs a welcome and history for audiences that are typically (although not always) composed of a non-Indigenous majority. It is, in the sense developed in chapter 4, a recent *fabrication*, and it has been received in a range of ways: as a significant political achievement, as an unwelcome imposition of "sorry culture" onto White Australians, or as an empty ritual or symbolic gesture—that is, as "only theater."

Charting the origins of this contemporary practice, Mark McKenna notes that the mainstream propagation of the Welcome to Country ceremony—as well as the related practice of Acknowledgement of Country (performed by a non-Indigenous speaker, about which I will say more below)—was largely due to the sustained campaigning efforts of the not-for-profit Reconciliation Australia and the Council for Aboriginal Reconciliation. The latter's National Strategy to Sustain the Reconciliation Process (1998) called for state and federal governments to "acknowledge the existence and/or presence of Aboriginal and Torres Strait Islander Elders at official events and ceremonies" and to "incorporate Indigenous ceremony into official events and ceremonies," including at new sessions of Parliament, as well as for "public officials, private executives, community leaders and individuals [to] take responsibility to include 'Acknowledgment of Country' in public speeches or public meetings where appropriate."[12] As McKenna notes, by 2006 key federal departments, major corporations,

universities, charities, and professional organizations had made a commitment to include these protocols.[13] The opening of the federal Parliament
with such a ceremony in 2008 was a significant milestone, followed in
2010 by the incorporation of the performance of an Acknowledgement
of Country in the official protocols of the Australian Senate, immediately
following the recitation of the Lord's Prayer:

> The President, on taking the chair each day, shall read the follow-
> ing prayer:
> Almighty God, we humbly beseech Thee to vouchsafe Thy
> special blessing upon this Parliament, and that Thou wouldst be
> pleased to direct and prosper the work of Thy servants to the
> advancement of Thy glory, and to the true welfare of the people
> of Australia.
> Our Father, which art in Heaven, Hallowed be Thy name. Thy
> kingdom come. Thy will be done in earth, as it is in Heaven. Give
> us this day our daily bread. And forgive us our trespasses, as we
> forgive them that trespass against us. And lead us not into tempta-
> tion; but deliver us from evil: For thine is the kingdom, and the
> power, and the glory, for ever and ever. Amen.
> The President shall then make an acknowledgement of country
> in the following terms:
> I acknowledge the Ngunnawal and Ngambri peoples who are
> the traditional custodians of the Canberra area and pay respect to
> the elders, past and present, of all Australia's Indigenous peoples.[14]

Although these rituals of acknowledgment have been subject to much
critique, which I will discuss below, it is worth dwelling on this juxtaposition of two forms of ritual citation: one is so deeply ingrained in European
and European colonial culture that it has normalized compulsory Christianity for elected politicians in Anglophone democracies; and the other,
even as it voices the names of peoples and languages that precede European culture by at least 70,000 years, is a relatively recent formulation,
becoming part of the fabric of Australian politics in just a decade of advo-
cacy by campaigners for Aboriginal recognition. As Emma Kowal writes,
"the WTC [Welcome to Country] and Acknowledgement rituals, along
with Kevin Rudd's apology to the Stolen Generations, may be the [recon-
ciliation] movement's greatest success story."[15]

In the decade following these parliamentary acknowledgments, the
standardization of these protocols as part of public gatherings has become
more pronounced. Elaborate Welcome to Country ceremonies are typically included at the launch of a festival or some other large-scale event:
the 2020 Biennale of Sydney, which was specifically organized around
work by Indigenous and First Nations artists, featured speeches in various

Indigenous languages, singing, poetry, and dancing. But for smaller events or talks, it is more common to see one of a handful of regular Aboriginal elders who are employed to welcome guests at the beginning of the event, and who typically leave once the event gets underway—rarely do they participate, whether through lack of invitation or lack of interest in the structure or content of the event. For smaller events where there is not a Welcome to Country, such as a staff meeting, a public talk, or the beginning of a university course, most organizations have developed a pro forma Acknowledgement of Country text which the non-Indigenous organizer may choose to read; often this is quite visibly the act of *reading* set words from a paper, in contrast, for example, to the remainder of the introduction, where the speaker will be more personal and specific with regard to the content of the event. These Acknowledgements of Country have a more or less standardized format, similar to the one used by the Australian Senate; while I worked in Australia, for example, this was the suggested text at my university's main campus:

> I would like to acknowledge the Bedegal people that are the Traditional Custodians of this land. I would also like to pay my respects to the Elders both past and present and extend that respect to other Aboriginal and Torres Strait Islanders who are present here today.[16]

Given this prevalence of prescriptive texts, and the newness of the protocols, it is not surprising that such ceremonies are frequently accused of tokenism. Right-wing figures resent being forced to speak them or hear them, and describe them as meaningless. For example, the counter-revisionist historian Keith Windschuttle—who has argued that the history of violence against Aboriginal peoples has been largely fabricated, and in turn has been roundly rebuffed by historians for his own shoddy scholarship[17]—describes feeling as if these ceremonies have been "foisted" upon persons whom he presumes feel as he does. These practices have been "introduced without any public debate, let alone public support, and [their] authors have never been named or their purposes justified," Windschuttle complains. "Nonetheless, since the passing of the Native Title Act in 1993, it has been foisted on a mystified public as though it had the sanction of deep indigenous tradition."[18] And as opposition leader—before his brief term as prime minister, and still later, his somewhat unbelievable appointment as special envoy on Indigenous affairs—Tony Abbott dismissed such ceremonies as an "empty gesture" and a "genuflection to political correctness."[19]

To speak of "foisting" in the context of settler-Aboriginal relations is hypocritical in the extreme, even if one were to disregard the history of forced displacement, outlawing of first languages, destruction of sacred

sites, and inexcusably disproportionate rates of incarceration of Aboriginal and Torres Strait Islander peoples, and were to focus only on how and
when certain words are compulsory. One might think about the example
of the song "Advance Australia Fair," another fabrication that has the
appearance of "deep tradition," written in 1878 and chosen by popular
plebiscite to replace "God Save the Queen" as the national anthem effective from 1984. Its opening lines, "Australians all let us rejoice, / For we
are young and free"—already refashioned in 1984 from the original "Australia's sons let us rejoice"—have been widely protested by Aboriginal and
Torres Strait Islander peoples. Given the more than 65,000-year history of
Aboriginal culture, what narrative is being "foisted" in the declaration of
"all" Australians as a "we" who are "young"?

In 2015, the soprano Deborah Cheetham—a member of the Stolen
Generations, taken from her mother when she was three weeks old and
raised by a White Baptist family—declined to sing the anthem at one of
the nation's largest sporting events after her request to change the second
line to "in peace and harmony" was refused.[20] Writing about this event,
and about the policing of Aboriginal speech more generally, Chelsea Bond,
Bryan Mukandi, and Shane Coghill write:

> The expectation that Blackfullas in Australia "rejoice" in being
> "young and free" goes further than calling for universal partici-
> pation in a white-washed mythic narrative around the birth of a
> nation. It is tantamount to demanding that Blackfullas be com-
> plicit in, and celebrate, the effacement of those who were here
> prior to 1788. That effacement is foundational to Australia.[21]

Drawing on Derrida's analysis of the political "fable" (discussed in chapter
4), they describe the fable of "Australia" as founded on "the legal fabrication that is *Terra Nullius*"—the materially false claim made by British
colonizers that the land was uninhabited, and no treaty needed to be
made.[22] In 2020, then Prime Minister Scott Morrison made a surprise uni-
lateral decision to change the words "young and free" to "one and free,"[23]
but for many this felt like a hollow gesture, an easy fix from a government that stubbornly ignored calls for treaty and refused to consider a
First Nations Voice for Parliament and a truth-telling process called for by
the 2017 Uluru Statement from the Heart, the result of an unprecedented
consultation and gathering of Aboriginal and Torres Strait Islander representatives.[24] Claire G. Coleman describes this as cowardice and "the most
tokenistic of nods": "When the prime minister could have announced a
new national day that does not insult Indigenous Australians, when a new
national anthem could be written, Morrison's courage extended to only
a single word."[25] All of this points to the ongoing work of fabrication
that is at work in the staging of a nation, including the Lord's Prayer, the

rituals of government, and the national anthem.[26] Welcome to Country and Acknowledgement of Country rituals are no more or less fabrications than these other forms, and so for right-wing critics to label them as fabricated is a flawed critique that reveals more than they intend about the constructed nature of nationhood.

But what about the other accusation, that they are tokenistic? Abbott's reactionary critique of them as "empty gesture" is one that has also been levied from the opposite direction by those who advocate for Indigenous recognition. With regard to Welcome to Country ceremonies, Emma Kowal quotes from personal correspondence with the Indigenous scholar Victor Hart, who describes the structure of the ceremony as "epistemological violence" that mirrors *Terra Nullius* mythology, "where blackfellas can appear at the beginning of the event (i.e., the beginning of history) and then conveniently disappear whilst whitefellas do their serious 'business.'"[27] And Kristina Everett describes these forms of recognition as "token," "a benign if not patronising *inclusion* of Aboriginality in state celebrations and rituals," in which "an *idea* of Aboriginal country can be included in state representations without legal or political consequences."[28]

That is to say, these words and rituals can be compared, as Kowal and others have done, to Sara Ahmed's idea of the "non-performative." In contrast to performatives, which do what they say, Ahmed writes that non-performatives do their work "by *not* bringing about the effects that they name."[29] Crucially, this is not the same as a *failed* performative; instead, the failure to bring about the effect *is* the intended effect, and in fact non-performatives are successful through their very failure: "Such speech acts are taken up *as if* they are performatives (as if they have brought about the effects they name), such that the names come to stand in for the effects," Ahmed writes. "As a result, naming can be a way of not bringing something into effect."[30] Ahmed's examples include diversity or antiracism statements issued by universities and other organizations, which appear to be actions taken, but in fact take the place of meaningful action. These examples are ones that set out to deliberately obfuscate, but Acknowledgement of Country performances can also be non-performative if their primary function is to assert the non-racism of the speaker in what is referred to as "virtue signaling"; Tanja Dreher and Poppy de Souza characterize such a view as one in which "Acknowledging Country does not produce Indigenous sovereignty but rather simply produces good feelings for White anti-racists."[31]

More than just being "empty" theater, then, the theatricality of these ceremonies can actively undermine the aims they were invented to support. Such is the risk. Nevertheless, once they have become a part of the fabric of cultural life, they remain full of potential for alternative actions. For some, they are useful merely as placeholders to mark the action that still needs to be taken. As Stephanie Convery comments, "there is a disconnect between political symbolism and action on Indigenous issues in Australia. The recognition of traditional owners, the welcome to country, is essential if only because it draws attention to this disconnect."[32] For others, they open up possibilities that cannot be closed down again: "Indigenous agency, once acknowledged in performance, cannot be fully directed by the nation state to serve its own ends," writes Kristina Everett.[33] For example, the Welcome to Country can be an opportunity for those who have not been heard to speak to those who have not listened. Dreher and de Souza describe a 2017 Welcome to Country during an Anzac Day memorial service for Australian soldiers, in which the Kaurna elder Katrina Ngaitlyala Power decried the slavery and dispossession of her ancestors—and which reportedly upset attendees who were apparently previously unaware that slavery was part of Australia's history of colonization.[34]

These ceremonies are representations of respect and acknowledgment, potentially (though not always) intervening in the structures of which they are a part and offering a view of a different set of relationships, or what has been excluded from the image of the public of which they are a part. In their very theatricality, they are also potentially (though not always) interventions in the structure of representation. As Dreher and de Souza argue, they perform a reconfiguring of roles, raising questions "around what it means for the settler to be recast as a guest and welcomed by a Sovereign, injured, and dispossessed party; or, in the case of Acknowledgements, what it means to acknowledge one's status as an uninvited guest on unceded Aboriginal land."[35] In the case of Welcomes, the form of the protocols turns the gathered speakers, temporarily at least, into listeners, with the possibility of some critical reflection on their own position as spectators—the *dédoublement* that Tracy Davis writes about (discussed in chapter 1).

And in the case of Acknowledgements, what becomes visible, even if just for a moment, is the stage of the "we," in all its compromises and unequal distributions of power, raising issues of "nation" and "sovereignty." Kowal suggests that these rituals "can most usefully be thought of as a *device to encourage reflection on belonging.*"[36] Rather than simply "appearing" as if from nowhere or on their own authority, the host of the event (literally) names the grounds of their appearance—and even the most basic form of prescribed text may at least introduce unfamiliar languages into the speaker's mouth, invoking different frames and contexts for their appearance. To return to Judith Butler's terms, discussed in chapter 3, these actions return speech to the body that is speaking: "The 'force' of the speech act . . . has everything to do with the status of speech as a bodily act."[37] The speech act of acknowledgment names and locates the speaker—even if, as they might, they exercise their privilege *not* to mean what they say. That is, it may be an infelicitous acknowledgment, and the *speaker* may not be sincere in their acknowledgment of the traditional owners of the land they occupy;

but the *act itself* acknowledges—makes visible and knowable—the status of the speaker and their capacity to either act or not act.

Even when the stage is occupied by people who are only pretending, the stage still appears. The stage in this case is the idea of nation, superimposed onto Country. As the practices of Acknowledgement of Country were criticized as being watered down in 2011, the Worimi elder Bev Manton, then chair of the New South Wales Aboriginal Land Council, responded with this defense:

> It's simply wrong to suggest that recognising the Aboriginal custodians of land in this country is tokenistic or impractical. Some have suggested the gesture does nothing for Aboriginal people, but they're mistaken. By showing a modicum of respect for traditional owners and their ancestors passed, you are doing a great deal to help bridge the gulf between black and white in this country. Using these words at official events may not heal the sick, or boost educational outcomes for Aboriginal kids, but it's not supposed to. It does however show that our elected leaders have an understanding and an admiration for Aboriginal culture and people. *It's symbolism, but it's essential symbolism.*[38]

If the theatrical experiments discussed in this book have been framed as a series of inquiries into the grounds on which appearance is possible, then this "essential symbolism," these small acts of theater that punctuate civic life in this nation of colonizers, raise the question, momentarily at least: What are the grounds on which one appears? Theatricality, as I have argued in this book, is an acknowledgment of the conditions that make action, speech, appearance possible. When we start to see and name the conditions that make action possible, the possibility of different action—that is, politics—appears. It is to that hope that this book has been dedicated.

I finish, then, by acknowledging the conditions that enabled the writing of this book, which began in London, where the beginning of this work was supported by the Arts and Humanities Research Council's Doctoral Awards Scheme, and where I benefited from that city's global positioning as a center of cultural and financial power that imports art and theater from around the world. The selection of work covered in this book was inevitably shaped by the choices made by curators, festivals, and funding bodies, as well as the availability of apparently "cheap" airfare (whose true cost is outsourced) that enabled me to see Rimini Protokoll in Dublin or Rabih Mroué in Athens. And the writing of this book was finished while I was an uninvited guest on unceded Gadigal and Bidjigal country, and I respectfully acknowledge the sovereignty and continuity of law, lore, and culture that will long outlast the memory of these words, the works discussed here, and the university where I worked while writing them.

Chapter 2 is derived in part from "Troublesome Professionals: On the Speculative Reality of Theatrical Labour," published in *Performance Research* 18, no. 2 (2013), edited by Mick Wallis and Joslin McKinney, copyright Taylor & Francis, available online: https://doi.org/10 .1080/13528165.2013.807161. Chapter 3 is derived in part from "Acting, Disabled: Back to Back Theatre and the Politics of Appearance" in *Postdramatic Theatre and the Political: International Perspectives on Contemporary Performance*, edited by Karen Jürs-Munby, Jerome Carroll, and Steve Giles (London: Methuen Drama, an imprint of Bloomsbury Publishing PLC, 2013). Chapter 4 is derived in part from "'We Say Sorry': Apology, the Law, and Theatricality," published in *Law Text Culture* 14 (2010), edited by Marett Leiboff and Sophie Nield; and also from "Christoph Schlingensief and the Bad Spectacle," published in *Performance Research* 16, no. 4 (2011), edited by Laura Cull Ó Maoilearca and Karoline Gritzner, copyright Taylor & Francis, available online: https://doi.org /10.1080/13528165.2011.606047. I first worked with combining ideas from Susan Sontag and Stanley Cavell, discussed here in the coda, in my performance-lecture "Some people will do anything to keep themselves from being moved," which was subsequently published in *Performance Research* 20, no. 5 (2015), coedited by myself and Eirini Kartsaki, copyright Taylor & Francis, available online: https://doi.org/10.1080 /13528165.2015.1095891. The description of Isabelle Dumont's *Regarding* is derived in part from "Playing with the Audience," first published in *RealTime* no. 86 (2008). My thanks to these editors and reviewers for supporting the development of this work; and especially to *RealTime*, the only of these publications to pay its authors for their work.

And I acknowledge the care and companionship of my peers, teachers, allies, collaborators, and co-spectators, those who have taken a chance on me and extended opportunities to me, and those who have offered their support and friendship across the long, long process of writing this book: Alan Read, Alex Tálamo, Amaara Raheem, Anika Marschall, Aoife Monks, Augusto Corrieri, Broderick Chow, Bryoni Trezise, Caroline Wake, CJ Mitchell, Claire Hicks, Clare Grant, Dan Harris, Deborah Kelly, Deborah Pollard, Diana Damian Martin, Doran George, Eirini Kartsaki, Erin Brannigan, Felipe Cervera, Francis Alexander, Gerry Harris, Hannah Ray, Helen Paris, Janine Randerson, Jazmin Llana, Jen Harvie, Jen Mitas, Jo McDonagh, Jo Pollitt, Joe Kelleher, Johanna Linsley, Jonathan Bollen, Julia Barclay-Morton, Julia Bardsley, Julie Vulcan, Julieanna Preston, Karen Christopher, Keith Gallasch, Kélina Gotman, Kim Solga, Konstantina Georgelou, Lara Shalson, Laura Cull Ó Maoilearca, Laura Karreman, Laurie Beth Clark, Leisa Shelton, Leslie Hill, Liesbeth Groot Nibbelink,

Lin Hixson, Lis Austin, Lois Keidan, Lois Weaver, Louise Owen, Lucy Cash, Maaike Bleeker, Mark Jeffery, Mark Mitchell, Martin Hargreaves, Mary Paterson, Matthew Goulish, Maurya Wickstrom, Meg Mumford, Michael Peterson, Mick Douglas, Nic Conibere, Nick Ridout, Patty White, Paul Matthews, Richard Gough, River Chua, Robert Pacitti, Sara Jane Bailes, Sigrid Merx, Sophie Nield, Stacy Holman-Jones, Su Goldfish, Taylan Halici, Tim Etchells, Tru Paraha, Una Bauer, Virginia Baxter, Will Daddario, and Rajni Shah.

For Gregory X (1947–2020).

NOTES

Introduction

1. Young Jean Lee, *The Shipment and LEAR* (New York: Theatre Communications Group, 2010), 11.

2. "So-called" because this is the name given by settlers to a continent of some 250 Aboriginal and Torres Strait Islander nations (see Australian Institute of Aboriginal and Torres Strait Islander Studies, "Map of Indigenous Australia"), with whom no treaty was signed and whose sovereignty was never ceded, and whose recognition via a constitutional Voice to Parliament was rejected by popular referendum in 2023. Without such recognition, it is the view of many, including this author, that the name "Australia" lacks legitimacy. The fabrication of nationhood and recognition of First Nations sovereignty in so-called Australia is discussed further in chapter 4 and the conclusion to this book.

3. Tim Etchells, "Step Off the Stage," in *The Live Art Almanac*, ed. Daniel Brine (London: Live Art Development Agency, 2008), 8–9.

4. Jérôme Bel and Yvane Chapuis, "Jérôme Bel—Interview—*The Show Must Go On* (2001)—Second Part," *Catalogue raisonné Jérôme Bel 1994–2005*, December 15, 2007, https://www.youtube.com/watch?v=9ZX7Hx15k_c. Famously, a disgruntled audience member at a 2002 performance of Jérôme Bel tried to sue the work's presenters, the International Dance Festival, with the claim that the work did not contain "a single step of dance." See Una Bauer, "The Movement of Embodied Thought: The Representational Game of the Stage Zero of Signification in Jérôme Bel," *Performance Research* 13, no. 1 (2008): 35–41, https://doi.org/10.1080/13528160802465508.

5. Claire Bishop, "The Social Turn: Collaboration and Its Discontents," *Artforum* 44, no. 6 (2006): 178–83.

6. Guy Debord, *The Society of the Spectacle* (*La Société du spectacle*, 1967), trans. Donald Nicholson-Smith (New York: Zone Books, 1994), 12.

7. Nicolas Bourriaud, *Relational Aesthetics* (*Esthétique relationnelle*, 1998), trans. Simon Pleasance (Dijon, France: Presses du Reél, 2002), 9.

8. Peter Handke and Artur Joseph, "Nauseated by Language: From an Interview with Peter Handke," trans. E. B. Ashton, *TDR/The Drama Review* 15, no. 1 (1970): 58, https://doi.org/10.2307/1144591.

9. Bourriaud, *Relational Aesthetics*, 83.

10. Claire Bishop, "Antagonism and Relational Aesthetics," *October* no. 110 (2004): 51–79, https://doi.org/10.1162/0162287042379810; Bishop, "The Social Turn."

11. Forced Entertainment, *Showtime* (1996), quoted in Tim Etchells, "A Six-Thousand-and-Forty-Seven-Word Manifesto on Liveness in Three Parts

with Interludes," in *Live: Art and Performance*, ed. Adrian Heathfield (London: Tate, 2004), 214.

12. Beth Hoffmann, review of *Bloody Mess*, by Forced Entertainment, *Theatre Journal* 58, no. 4 (2006): 702.

13. Michael Fried, "Art and Objecthood" (1967), in *Art and Objecthood: Essays and Reviews* (Chicago: University of Chicago Press, 1998), 163–64, 168.

14. Jacques Rancière, "The Emancipated Spectator," *Artforum* 45, no. 7 (2007): 271.

15. Sophie Nield, "The Rise of the Character Named Spectator," *Contemporary Theatre Review* 18, no. 4 (2008): 531–35, https://doi.org/10.1080/10486800802492855.

16. Adam Alston, *Beyond Immersive Theatre: Aesthetics, Politics and Productive Participation* (Basingstoke, UK: Palgrave Macmillan, 2016), 5ff., https://doi.org/10.1057/978-1-137-48044-6.

17. The spatial promises of these modes of immersive experience are discussed, and critiqued, in Gareth White, "On Immersive Theatre," *Theatre Research International* 37, no. 3 (2012): 221–35, https://doi.org/10.1017/S0307883312000880.

18. Bert O. States, "The Phenomenological Attitude" (1992), in *Critical Theory and Performance*, ed. Janelle G. Reinelt and Joseph R. Roach, 2nd ed. (Ann Arbor: University of Michigan Press, 2006), 28.

19. Josette Féral, foreword to "Theatricality," special issue, *SubStance* 31, no. 2/3, (2002): 10, https://doi.org/10.1353/sub.2002.0025.

20. Bel and Chapuis, "Jérôme Bel—Interview—*The Show Must Go On* (2001)—Second Part."

21. Tim Etchells, "More and More Clever Watching More and More Stupid," in *Live: Art and Performance*, ed. Adrian Heathfield (London: Tate, 2004), 198.

22. Etchells, "Step Off the Stage," 11–12.

23. Patricia Ybarra, "Young Jean Lee's Cruel Dramaturgy," *Modern Drama* 57, no. 4 (2014): 515, https://doi.org/10.3138/MD.0675.

24. Bertolt Brecht, "A Short Organum for the Theatre" (1948), in *Brecht on Theatre: The Development of an Aesthetic*, ed. and trans. John Willett (London: Methuen, 1964), 179–205.

25. Florian Malzacher, "No Organum to Follow: Possibilities of Political Theatre Today," in *Not Just a Mirror: Looking for the Political Theatre of Today*, ed. Florian Malzacher (Berlin and London: House on Fire; Alexander Verlag; Live Art Development Agency, 2015), 17.

26. Malzacher, "No Organum to Follow," 19.

27. Tom Sellar, "The City's Best (and Not So Best) Progressive Theater," *Village Voice*, January 5, 2010, https://www.villagevoice.com/2010/01/05/the-citys-best-and-not-so-best-progressive-theater/.

28. Chantal Mouffe, *The Democratic Paradox* (London: Verso, 2000), 20.

29. Judith Butler, *Notes Toward a Performative Theory of Assembly* (Cambridge, MA: Harvard University Press, 2015), 78.

30. Jacques Rancière, *Disagreement: Politics and Philosophy* (*La Mesentente: Politique et philosophie*, 1995), trans. Julie Rose (Minneapolis: University of Minnesota Press, 1999), 29, emphasis added.

31. Jacques Rancière, *The Politics of Aesthetics: The Distribution of the Sensible* (*Le Partage du sensible: Esthétique et politique*, 2000), trans. Gabriel Rockhill (London: Continuum, 2004).

32. Jacques Rancière, "Aesthetics and Politics: Rethinking the Link," presented at the University of California, Berkeley, September 2002, http://16beavergroup.org/mondays/2006/05/06/monday-night-05-08-06-discussion-on-rancieres-politics-of-aesthetics/.

33. Rancière, "Aesthetics and Politics."

34. Jacques Rancière, *Aisthesis: Scenes from the Aesthetic Regime of Art*, trans. Zakir Paul (London: Verso, 2013).

35. Leah Bassel, "Acting 'As' and Acting 'As If': Two Approaches to the Politics of Race and Migration," in *Theories of Race and Ethnicity: Contemporary Debates and Perspectives*, ed. John Solomos and Karim Murji (Cambridge: Cambridge University Press, 2015), 103, https://doi.org/10.1017/CBO9781139015431.009.

36. Ngũgĩ wa Thiong'o, "Enactments of Power," *TDR/The Drama Review* 41, no. 3 (1997): 13.

37. A similar tension between an individualist dissensus and a collective identity politics is briefly articulated in Janelle Reinelt, "'What I Came to Say': Raymond Williams, the Sociology of Culture and the Politics of (Performance) Scholarship," *Theatre Research International* 40, no. 3 (October 2015): 235–49, https://doi.org/10.1017/S0307883315000334.

38. Jane Bennett, *Vibrant Matter: A Political Ecology of Things* (Durham, NC: Duke University Press, 2010), 20–21ff. Similarly, Karen Barad describes agency in relation to "intra-acting": "it is an enactment, not something that someone or something has." Karen Barad, *Meeting the Universe Halfway: Quantum Physics and the Entanglement of Matter and Meaning* (Durham, NC: Duke University Press, 2007), 178.

39. Vinciane Despret, "From Secret Agents to Interagency," *History and Theory* 52, no. 4 (2013): 38, https://doi.org/10.1111/hith.10686. My thanks to Laura Cull Ó Maoilearca for drawing my attention to Despret's work.

40. Jean-Luc Nancy, *Being Singular Plural* (*Être singulier pluriel*, 1996), trans. Robert D. Richardson and Anne E. O'Byrne (Stanford, CA: Stanford University Press, 2000), 66.

41. I am grateful to Sophie Nield for teasing out these distinctions with me in a series of emails in 2012.

42. Aristotle, *Poetics*, trans. S. H. Butcher, http://classics.mit.edu/Aristotle/poetics.1.1.html.

43. Rancière, *Disagreement*, 102.

44. Nicholas Ridout, "Performance and Democracy," in *The Cambridge Companion to Performance Studies*, ed. Tracy C. Davis (Cambridge: Cambridge University Press, 2008), 19.

Chapter 1

1. The published text's opening note states, "*The Author* is set in the Jerwood Theatre Upstairs at the Royal Court Theatre—even when it's performed elsewhere." Tim Crouch, *Plays One: My Arm, An Oak Tree, ENGLAND, The Author* (London: Oberon, 2011), 164.

2. See Aleks Sierz, *In-Yer-Face: British Drama Today* (London: Faber and Faber, 2001).

3. Crouch, *Plays One*, 164.

4. Crouch, *Plays One*, 178–79.

5. Crouch, *Plays One*, 192.

6. Crouch, *Plays One*, 192.

7. Tim Crouch, "The Author: Response and Responsibility," *Contemporary Theatre Review* 21, no. 4 (2011): 416, https://doi.org/10.1080/10486801.2011.610312.

8. James Frieze, "Actualizing a Spectator Like You: The Ethics of the Intrusive-Hypothetical," *Performing Ethos: International Journal of Ethics in Theatre & Performance* 3, no. 1 (2012): 13, https://doi.org/10.1386/peet.3.1.7_1.

9. "We encourage the audience, at regular intervals, to consider whether they still want to be there. We even plant an audience member walking out—to suggest to the audience that they can do likewise." Crouch, "The Author: Response and Responsibility," 416–17.

10. Cristina Delgado-García, "'We're All in This Together': Reality, Vulnerability and Democratic Representation in Tim Crouch's *The Author*," in *Of Precariousness: Vulnerabilities, Responsibilities, Communities in 21st-Century British Drama and Theatre*, ed. Mireia Aragay and Martin Middeke (Berlin: De Gruyter, 2017), 102, 103, https://doi.org/10.1515/9783110548716–007, emphasis in original.

11. Crouch, *Plays One*, 182.

12. This event is hinted at in Rainer's journals, described in Catherine Wood, *Yvonne Rainer: The Mind Is a Muscle* (London: Afterall Books, 2007), 22.

13. Michael J. Arlen, *Living-Room War* (New York: Viking, 1969); Martha Rosler, *House Beautiful: Bringing the War Home, 1967–1972*, http://www.martharosler.net/house-beautiful-bringing-the-war-home-new-series-carousel-1.

14. Yvonne Rainer, "'Statement' from *The Mind Is a Muscle*, Anderson Theater, New York (April 1968)," in *Work 1961–73* (Halifax: Press of the Nova Scotia College of Art and Design, 1974), 70–71.

15. Debord, *Society of the Spectacle*, 22, emphasis in original.

16. Yvonne Rainer, "Some Retrospective Notes on a Dance for 10 People and 12 Mattresses Called 'Parts of Some Sextets' Performed at the Wadsworth Atheneum, Hartford, Connecticut, and Judson Memorial Church, New York, in March 1965," *Tulane Drama Review* 10, no. 2 (1965): 178, https://doi.org/10.2307/1125242.

17. Yvonne Rainer, "*Trio A*: Genealogy, Documentation, Notation," *Dance Research Journal* 41, no. 2 (2009): 13, https://doi.org/10.1017/S0149767700000619.

18. Rainer, "Notebook for *The Mind Is a Muscle*," 7.

19. Rainer, "Some Retrospective Notes," 170, emphasis in original.

20. Chantal Pontbriand, "The Eye Finds No Fixed Point on Which to Rest . . . ," trans. C. R. Parsons, *Modern Drama* 25, no. 1 (1982): 155, https://doi.org/10.3138/md.25.1.154.

21. Guy Debord, "Rapport sur la construction des situations et sur les conditions de l'organisation et de l'action de la tendance situationniste internationale" (1957), *Inter: Art Actuel*, no. 44 (1989): 1–11.

22. Debord, *Society of the Spectacle*, 12.

23. Sadie Plant, *The Most Radical Gesture: The Situationist International in a Postmodern Age* (London: Routledge, 1992), 1.

24. Guy Debord, "Report on the Construction of Situations and on the Terms of Organization and Action of the International Situationist Tendency" (1957), in *Guy Debord and the Situationist International: Texts and Documents*, ed. and trans. Tom McDonough (Cambridge, MA: MIT Press, 2002), 47.

25. Raoul Vaneigem, *The Revolution of Everyday Life* (*Traité de savoir-vivre à l'usage des jeunes générations*, 1967), trans. Donald Nicholson-Smith (Oakland, CA: PM, 2012), 93.

26. For more on the relationship between the Situationist International and experimental performances of the 1950s and 1960s, see Martin Puchner, "Society of the Counter-Spectacle: Debord and the Theatre of the Situationists," *Theatre Research International* 29, no. 1 (2004): 4–15, https://doi.org/10.1017/S0307883303001214.

27. Herbert Blau, "The Metaphysical Fight: Performative Politics and the Virus of Alienation," in *Performance, Identity, and the Neo-Political Subject*, ed. Fintan Walsh and Matthew Causey (London: Routledge, 2013), 28.

28. Michael Kirby, "On Acting and Not-Acting," *TDR/The Drama Review* 16, no. 1 (1972): 3, https://doi.org/10.2307/1144724.

29. Indeed, Kaprow includes Rainer's *Parts of Some Sextets* in his catalog of what he calls "operational art." See Allan Kaprow, "The Education of the Un-Artist, Part III" (1974), in Allan Kaprow, *Essays on the Blurring of Art and Life*, ed. Jeff Kelley, expanded ed. (Berkeley: University of California Press, 2003), 130–47.

30. Rainer, "'Statement' from *The Mind Is a Muscle*."

31. Pat Catterson, "I Promised Myself I Would Never Let It Leave My Body's Memory," *Dance Research Journal* 41, no. 2 (2009): 4, https://doi.org/10.1017/S0149767700000607.

32. Rainer quoted in Irving Sandler, "Gesture and Non-Gesture in Recent Sculpture" (1967), in *Minimal Art: A Critical Anthology*, ed. Gregory Battcock (New York: Dutton, 1968), 310.

33. Yvonne Rainer, *A Woman Who . . . : Essays, Interviews, Scripts* (Baltimore: Johns Hopkins University Press, 1999), 59–60.

34. Yvonne Rainer, Robert Alexander, and Sally Banes, *Trio A*, 1978, http://www.vdb.org/titles/trio.

35. Ramsay Burt, "'Don't Give the Game Away': Rainer's 1967 Reflections on Dance and the Visual Arts Revisited" (presentation at Yvonne Rainer: Intermedial Constellations Symposium, Ludwig Museum, Cologne, 2012), https://www.dora.dmu.ac.uk/xmlui/handle/2086/7344.

36. Carrie Lambert-Beatty, *Being Watched: Yvonne Rainer and the 1960s* (Cambridge, MA: October Books/MIT Press, 2008), 8.

37. Allan Kaprow, "The Happenings Are Dead: Long Live the Happenings!" (1966), in Allan Kaprow, *Essays on the Blurring of Art and Life*, ed. Jeff Kelley, expanded ed. (Berkeley: University of California Press, 2003), 64.

38. Lambert-Beatty, *Being Watched*, 14, emphasis in original.

39. Robert Morris, "Notes on Sculpture" (1966), in *Minimal Art: A Critical Anthology*, ed. Gregory Battcock (New York: Dutton, 1968), 221–35.

40. Yvonne Rainer, "A Quasi Survey of Some 'Minimalist' Tendencies in the Quantitatively Minimal Dance Activity midst the Plethora, or An Analysis of *Trio A*" (1966), in *Minimal Art: A Critical Anthology*, ed. Gregory Battcock (New York: Dutton, 1968), 263.

41. Rainer, "A Quasi Survey," 269, 271.

42. Fried, "Art and Objecthood," 155, emphasis in original.

43. Fried, "Art and Objecthood," 158.

44. Fried, "Art and Objecthood," 158.

45. Fried, "Art and Objecthood," 159, emphasis in original.

46. Fried, "Art and Objecthood," 160, emphasis in original.

47. Fried, "Art and Objecthood," 168.

48. Stephen Melville, "Notes on the Reemergence of Allegory, the Forgetting of Modernism, the Necessity of Rhetoric, and the Conditions of Publicity in Art and Criticism," *October* no. 19 (1981): 75, https://doi.org/10.2307/778660.

49. Michael Fried, *Absorption and Theatricality: Painting and Beholder in the Age of Diderot* (Berkeley: University of California Press, 1980).

50. Maaike Bleeker, "Absorption and Focalization: Performance and Its Double," *Performance Research* 10, no. 1 (January 1, 2005): 53, https://doi.org/10.1080/13528165.2005.10871396.

51. Fried, "Art and Objecthood," 163; Rainer quoted in Lambert-Beatty, *Being Watched*, vii.

52. Maaike Bleeker, "Movement as Lived Abstraction: The Logic of the Cut," in *Performance and Phenomenology: Traditions and Transformations*, ed. Maaike Bleeker, Jon Foley Sherman, and Eirini Nedelkopoulou (London: Routledge, 2015), 40.

53. Carrie Lambert-Beatty writes that Rainer's focus is "the relation between bodies and pictures in a changing culture of mediation." For Elise Archias, "Rainer's performance practice 'worked through' questions of spectacle by resembling the forms and structures of life in spectacle culture." And for Catherine Wood, "rather than proposing an outright rejection [of spectacle], however, Rainer grappled with image culture's inevitable presence, making space to inhabit it on her own terms." Lambert-Beatty, *Being Watched*, 131; Elise Archias, *The Concrete Body: Yvonne Rainer, Carolee Schneemann, Vito Acconci* (New Haven, CT: Yale University Press, 2016), 23; Wood, *The Mind Is a Muscle*, 22.

54. Rainer, "A Quasi Survey," 271.

55. Lambert-Beatty, *Being Watched*, 159.

56. Jens Richard Giersdorf, "*Trio A* Canonical," *Dance Research Journal* 41, no. 2 (2009): 19–24, https://doi.org/10.1017/S0149767700000620.

57. See Catterson, "I Promised Myself"; and Sally Gardner, "What Is a Transmitter?" *Choreographic Practices* 5, no. 2 (2014): 229–40, https://doi.org/10.1386/chor.5.2.229_1.

58. Bojana Kunst, *Artist at Work: Proximity of Art and Capitalism* (Winchester, UK: Zero Books, 2015), 118.

59. Yvonne Rainer, *Feelings Are Facts: A Life* (Cambridge, MA: MIT Press, 2006), 264.

60. Yvonne Rainer in *A Pamphlet for the Serpentine Gallery Manifesto Marathon 2008*, ed. Nicola Lees (London: Serpentine Gallery, 2008).

61. Rainer, "A Quasi Survey," 271.

62. Peter Handke and Artur Joseph, "Nauseated by Language: From an Interview with Peter Handke," trans. E. B. Ashton, *TDR/The Drama Review* 15, no. 1 (1970): 58, https://doi.org/10.2307/1144591.

63. See Jack Halstead, "Peter Handke's *Sprechstücke* and Speech-Act Theory," *Text and Performance Quarterly* 10, no. 3 (1990): 183–84, https://doi.org/10.1080/10462939009365969.

64. Peter Handke, "Peter Handke Bei Gruppe 47 in Princeton 1966" (transcript), ed. Thomas Gollas, September 29, 2014, http://hcolsezrawhcs.blogspot.com.au/2014/09/peter-handke-bei-der-gruppe-47-in.html; for a version in English, see Peter Handke, "Peter Handke's 1966 Speech at the Princeton Meeting of the Gruppe 47," trans. Scott Abbott, June 11, 2013, https://thegoaliesanxiety.wordpress.com/2013/06/11/peter-handkes-1966-speech-at-the-princeton-meeting-of-the-gruppe-47/.

65. Peter Handke, "Brecht, Play, Theatre, Agitation," trans. Nicholas Hern, *Theatre Quarterly* 1, no. 4 (1971): 89.

66. Handke, "Brecht, Play, Theatre, Agitation," 89–90, emphasis in original (in translation).

67. Handke, "Brecht, Play, Theatre, Agitation," 90.

68. Peter Handke, *Offending the Audience* (*Publikumsbeschimpfung*, 1966), trans. Michael Roloff, in *Plays: 1: Offending the Audience, Self-Accusation, Kaspar, My Foot My Tutor, The Ride across Lake Constance, They Are Dying Out* (London: Methuen Drama, 1997), 1–32, 4–6.

69. Bonnie Marranca, "The *Sprechstucke*: Peter Handke's Universe of Words," *PAJ: Performing Arts Journal* 1, no. 2 (1976): 53, https://doi.org/10.2307/3245038.

70. Handke, *Offending the Audience*, 6.

71. Handke, *Offending the Audience*, 16.

72. Handke and Joseph, "Nauseated by Language," 57.

73. Handke and Joseph, "Nauseated by Language," 57.

74. Handke, *Offending the Audience*, 19.

75. Bertolt Brecht, "On Form and Subject-Matter" (1929), in *Brecht on Theatre: The Development of an Aesthetic*, ed. and trans. John Willett (London: Methuen, 1964), 30.

76. David Barnett, *Brecht in Practice: Theatre, Theory and Performance* (London: Bloomsbury, 2015), 32, emphasis in original.

77. Bertolt Brecht, "Theatre for Pleasure or Theatre for Instruction" (1936?), in *Brecht on Theatre: The Development of an Aesthetic*, ed. and trans. John Willett (London: Methuen, 1964), 71.

78. Bertolt Brecht, "Showing Has to Be Shown" (1945), in *Bertolt Brecht Poems 1913—1956*, ed. John Willett, Ralph Manheim, and Erich Fried, trans. John Willett (London: Methuen, 1976), 341–42.

79. Bertolt Brecht, "On the Art of Spectatorship" ("Über die Zuschau-kunst," 1935), in *Brecht on Theatre*, ed. Marc Silberman, Steve Giles, and Tom Kuhn (London: Bloomsbury, 2018), 174.

80. Christine Kiebuzinska, *Intertextual Loops in Modern Drama* (Madison, NJ: Fairleigh Dickinson University Press, 2001), 173.

81. Müller quoted in Carl Weber, "Brecht in Eclipse?" *TDR/The Drama Review* 24, no. 1 (March 1980): 121, https://doi.org/10.2307/1145300.

82. Marranca, "The *Sprechstucke*," 57.

83. David Barnett, "Performing Dialectics in an Age of Uncertainty, or Why Post-Brechtian ≠ Postdramatic," in *Postdramatic Theatre and the Political*, ed. Karen Jürs-Munby, Jerome Carroll, and Steve Giles (London: Bloomsbury, 2013), 48.

84. Barnett describes this as a form of realism: not "the superficial imitation of reality" but "the laws under which the dialectic works, regardless of apparent differences among individuals." David Barnett, "Toward a Definition of Post-Brechtian Performance: The Example of *In the Jungle of the Cities* at the Berliner Ensemble, 1971," *Modern Drama* 54, no. 3 (2011): 334, https://doi.org/10.3138/md.54.3.333.

85. Peter Handke, "Note on Offending the Audience" (1972), in *Plays: 1: Offending the Audience, Self-Accusation, Kaspar, My Foot My Tutor, The Ride across Lake Constance, They Are Dying Out*, trans. Tom Kuhn (London: Methuen Drama, 1997), 309, emphasis added.

86. Handke, *Offending the Audience*, 14–15.

87. Hans-Thies Lehmann, *Postdramatic Theatre* (*Postdramatisch theater*, 1999), ed. and trans. Karen Jürs-Munby (London: Routledge, 2006), 134.

88. Hans-Thies Lehmann, "The Political in the Post-Dramatic," *Maska* 17, no. 74/75 (2002): 76, emphasis in original.

89. Tim Etchells, "On Risk and Investment" (1994), in *Certain Fragments: Contemporary Performance and Forced Entertainment* (London: Routledge, 1999), 49, emphasis added.

90. Bertolt Brecht, "The Street Scene: A Basic Model for an Epic Theatre" (1938), in *Brecht on Theatre: The Development of an Aesthetic*, ed. and trans. John Willett (London: Methuen, 1964), 121–29.

91. For a more thorough analysis of the various uses of the figure of the "witness" in ethical and aesthetic practices, see Caroline Wake, "The Accident and the Account: Towards a Taxonomy of Spectatorial Witness in Theatre and Performance Studies," in *Visions and Revisions: Performance, Memory, Trauma*, ed. Bryoni Trezise and Caroline Wake (Copenhagen: Museum Tuscu-lanum, 2013), 33–56.

92. Lehmann, *Postdramatic Theatre*, 185–86, emphasis in original.

93. Lehmann, *Postdramatic Theatre*, 99–104, 104–7.

94. Forced Entertainment, *Showtime* (1996), quoted in Tim Etchells, "A Six-Thousand-and-Forty-Seven-Word Manifesto on Liveness in Three Parts with Interludes," in *Live: Art and Performance*, ed. Adrian Heathfield (London: Tate, 2004), 214.

95. Handke, *Offending the Audience*, 12.

96. Janelle Reinelt, "Postdramatic Theatre and the Political: International Perspectives on Contemporary Performance (Review)," *Theatre Research*

International 40, no. 2 (2015): 203, https://doi.org/10.1017/S03078833150
00061.

97. Handke, "Brecht, Play, Theatre, Agitation," 90.

98. Alison Flood, "'Ignorant Questions': Nobel Winner Peter Handke
Refuses to Address Controversy," *Guardian*, December 6, 2019, http://www
.theguardian.com/books/2019/dec/06/peter-handke-questions-nobel-prize
-literature-milosevic.

99. Matthew Goulish, *39 Microlectures: In Proximity of Performance* (London: Routledge, 2000), 9–10.

100. Lambert-Beatty, *Being Watched*, vii.

101. Tim Etchells, "On Performance and Technology" (1995), in *Certain
Fragments: Contemporary Performance and Forced Entertainment* (London:
Routledge, 1999), 94.

102. Fabienne Arvers, "Jérôme Bel Par Jérôme Bel," Les Inrocks, January
31, 2001, http://www.lesinrocks.com/2001/01/31/musique/concerts/jerome
-bel-par-jerome-bel-11226045/. Augusto Corrieri builds on this exchange to
argue that for all his supposed radicalism, Bel is actually interested in the
apparatus of the classical theater; see Augusto Corrieri, "Watching People in
the Light: Jérôme Bel and the Classical Theatre," in *Contemporary French
Theatre and Performance*, ed. Clare Finburgh and Carl Lavery (Basingstoke,
UK: Palgrave Macmillan, 2011), 213–23.

103. In his history of the performances of Handke's *Offending the Audience*
(1966), Piet Defraeye gives a dismissive criticism of Forced Entertainment's
body of work, calling their *First Night* (2001) an "(unacknowledged) remake."
Piet Defraeye, "You! Hypocrite Spectateur: A Short History of the Production
and Reception of Peter Handke's *Publikumsbeschimpfung*," *Seminar: A Journal of Germanic Studies* 42, no. 4 (2006): 432.

104. RoseLee Goldberg, "Jerome Bel," *Artforum* 43, no. 10 (2005): 329.

105. Florian Malzacher, "There Is a Word for People Like You: Audience.
The Spectator as Bad Witness and Bad Voyeur," in *"Not Even a Game Anymore": The Theatre of Forced Entertainment*, ed. Judith Helmer and Florian
Malzacher (Berlin: Alexander Verlag, 2004), 137.

106. Fried, "Art and Objecthood," 164.

107. Hal Foster, "The Crux of Minimalism," in *The Return of the Real*
(Cambridge, MA: MIT Press, 1996), 40.

108. Rosalind Krauss, "Theories of Art after Minimalism and Pop," in *Discussions in Contemporary Culture*, ed. Hal Foster (Seattle: Bay, 1987), 59.

109. Douglas Crimp, "Pictures," *October* no. 8 (1979): 76.

110. Pontbriand, "The Eye Finds No Fixed Point," 154, emphasis added.

111. Pontbriand, "The Eye Finds No Fixed Point," 155.

112. Pontbriand, "The Eye Finds No Fixed Point," 155. Pontbriand
acknowledges the deconstructionist critiques of presence that had begun to
circulate at that time, but she argues that performance is less susceptible to
critiques of classical metaphysical presence because "performance unfolds in a
real time and a real place without any imaginary or transcendental space-time
a priori."

113. Pontbriand, "The Eye Finds No Fixed Point," 156.

114. Pontbriand, "The Eye Finds No Fixed Point," 157.

115. Josette Féral, "Performance and Theatricality: The Subject Demystified," trans. Terese Lyons, *Modern Drama* 25, no. 1 (1982): 176, https://doi.org/10.1353/mdr.1982.0036.

116. Féral, "Performance and Theatricality," 177.

117. Elin Diamond, "Introduction," in *Performance and Cultural Politics*, ed. Elin Diamond (London: Routledge, 1996), 3.

118. Elinor Fuchs, *The Death of Character: Perspectives on Theater after Modernism* (Bloomington: Indiana University Press, 1996), 79.

119. Richard Schechner, "A New Paradigm for Theatre in the Academy," *TDR/The Drama Review* 36, no. 4 (1992): 8, https://doi.org/10.2307/1146210.

120. Robert Ayers, "'The Knife Is Real, the Blood Is Real, and the Emotions Are Real': Robert Ayers in Conversation with Marina Abramović," March 10, 2010, http://www.askyfilledwithshootingstars.com/?p=1197 (site discontinued).

121. Parr quoted in Glen McGillivray, "The Discursive Formation of Theatricality as a Critical Concept," *Metaphorik.de*, no. 17 (2009): 102.

122. McGillivray, "Discursive Formation of Theatricality," 104–5. McGillivray is drawing on Krauss's 1987 reassessment of Fried: "Now theater and theatricality are precisely what is never defined in the pages of 'Art and Objecthood,' or in the one definition that is ventured we are told that theater is what lies between the arts, a definition that specifies the theater as a nonthing, and emptiness, a void. Theater is thus an empty term whose role is to set up a system founded upon the opposition between itself and another term." Krauss, "Theories of Art after Minimalism and Pop," 62–63.

123. Shannon Jackson, "Theatre . . . Again," *Art Lies* no. 60 (Winter 2008): 18.

124. Shannon Jackson, *Professing Performance: Theatre in the Academy from Philology to Performativity* (Cambridge: Cambridge University Press, 2004), 143, https://doi.org/10.1017/CBO9780511554247.

125. McGillivray, "Discursive Formation of Theatricality," 113.

126. Stephen Bottoms, "The Efficacy/Effeminacy Braid: Unpacking the Performance Studies/Theatre Studies Dichotomy," *Theatre Topics* 13, no. 2 (2003): 173–87, https://doi.org/10.1353/tt.2003.0029.

127. Amelia Jones, *Body Art/Performing the Subject* (Minneapolis: University of Minnesota Press, 1998), 111–12.

128. Fred Moten, *In the Break: The Aesthetics of the Black Radical Tradition* (Minneapolis: University of Minnesota Press, 2003), 235, 237.

129. Moten, *In the Break*, 234.

130. Diamond, "Introduction," 4. For more on the persistence of theater in performance art, see Lara Shalson, "On the Endurance of Theatre in Live Art," *Contemporary Theatre Review* 22, no. 1 (2012): 106–19, https://doi.org/10.1080/10486801.2011.645282.

131. Josette Féral, foreword to "Theatricality," special issue, *SubStance* 31, no. 2/3 (2002): 10, https://doi.org/10.1353/sub.2002.0025.

132. Tracy C. Davis and Thomas Postlewait, "Theatricality: An Introduction," in *Theatricality*, ed. Tracy C. Davis and Thomas Postlewait (Cambridge: Cambridge University Press, 2003), 5.

133. For example, Barish's critique of Plato is more a defense of an abstract idea of "individual expression" than it is a specific defense of theatricality. This vision of arts and artists standing up for individual expression might say more about Barish's own cultural circumstances than about what theatricality might actually be. Jonas Barish, *The Antitheatrical Prejudice* (Berkeley: University of California Press, 1981).

134. Davis and Postlewait, "Theatricality: An Introduction," 1.

135. Tracy C. Davis, "Theatricality and Civil Society," in *Theatricality*, ed. Tracy C. Davis and Thomas Postlewait (Cambridge: Cambridge University Press, 2003), 137.

136. Davis, "Theatricality and Civil Society," 141, emphasis in original. Davis's reference is to David Marshall, "Adam Smith and the Theatricality of Moral Sentiments," *Critical Inquiry* 10, no. 4 (1984): 592–613.

137. Davis, "Theatricality and Civil Society," 142.

138. Davis, "Theatricality and Civil Society," 145.

139. Elizabeth Burns, *Theatricality: A Study of Convention in the Theatre and in Social Life* (New York: Harper and Row, 1972), 13, emphasis added.

140. Robert Morris, "Blank Form" (1960–61), in *Blam! The Explosion of Pop, Minimalism, and Performance, 1958–1964*, ed. Barbara Haskell (New York: Whitney Museum of American Art in association with W. W. Norton, 1984), 101.

141. Jacques Rancière, "The Emancipated Spectator," *Artforum* 45, no. 7 (2007): 271–80.

142. Rancière, "The Emancipated Spectator," 271.

143. Rancière, "The Emancipated Spectator," 274.

144. Rancière, "The Emancipated Spectator," 274.

145. Rancière, "The Emancipated Spectator," 277.

146. Rancière, "The Emancipated Spectator," 276.

147. Crouch, *Plays One*, 111.

148. a smith, "Gentle Acts of Removal, Replacement and Reduction: Considering the Audience in Co-Directing the Work of Tim Crouch," *Contemporary Theatre Review* 21, no. 4 (2011): 415, https://doi.org/10.1080/10486801.2011.610311.

149. Handke, *Offending the Audience*, 27.

150. smith, "Gentle Acts of Removal," 412, emphasis added.

151. smith, "Gentle Acts of Removal," 413.

152. Tim Crouch and Caridad Svich, "Tim Crouch's Theatrical Transformations: A Conversation with Caridad Svich," 2006, http://www.hotreview.org/articles/timcrouchinterv.htm.

153. Crouch, *Plays One*, 167.

154. Tim Crouch, "Interview with Tim Crouch, Writer and Director of Royal Court's *Adler & Gibb*," *Aesthetica*, May 5, 2014, http://www.aestheticamagazine.com/interview-with-tim-crouch-writer-and-director-of-royal-courts-adler-and-gibb/.

155. Crouch and smith refer to reading Rancière during the making of *The Author* in Tim Crouch and a smith, "'How We Are Together': An Endless Conversation with Tim Crouch and a smith," *Thompson's Bank of Communicable*

Desire (blog), http://beescope.blogspot.com/2009/12/how-we-are-together
-endless.html (site discontinued).

156. Stephen Bottoms, "Authorizing the Audience: The Conceptual Drama
of Tim Crouch," *Performance Research* 14, no. 1 (2009): 69, 73, https://doi
.org/10.1080/13528160903113213.

157. Lucy R. Lippard and John Chandler, "The Dematerialization of Art"
(1968), in Lucy R. Lippard, *Changing: Essays in Art Criticism* (New York:
E. P. Dutton, 1971), 255–76.

158. Andy Smith, "This Is It: Notes on a Dematerialised Theatre," in *The
Twenty-First Century Performance Reader*, ed. Teresa Brayshaw, Anna Fenemore, and Noel Witts (London: Routledge, 2019), 498, https://doi.org/10
.4324/9780429283956.

159. Crouch, "Interview with Tim Crouch."

160. Crouch and Svich, "Tim Crouch's Theatrical Transformations."

161. Smith's presentation is described in Seda Ilter, "Andy Smith, 'Dematerialising Theatre' (Birkbeck Arts Week 2017)," *Birkbeck, Department of English
& Humanities Blog* (blog), May 25, 2017, http://blogs.bbk.ac.uk/english
/2017/05/25/seda-ilter-on-andy-smith-dematerialising-theatre-birkbeck-arts
-week-2017/.

162. Bottoms, "Authorizing the Audience," 67.

163. Tim Crouch, *ENGLAND* theater program (London: Whitechapel
Gallery, 2009); Brian O'Doherty, *Inside the White Cube: The Ideology of
the Gallery Space* (1976), expanded ed. (Berkeley: University of California
Press, 1999).

164. Crouch, *Plays One*, 127.

165. Tim Crouch, *Adler & Gibb* (London: Oberon, 2014), 29.

166. Crouch, *Adler & Gibb*, 72–73, emphasis added.

167. Such a project of distanciation is exemplified by visual arts exhibitions like *The World as a Stage* (Tate Modern, 2007) and *Audience as Subject*
(Yerba Buena, 2010), which featured numerous "relational" artworks but no
instances of theatrical performance; or in the very title of *A Theater without
Theater* (MACBA, 2007).

168. Crouch, *Adler & Gibb*, 39ff.

169. Crouch, *Adler & Gibb*, 60.

170. By "narrowly mimetic," I mean a representational relationship based
on imitation or verisimilitude between something on stage and a real or fictional reference, as in naturalist drama, as distinct from uses of "mimesis"
that emphasize its protean, transformative dynamics as analyzed in Michael
Taussig, *Mimesis and Alterity: A Particular History of the Senses* (London:
Routledge, 1993); or Elin Diamond, *Unmaking Mimesis: Essays on Feminism
and Theater* (London: Routledge, 1997). I address the diversity of meanings of
"representation" in chapter 3.

171. Tim Crouch, Dan Rebellato, and Louise LePage, "Tim Crouch and
Dan Rebellato in Conversation," *Platform* 6, no. 2 (2012): 14.

172. Aleks Sierz, "Navigating New Patterns of Power with an Audience: Tim
Crouch in Conversation with Aleks Sierz," *Journal of Contemporary Drama in
English* 2, no. 1 (2014): 66, https://doi.org/10.1515/jcde-2014–0006.

173. Crouch, *Plays One*, 59.

174. Crouch, *Plays One*, 60.
175. The idea of the hypnotist as charlatan is discussed in Crouch and Svich, "Tim Crouch's Theatrical Transformations."
176. Crouch, *Plays One*, 104.
177. Bottoms, "Authorizing the Audience," 75.
178. Crouch, *Plays One*, 114, 165, 181.
179. This association with talking to children has a sinister overture in *The Author*, with its themes of child sexual abuse. The character Vic describes the coaching he received from Tim about how to deliver a monologue: "You have to give the audience a character, a relationship to you. . . . Imagine them as a child—or a confessor. Enlisting is a good one! I'm enlisting you! Or they need seducing or pleasuring. Pleasing, I mean." Crouch, *Plays One*, 170–71.
180. Tim Crouch quoted in Seda Ilter, "'A Process of Transformation': Tim Crouch on *My Arm*," *Contemporary Theatre Review* 21, no. 4 (2011): 402, https://doi.org/10.1080/10486801.2011.610792.
181. Maxwell refers to Nield's phrase in an interview with Sarah Gorman, "Refusing Shorthand: Richard Maxwell," *Contemporary Theatre Review* 17, no. 2 (2007): 236.
182. Gregg Whelan and Gary Winters gave this description during a discussion as part of Lone Twin Theatre's *Catastrophe Trilogy*, Barbican Theatre, London, March 6, 2010.
183. Maxwell made these comments at a panel discussion with Tim Etchells and Phelim McDermott called "Re-Wiring / Re-Writing Theatre," facilitated by Adrian Heathfield, Riverside Studios, London, November 18, 2006.
184. Bonnie Marranca, "PerformanceContemporary: Dialogue with Richard Maxwell," LocationOne, 2002, http://www.location1.org/mediadb/artist.php#m (site discontinued).
185. Crouch and smith, "How We Are Together."
186. Crouch and smith, "How We Are Together."

Chapter 2
1. Peter Brook, *The Empty Space* (1968) (London: Penguin, 1990), 1.
2. The original live surtitles are in German. My quotations are taken from the English subtitles on the video documentation of the work that was provided to me.
3. Karl Marx, "Economic and Philosophical Manuscripts" (1844), in *Karl Marx: Early Writings*, trans. Gregor Benton and Rodney Livingstone (New York: Penguin, 1992), 324, 332, emphasis in original.
4. Bourriaud, *Relational Aesthetics*, 83.
5. Chantal Pontbriand, "Work: The Sharing of Experience," *Parachute*, no. 122 (2006): 7.
6. Stewart Martin, "Critique of Relational Aesthetics," *Third Text* 21, no. 4 (2007): 369–86, https://doi.org/10.1080/09528820701433323.
7. Maurizio Lazzarato, "Immaterial Labour," in *Radical Thought in Italy*, ed. Paolo Virno and Michael Hardt, trans. Paul Colilli and Ed Emory (Minneapolis: University of Minnesota Press, 1996), 132–46; Michael Hardt and Antonio Negri, *Empire* (Cambridge, MA: Harvard University Press, 2000); Michael Hardt, "Affective Labor," *Boundary 2* 26, no. 2 (1999): 89–100.

8. Claire Bishop, *Artificial Hells: Participatory Art and the Politics of Spectatorship* (London: Verso, 2012), 12.

9. Kunst, *Artist at Work*, 65.

10. Marx, "Economic and Philosophical Manuscripts," 328.

11. Nick Cumming-Bruce and Steven Erlanger, "Swiss Ban Building of Minarets on Mosques," *New York Times*, November 29, 2009, https://www.nytimes.com/2009/11/30/world/europe/30swiss.html.

12. Christiane Kühl, "Rimini Protokoll: A Live Archive of the Everyday," in *No More Drama*, ed. Peter Crawley and Willie White, trans. Rachel West (Dublin: Project/Carysfort, 2011), 39.

13. Jens Roselt, "Making an Appearance: On the Performance Practice of Self-Presentation," in *Experts of the Everyday: The Theatre of Rimini Protokoll*, ed. Miriam Dreysse and Florian Malzacher (Berlin: Alexander Verlag, 2008), 46.

14. For a comprehensive overview of the company, see Miriam Dreysse and Florian Malzacher, eds., *Experts of the Everyday: The Theatre of Rimini Protokoll* (Berlin: Alexander Verlag, 2008).

15. *Breaking News* is described in more detail in Katia Arfara, "Aspects of a New Dramaturgy of the Spectator—Rimini Protokoll's 'Breaking News,'" *Performance Research* 14, no. 3 (2009): 112–18, https://doi.org/10.1080/13528160903519575.

16. *Best Before* is described in more detail in a review by Alex Ferguson, "The Complicit Witness," *RealTime*, no. 96 (April 2010): 2–3, https://www.realtime.org.au/the-complicit-witness/.

17. Performers' words from *100% London*, quoted in Marissia Fragkou and Philip Hager, "Staging London: Participation and Citizenship on the Way to the 2012 Olympic Games," *Contemporary Theatre Review* 23, no. 4 (2013): 534, https://doi.org/10.1080/10486801.2013.839172.

18. In making this comparison, they critique *100% London* for its complicity with the state's desires for "managing diversity and difference" (Fragkou and Hager, "Staging London," 536). Keren Zaiontz follows a similar line of critique in relation to *100% Vancouver*, noting the project's imbrication in wider contexts of financialization and globalization. Keren Zaiontz, "Performing Visions of Governmentality: Care and Capital in *100% Vancouver*," *Theatre Research International* 39, no. 2 (2014): 101–19, https://doi.org/10.1017/S0307883314000030.

19. See Rimini Protokoll, "Annual Shareholder's Meeting," https://www.rimini-protokoll.de/website/en/project/hauptversammlung.

20. Quoted in Kühl, "Rimini Protokoll: A Live Archive of the Everyday," 31.

21. Florian Malzacher, "Dramaturgies of Care and Insecurity: The Story of Rimini Protokoll," in *Experts of the Everyday: The Theatre of Rimini Protokoll*, ed. Miriam Dreysse and Florian Malzacher (Berlin: Alexander Verlag, 2008), 16.

22. Thomas Irmer, "A Search for New Realities: Documentary Theatre in Germany," *TDR/The Drama Review* 30, no. 3 (2006): 17, https://doi.org/10.1162/dram.2006.50.3.16.

23. See, for example, Fintan O'Toole, "The Call of the Conscious in Reality Theatre," *Irish Times*, October 10, 2009, http://www.irishtimes.com/newspaper/weekend/2009/1010/1224256317409.html; and Lyn Gardner,

"How Real Is Reality Theatre?" *Guardian*, October 13, 2009, http://www .guardian.co.uk/stage/theatreblog/2009/oct/11/reality-verbatim-theatre.

24. Quote from Frankfurter Rundschau used in the publicity for *Best Before* at the LIFT festival in London, http://www.liftfest.com/events/past-events /2010-lift-festival/lift-2010-programme/best-before-rimini-protokoll (website discontinued).

25. Malzacher, "Dramaturgies of Care and Insecurity," 37.

26. Roselt, "Making an Appearance," 46.

27. Roselt, "Making an Appearance," 58.

28. Malzacher, "Dramaturgies of Care and Insecurity," 39, emphasis added.

29. Arfara, "Aspects of a New Dramaturgy of the Spectator," 114.

30. Matt Cornish, "Chat Room," *PAJ: A Journal of Performance and Art* 32, no. 1 (2009): 48, https://doi.org/10.1162/pajj.2010.32.1.46.

31. Gardner, "How Real Is Reality Theatre?"

32. Ulrike Garde and Meg Mumford, "Postdramatic Reality Theatre and Productive Insecurity: Destabilising Encounters with the Unfamiliar in Theatre from Sydney and Berlin," in *Postdramatic Theatre and the Political: International Perspectives on Contemporary Performance*, ed. Karen Jürs-Munby, Jerome Carroll, and Steve Giles (London: Bloomsbury, 2013), 151.

33. Giorgio Agamben, *What Is an Apparatus? and Other Essays*, trans. David Kishik (Stanford, CA: Stanford University Press, 2009), 14.

34. Shannon Jackson, *Social Works: Performing Art, Supporting Publics* (London: Routledge, 2011), 146.

35. Erin Hurley, *Theatre & Feeling* (Basingstoke, UK: Palgrave Macmillan, 2010), 9.

36. The embarrassment of the spectator as consumer is discussed in great detail by Nicholas Ridout in *Stage Fright, Animals, and Other Theatrical Problems* (Cambridge: Cambridge University Press, 2006), particularly in chapter 2, "Embarrassment: The Predicament of the Audience"; and in his "Performance in the Service Economy: Outsourcing and Delegation," in *Double Agent*, ed. Claire Bishop and Silvia Tramontana (London: ICA, 2009), 126–31.

37. Garde and Mumford, "Postdramatic Reality Theatre and Productive Insecurity," 148–49.

38. Tracy C. Davis, "Theatricality and Civil Society," in *Theatricality*, ed. Tracy C. Davis and Thomas Postlewait (Cambridge: Cambridge University Press, 2003), 145.

39. Jackson, *Social Works*, 43ff.

40. Jackson, *Social Works*, 31–32, 59ff., 211–13.

41. Maaike Bleeker, *Visuality in the Theatre: The Locus of Looking* (Basingstoke, UK: Palgrave, 2008), 9, emphasis in original.

42. Jackson, *Social Works*, 177.

43. Jackson, *Social Works*, 178.

44. Klaus Biesenbach and Hans Ulrich Obrist, "Foreword," in *11 Rooms* exhibition program (Manchester: Manchester International Festival, 2011).

45. Email from June 9, 2011, *11 Rooms* installation.

46. Email from June 2, 2011, *11 Rooms* installation.

47. Hardt and Negri, *Empire*, 290.

48. A more careful analysis than I am able to offer here would distinguish between the kinds and degrees of instability and agency that tend to get lumped together under the concept of "precarity": the situation of the contracted cleaner is quite different from that of the freelance project manager, as is that of the globe-trotting artist creating his/her own brand identity. For more nuanced considerations, see, for example, Shannon Jackson, "Just-in-Time: Performance and the Aesthetics of Precarity," *TDR/The Drama Review* 56, no. 4 (2012): 10–31; and Freee Art Collective, "When Work Is More Than Wages," *On Curating*, no. 16 (2014): 41–45.

49. Rancière, *The Politics of Aesthetics*, 18–23.

50. Mierle Laderman Ukeles, "Manifesto for Maintenance Art 1969! Proposal for an Exhibition 'CARE,' " https://www.wikiart.org/en/mierle-laderman-ukeles/manifesto-for-maintenance-art-1969-1969.

51. Nicolas Bourriaud, "Precarious Constructions: Answer to Jacques Rancière on Art and Politics," *Open*, no. 17 (2014): 23.

52. Liam Gillick, "The Good of Work," in *Are You Working Too Much? Post-Fordism, Precarity and the Labor of Art*, ed. Julieta Aranda, Brian Kuan Wood, and Anton Vidokle (Berlin: e-flux/Sternberg, 2011), 61.

53. Gillick, "The Good of Work," 70.

54. John Baldessari, "Unrealised Proposal for Cadavre Piece, 1970," in *11 Rooms* exhibition program (Manchester: Manchester International Festival, 2011).

55. Email from May 20, 2011, *11 Rooms* installation.

56. Karl Marx, *Capital, Volume 1* (1867), trans. Ben Fowkes (New York: Vintage, 1977), 171.

57. Marx, *Capital*, 206.

58. Marx, *Capital*, 163–64.

59. Nicholas Ridout, "A Make-Believe World" (presented at A Make-Believe World, Chelsea Theatre, London, November 13, 2010).

60. Jacques Derrida, *Specters of Marx* (*Spectres de Marx: L'État de la dette, le travail du deuil et la nouvelle Internationale*, 1993), trans. Peggy Kamuf (New York: Routledge, 2006).

61. Alice Rayner, "Rude Mechanicals and the *Specters of Marx*," *Theatre Journal* 54, no. 4 (2002): 541, https://doi.org/10.1353/tj.2002.0133.

62. Rayner, "Rude Mechanicals," 538–39, emphasis added.

63. Rayner, "Rude Mechanicals," 547.

64. Rayner, "Rude Mechanicals," 537.

65. Quarantine, *Entitled*, 2011, unpublished script provided to the author.

66. Kirby, "On Acting and Not-Acting," 3.

67. Kirby, "On Acting and Not-Acting," 3.

68. Quarantine, *Entitled* theater program (London: Sadler's Wells, 2011).

69. Geraldine Harris, "*Susan and Darren*: The Appearance of Authenticity," *Performance Research* 13, no. 4 (2008): 14, https://doi.org/10.1080/13528160902875580.

70. Quoted in Harris, "*Susan and Darren*," 9.

71. Bert O. States, *Great Reckonings in Little Rooms: On the Phenomenology of Theater* (Berkeley: University of California Press, 1985), 20.

72. Rayner, "Rude Mechanicals," 536.

73. My notes from Quarantine, *Entitled* screening and live discussion (online), May 29, 2020.

74. Ridout, *Stage Fright*, 33.

75. Pontbriand, "The Eye Finds No Fixed Point," 155.

76. John Roberts, *The Intangibilities of Form: Skill and Deskilling in Art after the Readymade* (London: Verso, 2007), 54, emphasis added.

77. Michael Shane Boyle, "Performance and Value: The Work of Theatre in Karl Marx's Critique of Political Economy," *Theatre Survey* 58, no. 1 (2017): 19, fn 62, https://doi.org/10.1017/S0040557416000661.

78. Boyle, "Performance and Value," 19.

79. Quarantine, *Entitled*, 2011.

80. Nicholas Ridout and Rebecca Schneider, "Precarity and Performance: An Introduction," *TDR/The Drama Review* 56, no. 4 (2012): 5, https://doi.org/10.1162/DRAM_a_00210.

81. Franco "Bifo" Berardi, *After the Future*, ed. Gary Genosko and Nicholas Thoburn (Oakland, CA: AK, 2011), 18.

82. Franz Kafka, *America* (*Der Verschollene*, written 1911–14, published posthumously 1927), trans. Edwin Muir (London: Vintage, 2005), 234.

83. Kafka, *America*, 235.

84. Kafka, *America*, 251.

85. Walter Benjamin, "What Is Epic Theater?" (1939), in Walter Benjamin, *Illuminations*, ed. Hannah Arendt, trans. Harry Zohn (New York: Schocken, 1969), 151.

86. Walter Benjamin, "Franz Kafka: On the Tenth Anniversary of His Death" (1934), in Walter Benjamin, *Illuminations*, ed. Hannah Arendt, trans. Harry Zohn (New York: Schocken, 1969), 121. And in turn, Benjamin's records of his conversations with Brecht reveal the significance of Kafka in each of their thinking about the role of art. See Walter Benjamin, "Conversations with Brecht" (1934), in *Understanding Brecht*, ed. Stanley Mitchell, trans. Anna Bostock (London: Verso, 1998), 106–12.

87. Benjamin, "Franz Kafka," 120.

88. Roland Barthes, "Baudelaire's Theater" (1954), in *A Barthes Reader*, ed. Susan Sontag, trans. Richard Howard (New York: Hill and Wang, 1982), 75.

89. Samuel Weber, *Theatricality as Medium* (New York: Fordham University Press, 2004), 90, emphasis in original.

90. Weber, *Theatricality as Medium*, x.

91. Weber, *Theatricality as Medium*, 92.

92. Kafka, *America*, 244.

93. Benjamin, "Franz Kafka," 124.

94. Alan Read, *Theatre and Everyday Life: An Ethics of Performance* (London: Routledge, 1993), 173.

95. Kafka, *America*, 255.

96. Nature Theater of Oklahoma, *Life and Times: Episode 1* (Chicago: 53rd State, 2013), 7.

97. Nature Theater of Oklahoma, *Life and Times: Episodes 1–5* theater program (Norwich, UK: Norfolk & Norwich Festival, 2013).

98. Nature Theater of Oklahoma, *Life and Times: Episode 1*, 79.

99. Nature Theater of Oklahoma, *Life and Times: Episode 1*, 21.

100. Nature Theater of Oklahoma, *Life and Times: Episode 1*, 50.

101. Nature Theater of Oklahoma, *Life and Times: Episode 2* (Chicago: 53rd State, 2013), 15.

102. Nature Theater of Oklahoma, *Life and Times: Episode 2*, 63.

103. Nature Theater of Oklahoma, *Life and Times: Episode 1*, 116–17.

104. Nature Theater of Oklahoma, *Life and Times: Episodes 3 & 4* (Chicago: 53rd State, 2013), 5–6.

105. Hilton Als, "Eight Hours of, Like, Life," *New Yorker*, January 23, 2013, http://www.newyorker.com/online/blogs/culture/2013/01/nature-theater-of -oklahoma-reviewed.html.

106. Charles Isherwood, "Theater Talkback: The Rough Beauty of Everyday Speech," *New York Times ArtsBeat* (blog), January 31, 2013, http:// artsbeat.blogs.nytimes.com/2013/01/31/theater-talkback-the-rough-beauty -of-everyday-speech/.

107. Maddy Costa, "How Everyone Who Ever Lived Eats and Drinks and Loves and Sleeps and Talks and Walks and Wakes and Forgets and Quarrels and Likes and Dislikes and Works and Sits: The Life and Times of Nature Theater of Oklahoma," *Deliq.* (blog), 2013, http://statesofdeliquescence.blogspot .co.uk/2013/06/how-everyone-who-ever-lived-eats-and.html.

108. Costa, "How Everyone Who Ever Lived Eats and Drinks." The italicized insertions are mine; the other is Costa's.

109. Rachel Anderson-Rabern, "The Nature Theater of Oklahoma's Aesthetics of Fun," *TDR/The Drama Review* 54, no. 4 (2010): 91.

110. Florian Malzacher, "Previously on Nature Theater of Oklahoma . . . ," in Nature Theater of Oklahoma, *Life and Times—Episode V* (Long Island City, NY: Nature Theater of Oklahoma, 2012), 125.

111. Yvonne Rainer, "A Quasi Survey of Some 'Minimalist' Tendencies in the Quantitatively Minimal Dance Activity midst the Plethora, or An Analysis of *Trio A*" (1966), in *Minimal Art: A Critical Anthology*, ed. Gregory Battcock (New York: Dutton, 1968), 263.

112. Young Jean Lee, "Nature Theater of Oklahoma," *Bomb*, no. 108 (2009): 89, https://bombmagazine.org/articles/nature-theater-of-oklahoma-1/.

113. Nature Theater of Oklahoma, *Life and Times: Episode 1*, 119.

114. Nature Theater of Oklahoma, *Life and Times: Episode 2*, 101.

115. Nature Theater of Oklahoma, *Life and Times: Episodes 3 & 4*, 10–11.

116. Nature Theater of Oklahoma, *Life and Times: Episode 2*, 16, 65.

117. Nature Theater of Oklahoma, *Life and Times: Episode 1*, 86.

118. Nature Theater of Oklahoma, *Life and Times: Episode 1*, 16.

119. Nature Theater of Oklahoma, *Life and Times: Episodes 3 & 4*, 68.

120. Malzacher, "Previously on Nature Theater of Oklahoma . . . ," 120.

121. Costa, "How Everyone Who Ever Lived Eats and Drinks."

122. Quoted in Lauren Grace Bakst, "Nature Theater of Oklahoma," *Bomb*, September 17, 2013, http://bombmagazine.org/article/7369/nature-theater-of -oklahoma.

123. Costa, "How Everyone Who Ever Lived Eats and Drinks."

124. For a discussion of *Marina Abramović Presents* in relation to cultural economies of temporality, see Lara Shalson, "On Duration and Multiplicity,"

Performance Research 17, no. 5 (2012): 98–106, https://doi.org/10.1080 /13528165.2012.728448. Abramović has continued to develop this "drill" as part of *512 Hours* (Serpentine Gallery, London, 2014) and *Marina Abramović: In Residence* (Kaldor Public Art Projects, Sydney, 2015).

125. Louise Owen, "Robert Wilson, *Walking* (Holkham Estate, 2012)," *Contemporary Theatre Review* 23, no. 4 (2013): 568–73, https://doi.org/10 .1080/10486801.2013.839177. Owen goes on to provocatively describe Wilson's work as "theatricalizing" the landscape, part of a lineage of such framings going back to the eighteenth century.

126. Nicholas Ridout, *Passionate Amateurs: Theatre, Communism, and Love* (Ann Arbor: University of Michigan Press, 2013), 131–32, 25.

127. Ridout, *Passionate Amateurs*, 124. A similar insistence on theater's proximity rather than separation from everyday life, or at least a model of what everyday life might be, is beautifully articulated by Alan Read: "To value theatre is to value life, not to escape from it. The everyday is at once the most habitual and demanding dimension of life which theatre has most responsibility to. Theatre does not tease people out of their everyday lives like other expressions of wish fulfilment but reminds them who they are and what is worth living and changing in their lives every day" (Read, *Theatre and Everyday Life*, 103).

128. Costa, "How Everyone Who Ever Lived Eats and Drinks." Though I haven't discussed it here, one might also think about their year-long podcast project, *OK Radio* (okradio.org, 2012–13), as a comparable project of opening and permeability. As a series of long-form, unedited conversations with theater-makers, duration was again a generative element, in that the length of the conversations meant they would inevitably depart from straightforward discussions of process, instead crossing over between many different kinds of activity (including thinking and reading) as part of the "work" of artists.

129. Bruno Gullì, *Earthly Plenitudes: A Study on Sovereignty and Labor* (Philadelphia: Temple University Press, 2010).

130. Kunst, *Artist at Work*, 79.

131. Costa, "How Everyone Who Ever Lived Eats and Drinks," emphasis added.

Chapter 3

1. States, *Great Reckonings in Little Rooms*, 29.

2. Karen Lury, *Tears, Fears and Fairy Tales* (London: I.B. Tauris, 2010), 147, 150.

3. Lury, *Tears, Fears and Fairy Tales*, 161.

4. Parr quoted in Glen McGillivray, "The Discursive Formation of Theatricality as a Critical Concept," *Metaphorik.de*, no. 17 (2009): 102; Robert Ayers, "'The Knife Is Real, the Blood Is Real, and the Emotions Are Real': Robert Ayers in Conversation with Marina Abramović," March 10, 2010, http://www.askyfilledwithshootingstars.com/?p=1197 (site discontinued); Tim Etchells, "On Risk and Investment" (1994), in Tim Etchells, *Certain Fragments: Contemporary Performance and Forced Entertainment* (London: Routledge, 1999).

5. Hans-Thies Lehmann, *Postdramatic Theatre* (*Postdramatisch theater*, 1999), ed. and trans. Karen Jürs-Munby (London: Routledge, 2006), 100.

6. Carol Martin, *Theatre of the Real* (Basingstoke, UK: Palgrave Macmillan, 2013), 5, https://doi.org/10.1057/9781137295729.

7. Ulrike Garde and Meg Mumford, *Theatre of Real People: Diverse Encounters from Berlin's Hebbel am Ufer and Beyond* (London: Bloomsbury, 2016), 5.

8. Paul Rae, *Real Theatre: Essays in Experience* (Cambridge: Cambridge University Press, 2019), 5.

9. States, *Great Reckonings in Little Rooms*, 37.

10. States, *Great Reckonings in Little Rooms*, 35.

11. States, *Great Reckonings in Little Rooms*, 35.

12. States, *Great Reckonings in Little Rooms*, 36.

13. For example, Artaud's fascination with Balinese puppet theater, Brecht's with Chinese opera, or, in the Australian context, Marina Abramović's primitivist othering and appropriation of Aboriginal peoples and cultures. See S. J. Norman, "Sarah Jane Norman Responds to Marina Abramovic," ABC Radio National, August 25, 2016, https://www.abc.net.au/radionational/programs/awaye/sarah-jane-norman-responds-to-marina-abramovic/7784750.

14. Ridout, *Stage Fright*, 97–100.

15. Brian Logan, "Edinburgh Festival: *Once and for All We're Gonna Tell You Who We Are So Shut Up and Listen*," *Guardian*, August 15, 2008, http://www.theguardian.com/culture/2008/aug/14/edinburghfestival.onceandforall.

16. For production history, see Ontroerend Goed, "*Once and For All* (2008)," http://www.ontroerendgoed.be/en/projecten/once-and-for-all/.

17. John Bailey, "Signatures and Signalling," *RealTime*, no. 93 (October–November 2009): 40, https://www.realtime.org.au/signatures-and-signalling/.

18. Tim Etchells, *That Night Follows Day* (Ghent, Belgium: Victoria, 2007), 13.

19. Etchells, *That Night Follows Day*, 16.

20. Etchells, *That Night Follows Day*, 34.

21. Etchells, *That Night Follows Day*, 32.

22. Joyce McMillan, "As Night Follows Day [*sic*]," *Scotsman*, May 3, 2008, http://www.scotsman.com/news/reviews-1–1166471.

23. Tim Etchells, "That Night Follows Day," http://timetchells.com/projects/that-night-follows-day/; Kate Wyver, "That Night Follows Day Review—Adults' Truths and Lies, Voiced by Children," *Guardian*, December 12, 2018, https://www.theguardian.com/stage/2018/dec/12/that-night-follows-day-review-southbank-centre-london-forced-entertainment.

24. Rayner, "Rude Mechanicals," 536.

25. Richard Schechner, *Between Theater and Anthropology* (Philadelphia: University of Pennsylvania Press, 1985), 111.

26. Clare Brennan, "That Night Follows Day," *Observer*, April 1, 2009, http://www.theguardian.com/stage/2009/apr/12/theatre-reviews-london.

27. Helen Freshwater, "Children and the Limits of Representation in the Work of Tim Crouch," in *Contemporary British Theatre: Breaking New Ground*, ed. Vicky Angelaki (Basingstoke, UK: Palgrave Macmillan, 2014), 170, https://doi.org/10.1057/9781137010131.

28. Freshwater, "Children and the Limits of Representation," 170–71. Freshwater is drawing upon Lee Edelman, *No Future: Queer Theory and the Death Drive* (Durham, NC: Duke University Press, 2004); and Robin Bernstein, *Racial Innocence: Performing American Childhood from Slavery to Civil Rights* (New York: New York University Press, 2011).

29. Freshwater, "Children and the Limits of Representation," 170, 171. Freshwater goes on to describe just such experimentation in the work of Tim Crouch, including *John, Antonio and Nancy* (2010), intended to be a one-off performance in which the words of British politicians are spoken by child performers. I discuss Crouch's use of child performers in *Adler & Gibb* (2014) in chapter 1.

30. Alex Marshall, "Is Milo Rau Really the Most Controversial Director in Theater?" *New York Times*, October 3, 2018, https://www.nytimes.com/2018 /10/03/theater/milo-rau-ntgent-controversy.html. No fighters responded to the ad, but tabloid newspapers picked up on it. Rau's provocation has precedent in Christoph Schlingensief's controversial recruitment of former neo-Nazis for his 2001 production of *Hamlet*. Schlingensief's provocative works are discussed further in chapter 4.

31. NTGent, "Ghent Manifesto," May 1, 2018, https://www.ntgent.be/en /manifest.

32. NTGent, "Ghent Manifesto." Other commitments extend to touring: the set for each production must be able to fit inside a single cargo van, and every production must be toured to at least three countries.

33. Quotations from dialogue are taken from the onstage projected English surtitles, transcribed from a video recording of the performance from July 2016 provided to me by CAMPO.

34. See Daniel Sack, "Festival d'Avignon (Review)," *Theatre Journal* 61, no. 1 (2009): 117–20, https://doi.org/10.1353/tj.0.0147.

35. See Antje Hildebrandt, "Soma-Conceptual Choreographic Strategies in Boris Charmatz's *Enfant*," *Journal of Dance & Somatic Practices* 9, no. 1 (2017): 95–103, https://doi.org/10.1386/jdsp.9.1.95_1; and Adrian Heathfield, "Glimmers in Limbo: Inhuman Animations, Child's Play, and the Coming Catastrophe," in *Boris Charmatz*, ed. Ana Janevski (New York: MoMA, 2017), 107–18.

36. Fevered Sleep, "Men & Girls Dance Newspaper, London Edition," 2019, 2, https://issuu.com/feveredsleep/docs/m_gd_6_londonnewspaper_f_issuu.

37. Other such works include Josse De Pauw's *üBUNG* (2002), Gob Squad's *Before Your Very Eyes* (2011), and Philippe Quesne's *Next Day* (2014).

38. Bella Todd, "Milo Rau: 'I'm Actually Not Trying to Break Any Taboos,' " WhatsOnStage, February 28, 2017, https://www.whatsonstage.com/brighton -theatre/news/milo-rau-interview-sick-festival-five-easy-pieces_43001.html.

39. Lehmann, *Postdramatic Theatre*, 22.

40. Debra Levine, "Not Just Adult Entertainment: Milo Rau and CAMPO's Collaborative *Five Easy Pieces*," *TDR/The Drama Review* 61, no. 4 (2017): 150, https://doi.org/10.1162/DRAM_a_00699.

41. States, *Great Reckonings in Little Rooms*, 36.

42. Andrew Haydon, "Five Easy Pieces—Sophiensæle (as TT17), Berlin," *Postcards from the Gods* (blog), May 16, 2017, http://postcardsgods.blogspot .com/2017/05/five-easy-pieces-sophiensle-as-tt17.html.

43. Pontbriand, "The Eye Finds No Fixed Point," 155.

44. Hanna Fenichel Pitkin, *The Concept of Representation* (Berkeley: University of California Press, 1967), 48. My thanks to one of the anonymous reviewers of an early draft of this book for drawing my attention to Pitkin's work.

45. Pitkin, *The Concept of Representation*, 61. Pitkin here quotes the US revolutionary John Adams, who argued that a representative legislature "should be an exact portrait, in miniature, of the people at large, as it should think, feel, reason and act like them."

46. Pitkin, *The Concept of Representation*, 67.

47. Pitkin, *The Concept of Representation*, 90.

48. Pitkin, *The Concept of Representation*, 7–8, emphasis in original.

49. Pitkin, *The Concept of Representation*, 141–43, 144, emphasis added.

50. Pitkin, *The Concept of Representation*, 105–6.

51. Pitkin, *The Concept of Representation*, 107–9.

52. Pitkin authored numerous analyses of Arendt, including the book *The Attack of the Blob: Hannah Arendt's Concept of the Social* (Chicago: University of Chicago Press, 1998).

53. Hannah Arendt, *The Human Condition*, 2nd ed. (1958; repr. Chicago: University of Chicago Press, 1998), 199.

54. Arendt, *The Human Condition*, 188.

55. Hannah Arendt, *The Life of the Mind* (New York: Harvest/HBJ, 1978), 19, emphasis in original.

56. Arendt, *The Life of the Mind*, 21, emphasis in original.

57. Arendt, *The Life of the Mind*, 23–26. Barad contrasts a representational idea of language, in which words are understood to describe preexisting phenomena, with a performative one, in which language is bound up in the phenomena being described: "representationalism is the belief in the ontological distinction between representations and that which they purport to represent; in particular, that which is represented is held to be independent of all practices of representing" (Barad, *Meeting the Universe Halfway*, 46).

58. An overview of Arendt's influence on contemporary political thought is outlined in Diana Damian Martin and Theron Schmidt, "Sites of Appearance, Matters of Thought: Hannah Arendt and Performance Philosophy," *Performance Philosophy* 5, no. 1 (2019): 1–7, https://doi.org/10.21476/PP.2019.51291.

59. Jean-Luc Nancy, *The Inoperative Community* (*La Communauté désoeuvrée*, 1986), ed. Peter Connor, trans. Peter Connor et al. (Minneapolis: University of Minnesota Press, 1991), 28.

60. Nancy, *The Inoperative Community*, 29, emphasis in original.

61. Nancy, *The Inoperative Community*, 29.

62. Nancy, *Being Singular Plural*, 66.

63. Nancy, *Being Singular Plural*, 67.

64. Nancy, *Being Singular Plural*, 68.

65. David Marshall, "Rousseau and the State of Theater," *Representations*, no. 13 (1986): 85.

66. Jean-Jacques Rousseau, *The Collected Writings of Rousseau*, vol. 10, *Letter to D'Alembert and Writings for the Theater*, trans. Allan Bloom

(Hanover, NH: Dartmouth College/University Press of New England, 2004), 343–48. Many commentators also refer to Rousseau's wistful evocation of the festival of the wine harvest in book 5 of *La Nouvelle Héloïse* (1761).

67. Barish, *The Antitheatrical Prejudice*, 290, emphasis in original.

68. Nancy, *Being Singular Plural*, 71.

69. Nancy, *Being Singular Plural*, 71.

70. Arendt, *The Life of the Mind*, 21.

71. Butler, *Notes Toward a Performative Theory*, 78.

72. Butler, *Notes Toward a Performative Theory*, 205.

73. Hannah Arendt, "We Refugees" (1943), in *Altogether Elsewhere: Writers on Exile*, ed. Marc Robinson (London: Faber and Faber, 1994), 110–19.

74. Chantal Mouffe, *The Democratic Paradox* (London: Verso, 2000), 33–34, emphasis added.

75. Rancière, *Disagreement*, 9ff.

76. Jacques Rancière, "Aesthetics and Politics: Rethinking the Link," presented at the University of California, Berkeley, September 2002, http://16beavergroup.org/mondays/2006/05/06/monday-night-05-08-06-discussion-on-rancieres-politics-of-aesthetics/.

77. Rancière, *The Politics of Aesthetics*, 39.

78. Peter Hallward, "Staging Equality: On Rancière's Theatrocracy," *New Left Review* 37 (2006): 111.

79. Judith Butler, *Excitable Speech: A Politics of the Performative* (London: Routledge, 1997), 1–2.

80. Butler, *Excitable Speech*, 5, emphasis added.

81. Rancière, *Disagreement*, 11.

82. Butler, *Excitable Speech*, 41.

83. Malzacher, "Dramaturgies of Care and Insecurity," 16.

84. In the video documentation of a different performance provided to me by the company, Deans carries a chair onto the stage, places it down, and then moves the spike to where he has placed the chair rather than moving the chair to the spike. In my viewing notes, however, the chairs were brought separately. Across these variations, what is consistent is Deans's playful use of winking, smiling, and other facial communication with the audience.

85. The published script for *Food Court* assigns fictional names to all the characters, but for simplicity and because these names are almost never seen or spoken in the play, I will refer to the performers by their real names. I am choosing to use first names because they indicate gender, which is important in *Food Court*, although the company also casts across gender. This is the case in *small metal objects*, discussed below, where I will use the characters' names rather than the actors'. In other shows discussed later, *Ganesh Versus the Third Reich* and *The Shadow Whose Prey the Hunter Becomes*, the actors play versions of themselves, indicated by their first names in the working and published scripts I am using for reference.

86. This part was originally developed and performed by Rita Halabarec but was played by Teuben in the production I saw.

87. The term "intellectual disability" is preferred in Australia, but there are regional variations in terminology, as Bree Hadley and Donna McDonald note: "In the UK, for example, scholars and practitioners will speak of

'learning disabled' to avoid use of 'intellectual disability' as a terminology they find problematic, whereas in the US and Australasia, 'learning disability' and 'intellectual disability' still mean different things, so scholars and practitioners will still speak of 'intellectual disability' in arts and media practice." Bree Hadley and Donna McDonald, "Introduction: Disability Arts, Culture, and Media Studies—Mapping a Maturing Field," in *The Routledge Handbook of Disability Arts, Culture, and Media*, ed. Bree Hadley and Donna McDonald (London: Routledge, 2019), 6.

88. Helena Grehan and Peter Eckersall, eds., *"We're People Who Do Shows": Back to Back Theatre: Performance Politics Visibility* (Aberystwyth, UK: Performance Research Books, 2013), 30.

89. Grehan and Eckersall, *"We're People Who Do Shows,"* 31.

90. Tony McCaffrey, "Institution, Care, and Emancipation in Contemporary Theatre Involving Actors with Intellectual Disabilities," in *The Routledge Handbook of Disability Arts, Culture, and Media*, ed. Bree Hadley and Donna McDonald (London: Routledge, 2019), 189.

91. Grehan and Eckersall, *"We're People Who Do Shows,"* 220. This version of the company statement is dated from 2008.

92. Responding to a previously published section of this chapter, Matthew Reason rightly points out that I write from this nondisabled perspective, and that I assume that I am writing for nondisabled readers. His own work deliberately includes other perspectives, based on interviews and conversations with learning disabled spectators to various theater works made by performers who also identify as learning disabled. See Matthew Reason, "Ways of Watching: Five Aesthetics of Learning Disability Theatre," in *The Routledge Handbook of Disability Arts, Culture, and Media*, ed. Bree Hadley and Donna McDonald (London: Routledge, 2019), 170.

93. Rosemarie Garland-Thomson, *Staring: How We Look* (Oxford: Oxford University Press, 2009), 9–10.

94. Garland-Thomson, *Staring*, 38, emphasis added.

95. Rosemarie Garland-Thomson, *Extraordinary Bodies: Figuring Physical Disability in American Culture and Literature* (New York: Columbia University Press, 1997), 8–9.

96. Garland-Thomson, *Staring*, 193, 83.

97. Bree Hadley, *Disability, Public Space Performance and Spectatorship: Unconscious Performers* (Basingstoke, UK: Palgrave Macmillan, 2014), 85. The quote from Tim Milful is from an online review published by MC Reviews which is no longer available.

98. Jen Harvie, *Theatre & the City* (Basingstoke, UK: Palgrave Macmillan, 2009), 4–5. Stratford, the region of East London, should not be confused with the more famous Stratford-upon-Avon in Warwickshire.

99. Back to Back Theatre, *small metal objects* (2005), in *"We're People Who Do Shows": Back to Back Theatre: Performance Politics Visibility*, ed. Helena Grehan and Peter Eckersall (Aberystwyth, UK: Performance Research Books, 2013), 59–72, 65–66.

100. Back to Back Theatre, *small metal objects*, 72.

101. Back to Back Theatre, *small metal objects*, 62.

102. Gladwin quoted in Matt Hargrave, "Pure Products Go Crazy," *Research in Drama Education: The Journal of Applied Theatre and Performance* 14, no. 1 (2009): 46.

103. Kirby, "On Acting and Not-Acting," 3.

104. Hargrave, "Pure Products Go Crazy," 47.

105. Hargrave, "Pure Products Go Crazy," 47–48; Kirby, "On Acting and Not-Acting," 5.

106. Garland-Thomson, *Staring*, 193.

107. Eve Kosofsky Sedgwick, *Touching Feeling: Affect, Pedagogy, Performativity* (Durham, NC: Duke University Press, 2003), 31, emphasis in original.

108. Back to Back Theatre, *Food Court* post-show discussion, Barbican Theatre, London, June 24, 2010. Participants: Lloyd Swanton, Bruce Gladwin, Sarah Mainwaring, Sonia Teuben, Mark Deans, Scott Price, Nicki Holland, moderated by Brian Logan.

109. Back to Back Theatre, *Food Court*, 2010.

110. Hargrave, "Pure Products Go Crazy," 48, emphasis in original.

111. Barish, *The Antitheatrical Prejudice*, 290, emphasis in original.

112. Diamond, *Unmaking Mimesis*, 52.

113. Diamond, *Unmaking Mimesis* 47.

114. Back to Back Theatre, *Food Court* (2008), in *"We're People Who Do Shows": Back to Back Theatre: Performance Politics Visibility*, ed. Helena Grehan and Peter Eckersall (Aberystwyth, UK: Performance Research Books, 2013), 95–101, 96. In the post-show discussion, Gladwin remarks that this section began as he overheard a conversation between two of the ensemble members about food, and was one of the starting places for the entire process.

115. Mainwearing has cerebral palsy as the result of an acquired brain injury.

116. Back to Back Theatre, *Food Court*, 2009, unpublished script provided to the author. The list of possible insults that I reproduce here is taken from the company's working script, and is more extensive than that subsequently published in *"We're People Who Do Shows,"* 97.

117. Back to Back Theatre, *Food Court*, 2013, 100.

118. Back to Back Theatre, *Food Court*, 2013, 101.

119. Elaine Scarry, *The Body in Pain: The Making and Unmaking of the World* (Oxford: Oxford University Press, 1985).

120. Butler, *Excitable Speech*, 6.

121. Toni Morrison, "Nobel Lecture," 1993, https://www.nobelprize.org/prizes/literature/1993/morrison/lecture/.

122. Butler, *Excitable Speech*, 27.

123. Butler, *Excitable Speech*, 69.

124. Lehmann, *Postdramatic Theatre*, 86–90.

125. Lehmann, *Postdramatic Theatre*, 147, emphasis in original.

126. Licia Carlson, *The Faces of Intellectual Disability: Philosophical Reflections* (Bloomington: Indiana University Press, 2010), 165.

127. Carlson, *The Faces of Intellectual Disability*, 164.

128. Carlson, *The Faces of Intellectual Disability*, 152.

129. Michael Oliver, *The Politics of Disablement* (London: Macmillan, 1990).

130. Carlson, *The Faces of Intellectual Disability*, 164, emphasis in original.

131. Disability Awareness in Action, *Overcoming Obstacles to the Integration of Disabled People*, UNESCO-sponsored report to the World Summit on Social Development (Copenhagen: Disability Awareness in Action, 1995). Cited in Peter Mittler, "Meeting the Needs of People with an Intellectual Disability: An International Perspective," in *The Human Rights of Persons with Intellectual Disabilities: Different but Equal*, ed. Stanley S. Herr, Lawrence O. Gostin, and Harold Hongju Koh (Oxford: Oxford University Press, 2003), 29.

132. Carlson, *The Faces of Intellectual Disability*, 86.

133. Tom Shakespeare, "Critiquing the Social Model," in *Disability Rights and Wrongs* (London: Routledge, 2006), 29–53.

134. Matt Hargrave, *Theatres of Learning Disability: Good, Bad, or Plain Ugly?* (Basingstoke, UK: Palgrave Macmillan, 2015), 30, emphasis in original.

135. Hargrave, *Theatres of Learning Disability*, 31; John Swain and Sally French, "Towards an Affirmation Model of Disability," *Disability & Society* 15, no. 4 (2000): 569–82, https://doi.org/10.1080/09687590050058189.

136. Swain and French, "Towards an Affirmation Model of Disability," 577.

137. Grehan and Eckersall, *"We're People Who Do Shows,"* 8.

138. Grehan and Eckersall, *"We're People Who Do Shows,"* 11.

139. Bruce Gladwin, "On Making Theatre," in *The Twenty-First Century Performance Reader*, ed. Teresa Brayshaw, Anna Fenemore, and Noel Witts (London: Routledge, 2019), 30, https://doi.org/10.4324/9780429283956.

140. In reporting on the post-show discussion, I am drawing mainly on Gladwin's comments. My selective quotation is not indicative, however, and obscures the extent to which Gladwin deferred to the comments and experience of the actors, who shared the stage with him, and who repeatedly articulated their experience of sharing authorship and ownership of the work.

141. Reported in Gabriella Coslovich, "The Elephant in the Room," *Sydney Morning Herald*, September 23, 2011, https://www.smh.com.au/entertainment/theatre/the-elephant-in-the-room-20110923-1kout.html.

142. Back to Back Theatre, "About Us," https://backtobacktheatre.com/about/about-us/.

143. Coslovich, "The Elephant in the Room."

144. Back to Back Theatre, *Ganesh Versus the Third Reich* (2011), in *"We're People Who Do Shows": Back to Back Theatre: Performance Politics Visibility*, ed. Helena Grehan and Peter Eckersall (Aberystwyth, UK: Performance Research Books, 2013), 159–94, 182.

145. Back to Back Theatre, *Ganesh Versus the Third Reich*, 183.

146. Back to Back Theatre, *Ganesh Versus the Third Reich*, 183–84.

147. Back to Back Theatre, *The Shadow Whose Prey the Hunter Becomes*, 2019, unpublished script provided to the author. The production toured with a smaller company, so the lines and actions that Mark performed were given to others in later performances, including in the script that was provided to me, but my description is based on the full-cast performance that I saw at Carriageworks, Sydney (2019).

148. Back to Back Theatre, *The Shadow Whose Prey*, 5–6.

149. Carlson, *The Faces of Intellectual Disability*, 152.

150. Back to Back Theatre, *The Shadow Whose Prey*, 8.

151. JP O'Malley, "Convent 'Paid Pocket Money' to Toy Packers," *Sunday Times*, March 27, 2016, https://www.thetimes.co.uk/article/convent-paid-pocket-money-to-toy-packers-69fxndmgkms.

152. Dan Barry, "The 'Boys' in the Bunkhouse," *New York Times*, March 8, 2014, https://www.nytimes.com/interactive/2014/03/09/us/the-boys-in-the-bunkhouse.html.

153. McCaffrey, "Institution, Care, and Emancipation," 192.

Chapter 4

1. J. L. Austin, *How to Do Things with Words*, ed. J. O. Urmson, 2nd ed. (1955; repr. New York: Oxford University Press, 1975), 22, 104.

2. Austin, *How to Do Things with Words*, 14.

3. Gay McAuley, "Unsettled Country: Coming to Terms with the Past," *About Performance*, no. 9 (2009): 48.

4. Kevin Rudd, "Apology to Australia's Indigenous Peoples," February 13, 2008, Parliament of Australia, https://parlinfo.aph.gov.au/parlInfo/search/display/display.w3p;query=Id%3A%22chamber%2Fhansardr%2F2008-02-13%2F0003%22.

5. Nick Smith, *I Was Wrong: The Meanings of Apologies* (Cambridge: Cambridge University Press, 2008), 5–6.

6. Smith, *I Was Wrong*, 140–45.

7. John Howard, "Motion of Reconciliation," August 26, 1999, Parliament of Australia, https://parlinfo.aph.gov.au/parlInfo/search/display/display.w3p;query=Id:%22media/pressrel/23E06%22.

8. John Howard, "Interview with Mike Munro, *A Current Affair*, Channel Nine," PM Transcripts, August 26, 1999, https://pmtranscripts.pmc.gov.au/release/transcript-11129.

9. Tara McCormack, "Aboriginal Apology: A Sorry Spectacle," *Spiked*, February 19, 2008, https://www.spiked-online.com/2008/02/19/aboriginal-apology-a-sorry-spectacle/.

10. McAuley, "Unsettled Country," 60–62.

11. Austin, *How to Do Things with Words*, 147, also 52.

12. On "so-called Australia," see "Introducing the Lineup," note 2.

13. Rudd, "Apology to Australia's Indigenous Peoples."

14. Austin, *How to Do Things with Words*, 79, 134.

15. Austin, *How to Do Things with Words*, 91, 99.

16. Austin, *How to Do Things with Words*, 83.

17. Austin, *How to Do Things with Words*, 150.

18. Austin, *How to Do Things with Words*, 156–57.

19. Austin, *How to Do Things with Words*, 151, 159.

20. Jacques Derrida, "Signature Event Context" (1972), in Jacques Derrida, *Limited Inc*, ed. Gerald Graff and Jeffrey Mehlman, trans. Samuel Weber (Evanston IL: Northwestern University Press, 1988), 15, emphasis in original.

21. Derrida, "Signature Event Context," 17.

22. Jacques Derrida, "Declarations of Independence" (1976), in Jacques Derrida, *Negotiations: Interventions and Interviews, 1971–2001*, ed. Elizabeth Rottenberg and Tom Pepper, trans. Tom Keenan (Stanford, CA: Stanford University Press, 2002), 47.

23. Derrida, "Declarations of Independence," 50. See also Jacques Derrida, "Force of Law: The 'Mystical Foundation of Authority'" (1989), in *Deconstruction and the Possibility of Justice*, ed. Drucilla Cornell, Michel Rosenfeld, and David Gray Carlson, trans. Mary Quaintance (London: Routledge, 1992), 3–67.

24. Derrida, "Declarations of Independence," 49, emphasis in original.

25. Stanley Fish, *Doing What Comes Naturally: Change, Rhetoric, and the Practice of Theory in Literary and Legal Studies* (Durham, NC: Duke University Press, 1989), 49, emphasis in original.

26. Fish, *Doing What Comes Naturally*, 49.

27. Stanley Fish, *Is There a Text in This Class? The Authority of Interpretive Communities* (Cambridge, MA: Harvard University Press, 1980), 231–44.

28. Alan Read, *Theatre & Law* (Basingstoke, UK: Palgrave, 2016), 8.

29. Rudd, "Apology to Australia's Indigenous Peoples."

30. Butler, *Excitable Speech*, 51, emphasis in original.

31. Butler, *Excitable Speech*, 51, emphasis added.

32. Judith Butler, Gary A. Olson, and Lynn Worsham, "Changing the Subject: Judith Butler's Politics of Radical Resignification" (2000), in *The Judith Butler Reader*, ed. Judith Butler and Sara Salih (Oxford: Blackwell, 2004), 335.

33. Butler, *Excitable Speech*, 146–47, emphasis in original.

34. Carey Young, *Disclaimer Series*, 2004, three inkjet prints on board.

35. Fried, "Art and Objecthood," 155.

36. Fried, "Art and Objecthood," 155.

37. Austin, *How to Do Things with Words*, 22.

38. See Marett Leiboff, "Art, Actually! The Courts and the Imposition of Taste," *Public Space: The Journal of Law and Social Justice*, no. 3 (2009): 1–23.

39. Carey Young, *Mutual Release*, 2008, inkjet print on paper.

40. Rabih Mroué, *I, the Undersigned*, 2007, printed statement and video. I first saw this work at the highly commercialized Frieze Art Fair in London, and later as part of the exhibition ~~I, the Undersigned~~—*The People Are Demanding* (London: Iniva, 2011).

41. Austin, *How to Do Things with Words*, 15–16.

42. Rabih Mroué, *Theater with Dirty Feet: A Talk on Theater into Art* (Sharjah: Sharjah Biennial, 2009), http://sharjahart.org/sharjah-art-foundation /projects/theater-with-dirty-feet-a-talk-on-theater-into-art.

43. Rabih Mroué, "The Fabrication of Truth," *Afterall: A Journal of Art, Context and Enquiry* 25 (2010): 89, https://doi.org/10.1086/657466.

44. Aurora F. Polanco, "Fabrication: Image(s), Mon Amour," trans. David Sánchez, in *Rabih Mroué: Image(s), Mon Amour. Fabrications*, exhibition catalog (Madrid: CA2M, 2013), 49.

45. Rabih Mroué, "The Pixelated Revolution," intro. Carol Martin, trans. Ziad Nawfal, *TDR/The Drama Review*, 56, no. 3 (2012): 18–35, 25.

46. Mroué, "The Pixelated Revolution," 31.

47. Mroué, "The Pixelated Revolution," 35.

48. Maaike Bleeker, "Resistance to Representation and the Fabrication of Truth: Performance as Thought-Apparatus," in *Artists in the Archive: Creative and Curatorial Engagements with Documents of Art and Performance*, ed. Paul Clarke et al. (London: Routledge, 2018), 248.

49. Jacques Rancière, *The Emancipated Spectator*, trans. Gregory Elliott (London: Verso, 2009), 102.

50. Alan Gilbert, "Walid Ra'ad," *Bomb*, no. 81 (2002), https://bombmagazine .org/articles/walid-raad/.

51. André Lepecki, "'After All, This Terror Was Not without Reason': Unfiled Notes on the Atlas Group Archive," *TDR/The Drama Review* 30, no. 3 (2006): 90, 98.

52. Lepecki, "After All, This Terror," 90, emphasis in original.

53. Britta Schmitz, "Not a Search for Truth," in *The Atlas Group (1989–2004): A Project by Walid Raad*, ed. Kassandra Nakas and Britta Schmitz, trans. Paul Bowman (Cologne: Walther König, 2006), 42.

54. Walid Raad, "Artist Talk," Walker Art Center, Minneapolis, October 25, 2007, http://www.walkerart.org/channel/2007/artist-talk-walid-raad (video no longer available). The transcription is mine based on this video, to which I have added emphasis.

55. Raad, "Artist Talk."

56. Gilbert, "Walid Ra'ad."

57. Lee Smith, "Missing in Action: The Art of the Atlas Group / Walid Raad," *Artforum* 41, no. 6 (2003): 124–29.

58. Bruno Latour, *Pandora's Hope: Essays on the Reality of Science Studies* (Cambridge, MA: Harvard University Press, 1999), 290–91.

59. Raad, "Artist Talk."

60. Walid Raad, *Let's Be Honest, The Weather Helped* (Amsterdam: Roma, 2020), 44.

61. Rabih Mroué, *The Pixelated Revolution* post-show discussion, Fast Forward Festival, Athens, May 4, 2014.

62. Rabih Mroué, in discussion with the author, May 6, 2014.

63. Pablo Martínez, "When Images Shoot," trans. David Sánchez, in *Rabih Mroué: Image(s), Mon Amour*, exhibition catalog (Madrid: CA2M, 2013), 91.

64. Rabih Mroué, in discussion with the author, May 6, 2014.

65. Ariella Azoulay, *The Civil Contract of Photography* (New York: Zone Books, 2008), 81.

66. Comprehensive surveys of Schlingensief's body of work are provided by Tara Forrest and Anna Teresa Scheer, eds., *Christoph Schlingensief: Art without Borders* (Bristol, UK: Intellect, 2010); and Anna Teresa Scheer, *Christoph Schlingensief: Staging Chaos, Performing Politics and Theatrical Phantasmagoria* (London: Bloomsbury, 2018).

67. *Chance 2000* is described in more detail in Solveig Gade, "Putting the Public Sphere to the Test: On Publics and Counter-Publics in *Chance 2000*," in *Christoph Schlingensief: Art without Borders*, ed. Tara Forrest and Anna Teresa Scheer (Bristol, UK: Intellect, 2010), 89–90.

68. Gade, "Putting the Public Sphere to the Test," 91. Gade's original source is Irene Albers, "Scheitern als Chance—Die Kunst des Krisenexperiments," in *Die Dokumentation—Chance 2000*, ed. Johannes Finke and Matthias Wulff (Berlin: Lautsprecher Verlag, 1999), 43–72, 44.

69. Gade, "Putting the Public Sphere to the Test," 91, and footnote.

70. Thomas Irmer, "Out with the Right! or, Let's Not Let Them in Again," *Theater* 32, no. 3 (2002): 62.

71. *Ausländer Raus! Schlingensief's Container*, directed by Paul Poet (Austria: Bonusfilm, 2002), DVD.

72. *Bitte Liebt Österreich* website, quoted in Poet, *Ausländer Raus!*

73. The influence of Haider and the FPÖ waned in the years after this European intervention, but the party has only grown stronger in recent years, capitalizing on rising anti-Muslim sentiment. Under Haider's successor, Heinz-Christian Strache, the FPÖ won 26 percent of the national vote in 2017 and again formed a coalition government with the ÖVP, before scandals over Strache's use of party funds for private expenses split the coalition in 2019, with the FPÖ returned to opposition in a subsequent snap election.

74. Poet, *Ausländer Raus!*

75. Here and in subsequent quotations from Poet's documentary, I am generally taking the text from the translated subtitles, with occasional adjustments for punctuation and minor word changes.

76. Scheer, *Christoph Schlingensief*.

77. Poet, *Ausländer Raus!*

78. Poet, *Ausländer Raus!*

79. Irmer, "Out with the Right!" 63.

80. Denise Varney, "Being Political in German Theatre and Performance: Anna Langhoff and Christoph Schlingensief," in *Proceedings of the 2006 Conference of the Australasian Association for Drama, Theatre and Performance Studies*, 2014, 1–2, http://ses.library.usyd.edu.au/bitstream/2123/2484/1/ADSA2006_Varney.pdf. Varney's reference is to Janelle Reinelt, "Notes for a Radical Democratic Theater: Productive Crises and the Challenge of Indeterminacy," in *Staging Resistance: Essays on Political Theater*, ed. Jeanne Colleran and Jenny S. Spencer (Ann Arbor: University of Michigan Press, 1998), 289.

81. Tara Forrest, "Mobilizing the Public Sphere: Schlingensief's Reality Theatre," *Contemporary Theatre Review* 18, no. 1 (2008): 91.

82. Forrest, "Mobilizing the Public Sphere," 98. Forrest's source for Schlingensief's phrase "Wir sind zwar nicht gut, aber wir sind da," in *Schlingensief! Notruf für Deutschland: Über die Mission, das Theater und die Welt des Christoph Schlingensief*, ed. Julia Lochte and Wilfried Schulz (Hamburg: Rotbuch Verlag, 1998), 12–39, 12.

83. BAVO, "Always Choose the Worst Option: Artistic Resistance and the Strategy of Over-Identification," in *Cultural Activism Today: The Art of Over-Identification*, ed. BAVO (Rotterdam: Episode, 2007), 21.

84. BAVO, "Always Choose the Worst Option," 18.

85. BAVO, "Always Choose the Worst Option," 23. Incidentally, "Art without Borders" is the subtitle to Forrest and Scheer's collection of essays on Schlingensief.

86. BAVO, "Always Choose the Worst Option," 27–28, emphasis in original.

87. BAVO, "Always Choose the Worst Option," 34, emphasis in original.

88. Forrest, "Mobilizing the Public Sphere," 94.

89. Poet, *Ausländer Raus!*

90. Poet, *Ausländer Raus!*

91. Kirsten Weiss, "Recycling the Image of the Public Sphere in Art," *Thresholds*, no. 23 (2001): 58.

92. Weiss, "Recycling the Image," 59, emphasis added.

93. Walter Benjamin, "The Work of Art in the Age of Mechanical Reproduction" (1935), in Walter Benjamin, *Illuminations*, ed. Hannah Arendt, trans. Harry Zohn (London: Cape, 1970), 243.

94. Philippe Lacoue-Labarthe, *Heidegger, Art and Politics: The Fiction of the Political*, trans. Chris Turner (Oxford: Basil Blackwell, 1990), 103.

95. Lacoue-Labarthe, *Heidegger, Art and Politics*, 94.

96. Michael Hirsch, "Politics of Fiction," *Parachute*, no. 101 (2001): 135.

97. "Hyper-authenticity" is how Silvija Jestrović describes the predicament of the asylum seeker: "It is not only a matter of being an asylum seeker, a refugee, or an immigrant, but also of performing accordingly in order not to be considered bogus." Silvija Jestrović, "Performing like an Asylum Seeker: Paradoxes of Hyper-Authenticity in Schlingensief's *Please Love Austria*," in *Double Agent*, ed. Claire Bishop and Silvia Tramontana (London: ICA, 2009), 57, emphasis in original.

Coda

1. Susan Sontag, *Regarding the Pain of Others* (London: Penguin, 2003), 97.

2. Sontag, *Regarding the Pain of Others*, 98–99.

3. Sontag, *Regarding the Pain of Others*, 99, emphasis added.

4. Sontag, *Regarding the Pain of Others*, 91.

5. Sontag, *Regarding the Pain of Others*, 109.

6. Sontag, *Regarding the Pain of Others*, 113.

7. Stanley Cavell, "The Avoidance of Love: A Reading of King Lear" (1967), in *Must We Mean What We Say?* updated ed. (Cambridge: Cambridge University Press, 2002), 338.

8. Stanley Cavell, "Knowing and Acknowledging" (1969), in *Must We Mean What We Say?* updated ed. (Cambridge: Cambridge University Press, 2002), 257.

9. Cavell, "The Avoidance of Love," 339.

10. Cavell, "Knowing and Acknowledging," 263.

11. Deborah Bird Rose, *Nourishing Terrains: Australian Aboriginal Views of Landscape and Wilderness* (Canberra: Australian Heritage Commission, 1996), 7.

12. Cited in Mark McKenna, "Tokenism or Belated Recognition? Welcome to Country and the Emergence of Indigenous Protocol in Australia, 1991–2014," *Journal of Australian Studies* 38, no. 4 (2014): 482, https://doi.org/10.1080/14443058.2014.952765.

13. McKenna, "Tokenism or Belated Recognition?" 483–84.

14. Parliament of Australia, "Annotated Standing Orders of the Australian Senate: Chapter 8, Sittings, Quorum and Adjournment of the Senate," October 26, 2010, https://www.aph.gov.au/About_Parliament/Senate/Powers_practice_n_procedures/aso/so050.

15. Emma Kowal, "Welcome to Country: Acknowledgement, Belonging and White Anti-Racism," *Cultural Studies Review* 21, no. 2 (2015): 189.

16. UNSW Sydney, "Welcome to Country and Acknowledgement of Country Protocol," Nura Gili—Centre for Indigenous Programs, https://www.nuragili.unsw.edu.au/about-us/welcome-country-and-acknowledgement-country-protocol.

17. See Robert Manne, ed., *Whitewash: On Keith Windschuttle's Fabrication of Aboriginal History* (Melbourne: Black Inc. Agenda, 2003).

18. Keith Windschuttle, "Welcomes to Country Are Being Foisted on Us in Error," *The Australian*, November 30, 2012, http://at.theaustralian.com.au /link/82b9749840792d606b4115c9772.

19. Samantha Maiden, "Indigenous Tokenism an Empty Gesture, Says Tony Abbott," *The Australian*, March 15, 2010, https://www.news.com.au/breaking -news/indigenous-tokenism-an-empty-gesture-says-tony-abbott/news-story /533218b71f5cafe28956bb2c61d55d01.

20. Deborah Cheetham, "Young and Free? Why I Declined to Sing the National Anthem at the 2015 AFL Grand Final," The Conversation, October 20, 2015, http://theconversation.com/young-and-free-why-i-declined-to-sing -the-national-anthem-at-the-2015-afl-grand-final-49234.

21. Chelsea Bond, Bryan Mukandi, and Shane Coghill, "'You Cunts Can Do as You Like': The Obscenity and Absurdity of Free Speech to Blackfullas," *Continuum* 32, no. 4 (2018): 416, https://doi.org/10.1080/10304312.2018 .1487126.

22. Bond et al., "You Cunts Do What You Like," 416–17.

23. Scott Morrison, "Now Is the Time to Recognise That Australia Is 'One and Free,'" *Sydney Morning Herald*, December 31, 2020, https://www.smh .com.au/national/now-is-the-time-to-recognise-that-australia-is-one-and-free -20201231-p56r39.html.

24. Uluru Statement from the Heart, 2017, https://ulurustatement.org.

25. Claire G. Coleman, "A Single Word: How Political Fear Erodes Indigenous Rights," *The Saturday Paper*, January 23, 2021, https://www .thesaturdaypaper.com.au/opinion/topic/2021/01/23/how-political-fear -erodes-indigenous-rights/161132040010968.

26. The Australian fables around Whiteness and Christianity converge in the name of the Grammy-nominated Christian musical group Hillsong Young & Free, part of the Pentecostal megachurch Hillsong, of which the former Australian prime minister Scott Morrison was an outspoken member.

27. Kowal, "Welcome to Country," 189.

28. Kristina Everett, "Welcome to Country . . . Not," *Oceania* 79, no. 1 (2009): 58, https://doi.org/10.1002/j.1834-4461.2009.tb00050.x, emphasis in original.

29. Sara Ahmed, "The Non-Performativity of Anti-Racism," *Borderlands* 5, no. 3 (2006), http://www.borderlands.net.au/vol5no3_2006/ahmed _nonperform.htm, emphasis added.

30. Sara Ahmed, *On Being Included: Racism and Diversity in Institutional Life* (Durham, NC: Duke University Press, 2012), 117.

31. Tanja Dreher and Poppy de Souza, "Locating Listening," in *Ethical Responsiveness and the Politics of Difference*, ed. Tanja Dreher and Anshuman A. Mondal (Cham, Switz.: Palgrave Macmillan, 2018), 28.

32. Stephanie Convery, "Lip Service," *Overland Literary Journal*, March 16, 2010, https://overland.org.au/2010/03/lip-service/.

33. Everett, "Welcome to Country . . . Not," 53.

34. Dreher and de Souza, "Locating Listening," 29.

35. Dreher and Souza, "Locating Listening," 28.

36. Kowal, "Welcome to Country," 181, emphasis in original.

37. Butler, *Excitable Speech*, 152.

38. New South Wales Aboriginal Land Council, "Council Defends Welcome to Country," *Deadly Vibe* (blog), May 22, 2011, https://www.deadlyvibe.com .au/2011/05/council-defends-welcome-to-country/, emphasis added.

BIBLIOGRAPHY

Agamben, Giorgio. *What Is an Apparatus? and Other Essays*. Translated by David Kishik. Stanford, CA: Stanford University Press, 2009.

Ahmed, Sara. "The Non-Performativity of Anti-Racism." *Borderlands* 5, no. 3 (2006). http://www.borderlands.net.au/vol5no3_2006/ahmed_nonperform .htm.

———. *On Being Included: Racism and Diversity in Institutional Life*. Durham, NC: Duke University Press, 2012.

Als, Hilton. "Eight Hours of, Like, Life." *New Yorker*, January 23, 2013. http://www.newyorker.com/online/blogs/culture/2013/01/nature-theater-of -oklahoma-reviewed.html.

Alston, Adam. *Beyond Immersive Theatre: Aesthetics, Politics and Productive Participation*. Basingstoke, UK: Palgrave Macmillan, 2016. https://doi.org /10.1057/978-1-137-48044-6.

Anderson-Rabern, Rachel. "The Nature Theater of Oklahoma's Aesthetics of Fun." *TDR/The Drama Review* 54, no. 4 (2010): 81–98.

Archias, Elise. *The Concrete Body: Yvonne Rainer, Carolee Schneemann, Vito Acconci*. New Haven, CT: Yale University Press, 2016.

Arendt, Hannah. *The Human Condition*. 2nd ed. 1958. Reprint, Chicago: University of Chicago Press, 1998.

———. *The Life of the Mind*. New York: Harvest/HBJ, 1978.

———. "We Refugees" (1943). In *Altogether Elsewhere: Writers On Exile*, edited by Marc Robinson, 110–19. London: Faber and Faber, 1994.

Arfara, Katia. "Aspects of a New Dramaturgy of the Spectator—Rimini Protokoll's 'Breaking News.'" *Performance Research* 14, no. 3 (2009): 112–18. https://doi.org/10.1080/13528160903519575.

Aristotle. *Poetics*. Translated by S. H. Butcher. http://classics.mit.edu/Aristotle /poetics.1.1.html.

Arlen, Michael J. *Living-Room War*. New York: Viking, 1969.

Arvers, Fabienne. "Jérôme Bel Par Jérôme Bel." Les Inrocks, January 31, 2001. http://www.lesinrocks.com/2001/01/31/musique/concerts/jerome-bel-par -jerome-bel-11226045/.

Austin, J. L. *How to Do Things with Words*. Edited by J. O. Urmson. 2nd ed. 1955. Reprint, New York: Oxford University Press, 1975.

Australian Institute of Aboriginal and Torres Strait Islander Studies. "Map of Indigenous Australia." https://aiatsis.gov.au/explore/map-indigenous -australia.

Ayers, Robert. "'The Knife Is Real, the Blood Is Real, and the Emotions Are Real': Robert Ayers in Conversation with Marina Abramović." March 10, 2010. http://www.askyfilledwithshootingstars.com/?p=1197 (site discontinued).

Azoulay, Ariella. *The Civil Contract of Photography*. New York: Zone Books, 2008.

Back to Back Theatre. "About Us." https://backtobacktheatre.com/about/about-us/.

———. *Food Court* (2008). In *"We're People Who Do Shows": Back to Back Theatre: Performance Politics Visibility*, edited by Helena Grehan and Peter Eckersall, 95–101. Aberystwyth, UK: Performance Research Books, 2013.

———. *Food Court*. 2009. Unpublished script provided to the author.

———. *Food Court* post-show discussion, Barbican Theatre, London, June 24, 2010. Participants: Lloyd Swanton, Bruce Gladwin, Sarah Mainwaring, Sonia Teuben, Mark Deans, Scott Price, and Nicki Holland. Moderated by Brian Logan.

———. *Ganesh Versus the Third Reich* (2011). In *"We're People Who Do Shows": Back to Back Theatre: Performance Politics Visibility*, edited by Helena Grehan and Peter Eckersall, 159–94. Aberystwyth, UK: Performance Research Books, 2013.

———. *The Shadow Whose Prey the Hunter Becomes*. 2019. Unpublished script provided to the author.

———. *Small Metal Objects* (2005). In *"We're People Who Do Shows": Back to Back Theatre: Performance Politics Visibility*, edited by Helena Grehan and Peter Eckersall, 59–72. Aberystwyth, UK: Performance Research Books, 2013.

Bailey, John. "Signatures and Signalling." *RealTime*, no. 93 (October–November 2009): 40. https://www.realtime.org.au/signatures-and-signalling/.

Bakst, Lauren Grace. "Nature Theater of Oklahoma." *Bomb*, September 17, 2013. http://bombmagazine.org/article/7369/nature-theater-of-oklahoma.

Baldessari, John. "Unrealised Proposal for Cadavre Piece, 1970." In *11 Rooms* exhibition program. Manchester: Manchester International Festival, 2011.

Barad, Karen. *Meeting the Universe Halfway: Quantum Physics and the Entanglement of Matter and Meaning*. Durham, NC: Duke University Press, 2007.

Barish, Jonas. *The Antitheatrical Prejudice*. Berkeley: University of California Press, 1981.

Barnett, David. *Brecht in Practice: Theatre, Theory and Performance*. London: Bloomsbury, 2015.

———. "Performing Dialectics in an Age of Uncertainty, or Why Post-Brechtian ≠ Postdramatic." In *Postdramatic Theatre and the Political*, edited by Karen Jürs-Munby, Jerome Carroll, and Steve Giles, 47–66. London: Bloomsbury, 2013.

———. "Toward a Definition of Post-Brechtian Performance: The Example of *In the Jungle of the Cities* at the Berliner Ensemble, 1971." *Modern Drama* 54, no. 3 (2011): 333–56. https://doi.org/10.3138/md.54.3.333.

Barry, Dan. "The 'Boys' in the Bunkhouse." *New York Times*, March 8, 2014. https://www.nytimes.com/interactive/2014/03/09/us/the-boys-in-the-bunkhouse.html.

Barthes, Roland. "Baudelaire's Theater" (1954). In *A Barthes Reader*, edited by Susan Sontag, translated by Richard Howard, 74–81. New York: Hill and Wang, 1982.

Bassel, Leah. "Acting 'As' and Acting 'As If': Two Approaches to the Politics of Race and Migration." In *Theories of Race and Ethnicity: Contemporary Debates and Perspectives*, edited by John Solomos and Karim Murji, 94–113. Cambridge: Cambridge University Press, 2015. https://doi.org/10.1017/CBO9781139015431.009.

Bauer, Una. "The Movement of Embodied Thought: The Representational Game of the Stage Zero of Signification in *Jérôme Bel*." *Performance Research* 13, no. 1 (2008): 35–41. https://doi.org/10.1080/13528160802465508.

BAVO. "Always Choose the Worst Option: Artistic Resistance and the Strategy of Over-Identification." In *Cultural Activism Today: The Art of Over-Identification*, edited by BAVO, 18–39. Rotterdam: Episode, 2007.

Bel, Jérôme, and Yvane Chapuis. "Jérôme Bel—Interview—*The Show Must Go On* (2001)—Second Part." *Catalogue raisonné Jérôme Bel 1994–2005*, December 15, 2007. https://www.youtube.com/watch?v=9ZX7Hx15k_c.

Benjamin, Walter. "Conversations with Brecht" (1934). In *Understanding Brecht*, edited by Stanley Mitchell, translated by Anna Bostock, 105–21. London: Verso, 1998.

———. "Franz Kafka: On the Tenth Anniversary of His Death" (1934). In Walter Benjamin, *Illuminations*, edited by Hannah Arendt, translated by Harry Zohn, 111–40. New York: Schocken, 1969.

———. "What Is Epic Theater?" (1939). In Walter Benjamin, *Illuminations*, edited by Hannah Arendt, translated by Harry Zohn, 147–54. New York: Schocken, 1969.

———. "The Work of Art in the Age of Mechanical Reproduction" (1935). In Walter Benjamin, *Illuminations*, edited by Hannah Arendt, translated by Harry Zohn, 219–53. London: Cape, 1970.

Bennett, Jane. *Vibrant Matter: A Political Ecology of Things*. Durham, NC: Duke University Press, 2010.

Berardi, Franco "Bifo." *After the Future*. Edited by Gary Genosko and Nicholas Thoburn. Oakland, CA: AK, 2011.

Bernstein, Robin. *Racial Innocence: Performing American Childhood from Slavery to Civil Rights*. New York: New York University Press, 2011.

Biesenbach, Klaus, and Hans Ulrich Obrist. "Foreword." In *11 Rooms* exhibition program. Manchester: Manchester International Festival, 2011.

Bishop, Claire. "Antagonism and Relational Aesthetics." *October*, no. 110 (2004): 51–79. https://doi.org/10.1162/0162287042379810.

———. *Artificial Hells: Participatory Art and the Politics of Spectatorship*. London: Verso, 2012.

———. "The Social Turn: Collaboration and Its Discontents." *Artforum* 44, no. 6 (2006): 178–83.

Blau, Herbert. "The Metaphysical Fight: Performative Politics and the Virus of Alienation." In *Performance, Identity, and the Neo-Political Subject*, edited by Fintan Walsh and Matthew Causey, 21–32. London: Routledge, 2013.

Bleeker, Maaike. "Absorption and Focalization: Performance and Its Double." *Performance Research* 10, no. 1 (January 1, 2005): 48–60. https://doi.org/10.1080/13528165.2005.10871396.

———. "Movement as Lived Abstraction: The Logic of the Cut." In *Performance and Phenomenology: Traditions and Transformations*, edited by

Maaike Bleeker, Jon Foley Sherman, and Eirini Nedelkopoulou, 35–53. London: Routledge, 2015.

———. "Resistance to Representation and the Fabrication of Truth: Performance as Thought-Apparatus." In *Artists in the Archive: Creative and Curatorial Engagements with Documents of Art and Performance*, edited by Paul Clarke, Simon Jones, Nick Kaye, and Johanna Linsley, 247–69. London: Routledge, 2018.

———. *Visuality in the Theatre: The Locus of Looking*. Basingstoke, UK: Palgrave, 2008.

Bond, Chelsea, Bryan Mukandi, and Shane Coghill. "'You Cunts Can Do as You Like': The Obscenity and Absurdity of Free Speech to Blackfullas." *Continuum* 32, no. 4 (2018): 415–28. https://doi.org/10.1080/10304312.2018.1487126.

Bottoms, Stephen. "Authorizing the Audience: The Conceptual Drama of Tim Crouch." *Performance Research* 14, no. 1 (2009): 65–76. https://doi.org/10.1080/13528160903113213.

———. "The Efficacy/Effeminacy Braid: Unpacking the Performance Studies/Theatre Studies Dichotomy." *Theatre Topics* 13, no. 2 (2003): 173–87. https://doi.org/10.1353/tt.2003.0029.

Bourriaud, Nicolas. "Precarious Constructions: Answer to Jacques Rancière on Art and Politics." *Open*, no. 17 (2014): 17–37.

———. *Relational Aesthetics (Esthétique relationnelle*, 1998). Translated by Simon Pleasance. Dijon, Fr.: Presses du Reél, 2002.

Boyle, Michael Shane. "Performance and Value: The Work of Theatre in Karl Marx's Critique of Political Economy." *Theatre Survey* 58, no. 1 (2017): 3–23. https://doi.org/10.1017/S0040557416000661.

Brecht, Bertolt. "A Short Organum for the Theatre" (1948). In *Brecht on Theatre: The Development of an Aesthetic*, edited and translated by John Willett, 179–205. London: Methuen, 1964.

———. "On Form and Subject-Matter" (1929). In *Brecht on Theatre: The Development of an Aesthetic*, edited and translated by John Willett, 29–30. London: Methuen, 1964.

———. "On the Art of Spectatorship" ("Über die Zuschaukunst," 1935). In *Brecht on Theatre*, edited by Marc Silberman, Steve Giles, and Tom Kuhn, 174. London: Bloomsbury, 2018.

———. "Showing Has to Be Shown" (1945). In *Bertolt Brecht Poems 1913– 1956*, edited by John Willett, Ralph Manheim, and Erich Fried, translated by John Willett, 341–42. London: Methuen, 1976.

———. "The Street Scene: A Basic Model for an Epic Theatre" (1938). In *Brecht on Theatre: The Development of an Aesthetic*, edited and translated by John Willett, 121–29. London: Methuen, 1964.

———. "Theatre for Pleasure or Theatre for Instruction" (1936?). In *Brecht on Theatre: The Development of an Aesthetic*, edited and translated by John Willett, 69–77. London: Methuen, 1964.

Brennan, Clare. "That Night Follows Day." *Observer*, April 1, 2009. http://www.theguardian.com/stage/2009/apr/12/theatre-reviews-london.

Brook, Peter. *The Empty Space*. 1968. Reprint, London: Penguin, 1990.

Burns, Elizabeth. *Theatricality: A Study of Convention in the Theatre and in Social Life.* New York: Harper and Row, 1972.

Burt, Ramsay. "'Don't Give the Game Away': Rainer's 1967 Reflections on Dance and the Visual Arts Revisited." Presented at Yvonne Rainer: Intermedial Constellations Symposium, Ludwig Museum, Cologne, 2012. https://www.dora.dmu.ac.uk/xmlui/handle/2086/7344.

Butler, Judith. *Excitable Speech: A Politics of the Performative.* London: Routledge, 1997.

———. *Notes Toward a Performative Theory of Assembly.* Cambridge, MA: Harvard University Press, 2015.

Butler, Judith, Gary A. Olson, and Lynn Worsham. "Changing the Subject: Judith Butler's Politics of Radical Resignification" (2000). In *The Judith Butler Reader,* edited by Judith Butler and Sara Salih, 325–56. Oxford: Blackwell, 2004.

Carlson, Licia. *The Faces of Intellectual Disability: Philosophical Reflections.* Bloomington: Indiana University Press, 2010.

Catterson, Pat. "I Promised Myself I Would Never Let It Leave My Body's Memory." *Dance Research Journal* 41, no. 2 (2009): 3–11. https://doi.org/10.1017/S0149767700000607.

Cavell, Stanley. "The Avoidance of Love: A Reading of *King Lear*" (1967). In *Must We Mean What We Say?* updated edition, 267–353. Cambridge: Cambridge University Press, 2002.

———. "Knowing and Acknowledging" (1969). In *Must We Mean What We Say?* updated edition, 238–66. Cambridge: Cambridge University Press, 2002.

Cheetham, Deborah. "Young and Free? Why I Declined to Sing the National Anthem at the 2015 AFL Grand Final." The Conversation, October 20, 2015. http://theconversation.com/young-and-free-why-i-declined-to-sing-the-national-anthem-at-the-2015-afl-grand-final-49234.

Coleman, Claire G. "A Single Word: How Political Fear Erodes Indigenous Rights." *The Saturday Paper,* January 23, 2021. https://www.thesaturdaypaper.com.au/opinion/topic/2021/01/23/how-political-fear-erodes-indigenous-rights/161132040010968.

Convery, Stephanie. "Lip Service." *Overland Literary Journal,* March 16, 2010. https://overland.org.au/2010/03/lip-service/.

Cornish, Matt. "Chat Room." *PAJ: A Journal of Performance and Art* 32, no. 1 (2009): 45–52. https://doi.org/10.1162/pajj.2010.32.1.46.

Corrieri, Augusto. "Watching People in the Light: Jérôme Bel and the Classical Theatre." In *Contemporary French Theatre and Performance,* edited by Clare Finburgh and Carl Lavery, 213–23. Basingstoke, UK: Palgrave Macmillan, 2011.

Coslovich, Gabriella. "The Elephant in the Room." *Sydney Morning Herald,* September 23, 2011. https://www.smh.com.au/entertainment/theatre/the-elephant-in-the-room-20110923-1kout.html.

Costa, Maddy. "How Everyone Who Ever Lived Eats and Drinks and Loves and Sleeps and Talks and Walks and Wakes and Forgets and Quarrels and Likes and Dislikes and Works and Sits: The Life and Times of Nature Theater

of Oklahoma." *Deliq.* (blog), 2013. http://statesofdeliquescence.blogspot.co
.uk/2013/06/how-everyone-who-ever-lived-eats-and.html.

Crimp, Douglas. "Pictures." *October*, no. 8 (1979): 75–88.

Crouch, Tim. *Adler & Gibb.* London: Oberon, 2014.

———. "*The Author*: Response and Responsibility." *Contemporary Theatre Review* 21, no. 4 (2011): 416–22. https://doi.org/10.1080/10486801.2011
.610312.

———. *ENGLAND* theater program. London: Whitechapel Gallery, 2009.

———. "Interview with Tim Crouch, Writer and Director of Royal Court's *Adler & Gibb.*" *Aesthetica*, May 5, 2014. http://www.aestheticamagazine
.com/interview-with-tim-crouch-writer-and-director-of-royal-courts-adler
-and-gibb/.

———. *Plays One: My Arm, An Oak Tree, ENGLAND, The Author.* London: Oberon, 2011.

Crouch, Tim, Dan Rebellato, and Louise LePage. "Tim Crouch and Dan Rebellato in Conversation." *Platform* 6, no. 2 (2012): 13–27.

Crouch, Tim, and a smith. "'How We Are Together': An Endless Conversation with Tim Crouch and a smith." *Thompson's Bank of Communicable Desire* (blog). http://beescope.blogspot.com/2009/12/how-we-are-together-endless
.html (site discontinued).

Crouch, Tim, and Caridad Svich. "Tim Crouch's Theatrical Transformations: A Conversation with Caridad Svich," 2006. http://www.hotreview.org
/articles/timcrouchinterv.htm.

Cumming-Bruce, Nick, and Steven Erlanger. "Swiss Ban Building of Minarets on Mosques." *New York Times*, November 29, 2009. https://www.nytimes
.com/2009/11/30/world/europe/30swiss.html.

Damian Martin, Diana, and Theron Schmidt. "Sites of Appearance, Matters of Thought: Hannah Arendt and Performance Philosophy." *Performance Philosophy* 5, no. 1 (2019): 1–7. https://doi.org/10.21476/PP.2019.51291.

Davis, Tracy C. "Theatricality and Civil Society." In *Theatricality*, edited by Tracy C. Davis and Thomas Postlewait, 127–55. Cambridge: Cambridge University Press, 2003.

Davis, Tracy C., and Thomas Postlewait. "Theatricality: An Introduction." In *Theatricality*, edited by Tracy C. Davis and Thomas Postlewait, 1–39. Cambridge: Cambridge University Press, 2003.

Debord, Guy. "Rapport sur la construction des situations et sur les conditions de l'organisation et de l'action de la tendance situationniste internationale" (1957). *Inter: Art Actuel*, no. 44 (1989): 1–11.

———. "Report on the Construction of Situations and on the Terms of Organization and Action of the International Situationist Tendency" (1957). In *Guy Debord and the Situationist International: Texts and Documents*, edited and translated by Tom McDonough, 29–50. Cambridge, MA: MIT Press, 2002.

———. *The Society of the Spectacle* (*La Société du spectacle*, 1967). Translated by Donald Nicholson-Smith. New York: Zone Books, 1994.

Defraeye, Piet. "You! Hypocrite Spectateur. A Short History of the Production and Reception of Peter Handke's *Publikumsbeschimpfung.*" *Seminar: A Journal of Germanic Studies* 42, no. 4 (2006): 412–38.

Delgado-García, Cristina. "'We're All in This Together': Reality, Vulnerability and Democratic Representation in Tim Crouch's *The Author.*" In *Of Precariousness: Vulnerabilities, Responsibilities, Communities in 21st-Century British Drama and Theatre*, edited by Mireia Aragay and Martin Middeke, 91–107. Berlin: De Gruyter, 2017. https://doi.org/10.1515/9783110548716 -007.

Derrida, Jacques. "Declarations of Independence" (1976). In Jacques Derrida, *Negotiations: Interventions and Interviews, 1971–2001*, edited by Elizabeth Rottenberg and Tom Pepper, translated by Tom Keenan, 46–54. Stanford, CA: Stanford University Press, 2002.

———. "Force of Law: The 'Mystical Foundation of Authority'" (1989). In *Deconstruction and the Possibility of Justice*, edited by Drucilla Cornell, Michel Rosenfeld, and David Gray Carlson, translated by Mary Quaintance, 3–67. London: Routledge, 1992.

———. "Signature Event Context" (1972). In Jacques Derrida, *Limited Inc*, edited by Gerald Graff and Jeffrey Mehlman, translated by Samuel Weber, 1–23. Evanston, IL: Northwestern University Press, 1988.

———. *Specters of Marx* (*Spectres de Marx: L'État de la dette, le travail du deuil et la nouvelle Internationale*, 1993). Translated by Peggy Kamuf. New York: Routledge, 2006.

Despret, Vinciane. "From Secret Agents to Interagency." *History and Theory* 52, no. 4 (2013): 29–44. https://doi.org/10.1111/hith.10686.

Diamond, Elin. "Introduction." In *Performance and Cultural Politics*, edited by Elin Diamond, 1–12. London: Routledge, 1996.

———. *Unmaking Mimesis: Essays on Feminism and Theater*. London: Routledge, 1997.

Disability Awareness in Action. *Overcoming Obstacles to the Integration of Disabled People*. UNESCO-sponsored report to the World Summit on Social Development. Copenhagen: Disability Awareness in Action, 1995.

Dreher, Tanja, and Poppy de Souza. "Locating Listening." In *Ethical Responsiveness and the Politics of Difference*, edited by Tanja Dreher and Anshuman A. Mondal, 21–39. Cham, Switz.: Palgrave Macmillan, 2018.

Dreysse, Miriam, and Florian Malzacher, eds. *Experts of the Everyday: The Theatre of Rimini Protokoll*. Berlin: Alexander Verlag, 2008.

Edelman, Lee. *No Future: Queer Theory and the Death Drive*. Durham, NC: Duke University Press, 2004.

Etchells, Tim. "More and More Clever Watching More and More Stupid." In *Live: Art and Performance*, edited by Adrian Heathfield, 198–99. London: Tate, 2004.

———. "On Performance and Technology" (1995). In *Certain Fragments: Contemporary Performance and Forced Entertainment*, 94–97. London: Routledge, 1999.

———. "On Risk and Investment" (1994). In *Certain Fragments: Contemporary Performance and Forced Entertainment*, 48–49. London: Routledge, 1999.

———. "A Six-Thousand-and-Forty-Seven-Word Manifesto on Liveness in Three Parts with Interludes." In *Live: Art and Performance*, edited by Adrian Heathfield, 210–17. London: Tate, 2004.

———. "Step Off the Stage." In *The Live Art Almanac*, edited by Daniel Brine, 7–16. London: Live Art Development Agency, 2008.

———. *That Night Follows Day*. Ghent, Belgium: Victoria, 2007.

———. "That Night Follows Day." http://timetchells.com/projects/that-night -follows-day/.

Etchells, Tim, Richard Maxwell, and Phelim McDermott. "Re-Wiring / Re-Writing Theatre," panel facilitated by Adrian Heathfield, Riverside Studios, London, November 18, 2006.

Everett, Kristina. "Welcome to Country . . . Not." *Oceania* 79, no. 1 (2009): 53–64. https://doi.org/10.1002/j.1834-4461.2009.tb00050.x.

Féral, Josette. Foreword. "Theatricality." Special issue, *SubStance* 31, no. 2/3 (2002): 3–13. https://doi.org/10.1353/sub.2002.0025.

———. "Performance and Theatricality: The Subject Demystified." Translated by Terese Lyons. *Modern Drama* 25, no. 1 (1982): 170–81. https://doi.org /10.1353/mdr.1982.0036.

Ferguson, Alex. "The Complicit Witness." *RealTime*, April 2010. https://www .realtime.org.au/the-complicit-witness/.

Fevered Sleep. Men & Girls Dance Newspaper, London Edition, 2019. https:// issuu.com/feveredsleep/docs/m_gd_6_londonnewspaper_f_issuu.

Fish, Stanley. *Doing What Comes Naturally: Change, Rhetoric, and the Practice of Theory in Literary and Legal Studies*. Durham, NC: Duke University Press, 1989.

———. *Is There a Text in This Class? The Authority of Interpretive Communities*. Cambridge, MA: Harvard University Press, 1980.

Flood, Alison. "'Ignorant Questions': Nobel Winner Peter Handke Refuses to Address Controversy." *Guardian*, December 6, 2019. http://www .theguardian.com/books/2019/dec/06/peter-handke-questions-nobel-prize -literature-milosevic.

Forrest, Tara. "Mobilizing the Public Sphere: Schlingensief's Reality Theatre." *Contemporary Theatre Review* 18, no. 1 (2008): 90–98.

Forrest, Tara, and Anna Teresa Scheer, eds. *Christoph Schlingensief: Art without Borders*. Bristol, UK: Intellect, 2010.

Foster, Hal. "The Crux of Minimalism." In *The Return of the Real*, 35–70. Cambridge, MA: MIT Press, 1996.

Fragkou, Marissia, and Philip Hager. "Staging London: Participation and Citizenship on the Way to the 2012 Olympic Games." *Contemporary Theatre Review* 23, no. 4 (2013): 532–41. https://doi.org/10.1080/10486801.2013 .839172.

Freee Art Collective. "When Work Is More Than Wages." *On Curating*, no. 16 (2014): 41–45.

Freshwater, Helen. "Children and the Limits of Representation in the Work of Tim Crouch." In *Contemporary British Theatre: Breaking New Ground*, edited by Vicky Angelaki, 167–88. Basingstoke, UK: Palgrave Macmillan, 2014. https://doi.org/10.1057/9781137010131.

Fried, Michael. *Absorption and Theatricality: Painting and Beholder in the Age of Diderot*. Berkeley: University of California Press, 1980.

———. "Art and Objecthood" (1967). In *Art and Objecthood: Essays and Reviews*, 148–72. Chicago: University of Chicago Press, 1998.

Frieze, James. "Actualizing a Spectator Like You: The Ethics of the Intrusive-Hypothetical." *Performing Ethos: International Journal of Ethics in Theatre & Performance* 3, no. 1 (2012): 7–22. https://doi.org/10.1386/peet.3.1.7_1.

Fuchs, Elinor. *The Death of Character: Perspectives on Theater after Modernism.* Bloomington: Indiana University Press, 1996.

Gade, Solveig. "Putting the Public Sphere to the Test: On Publics and Counter-Publics in *Chance 2000.*" In *Christoph Schlingensief: Art without Borders,* edited by Tara Forrest and Anna Teresa Scheer, 89–103. Bristol, UK: Intellect, 2010.

Garde, Ulrike, and Meg Mumford. "Postdramatic Reality Theatre and Productive Insecurity: Destabilising Encounters with the Unfamiliar in Theatre from Sydney and Berlin." In *Postdramatic Theatre and the Political: International Perspectives on Contemporary Performance,* edited by Karen Jürs-Munby, Jerome Carroll, and Steve Giles, 147–64. London: Bloomsbury, 2013.

———. *Theatre of Real People: Diverse Encounters from Berlin's Hebbel am Ufer and Beyond.* London: Bloomsbury, 2016.

Gardner, Lyn. "How Real Is Reality Theatre?" *Guardian,* October 13, 2009. http://www.guardian.co.uk/stage/theatreblog/2009/oct/11/reality-verbatim-theatre.

Gardner, Sally. "What Is a Transmitter?" *Choreographic Practices* 5, no. 2 (2014): 229–40. https://doi.org/10.1386/chor.5.2.229_1.

Garland-Thomson, Rosemarie. *Extraordinary Bodies: Figuring Physical Disability in American Culture and Literature.* New York: Columbia University Press, 1997.

———. *Staring: How We Look.* Oxford: Oxford University Press, 2009.

Giersdorf, Jens Richard. "*Trio A* Canonical." *Dance Research Journal* 41, no. 2 (2009): 19–24. https://doi.org/10.1017/S0149767700000620.

Gilbert, Alan. "Walid Ra'ad." *Bomb,* no. 81 (2002). https://bombmagazine.org/articles/walid-raad/.

Gillick, Liam. "The Good of Work." In *Are You Working Too Much? Post-Fordism, Precarity and the Labor of Art,* edited by Julieta Aranda, Brian Kuan Wood, and Anton Vidokle, 30–73. Berlin: e-flux/Sternberg, 2011.

Gladwin, Bruce. "On Making Theatre." In *The Twenty-First Century Performance Reader,* edited by Teresa Brayshaw, Anna Fenemore, and Noel Witts, 30–34. London: Routledge, 2019. https://doi.org/10.4324/9780429283956.

Goldberg, RoseLee. "Jerome Bel." *Artforum* 43, no. 10 (2005): 329.

Gorman, Sarah. "Refusing Shorthand: Richard Maxwell." *Contemporary Theatre Review* 17, no. 2 (2007): 235–41.

Goulish, Matthew. *39 Microlectures: In Proximity of Performance.* London: Routledge, 2000.

Grehan, Helena, and Peter Eckersall, eds. *"We're People Who Do Shows": Back to Back Theatre: Performance Politics Visibility.* Aberystwyth, UK: Performance Research Books, 2013.

Gullì, Bruno. *Earthly Plenitudes: A Study on Sovereignty and Labor.* Philadelphia: Temple University Press, 2010.

Hadley, Bree. *Disability, Public Space Performance and Spectatorship: Unconscious Performers.* Basingstoke, UK: Palgrave Macmillan, 2014.

Hadley, Bree, and Donna McDonald. "Introduction: Disability Arts, Culture, and Media Studies—Mapping a Maturing Field." In *The Routledge Handbook of Disability Arts, Culture, and Media*, edited by Bree Hadley and Donna McDonald, 1–18. London: Routledge, 2019.

Hallward, Peter. "Staging Equality: On Rancière's Theatrocracy." *New Left Review*, no. 37 (2006): 109–29.

Halstead, Jack. "Peter Handke's *Sprechstücke* and Speech-Act Theory." *Text and Performance Quarterly* 10, no. 3 (1990): 183–93. https://doi.org/10.1080/10462939009365969.

Handke, Peter. "Brecht, Play, Theatre, Agitation." Translated by Nicholas Hern. *Theatre Quarterly* 1, no. 4 (1971): 89–90.

———. "Note on Offending the Audience" (1972). In *Plays: 1: Offending the Audience, Self-Accusation, Kaspar, My Foot My Tutor, The Ride across Lake Constance, They Are Dying Out*, translated by Tom Kuhn, 309. London: Methuen Drama, 1997.

———. *Offending the Audience* (*Publikumsbeschimpfung*, 1966). Translated by Michael Roloff. In *Plays: 1: Offending the Audience, Self-Accusation, Kaspar, My Foot My Tutor, The Ride across Lake Constance, They Are Dying Out*, 1–32. London: Methuen Drama, 1997.

———. "Peter Handke Bei Gruppe 47 in Princeton 1966" (transcript). Edited by Thomas Gollas, September 29, 2014. http://hcolsezrawhcs.blogspot.com.au/2014/09/peter-handke-bei-der-gruppe-47-in.html.

———. "Peter Handke's 1966 Speech at the Princeton Meeting of the Gruppe 47." Translated by Scott Abbott, June 11, 2013. https://thegoaliesanxiety.wordpress.com/2013/06/11/peter-handkes-1966-speech-at-the-princeton-meeting-of-the-gruppe-47/.

Handke, Peter, and Artur Joseph. "Nauseated by Language: From an Interview with Peter Handke." Translated by E. B. Ashton. *TDR/The Drama Review* 15, no. 1 (1970): 57–61. https://doi.org/10.2307/1144591.

Hardt, Michael. "Affective Labor." *Boundary 2* 26, no. 2 (1999): 89–100.

Hardt, Michael, and Antonio Negri. *Empire*. Cambridge, MA: Harvard University Press, 2000.

Hargrave, Matt. "Pure Products Go Crazy." *Research in Drama Education: The Journal of Applied Theatre and Performance* 14, no. 1 (2009): 37–54.

———. *Theatres of Learning Disability: Good, Bad, or Plain Ugly?* Basingstoke, UK: Palgrave Macmillan, 2015.

Harris, Geraldine. "*Susan and Darren*: The Appearance of Authenticity." *Performance Research* 13, no. 4 (2008): 4–15. https://doi.org/10.1080/13528160902875580.

Harvie, Jen. *Theatre & the City*. Basingstoke, UK: Palgrave Macmillan, 2009.

Haydon, Andrew. "Five Easy Pieces—Sophiensæle (as TT17), Berlin." *Postcards from the Gods* (blog), May 16, 2017. http://postcardsgods.blogspot.com/2017/05/five-easy-pieces-sophiensle-as-tt17.html.

Heathfield, Adrian. "Glimmers in Limbo: Inhuman Animations, Child's Play, and the Coming Catastrophe." In *Boris Charmatz*, edited by Ana Janevski, 107–18. New York: MoMA, 2017.

Hildebrandt, Antje. "Soma-Conceptual Choreographic Strategies in Boris Charmatz's *Enfant.*" *Journal of Dance & Somatic Practices* 9, no. 1 (2017): 95–103. https://doi.org/10.1386/jdsp.9.1.95_1.

Hirsch, Michael. "Politics of Fiction." *Parachute*, no. 101 (2001): 124–36.

Hoffmann, Beth. Review of *Bloody Mess*, by Forced Entertainment. *Theatre Journal* 58, no. 4 (2006): 701–3.

Howard, John. "Interview with Mike Munro, *A Current Affair*, Channel Nine." PM Transcripts, August 26, 1999. https://pmtranscripts.pmc.gov.au /release/transcript-11129.

———. "Motion of Reconciliation," August 26, 1999. Parliament of Australia. https://parlinfo.aph.gov.au/parlInfo/search/display/display.w3p;query= Id:%22media/pressrel/23E06%22.

Hurley, Erin. *Theatre & Feeling*. Basingstoke, UK: Palgrave Macmillan, 2010.

Ilter, Seda. "Andy Smith, 'Dematerialising Theatre' (Birkbeck Arts Week 2017)." *Birkbeck, Department of English & Humanities Blog* (blog), May 25, 2017. http://blogs.bbk.ac.uk/english/2017/05/25/seda-ilter-on-andy -smith-dematerialising-theatre-birkbeck-arts-week-2017/.

———. "'A Process of Transformation': Tim Crouch on *My Arm.*" *Contemporary Theatre Review* 21, no. 4 (2011): 394–404. https://doi.org/10.1080 /10486801.2011.610792.

Irmer, Thomas. "Out with the Right! or, Let's Not Let Them in Again." *Theater* 32, no. 3 (2002): 61–67.

———. "A Search for New Realities: Documentary Theatre in Germany." *TDR/The Drama Review* 30, no. 3 (2006): 16–28. https://doi.org/10.1162 /dram.2006.50.3.16.

Isherwood, Charles. "Theater Talkback: The Rough Beauty of Everyday Speech." *New York Times ArtsBeat* (blog), January 31, 2013. http://artsbeat .blogs.nytimes.com/2013/01/31/theater-talkback-the-rough-beauty-of -everyday-speech/.

Jackson, Shannon. "Just-in-Time: Performance and the Aesthetics of Precarity." *TDR/The Drama Review* 56, no. 4 (2012): 10–31.

———. *Professing Performance: Theatre in the Academy from Philology to Performativity*. Cambridge: Cambridge University Press, 2004. https://doi .org/10.1017/CBO9780511554247.

———. *Social Works: Performing Art, Supporting Publics*. London: Routledge, 2011.

———. "Theatre . . . Again." *Art Lies*, no. 60 (2008): 18–21.

Jestrovic, Silvija. "Performing like an Asylum Seeker: Paradoxes of Hyper-Authenticity in Schlingensief's *Please Love Austria.*" In *Double Agent*, edited by Claire Bishop and Silvia Tramontana, 56–61. London: ICA, 2009.

Jones, Amelia. *Body Art/Performing the Subject*. Minneapolis: University of Minnesota Press, 1998.

Kafka, Franz. *America* (*Der Verschollene*, written 1911–14, published posthumously 1927). Translated by Edwin Muir. London: Vintage, 2005.

Kaprow, Allan. "The Education of the Un-Artist, Part III" (1974). In Allan Kaprow, *Essays on the Blurring of Art and Life*, edited by Jeff Kelley, expanded edition, 130–47. Berkeley: University of California Press, 2003.

————. "The Happenings Are Dead: Long Live the Happenings!" (1966). In Allan Kaprow, *Essays on the Blurring of Art and Life*, edited by Jeff Kelley, expanded edition, 59–65. Berkeley: University of California Press, 2003.

Kiebuzinska, Christine. *Intertextual Loops in Modern Drama*. Madison, NJ: Fairleigh Dickinson University Press, 2001.

Kirby, Michael. "On Acting and Not-Acting." *TDR/The Drama Review* 16, no. 1 (1972): 3–15. https://doi.org/10.2307/1144724.

Kowal, Emma. "Welcome to Country: Acknowledgement, Belonging and White Anti-Racism." *Cultural Studies Review* 21, no. 2 (2015): 173–204.

Krauss, Rosalind. "Theories of Art after Minimalism and Pop." In *Discussions in Contemporary Culture*, edited by Hal Foster, 59–64. Seattle: Bay, 1987.

Kühl, Christiane. "Rimini Protokoll: A Live Archive of the Everyday." In *No More Drama*, edited by Peter Crawley and Willie White, translated by Rachel West, 29–41. Dublin: Project/Carysfort, 2011.

Kunst, Bojana. *Artist at Work: Proximity of Art and Capitalism*. Winchester, UK: Zero Books, 2015.

Lacoue-Labarthe, Philippe. *Heidegger, Art and Politics: The Fiction of the Political*. Translated by Chris Turner. Oxford: Basil Blackwell, 1990.

Lambert-Beatty, Carrie. *Being Watched: Yvonne Rainer and the 1960s*. Cambridge, MA: October Books/MIT Press, 2008.

Latour, Bruno. *Pandora's Hope: Essays on the Reality of Science Studies*. Cambridge, MA: Harvard University Press, 1999.

Lazzarato, Maurizio. "Immaterial Labour." In *Radical Thought in Italy*, edited by Paolo Virno and Michael Hardt, translated by Paul Colilli and Ed Emory, 132–46. Minneapolis: University of Minnesota Press, 1996.

Lee, Young Jean. "Nature Theater of Oklahoma." *Bomb*, no. 108 (2009). https://bombmagazine.org/articles/nature-theater-of-oklahoma-1/.

Lees, Nicola, ed. *A Pamphlet for the Serpentine Gallery Manifesto Marathon 2008*. London: Serpentine Gallery, 2008.

————. *The Shipment and LEAR*. New York: Theatre Communications Group, 2010.

Lehmann, Hans-Thies. "The Political in the Post-Dramatic." *Maska* 17, no. 74/75 (2002): 74–76.

————. *Postdramatic Theatre (Postdramatisch Theater*, 1999). Edited and translated by Karen Jürs-Munby. London: Routledge, 2006.

Leiboff, Marett. "Art, Actually! The Courts and the Imposition of Taste." *Public Space: The Journal of Law and Social Justice*, no. 3 (2009): 1–23.

Lepecki, André. "'After All, This Terror Was Not without Reason': Unfiled Notes on the Atlas Group Archive." *TDR/The Drama Review* 30, no. 3 (2006): 88–99.

Levine, Debra. "Not Just Adult Entertainment: Milo Rau and CAMPO's Collaborative *Five Easy Pieces*." *TDR/The Drama Review* 61, no. 4 (2017): 147–55. https://doi.org/10.1162/DRAM_a_00699.

Lippard, Lucy R., and John Chandler. "The Dematerialization of Art" (1968). In Lucy R. Lippard, *Changing: Essays in Art Criticism*, 255–76. New York: E. P. Dutton, 1971.

Logan, Brian. "Edinburgh Festival: *Once and for All We're Gonna Tell You Who We Are So Shut Up and Listen.*" *Guardian*, August 15, 2008. http://www .theguardian.com/culture/2008/aug/14/edinburghfestival.onceandforall.

Lury, Karen. *The Child in Film: Tears, Fears and Fairy Tales.* London: I. B. Tauris, 2010.

Maiden, Samantha. "Indigenous Tokenism an Empty Gesture, Says Tony Abbott." *The Australian*, March 15, 2010. https://www.news.com.au/breaking -news/indigenous-tokenism-an-empty-gesture-says-tony-abbott/news-story/ 533218b71f5cafe28956bb2c61d55d01.

Malzacher, Florian. "Dramaturgies of Care and Insecurity: The Story of Rimini Protokoll." In *Experts of the Everyday: The Theatre of Rimini Protokoll*, edited by Miriam Dreysse and Florian Malzacher, 14–43. Berlin: Alexander Verlag, 2008.

———. "No Organum to Follow: Possibilities of Political Theatre Today." In *Not Just a Mirror: Looking for the Political Theatre of Today*, edited by Florian Malzacher, 16–30. Berlin and London: House on Fire; Alexander Verlag; Live Art Development Agency, 2015.

———. "Previously on Nature Theater of Oklahoma . . ." In Nature Theater of Oklahoma, *Life and Times—Episode V*, 113–28. Long Island City, NY: Nature Theater of Oklahoma, 2012.

———. "There Is a Word for People Like You: Audience: The Spectator as Bad Witness and Bad Voyeur." In *"Not Even a Game Anymore": The Theatre of Forced Entertainment*, edited by Judith Helmer and Florian Malzacher, 127–41. Berlin: Alexander Verlag, 2004.

Manne, Robert, ed. *Whitewash: On Keith Windschuttle's Fabrication of Aboriginal History.* Melbourne: Black Inc. Agenda, 2003.

Marranca, Bonnie. "PerformanceContemporary: Dialogue with Richard Maxwell." LocationOne, 2002. http://www.location1.org/mediadb/artist.php #m (site discontinued).

———. "The *Sprechstucke*: Peter Handke's Universe of Words." *PAJ: Performing Arts Journal* 1, no. 2 (1976): 52–62. https://doi.org/10.2307/3245038.

Marshall, Alex. "Is Milo Rau Really the Most Controversial Director in Theater?" *New York Times*, October 3, 2018. https://www.nytimes.com/2018 /10/03/theater/milo-rau-ntgent-controversy.html.

Marshall, David. "Adam Smith and the Theatricality of Moral Sentiments." *Critical Inquiry* 10, no. 4 (1984): 592–613.

———. "Rousseau and the State of Theater." *Representations*, no. 13 (1986): 84–114.

Martin, Carol. *Theatre of the Real.* Basingstoke, UK: Palgrave Macmillan, 2013. https://doi.org/10.1057/9781137295729.

Martin, Stewart. "Critique of Relational Aesthetics." *Third Text* 21, no. 4 (2007): 369–86. https://doi.org/10.1080/09528820701433323.

Martínez, Pablo. "When Images Shoot." Translated by David Sánchez. In *Rabih Mroué: Image(s), Mon Amour*, 86–97. Exhibition catalog. Madrid: CA2M, 2013.

Marx, Karl. *Capital, Volume 1.* Translated by Ben Fowkes. New York: Vintage, 1977.

———. "Economic and Philosophical Manuscripts" (1844). In *Karl Marx: Early Writings*, translated by Gregor Benton and Rodney Livingstone, 279–400. New York: Penguin, 1992.

McAuley, Gay. "Unsettled Country: Coming to Terms with the Past." *About Performance* 9 (2009): 45–65.

McCaffrey, Tony. "Institution, Care, and Emancipation in Contemporary Theatre Involving Actors with Intellectual Disabilities." In *The Routledge Handbook of Disability Arts, Culture, and Media*, edited by Bree Hadley and Donna McDonald, 189–202. London: Routledge, 2019.

McCormack, Tara. "Aboriginal Apology: A Sorry Spectacle." *Spiked*, February 19, 2008. https://www.spiked-online.com/2008/02/19/aboriginal-apology -a-sorry-spectacle/.

McGillivray, Glen. "The Discursive Formation of Theatricality as a Critical Concept." *Metaphorik.de*, no. 17 (2009): 101–14.

McKenna, Mark. "Tokenism or Belated Recognition? Welcome to Country and the Emergence of Indigenous Protocol in Australia, 1991–2014." *Journal of Australian Studies* 38, no. 4 (2014): 476–89. https://doi.org/10.1080 /14443058.2014.952765.

McMillan, Joyce. "As Night Follows Day [*sic*]." *Scotsman*, May 3, 2008. http://www.scotsman.com/news/reviews-1-1166471.

Melville, Stephen. "Notes on the Reemergence of Allegory, the Forgetting of Modernism, the Necessity of Rhetoric, and the Conditions of Publicity in Art and Criticism." *October*, no. 19 (1981): 55–92. https://doi.org/10.2307 /778660.

Mittler, Peter. "Meeting the Needs of People with an Intellectual Disability: An International Perspective." In *The Human Rights of Persons with Intellectual Disabilities: Different but Equal*, edited by Stanley S. Herr, Lawrence O. Gostin, and Harold Hongju Koh, 25–48. Oxford: Oxford University Press, 2003.

Morris, Robert. "Blank Form" (1960–61). In *Blam! The Explosion of Pop, Minimalism, and Performance, 1958–1964*, edited by Barbara Haskell, 101. New York: Whitney Museum of American Art in association with W. W. Norton, 1984.

———. "Notes on Sculpture" (1966). In *Minimal Art: A Critical Anthology*, edited by Gregory Battcock, 221–35. New York: Dutton, 1968.

Morrison, Scott. "Now Is the Time to Recognise That Australia Is 'One and Free.'" *Sydney Morning Herald*, December 31, 2020. https://www.smh.com .au/national/now-is-the-time-to-recognise-that-australia-is-one-and-free -20201231-p56r39.html.

Morrison, Toni. "Nobel Lecture." 1993. https://www.nobelprize.org/prizes /literature/1993/morrison/lecture/.

Moten, Fred. *In the Break: The Aesthetics of the Black Radical Tradition*. Minneapolis: University of Minnesota Press, 2003.

Mouffe, Chantal. *The Democratic Paradox*. London: Verso, 2000.

Mroué, Rabih. "The Fabrication of Truth." *Afterall: A Journal of Art, Context and Enquiry* 25 (2010): 86–89. https://doi.org/10.1086/657466.

———. *I, the Undersigned*. 2007. Printed statement and video.

———. In discussion with the author, May 6, 2014.

————. "The Pixelated Revolution." Introduced by Carol Martin, translated by Ziad Nawfal. *TDR/The Drama Review* 56, no. 3 (2012): 18–35. https://doi.org/10.1162/DRAM_a_00186.

————. *The Pixelated Revolution* post-show discussion. Fast Forward Festival, Athens, May 4, 2014.

————. *Theater with Dirty Feet: A Talk on Theater into Art*. Sharjah: Sharjah Biennial, 2009. http://sharjahart.org/sharjah-art-foundation/projects/theater-with-dirty-feet-a-talk-on-theater-into-art.

Nancy, Jean-Luc. *Being Singular Plural (Être singulier pluriel*, 1996). Translated by Robert D. Richardson and Anne E. O'Byrne. Stanford, CA: Stanford University Press, 2000.

————. *The Inoperative Community (La Communauté désoeuvrée*, 1986). Edited by Peter Connor, translated by Peter Connor, Lisa Garbus, Michael Holland, and Simona Sawhney. Minneapolis: University of Minnesota Press, 1991.

Nature Theater of Oklahoma. *Life and Times: Episode 1*. Chicago: 53rd State, 2013.

————. *Life and Times: Episode 2*. Chicago: 53rd State, 2013.

————. *Life and Times: Episodes 3 & 4*. Chicago: 53rd State, 2013.

————. *Life and Times: Episodes 1–5* theater program. Norwich, UK: Norfolk & Norwich Festival, 2013.

New South Wales Aboriginal Land Council. "Council Defends Welcome to Country." *Deadly Vibe* (blog), May 22, 2011. https://www.deadlyvibe.com.au/2011/05/council-defends-welcome-to-country/.

Nield, Sophie. "The Rise of the Character Named Spectator." *Contemporary Theatre Review* 18, no. 4 (2008): 531–35. https://doi.org/10.1080/10486800802492855.

Norman, S. J. "Sarah Jane Norman Responds to Marina Abramovic." ABC Radio National, August 25, 2016. https://www.abc.net.au/radionational/programs/awaye/sarah-jane-norman-responds-to-marina-abramovic/7784750.

NTGent. "Ghent Manifesto," May 1, 2018. https://www.ntgent.be/en/manifest.

O'Doherty, Brian. *Inside the White Cube: The Ideology of the Gallery Space*, expanded edition. 1976. Reprint, Berkeley: University of California Press, 1999.

Oliver, Michael. *The Politics of Disablement*. London: Macmillan, 1990.

O'Malley, JP. "Convent 'Paid Pocket Money' to Toy Packers." *Sunday Times*, March 27, 2016. https://www.thetimes.co.uk/article/convent-paid-pocket-money-to-toy-packers-69fxndmgkms.

Ontroerend Goed. "*Once and for All* (2008)." http://www.ontroerendgoed.be/en/projecten/once-and-for-all/.

O'Toole, Fintan. "The Call of the Conscious in Reality Theatre." *Irish Times*, October 10, 2009. http://www.irishtimes.com/newspaper/weekend/2009/1010/1224256317409.html.

Owen, Louise. "Robert Wilson, *Walking* (Holkham Estate, 2012)." *Contemporary Theatre Review* 23, no. 4 (2013): 568–73. https://doi.org/10.1080/10486801.2013.839177.

Parliament of Australia. "Annotated Standing Orders of the Australian Senate: Chapter 8, Sittings, Quorum and Adjournment of the Senate," October 26, 2010. https://www.aph.gov.au/About_Parliament/Senate/Powers_practice _n_procedures/aso/so050.

Pitkin, Hanna Fenichel. *The Attack of the Blob: Hannah Arendt's Concept of the Social*. Chicago: University of Chicago Press, 1998.

———. *The Concept of Representation*. Berkeley: University of California Press, 1967.

Plant, Sadie. *The Most Radical Gesture: The Situationist International in a Postmodern Age*. London: Routledge, 1992.

Poet, Paul, dir. *Ausländer Raus! Schlingensief's Container*. Austria: Bonusfilm, 2002. DVD.

Polanco, Aurora F. "Fabrication: Image(s), Mon Amour." Translated by David Sánchez. In *Rabih Mroué: Image(s), Mon Amour. Fabrications*, 36–59. Exhibition catalog. Madrid: CA2M, 2013.

Pontbriand, Chantal. "The Eye Finds No Fixed Point on Which to Rest . . ." Translated by C. R. Parsons. *Modern Drama* 25, no. 1 (1982): 154–62. https://doi.org/10.3138/md.25.1.154.

———. "Work: The Sharing of Experience." *Parachute*, no. 122 (2006): 6–9.

Puchner, Martin. "Society of the Counter-Spectacle: Debord and the Theatre of the Situationists." *Theatre Research International* 29, no. 1 (2004): 4–15. https://doi.org/10.1017/S0307883303001214.

Quarantine. *Entitled*. 2011. Unpublished script provided to the author.

———. *Entitled* theater program. London: Sadler's Wells, 2011.

———. *Entitled* screening and live discussion (online), May 29, 2020.

Raad, Walid. "Artist Talk." Walker Art Center, Minneapolis, October 25, 2007. http://www.walkerart.org/channel/2007/artist-talk-walid-raad (video no longer available).

———. *Let's Be Honest, The Weather Helped*. Amsterdam: Roma, 2020.

Rae, Paul. *Real Theatre: Essays in Experience*. Cambridge: Cambridge University Press, 2019.

Rainer, Yvonne. *Feelings Are Facts: A Life*. Cambridge, MA: MIT Press, 2006.

———. "A Quasi Survey of Some 'Minimalist' Tendencies in the Quantitatively Minimal Dance Activity midst the Plethora, or An Analysis of *Trio A*" (1966). In *Minimal Art: A Critical Anthology*, edited by Gregory Battcock, 263–73. New York: Dutton, 1968.

———. *A Woman Who . . . : Essays, Interviews, Scripts*. Baltimore: Johns Hopkins University Press, 1999.

———. "Notebook for *The Mind Is a Muscle*, Anderson Theatre, New York, 1968." In *Yvonne Rainer: The Mind Is a Muscle*, by Catherine Wood, 6–9. London: Afterall Books, 2007.

———. "Some Retrospective Notes on a Dance for 10 People and 12 Mattresses Called 'Parts of Some Sextets' Performed at the Wadsworth Atheneum, Hartford, Connecticut, and Judson Memorial Church, New York, in March 1965." *Tulane Drama Review* 10, no. 2 (1965): 168–78. https://doi.org/10.2307/1125242.

———. "'Statement' from *The Mind Is a Muscle*, Anderson Theater, New York (April 1968)." In *Work 1961–73*, 70–71. Halifax: Press of the Nova Scotia College of Art and Design, 1974.

———. "*Trio A*: Genealogy, Documentation, Notation." *Dance Research Journal* 41, no. 2 (2009): 12–18. https://doi.org/10.1017/S0149767700000619.

Rainer, Yvonne, Robert Alexander, and Sally Banes. *Trio A*. 1978. http://www.vdb.org/titles/trio.

Rancière, Jacques. "Aesthetics and Politics: Rethinking the Link." Presented at the University of California, Berkeley, September 2002. http://16beavergroup.org/mondays/2006/05/06/monday-night-05-08-06-discussion-on-rancieres-politics-of-aesthetics/.

———. *Aisthesis: Scenes from the Aesthetic Regime of Art*. Translated by Zakir Paul. London: Verso, 2013.

———. *Disagreement: Politics and Philosophy* (*La Mesentente: Politique et philosophie*, 1995). Translated by Julie Rose. Minneapolis: University of Minnesota Press, 1999.

———. "The Emancipated Spectator." *Artforum* 45, no. 7 (2007): 271–80.

———. *The Emancipated Spectator*. Translated by Gregory Elliott. London: Verso, 2009.

———. *The Politics of Aesthetics: The Distribution of the Sensible* (*Le Partage du sensible: Esthétique et politique*, 2000). Translated by Gabriel Rockhill. London: Continuum, 2004.

Rayner, Alice. "Rude Mechanicals and the *Specters of Marx*." *Theatre Journal* 54, no. 4 (2002): 535–54. https://doi.org/10.1353/tj.2002.0133.

Read, Alan. *Theatre and Everyday Life: An Ethics of Performance*. London: Routledge, 1993.

———. *Theatre & Law*. Basingstoke, UK: Palgrave, 2016.

Reason, Matthew. "Ways of Watching: Five Aesthetics of Learning Disability Theatre." In *The Routledge Handbook of Disability Arts, Culture, and Media*, edited by Bree Hadley and Donna McDonald, 163–75. London: Routledge, 2019.

Reinelt, Janelle. "Notes for a Radical Democratic Theater: Productive Crises and the Challenge of Indeterminacy." In *Staging Resistance: Essays on Political Theater*, edited by Jeanne Colleran and Jenny S. Spencer, 283–300. Ann Arbor: University of Michigan Press, 1998.

———. "*Postdramatic Theatre and the Political: International Perspectives on Contemporary Performance* (Review)." *Theatre Research International* 40, no. 2 (2015): 201–3. https://doi.org/10.1017/S0307883315000061.

———. "'What I Came to Say': Raymond Williams, the Sociology of Culture and the Politics of (Performance) Scholarship." *Theatre Research International* 40, no. 3 (2015): 235–49. https://doi.org/10.1017/S0307883315000334.

Ridout, Nicholas. "A Make-Believe World." Presented at A Make-Believe World, Chelsea Theatre, London, November 13, 2010.

———. *Passionate Amateurs: Theatre, Communism, and Love*. Ann Arbor: University of Michigan Press, 2013.

———. "Performance and Democracy." In *The Cambridge Companion to Performance Studies*, edited by Tracy C. Davis, 11–22. Cambridge: Cambridge University Press, 2008.

———. "Performance in the Service Economy: Outsourcing and Delegation." In *Double Agent*, edited by Claire Bishop and Silvia Tramontana, 126–31. London: ICA, 2009.

———. *Stage Fright, Animals, and Other Theatrical Problems*. Cambridge: Cambridge University Press, 2006.

Ridout, Nicholas, and Rebecca Schneider. "Precarity and Performance: An Introduction." *TDR/The Drama Review* 56, no. 4 (2012): 5–9. https://doi .org/10.1162/DRAM_a_00210.

Rimini Protokoll. "Annual Shareholder's Meeting." https://www.rimini -protokoll.de/website/en/project/hauptversammlung

Roberts, John. *The Intangibilities of Form: Skill and Deskilling in Art after the Readymade*. London: Verso, 2007.

Rose, Deborah Bird. *Nourishing Terrains: Australian Aboriginal Views of Landscape and Wilderness*. Canberra: Australian Heritage Commission, 1996.

Roselt, Jens. "Making an Appearance: On the Performance Practice of Self-Presentation." In *Experts of the Everyday: The Theatre of Rimini Protokoll*, edited by Miriam Dreysse and Florian Malzacher, 46–63. Berlin: Alexander Verlag, 2008.

Rosler, Martha. *House Beautiful: Bringing the War Home, 1967–1972*. http:// www.martharosler.net/house-beautiful-bringing-the-war-home-new-series -carousel-1.

Rousseau, Jean-Jacques. *The Collected Writings of Rousseau*. Vol. 10, *Letter to D'Alembert and Writings for the Theater*, translated by Allan Bloom. Hanover, NH: Dartmouth College/University Press of New England, 2004.

Rudd, Kevin. "Apology to Australia's Indigenous Peoples," February 13, 2008. Parliament of Australia. https://parlinfo.aph.gov.au/parlInfo/search/display /display.w3p;query=Id%3A%22chamber%2Fhansardr%2F2008-02-13 %2F0003%22.

Sack, Daniel. "Festival d'Avignon (Review)." *Theatre Journal* 61, no. 1 (2009): 117–20. https://doi.org/10.1353/tj.0.0147.

Sandler, Irving. "Gesture and Non-Gesture in Recent Sculpture" (1967). In *Minimal Art: A Critical Anthology*, edited by Gregory Battcock, 308–16. New York: Dutton, 1968.

Scarry, Elaine. *The Body in Pain: The Making and Unmaking of the World*. Oxford: Oxford University Press, 1985.

Schechner, Richard. *Between Theater and Anthropology*. Philadelphia: University of Pennsylvania Press, 1985.

———. "A New Paradigm for Theatre in the Academy." *TDR/The Drama Review* 36, no. 4 (1992): 7–10. https://doi.org/10.2307/1146210.

Scheer, Anna Teresa. *Christoph Schlingensief: Staging Chaos, Performing Politics and Theatrical Phantasmagoria*. London: Bloomsbury, 2018.

Schmitz, Britta. "Not a Search for Truth." In *The Atlas Group (1989–2004): A Project by Walid Raad*, edited by Kassandra Nakas and Britta Schmitz, translated by Paul Bowman, 41–46. Cologne: Walther König, 2006.

Sedgwick, Eve Kosofsky. *Touching Feeling: Affect, Pedagogy, Performativity*. Durham, NC: Duke University Press, 2003.

Sellar, Tom. "The City's Best (and Not So Best) Progressive Theater." *The Village Voice*, January 5, 2010. https://www.villagevoice.com/2010/01/05/the-citys-best-and-not-so-best-progressive-theater/.

Shakespeare, Tom. "Critiquing the Social Model." In *Disability Rights and Wrongs*, 29–53. London: Routledge, 2006.

Shalson, Lara. "On Duration and Multiplicity." *Performance Research* 17, no. 5 (2012): 98–106. https://doi.org/10.1080/13528165.2012.728448.

———. "On the Endurance of Theatre in Live Art." *Contemporary Theatre Review* 22, no. 1 (2012): 106–19. https://doi.org/10.1080/10486801.2011.645282.

Sierz, Aleks. *In-Yer-Face: British Drama Today*. London: Faber and Faber, 2001.

———. "Navigating New Patterns of Power with an Audience: Tim Crouch in Conversation with Aleks Sierz." *Journal of Contemporary Drama in English* 2, no. 1 (2014): 63–77. https://doi.org/10.1515/jcde-2014–0006.

smith, a. "Gentle Acts of Removal, Replacement and Reduction: Considering the Audience in Co-Directing the Work of Tim Crouch." *Contemporary Theatre Review* 21, no. 4 (2011): 410–15. https://doi.org/10.1080/10486801.2011.610311.

Smith, Andy. "This Is It: Notes on a Dematerialised Theatre." In *The Twenty-First Century Performance Reader*, edited by Teresa Brayshaw, Anna Fenemore, and Noel Witts, 497–504. London: Routledge, 2019. https://doi.org/10.4324/9780429283956.

Smith, Lee. "Missing in Action: The Art of The Atlas Group / Walid Raad." *Artforum* 41, no. 6 (2003): 124–29.

Smith, Nick. *I Was Wrong: The Meanings of Apologies*. Cambridge: Cambridge University Press, 2008.

Sontag, Susan. *Regarding the Pain of Others*. London: Penguin, 2003.

States, Bert O. *Great Reckonings in Little Rooms: On the Phenomenology of Theater*. Berkeley: University of California Press, 1985.

———. "The Phenomenological Attitude" (1992). In *Critical Theory and Performance*, edited by Janelle G. Reinelt and Joseph R. Roach, 26–36. 2nd ed. Ann Arbor: University of Michigan Press, 2006.

Swain, John, and Sally French. "Towards an Affirmation Model of Disability." *Disability & Society* 15, no. 4 (2000): 569–82. https://doi.org/10.1080/09687590050058189.

Taussig, Michael. *Mimesis and Alterity: A Particular History of the Senses*. London: Routledge, 1993.

Thiong'o, Ngũgĩ wa. "Enactments of Power." *TDR/The Drama Review* 41, no. 3 (1997): 11–30.

Todd, Bella. "Milo Rau: 'I'm Actually Not Trying to Break Any Taboos.'" WhatsOnStage, February 28, 2017. https://www.whatsonstage.com/brighton-theatre/news/milo-rau-interview-sick-festival-five-easy-pieces_43001.html.

Ukeles, Mierle Laderman. "Manifesto for Maintenance Art 1969! Proposal for an Exhibition 'CARE.'" https://www.wikiart.org/en/mierle-laderman-ukeles/manifesto-for-maintenance-art-1969–1969.

Uluru Statement from the Heart, 2017. https://ulurustatement.org.

UNSW Sydney. "Welcome to Country and Acknowledgement of Country Protocol." Nura Gili—Centre for Indigenous Programs. https://www.nuragili.unsw.edu.au/about-us/welcome-country-and-acknowledgement-country-protocol.

Vaneigem, Raoul. *The Revolution of Everyday Life* (*Traité de savoir-vivre à l'usage des jeunes générations*, 1967). Translated by Donald Nicholson-Smith. Oakland, CA: PM, 2012.

Varney, Denise. "Being Political in German Theatre and Performance: Anna Langhoff and Christoph Schlingensief." In *Proceedings of the 2006 Conference of the Australasian Association for Drama, Theatre and Performance Studies*, 2014. http://ses.library.usyd.edu.au/bitstream/2123/2484/1/ADSA2006_Varney.pdf.

Wake, Caroline. "The Accident and the Account: Towards a Taxonomy of Spectatorial Witness in Theatre and Performance Studies." In *Visions and Revisions: Performance, Memory, Trauma*, edited by Bryoni Trezise and Caroline Wake, 33–56. Copenhagen: Museum Tusculanum, 2013.

Weber, Carl. "Brecht in Eclipse?" *TDR/The Drama Review* 24, no. 1 (1980): 115–24. https://doi.org/10.2307/1145300.

Weber, Samuel. *Theatricality as Medium*. New York: Fordham University Press, 2004.

Weiss, Kirsten. "Recycling the Image of the Public Sphere in Art." *Thresholds*, no. 23 (2001): 58–63.

White, Gareth. "On Immersive Theatre." *Theatre Research International* 37, no. 3 (2012): 221–35. https://doi.org/10.1017/S0307883312000880.

Windschuttle, Keith. "Welcomes to Country Are Being Foisted on Us in Error." *The Australian*, November 30, 2012. http://at.theaustralian.com.au/link/82b9749840792d606b4115c9772.

Wood, Catherine. *Yvonne Rainer: The Mind Is a Muscle*. London: Afterall Books, 2007.

Wyver, Kate. "*That Night Follows Day* Review—Adults' Truths and Lies, Voiced by Children." *Guardian*, December 12, 2018. https://www.theguardian.com/stage/2018/dec/12/that-night-follows-day-review-southbank-centre-london-forced-entertainment.

Ybarra, Patricia. "Young Jean Lee's Cruel Dramaturgy." *Modern Drama* 57, no. 4 (2014): 513–33. https://doi.org/10.3138/MD.0675.

Young, Carey. *Disclaimer Series*. 2004. Three inkjet prints on board.

———. *Mutual Release*. 2008. Inkjet print on paper.

Zaiontz, Keren. "Performing Visions of Governmentality: Care and Capital in *100% Vancouver*." *Theatre Research International* 39, no. 2 (2014): 101–19. https://doi.org/10.1017/S0307883314000030.